PRAISE FOR
SUCH A GOOD MOTHER

"I picked up *Such a Good Mother* and was absolutely transfixed. What mother hasn't considered doing absolutely anything to get into a circle of friends who can make her life more bearable, and give her children access to the best things in life? I completely identified with Monks Takhar's heroine, Rose . . . until I couldn't believe what I was reading. Mothers and hustlers can be a lethal combination—and the perfect recipe for a novel to keep you up all night."

—Amanda Eyre Ward, *New York Times* bestselling author of *The Jetsetters*

"Wickedly paced and devilishly clever, *Such a Good Mother* showcases the terrifying lengths some parents will go to secure privileges for their children. A delicious and addictive read that goes straight for the jugular of modern motherhood."

—Lindsay Cameron, author of *Just One Look*

"Everyone wants to join The Circle. But is it all that it's cracked up to be? Who is conning who? And can one woman outplay them all? If you're looking for smart, suspenseful prose, look no further. Helen Monks Takhar is now on my favorite list of authors. Exceptional, taut, and emotional storytelling in *Such a Good Mother*."

—Georgina Cross, author of *Nanny Needed*

PRAISE FOR THE WORK OF HELEN MONKS TAKHAR

"An addictive thriller . . . A hypnotic dance . . . that doesn't let up until its final unnerving reveal."

—*People*

"Delicious."

—*New York Post*

"Chilling, smart, and brutal . . . A triumph of a debut."

—*Harper's Bazaar*

"Absolutely haunting . . . I don't believe I will forget these characters, nor their story, anytime soon."

—*The Nerd Daily*

"Epic."

—*CrimeReads*

"Enjoyably poisonous."

—*The Independent*

"Enthralling."

—*The Sunday Times*

"An impressive, unsettling debut."

—*Woman & Home*

"Dark and totally gripping."

—*Bella*

"[A] clever, truly creepy, and uniquely modern tale."

—*Woman's Own*

"We were hooked from the first page—a brilliant and dark story."

—*Closer*

"Tightly plotted and gripping."

—*Woman's Weekly*

"Sexy, scary, and satirical, [it's] a cat-and-mouse tale on steroids."

—*The Bookseller*

"Wickedly sharp."

—*Kirkus Reviews* (starred review)

BY HELEN MONKS TAKHAR

Such a Good Mother
Precious You

SUCH a GOOD MOTHER

A NOVEL

HELEN MONKS TAKHAR

RANDOM HOUSE
NEW YORK

A Random House Trade Paperback Original

Copyright © 2022 by Helen Monks Takhar
Book club guide copyright © 2022 by
Penguin Random House LLC

Published in the United States by Random House, an imprint and division of Penguin Random House LLC, New York.

RANDOM HOUSE and the HOUSE colophon are registered trademarks of Penguin Random House LLC.

RANDOM HOUSE BOOK CLUB and colophon are trademarks of Penguin Random House LLC.

Library of Congress Cataloging-in-Publication Data
Names: Monks Takhar, Helen, author.
Title: Such a good mother: a novel / Helen Monks Takhar.
Description: First edition. | New York: Random House, [2022]
Identifiers: LCCN 2022010403 (print) |
LCCN 2022010404 (ebook) | ISBN 9781984855992 (trade paperback; acid-free paper) | ISBN 9781984856005 (ebook)
Subjects: LCGFT: Novels.
Classification: LCC PR6113.O534 S83 2022 (print) |
LCC PR6113.O534 (ebook) | DDC 823/.92—dc23/eng/20220303
LC record available at https://lccn.loc.gov/2022010403
LC ebook record available at https://lccn.loc.gov/2022010404

PRINTED IN THE UNITED STATES OF AMERICA ON ACID-FREE PAPER

randomhousebooks.com

2 4 6 8 9 7 5 3 1

First Edition

For Ruth,
and working mothers everywhere

While more women than ever are working, they're also bearing the brunt of household chores and feeling the pressure to raise perfect children . . . It's exhausting for them.

—*Cary Cooper, professor of psychology, Manchester Business School*

"Your baby has gone down the plug
The poor little thing was so skinny and thin
It should have been washed in a jug
Your baby is ever so happy
He won't need a bath any more"

—*"A Mother's Lament," music hall song, unknown writer*

SUCH A GOOD MOTHER

HER BODY HAS BARELY BEGUN TO COOL. SHE AWAITS DISCOVERY on the playground's tarmac, hidden behind the wide metal gate that leads into The Woolf Academy where Ginny Kirkbride is currently punching the wrong sequence of digits into the entrance's keypad.

The chatter among the cluster of parents amassed behind Ginny appears polite enough, but tension is starting to build. Each parent is primed, ready to follow her into the school for tonight's fundraising auction, mentally preparing themselves to race inside to secure the front-row seats where their generosity might be best observed, but, of course, without appearing as though they are running at all.

Everyone senses the weight of the twisted steel words over their heads.

Magis et Magis.

More and more.

The school's motto is both pledge and demand. Because The Woolf is more than a place of education. The once-humble outer-city neighborhood around it has gentrified at warp speed because of its allure, the school providing the sharpest-elbowed parents in town with a platform to shape their children to their sky-high specifications. And The Woolf has achieved this by promising as much as it asks—from its pupils, yes, but from their parents too. Could they ever expect the excellence they seek without The Woolf asking for a little extra here and there?

Take tonight's event: on the surface, a well-intentioned gathering for established members of the parental community, the first of the new school year and one of a great many conceived of to keep the school's coffers enviably replete. Parents, their businesses, and their employers have been relieved of highly valuable time, services, and goods, all lots for the evening's auction donated voluntarily, though not always exactly willingly. *Magis et Magis.* Unshackled from local authority control, The Woolf has, officially, no fees to pay, but for a free school to be this outstanding, Woolf parents are made to understand there is always a cost.

Many of the women in the crowd attempt to secure Ginny's attention with ingratiating small talk as the gate refuses to release. Perhaps it's the distracting efforts of these Woolf Mothers that causes Ginny to mistype the security code for a second time. More likely it's the half bottle of Viognier she downed between settling her six-year-old twins and leaving the house that is to blame for her finger missing its target again.

As Ginny finally enters the correct sequence, the swollen knot of parents waiting on the pavement falls into determined silence before barely resisting the compulsion to surge ungraciously across the playground toward the entrance to the building.

But Ginny has stopped dead.

The parents are oblivious at first, jostling and banging into her and one another, still hell-bent on bagging their premium positions in the school hall. But a second later, the brittle stillness of the September air is snapped by a shriek from somewhere behind Ginny.

However, it was Ginny who laid eyes on the body first. Ginny, who has now forgotten how to breathe.

Manicured hands clamp over horrified faces as parents spill

past her, before stopping to look back to Ginny for a cue on what they should do next. Everyone knows she's used to leading them and expects to be followed. But Ginny remains frozen. Some parents start to break into sprints to get to their new target first, ignoring her inaction. Order is already collapsing.

And at this race's finish line: a woman lying in a contorted S-shape on the black ground next to the outdoor gym equipment.

Ginny finally makes her feet take her to the dead woman and registers such a profound lack of motion about her: eyes still and open, the sand-colored silk of her shirt soaked darkest red and unmoved by the rise and fall of breath. And the pool of blood under her head, so sickeningly rich and glossy—two words that themselves may have described the deceased, until recently.

"Oh God, she must have fallen!" a dad cries.

Two mums exchange a glance and immediately check no one saw their shared, silent challenge to this benign assumption. True, the woman may well have somehow fallen five stories from the school's "sensory roof garden" to the playground. Perhaps she was decorating the space for the post-auction cocktails when a freak accident caused her to tumble; maybe a book of Woolf lottery tickets flew out of her hand only for her to instinctively pursue it into thin air. Sure, she *may* have fallen, but given the state of her in recent weeks, some are wondering if a tumble without intention is too innocent a conclusion after all.

And there's no denying one further suspicion seeping silently into the imaginations of the assembled. It's often heard at the school gates and on playdates: "I'd kill to be *on the inside.*" She was one of *Those Women,* the luckiest of Woolf Mothers, but of late she'd begun to appear ungrateful for her gilded status.

Before her flesh is even cold, some parents are troubled less with the dead woman's fate and the three children she has left behind than with what a body in the playground will do to the reputation of the school and the hitherto skyward trajectory of local property prices. And, as the emergency call is placed and the police officers and paramedics speed across town, each woman on the scene quietly eyes the small brooch, an outline of a thin golden circle, pinned to the collar of her Stella Mc-Cartney blouse.

Because the snap of this woman's spine was the firing of a starting gun. Like it or not, there is now an unexpected vacancy at The Woolf's top table. The race to fill it is on. Despite the rumble of misgivings, the rumor mill already grinding into action about what happened to her, each woman here wants to be anointed in the dead woman's place; each furtively watching Ginny with the words "Pick me" burning in their throats as she makes the call to the one woman more powerful than she is, her leader, and, by extension, theirs.

But, as all these desperate Woolf Mothers know, the only way to get invited inside The Circle is to never ask.

PART ONE

OUTSIDE THE CIRCLE

1

DECEMBER

THE BOY'S GOLD-AND-MAROON CAP DISAPPEARS AROUND THE corner. Jacq and I follow it and the squeak-squeak of his brogues as he turns down yet another dark, wood-paneled corridor. I'm trying my best to be more sure-footed, anticipate the turns ahead, ones I should know are coming. This was once my old high school and I must have been this way hundreds of times before, but either I've blocked my memories in the nearly twenty years since I last set foot inside this building, or everything about the place is as different as they say it is. I begin to wonder, if I was left alone here right now, whether I'd know how to get back out again.

My sister-in-law tracks the fast-walking boy, oblivious to my queasy disorientation. "You'll be walking miles tonight!" Jacq calls behind him, but the boy doesn't seem to register her attempt at lightheartedness as he comes to an abrupt stop in front of a set of double doors.

"This is the registration zone. Welcome again to The Woolf Academy. We hope tonight helps you find the most appropriate setting to educate your child." The boy can't be more than ten, but he sounds like a gentleman from the 1940s. He has what people say is the *Woolf polish*. The boys and girls who go here emerge with the combination of manners and confidence,

not to mention grades, they'd normally achieve only from attending some ancient public school, not a free school that's
been open only a few years. He shakes my hand, then Jacq's.

"Cheers, little man. You like it here, then?" Jacq asks, causing the boy to blink and look about him nervously.

"The Woolf is the top-performing school in the region. It
strives to instill confidence and aspiration in every pupil." The
boy pauses, then nods at the ceiling with his eyes wide open,
before snapping them shut, as if he's trapping the words he
needs to remember from somewhere above him. "Attending
this school is a privilege."

"Is that so?" Jacq sends raised eyebrows my way, the kind
that say, *Well, la-di-da!,* then goes to peer through one of the
door's small rectangular windows. "Better get ourselves in
there, then."

I go to peek through the other window and fail to still the
gasp in my throat.

Now, at least, I know exactly where I am.

It's the old school hall: double-height ceiling and more
wood paneling, a large open space with nowhere to hide. My
insides twist, my body now unable to deny that the worst years
of my life happened within these walls.

But that was then, this is the here and now, I tell myself. I'm
not the same person the girls bullied here. I'm a mum, married
to the man I love, with a respectable job at the bank. I'm not
who those girls said I was.

Through the window, I can see in front of the hall's stage
two empty chairs waiting behind a long desk. Jacq pushes one
of the double doors slightly ajar and a waft of familiar odors
hits me: floor wax, snapped pencils, disinfectant. Whispers
reach me from the freed air.

Rotten Rosie. Rotten Rosie.

I steady myself against the doorframe.

"You OK? Rose?"

"I'm fine."

I push the door on my side open and approach the deserted desk as confidently as I can manage, but the heels of my boots seem to make a terrible clatter, rupturing the silence. The hall's lights heat the crown of my head so intensely it's as if a spotlight is tracking my every step, and while I realize the ridiculousness of this paranoia, something inside tells me not to turn around, in case someone does indeed have me in their sights. Old habits.

"Hello?" I make myself speak, fearing Jacq's about to shout something like, *Come out, come out, wherever you are!* But my voice is too quiet to be heard.

Laughter from somewhere needles my ears. My stomach squirms, memories I'm desperate not to disturb agitating closer to the surface. Me, alone, looking over my shoulder, then suddenly surrounded, stiff in the dead center of a ring of my tormentors.

"Anybody there?" Jacq calls.

"Good evening."

A very thin blond woman emerges from another pair of double doors to the left of the stage. I breathe out, stealing a quick glimpse of the room behind her before the doors swing shut. I can see parents laughing loudly, people seeming to fizz with a confidence they wear so lightly they don't even realize they have it. The doors close with a swish.

The blond woman wears a white boiler suit and huge silver bracelets that clunk as she walks toward the desk without even giving us a glance. It's the first day of December and freezing, so I threw on my old three-quarter-length Puffa over my smartish black trousers and trusty (if faded) charcoal polo neck. But as the blond woman turns her eyes to me, my coat suddenly feels like a twenty-tog duvet, shapeless and drab. I can sense a slight hesitation in her final step, as if she's not keen on coming forward to us. I send an on-duty smile to my face as the chair scrapes behind her and she sits, impatiently gesturing for me and Jacq to do the same.

"You're thinking about applying to The Woolf Academy for your child?"

"That's right." I'm almost whispering, the old instinct to remain unnoticed and therefore safe is so strong. I need to regroup and fast. The blond woman hasn't even bothered to introduce herself. She doesn't look teacherly; her clothes suggest high levels of disposable income.

"Are you part of the teaching staff?" says Jacq before I can shake my shyness and ask myself.

"Ginny Kirkbride, clerk to the governors, admissions, and legal officer." I'm taken aback by a gust of what smells like distinctly alcohol-laden breath she releases as she speaks. "Boy or girl?" she asks no one in particular, eyes down on her tablet.

"My boy, Charlie," I tell her. "He's four next August, probably the youngest in his year, I'd imagine."

Not a flicker on her face as she taps my responses into her tablet, while I berate myself for letting my worries over Charlie's age bubble into the open.

"And how did you hear about The Woolf?"

"I live over the road. We rent the flat above the natural food and wine shop." Ginny appears, for a moment, as if she has a nasty taste in her mouth. I can't help but want her to think well of me. "I actually used to go here myself, only back when it was Amhurst Middleton High School, so you might say my son could be the second generation of O'Connells who've had the privilege of attending this school." A flash of a grimace on her face leaves me in no doubt she disagrees with this perspective.

"And you are?" Ginny turns her chin and attention to Jacq, who's been watching quietly with a patience I can sense thinning.

"I'm Charlie's auntie," Jacq tells Ginny unsmilingly.

"Is the father not involved in his life?" Ginny looks at me directly for the first time.

"Yes. My husband, Pete, he's looking after Charlie as we speak."

"He doesn't want to be involved in finding the right school for his son?"

"Of course he does, it's only that . . ." I can't seem to remember why we agreed Jacq would come with me tonight, not Pete. Whatever I say feels like it's going to damn him, and me.

"In our family, we play to our strengths." Jacq leans forward with a forgiving smile that isn't returned, while I try to pick the words that will put Ginny right about Pete.

"My husband has a very strong interest in his son's education, but Jacq's studying for her degree at night school, anthropology. I suppose it made sense to bring the most educated person in the family." My chest prickles with adrenaline, and while Ginny's eyes return to her tablet, Jacq gives me a modest little nod. At least I've said the right thing in her eyes.

"And what is it you think your family might bring to our school community?"

I fluster. I don't know what the right answer is. I'm not even sure I understand the question. Is this code for something I should know about?

"The Woolf is more than a school." Impatience ices her words. "Where appropriate, we expect our families to contribute their skills and other resources to sustain the unique quality of academic and pastoral care our children enjoy. So, do you or anyone in your family have anything in particular you think may prove beneficial to the school and its governing and fundraising apparatus?"

Before I can answer, another woman enters the hall through a single door to the right. Behind it, I see a snapshot of more parents, but they don't seem anything like as shiny as the people on the other side of the hall. I spy a couple who look a bit like me and Pete. She's petite and pale, light brown hair, short and choppy. Her partner looks mixed white and African-Caribbean heritage, not as gorgeous as Pete, but not bad-looking either. The two of them stand very close to each other.

As the second woman takes the seat opposite mine, she, too, avoids looking at me directly. Perhaps she's embarrassed because she can tell I've clocked The Woolf puts all the posh parents in one lavish room and sends the rest to some kind of holding pen until it's time to go. Or perhaps my paranoia is getting out of control and she's simply tired after a long day, which she certainly looks like she's had.

"Bea, I was just asking this parent what she might be in a position to contribute to The Woolf community."

Bea's expression becomes even more weary. From a distance, she looked as sleek and moneyed as Ginny, but up close I can see a dry inch of gray at her roots and her blouse, a clearly expensive beige silk affair, is creased, a faint tea stain near the pocket detail. The only thing about her that's not dulled is a small brooch on her lapel, a thin golden circle, glinting in the stage lights. I notice now that Ginny is wearing exactly the same gold circular pin.

"Well?" Ginny snaps me back to the moment.

"My husband fits bathrooms for a living and I'm just a bank cashier," I blurt out before I can think of any way I might frame our lives more impressively.

"You're not *just* anything." Jacq looks at me, then back at Ginny. "Rose is brilliant with numbers and amazing with people."

I should be thanking Jacq for being in my corner, but what she's told Ginny makes my life sound so small. It already feels as though tonight couldn't be going much worse. I try to pull it round. "I'm very confident I have skills that would be useful to the school community and its governing body." I clear my throat in the gaps between the words. "I work at the bank over on the high street, but I'm actually a partly trained accountant, but, well, now, that's . . . that's another story." It's actually the story of my life.

Bea's head shoots up at the word "accountant." I go to fiddle with the bright red neck scarf that's part of my work uniform, something I know I do when I'm nervous, but it's not there.

"Accountancy. OK. At the bank, your responsibilities are . . . ?" Ginny asks while Bea's eyes zero in on me.

"Well," I call up a line from my training, "the key skills for any cashier are numeracy, accuracy, but above all, honesty, so . . ." I try to catch Ginny's eye, but she's flicked her sight to the back of the hall. Her eyes narrow. The tiniest shake of her head.

"Thank you for sharing that." She retrieves a thin, monochrome pamphlet from a pack below the desk and thrusts it into my hand. "You'll know, of course, we are the most oversubscribed school in the region and this very fact means The Woolf cannot be for everyone. Bea, will you please escort them to the room on the right?"

Bea looks relieved. Picking up her tablet, she rises and walks toward the room where I saw my doppelgänger, expecting us to follow. My stomach falls. I want to know why I'm not being sent to the other room. What is it about me they don't like, wasn't good enough? Or perhaps it's a simple case of our arriving too late to get into the other room? And yet I can't get past the feeling I've been deselected.

"If I could just make a note of your names for our records?" Bea asks.

"Jacqueline Jacobs."

If Jacq's seen what I've seen, she doesn't appear to be at all bothered about being shunted toward "the other room" as she obediently follows in Bea's wake. I move to do the same, figur-

ing that even if Jacq or I were to object, it wouldn't change
their minds about me. The least I can do is leave here tonight
with some dignity.

"I'm Rose, Rose O'Connell."

My name catches in my throat. I could have changed it
when I got married, thought I'd be dying to. Rose Jacobs
could let go of all the fear and shame of being Rose O'Connell,
but I chose not to set myself free of my father's name. Turns
out I wasn't ready to cut ties with him. Maybe I never will.

"Sorry, I didn't catch that."

"I'm Rose O'Connell."

This time it comes out too loudly, my name bouncing back
at me off the dark walls. Even Ginny looks up from her tablet.
Bea, meanwhile, taps at her screen while the unexpected volume of my voice makes my blood scald my cheeks.

We're almost at the door to the room on the right when
Bea's phone goes off in her pocket, startling her. I see her
check who the caller is, then swipe quickly to answer.

"Yep . . . Really? I don't think there's any . . . Fine." She
sighs and hangs up, her expression leaden. "This way."

Bea starts to cross the hall, her head bowed, as we're redi-
rected to the left, to be with the better-dressed people. Maybe
there's a chance we *are* a Woolf family, or we could be. I feel a
sense of approval recharging me as the double doors to the
other room appear to fly open. Before I can think about what's
happening, we're immediately immersed in an atmosphere of
confident chatter that seems to make the air vibrate with a
specific sort of energy: excitable, hopeful. This is where I want
to be. This is what I thought tonight would be like. I reach for
a glass of orange juice from the table by the door, but I'm
stopped.

Bea's hand is shockingly firm around my wrist, her eyes on
mine.

"Don't forget, when you're offered a place for your child, you still have a choice. One day you might not have options, you may end up with no freedom at all." Bea's teeth are gritted, the tendons in her neck pulling through her skin. I'm stunned into frozen silence.

"That's enough of that, thanks." Jacq prizes Bea's hand from my arm, her jaw strong, shoulders square. Bea registers her as if she's been brought round from a trance. She mutters something like an apology and disappears back into the main hall.

"What the hell was *that* about?" Jacq asks, watching Bea leave.

"Forget about it." I'm completely confused by Bea's actions but don't want to bring any unwelcome attention on us. "Let's get a proper handle on this place, shall we? Go grab us a prospectus." I point to the shiny stack of full-color brochures on a table nearby, shoving Ginny's pictureless pamphlet into the bottom of my bag.

"Right you are," Jacq keeps her eyes on Bea, making sure she's safely out of the room before collecting a shiny catalog better matched to the glossy people before us and handing it to me as I survey the crowd. Their clothes are all individually stylish and colorful, but somehow all the same. Each person also seems so well nourished, so lofty. Not for the first time, I curse my five-foot-one frame, how my body forces me to look up to people like these.

"Are we really thinking about sending Charlie here, after all that?" Jacq ticks her head back in the direction of the registration zone. "I know you wanted to check this place out, but, I don't know, the Stepford child, that snooty Ginny, batshit Bea, it's all a bit much, isn't it?" Jacq gestures at the well-heeled crowd, buzzing loudly with their entitlement to be part of The Woolf. "I mean, Charlie'll get eaten alive by this lot's Jocastas and Tarquins, won't he?"

Not completely sure whether I'm feeling exasperated by what we've experienced at The Woolf so far, or Jacq's defeatism, I rub the feel of Bea's grip off my wrist and flick through the prospectus's images of immaculate children, imagining how smart my son will look in a gold-and-maroon cap and uniform.

2

WHEN JACQ HEADS OFF TO FIND A LOO A FEW MINUTES LATER, I
feel suddenly very alone. Everyone seems to already know
one another. As I think about breaking into one of the cozy
clusters of parents, my stomach fills with anxiety. How will my
son hold his own here if I can't? I steel myself to start a conversation with a mousy-looking woman standing on her own.

"Amazing school, isn't it?"

The woman turns to me, but the hopeful smile in her eyes
seems to evaporate the second she sees it's me doing the asking.
I look down at myself through her eyes, too, noticing how the
black leather of my boots, which I'd shined earlier today, is still
scuffed. I must smell like shoe polish, too, while she is fragrant
with sandalwood. A lot of women in here seem to carry the
same sweet, organic note. She wears a long white-and-black
polka-dot dress, drawn in at the waist with a brown leather
men's belt tucked around itself, and gleaming white trainers.
How do women like her know what to wear, how to smell;
where do they find it all out?

"Sure. I mean, yeah, it definitely is." The woman's fine hair
twitches about her ears as she shakes her head dismissively,
clearly searching for someone better to talk to. In front of us,
the chatter gets louder, almost raucous. The woman next to
me cranes her neck to see.

In a gap between bodies is a woman, dark brown skin, high gloss on her cheeks, short black hair in marcel curls around her face. She wears a loose-fitting, powder-pink jumpsuit and a single red plexiglass earring the shape of a hacksaw in her left ear. Her whole look is also finished off with those ubiquitous chunky, pure-white trainers. I watch one mother ask her to pose for a selfie, while a couple of others snap pictures of her as she moves through the crowd.

"Who's she?" I dare to ask.

"You don't know?" The mousy woman sounds scornful. "It's Ruby, as in @RubyWins. Half a million followers plus on Insta. You haven't followed her yet? She's an inspiration."

Something on Ruby's collar catches the flash of a phone camera. I see the same small golden circle the pair who "registered" me wore. "Oh, she's got one of those circle pins," I say, half to myself. "What are *they* about?"

The other woman seems suddenly flabbergasted. "You don't . . . I wouldn't . . ." She silences herself before sighing and offering, "Look, if I have to explain it to you, chances are, you wouldn't understand."

Chances are, you wouldn't understand. I feel winded, weak. Clearly, she thinks I should be over in the rejects' room. Looking around again, maybe I agree with her. Chummy laughter, all the dads in Boden cashmere V-necks, pops of bright colors on the women, everyone smelling the same, except for me.

Rotten Rosie.

I think perhaps I never should have come here tonight. Jacq's right. This isn't the place for my son. I grab my Puffa and go to find her. I'm nearly out of the room, about to push open the double doors back into the main hall, when they burst open, slamming into my hands. I stagger backward, my palms on fire.

In that moment, I think I hear it, the whoops of rowdy glee rippling through the other kids while I crash to the floor, right

SUCH A GOOD MOTHER 21

before, to my surprise, I feel someone's hand in mine, another firmly but gently finding its way around my back.

I'm put on my feet again, my head brought parallel to my savior, who has bent herself to be at my level.

She is absolutely beautiful. Her pale brown skin shines as though there's a light inside her radiating through her cheeks. Health personified, like someone who sleeps nine hours straight every night. Her long black-brown hair lies flat, every strand doing what it's told, pouring out of a clean line of paler skin scoring the center of her head. Her lips are full, but tasteful, not inflated, or fake. Deep brown irises glisten against the whites of her eyes. She, too, wears a boiler suit, but this one is black and tailored, clinging to the curves of a body that's narrow overall, but curvy where it counts. Her elegant arms end in fingers ringed with gold and diamonds, not that she needs the extra gilding to grab your attention, but purely to underscore she's the kind of desirable that comes from a place of luxury, somewhere you can never reach, though you'd kill to get even close.

I see a flash of something as she looks into my eyes. Appreciation, or intrigue at least. *Are they real?* People have often assumed the shocking green of my eyes means they are somehow fake. She composes her features and goes to speak.

"Did I hurt you?"

I realize I have lost some skin off the heel of one of my wrists, and there might be blood. But my mind empties of the words I need to lie to her: *No, you didn't hurt me.*

"Well, that's what you get for trying to leave before the part where I tell you The Woolf is the best school in this and all surrounding postcodes. Who'd want to dodge *that* now the free bar's about to run dry!" She talks to me, but plays to the crowd. A ripple of laughter behind my back. If my blood pumps any harder in my veins, I'm sure she'll hear it. Still, no words find their way into my mouth.

"I'm so sorry to have knocked you. I won't stop you from getting where you need to go." Then she says softly and to me alone, "Everything all right?"

"Yeah, it's fine, I'm sure. It's only my son's taken ill I think, I mean not badly, but he's asking for me."

As the lie tumbles out, the woman's eyes open wide, a faint smile holding up her cheeks, but the lightning-quick way she examines every millimeter of my face betrays her hunt for whether I'm telling the truth. The muscles in my cheeks go cold as the pause after my lie stretches.

"Well, thanks so much for making the effort," she says, and I can't tell if she's being sarcastic or not.

"Thank *you* for having me," I tell her.

Another unbearable wait.

"Fanks for 'aving me!" She releases a silent laugh at her own impersonation of my accent, making the crowd around me snort and my body cringe in shame. Then, she's right by my side. I find my torso tightening further, but before I know what's happening, an arm wraps itself around me. I'm brought into a hard sideways hug, hit by the woman's sudden warmth and her scent: complicated, challenging, like nothing I've smelled before. She must be more than half a foot taller than I am; I find I'm nestled in the crook of her shoulder. Does it look to everyone watching that I'm being taken under her wing, or that I'm being told I can only leave when she says I can? Either way, I think it would be almost impossible to wriggle free of her grasp, even if I tried.

"Oh my *God,* I *love* your accent!" She says it loudly, and for a second I feel like she's mocking me, before she drops her voice and it switches once more into something entirely friendly. "You don't have to stay to listen to me, but say you'll put my school down as your first choice, won't you?" Her eyes see into mine through lush black lashes.

I gaze up at her, dumbstruck, and silently nod.

Seemingly from nowhere, a very tall, heavily pregnant, handsome-looking woman appears. She has hair the color of licorice spilling extravagantly free of the grips attempting to hold it in place. She goes to whisper in the ear of the woman whose grip I'm in.

"Amala . . ." she begins in a voice that sounds as if it's powered by country air. She has one of those accents that's so round and resonant, it's almost manly, and her face is ageless, timeless, like she could be thirty, or fifty.

"Tamsin. I'm just in the middle of talking to a new parent, in case you didn't notice?"

Tamsin swallows down whatever it is she believes Amala urgently needs to know and finally notices me. Seeming admonished now, she goes to fiddle with what looks like her cuff, before I realize she's pulling on a thick red elastic band around her wrist, incongruous with the rest of her immaculate outfit. She snaps it back so hard it makes her flinch. I'm a little taken aback, but Amala ignores the motion and focuses on angling her face away from the crowd, her smile gone.

"Come up to my office when we're finished tonight if there's something you think we need to discuss." Amala, her head turned to me, gives me a conspiratorial half eye roll at Tamsin's apparent neediness. The gesture leaves me ringing with a powerful sense of inclusion, endorsement even. Amala finally releases me.

"I'm going to take that little nod of yours just now as a yes." She leans into my space once more and whispers, "You won't regret it."

Amala's voice is still in my ear as she sashays to the front of the room, rolling up her sleeves in a practiced, workmanlike way, readying herself to address the crowd, which has broken out into spontaneous applause.

I watch her go stand in front of a row of five stools, where Ruby, Ginny, and Bea are already seated. The licorice-haired woman, Tamsin, takes an empty seat at the far end as the audience bathes Amala with pure adoration. Standing front and center of the row, Amala opens her arms like some kind of messiah and repays the audience's kindness with a beatific smile.

When she finally sits, on the central stool, through the crowd I see Amala, too, wears a circle pin. It may be the distance, but the gold outline of her pin appears to be thicker. From here, Amala's brooch appears significantly bigger and better than anyone else's.

I'M NEARLY AT the exit when Jacq comes down the corridor.

"Let's get out of here." I hand over her coat.

"That's the most sensible thing you've said all night."

But as we turn to leave together, Bea rushes past, followed out into the main hall by a stony-faced Ginny. Something inside me has to know more about the weird dynamic among this group of women, their mysterious brooches.

"Actually, Jacq, would you wait there a sec? Let me just pop to the loo, too, then we'll head out."

I leave the hall stealthily, trying to move quickly enough to keep the two women in my sights but without being noticed. Bea seems to look in my direction for half a second, and I fear I've been found out, but instead she turns and starts speaking to Ginny. Before I can stop myself, I slip behind a curtain at the side of the stage. What I'm doing feels ridiculous, but I tell myself that if I'm considering this school for Charlie, it's only right I gather all the insight I can and by any means.

"Like I told Tam, I can't listen to another word from her tonight," I hear Bea say to Ginny.

A harsh whisper in reply from Ginny.

Bea speaks louder in response. "*Magis et magis.* More and more and more and *more,* that's what she wants, but it's too much; too far."

Metallic clunking. The clatter of Ginny's bangles grows louder. My heart thumps as the sound comes to a stop only a couple of meters away. I panic, working out whether it would be more mortifying to reveal myself now, try to make like I've lost something, or risk having Ginny pull back the curtain on me in some horrifying *gotcha* moment.

A draft hits me, the curtain catching a breeze. I'm on the verge of being exposed. I hold myself dead still, muscles remembering how I used to hide when the bullies were looking for me.

I see their faces: Michela, Hazel, Jade, and the most fearsome of them all, the nightmarish Whichello twins, Emma and Gaby, with their dyed black hair, round paint-white faces, and shared love of encouraging everyone to chant *Rotten Rosie* wherever I turned. Apparently, my father had wronged their uncle, so I was to pay the price. I hold my breath, every tendon tense and still, as if the last two decades never happened. Aged thirty-six, and I can barely believe I'm here again, cringing behind the school hall curtains willing myself not to be seen.

"Well, you've got some explaining to do."

Oh God, oh God, oh God. Ginny is so close I can smell the wine on her breath once more.

"Amala will want to know what you think your game is."

I still my lungs.

Bea calls after Ginny, "Well, you can tell her this: I know all about *her* game. First, she asks for your time, plus maybe something extra, and then, if you've *really* caught her attention, that's when she asks you for something you don't want to give. And if you get *that* far, the next thing she doesn't ask for, she takes."

A pause. I will them to keep speaking. I have to know more.

"Bea. I've too much shit on my own plate for yours too," Ginny replies.

A stronger gust of air now, as Ginny opens the door into the side room where Amala's adoring fans have just erupted into overexcited laughter. When the door closes and the curtain is still again, I decide I can finally exhale.

"You can come out now." Bea's voice reverberates around me. "I'm not going to . . . do whatever it is you think I'm going to."

I'm frozen but know I have to face her. I make myself straighten my Puffa and take a deep breath before stepping out. "I'm so sorry, I didn't mean to—"

"Hide behind a curtain so you could hear me and Ginny rowing about Herself?" Bea starts to shuffle toward me.

"I was only . . ." I have no idea how I'm going to finish this sentence.

Bea is close now. Under the harsh stage lights, I can see her eyes sit atop two purplish pockets of skin, with the gleam of a woman on the edge.

"It's all right." She looks me up and down, as if appraising my suitability to a task I'm yet to be told about. "I wanted you to hear."

"I don't understand." The words leave me like a whisper.

Bea regards me for one further moment before turning her back on me with a sigh and walking once more toward the exit. Her next words are more forceful than I've heard her speak all evening: "I was trying to do you a fucking favor."

Before I can get any more clues on what she's talking about, Bea disappears down one of the corridors spidering off the hall.

I level my breathing and return to Jacq, finding her half listening at the back of the room while Amala continues to hold court.

"What took you so long?" Jacq wants to know.

"Nothing. I got a bit lost."

3

THE NEXT MORNING, I TAKE MY CUP OF TEA TO THE WINDOW, leaning against my usual spot on the short dividing wall between our kitchenette and living space, and watch trickles of parents dropping off their children at The Woolf. I spot two mums meeting on the pavement in front of the metal gates, both clutching coffees in reusable cups. They give each other a double air-kiss and begin to chat, self-importantly blocking the pavement with the impeccable duo of girls at each of their sides who seem to jabber at each other with a self-assured entitlement that mirrors their mothers'.

I see kids like that all the time, running in and out of The Woolf, shoving themselves in front of Charlie in the queue for the zip wire at the park. Like me, those children can say they were raised round here. They'll call this part of town home just like I do, but without ever knowing where they're really from. Unlike Charlie, they won't have anyone to educate them on the realities of this neighborhood before The Woolf and Amala Kaur came along. They'll assume the high street was always clean, the pubs always catered to their clientele with coloring-in and babyccinos, and that it's normal to spend more than five pounds on a loaf of bread. Those posh kids will know nothing about the smashed-windowed boozers and bookies my dad frequented, the smoke-filled greasy spoons, and all the years when the high street didn't thrum with civic smugness and the waft of yeast from artisanal bakeries, but with litter, menace, and dog shit.

"Morning, you." Pete flicks the kettle on behind me in the kitchenette. "You've been up awhile."

"Sorry, did I wake you?"

Pete comes up behind me. I close my eyes, breathe in his morning deodorant and the traces of shaving cream on the skin below his ear lobe as he tucks his head onto my shoulder. "I just missed you when you weren't there." He kisses my cheek and spots the book I'm holding. "You got that old thing out again? You only ever look at it when something's getting to you. What's up?"

I don't respond to Pete's question, simply thumb the frayed claret string coming away from the spine of the book and give a dismissive shrug. *Tricks of Confidence* was written in the late 1800s. It's essentially a handbook for con artists. I remember my childish fascination with the at turns benign and bizarre names for each stage of the long con it details: The Foundation, The Society, The Approach, The Convincer, The Come In, The Distraction, and The Hurrah. It made the immoral and illegal sound like a kind of magic practiced down the ages. It was my father's most treasured possession.

"If you're missing your dad—"

"It's not that." I say it quickly, keen to shut down this avenue of conversation.

"I'd bet your big bro and sister would love it if you tracked them down now. Time heals, and all that."

"I don't think so." Months or years might be enough to repair some families. For mine, time seems only to provide the space for wounds to fester. Pete has never really understood how I felt when my older siblings got away from our dad as soon as they could and abandoned me in the process, probably because I've spared him the details. He gives me a squeeze of a hug and before he can keep on at me about my family, I toss my dad's damned book onto our tiny dining table, but snatch it back when I see Charlie's sticky little hand dropping his jammy toast to reach for it.

"How're you doing there, sweetheart?" I ask him.

"Great, fanks!" Charlie sends me a happy, jammy smile, but my face falls as I shoo him toward the bathroom to clean the jam off his face and hands. If we send Charlie to The Woolf, will I be securing sky-high grades but cripplingly low self-esteem for him? Will some posh kid laugh in his face but get away with it by saying they *loved* his accent?

Pete waves his hand in front of my face. "And you've been staring over there. Did you like the place or not?"

I came home last night to find Pete half asleep on the sofa after a big workout and a bath, so I haven't had the chance to update him on the evening, not that I plan to bother him with every strange detail.

"It's like what's happened to everything round here: It's top drawer now."

I know Pete trusts me to make all the big decisions for our family—including where Charlie will go to school—and has complete faith I'll choose the right ones. I tell myself, yes, there were some odd parts of the night, but this should be about what's best for Charlie. I can't let my own insecurities block the path to my son's best possible future.

"There was this woman, she's the CEO of the school's trust, Amala Kaur, well—"

"Who?"

"Amala. Amala Kaur. You know her?"

Pete rubs the back of his neck, bites the inside of his cheek, and goes to say something, but our buzzer rings and he leaps up to open the door.

As Jacq walks in, she gives Pete a flick on his ear before he pretends to punch her on the arm while I let the smell of Jacq's hair wax and her clean blouse, pressed with a too hot iron that's nearly singed the cotton, bring me a moment of familial comfort. It doesn't last long.

"So, what did *you* make of it over the road last night?" Pete asks Jacq.

"This one tell you about the mad woman who grabbed her?"

"What? Who?" Pete looks to me, shocked.

"It was hardly a *grab*. She was just one of the parents helping out and a bit . . . intense."

"Intense? She had you like this." Jacq mimes the seizing of her own wrist, much more roughly than Bea did mine, and then bites the inside of her cheek. She looks just like Pete when she does it, despite the fact she has a mass of black curls that she keeps in a tense updo and Pete has a grade-two fade. They both have the same beautifully symmetrical features, each with a firm-set jaw that clenches and unclenches when they worry the flesh in their mouths. For Pete, I know it's a tell powered by guilt, usually because he's not done something I've asked him to do; for Jacq, a signal of annoyance.

"Forget it," I say, but I don't think Jacq hears me. Even aside from my naturally quiet voice, sometimes I think it suits her to not tune in to what I want to say about something.

"Dirt is matter out of place," Jacq says declaratively. I know she's about to dispense some kind of anthropological insight on the situation I think I'd rather not hear. "Humans only decide something's dirt if it's not where they think it should be. Say, if it's on the inside when it should be on the outside."

"Come again?" Pete says.

"Outside, in your garden, compost makes your roses bloom. Marvelous, right? But once it gets inside, where it's not wanted, that same compost is muck. Blood in your veins? Good thing. But blood on a bandage: unclean. It's not where it's supposed to be. Being where you're not supposed to be is the only difference to being viewed as clean or—"

"What are you saying, Jacq? They'll class us and Charlie as dirt at The Woolf?" I can't bear disagreeing with Jacq, but I can't let this slide.

"Rose, from day one, you've been blood to me, in the right way, in the right place. Find yourself inside someplace people think you shouldn't be, there might be a harsher view."

I don't want to hear any more of Jacq's perspectives on why my family won't fit in at The Woolf or have her question my motivations for considering it for Charlie. I know once he's back in the room, the mood will lighten and maybe somewhere inside, Jacq will understand why I want more for him than some bog-standard primary school.

"Now, where's Charlie got to? Charlie!"

Sure enough, when he bursts into the room and takes a running jump into Jacq's arms, both their faces light up. The strangeness at The Woolf last night has been smoothed over, for now at least.

"Here, Jacq, let me give you a few quid for something from the gift shop for him." Jacq's taking Charlie to the museum today. She looks after him on Fridays to give him a break from nursery, and usually takes him somewhere educational. I take my purse down from the shelf near me to grab a tenner, before remembering I spent it on food shopping earlier in the week. "Damn, I'm out." I don't bother embarrassing Pete, knowing he'll have little more than coppers lurking in his wallet.

"It's all right, Rose. I've got this." Jacq gives me a sympathetic touch on the shoulder.

"Don't spoil him, will you?"

Jacq shakes her head with a smile while I feel sick with myself for taking advantage of her generosity, especially as I know her income is declining by the day. She runs a café nearby, but it seems locals who want a full English breakfast and a mug of builder's tea have been all but priced out of the postcode, immediately replaced by the smashed avocado and oat latte brigade, who'd likely rather die than take a seat at one of her sticky tables.

Pete leaves for a meeting about a potential new job—one that looks promising but will probably go nowhere. His work hasn't been too good these days, either, as he apparently struggles to find favor with the newcomers to the area. Jacq and Charlie follow him out.

In the last half hour before I leave for work, I should be getting the drying done, thinking about defrosting something for dinner, changing Charlie's bed for the weekend, but left alone, all I do is watch more mums come and go at The Woolf's main, ornate metalwork gate.

I spot Ruby, Bea, and Tamsin. Ruby arrives with a photogenic little boy who I assume is her son, Bea with a lanky, sandy-haired lad and a younger boy. Tamsin appears with a maroon-and-gold crocodile of no fewer than four children in ascending order of size, trailing behind her at the gate, and a harassed-looking woman I assume to be the nanny at the rear of all of them. I watch Ginny turn up twenty minutes after the other three, twin girls panting behind her. I'm surprised at the strange satisfaction I feel when I eventually see her, like a bird-watcher's delight as she ticks off yet another species on her wish list.

I try to keep watch long enough to secure a sighting of Amala, but my efforts aren't rewarded, even though I make myself late for work in trying to do so. Amala must get to school before anyone else. Seems like you have to be up before dawn to get ahead of her.

4

AFTER A BUSY MORNING AT THE BANK, I END UP TAKING A LONger break than I meant to, minutes whizzing by while I create photo-free but benign-sounding profiles to follow Amala and the other four on every social platform I find them on. Through my lunchtime scrolling, I learn about Amala's many awards and accolades on LinkedIn and find links to interviews with local and national newspapers, all fixated on the success of the school under her leadership, how The Woolf has transformed our once dodgy corner of town.

Meanwhile, Amala's Instagram showcases how being CEO of a school trust seems to have put her in the slipstream of some great current that's deposited her from the shores of one gilded territory to another, from brilliant student to senior advertising exec to revered educationalist. I scroll through her feed: incredible-looking holidays, a second home somewhere in France, designer shoes and jewelry brands I've never heard of. Each post is punctuated with hashtags like #DreamandDeliver and, in the case of a "preloved gold Vacheron Constantin watch," a gift from her husband, Darius, that would have set him back no less than ten thousand pounds, #HardWorkPays. I google him and note the school's doubtless lucrative cleaning and IT services are supplied by a company where the director is one Darius Harcross.

I pause on a post of a helicopter ride followed by a "private dining experience" on Darius's fortieth birthday last year, and then scroll to another from her "four times a week" sessions with a celebrity trainer I recognize from the TV. I can't imagine how much that must cost, until I google it and find a week's sessions are the equivalent of half our rent. The same is true of her "regime" of facial acupuncture, protein hair treatments, and scientific-sounding procedures at a swanky salon on a discreet side road off the high street, which she also proudly documents. Maintaining "Amala Kaur" seems to be a punitively expensive process. I find myself wondering, what would happen if she weren't able to pay her way on the merry-go-round of luxury experiences and personal care? Might she suddenly age ten years?

Ginny posts articles mostly related to her legal profession on LinkedIn, while on Insta, I avoid her stories and view posts mostly about being the mother of twins, Xanthe and Idabelle, six. Their every movement is documented in a hazy, sentimental style, often with reference to the fact she's hard-pressed for time, but nevertheless faultless in each moment, in every task she executes. The results are not entirely convincing. One post with the words "Ninety seconds before my next Zoom. Enough time to help the twins learn the basics!" accompanies a photo whose heavy filter can't disguise the exhaustion and stress involved in trying to smuggle the difference between "noun" and "adjective" into the brains of the squirming blur of blond poppets clearly not taking a blind bit of notice.

Ginny's husband barely features in any of her posts, though there is a smattering of references to his "business venture in Dubai" and her caring responsibilities to his father, described more than once as "her privilege to support the most vulnerable." All of it feels as cold and hollow as what I've seen of Ginny herself.

I spend a good amount of time in Ruby's life as she lives it publicly. As a lifestyle and parenting blogger, she pumps out the most amount of content of all the women. The camera appears to love both Ruby and her beautiful, androgynous-looking son Elvis, who, I learn, was conceived with a donor. Ruby, who also describes herself as The Woolf's publicity and social media consultant, built her platform initially by showcasing the big fashion PR campaigns she used to devise in her job at an agency, but she doesn't seem to work anymore. Being "@RubyWins" must pay the bills, but I can't imagine the hours she surely spends every day ensuring she's ten times cooler than everyone else and supplying the endless, quasi-spiritual positivity her followers demand from her, in addition to being a single mum. It's a testament to her skills of presentation that Ruby makes the whole setup look anything less than exhausting.

Tamsin McCandless leads The Woolf's fundraising efforts. Her family owns one of the largest paper manufacturers in Europe, and its associated philanthropic institution, The McCandless Foundation, no doubt extends its generosity to The Woolf and, almost certainly, to Tamsin herself, who has no discernible job. There are big houses with short names on both her horse breeder mother's and her paper magnate father's sides. Some determined clicking reveals Tamsin is married to a much older man, Howard, a sixty-year-old minor aristocrat who runs the Oriental rug shop that opened a couple of years ago on the high street. Some time spent digging for his biography reveals spells in North Africa, Ibiza, and rehab. I wonder in which of these locations, if any, Tamsin met her life partner.

Finally, Bea doesn't appear to be very active on social media, though she has recently posted a sweet throwback photo of her on Facebook with a daughter aged about nine or ten, a toddler boy, and a newborn in matching Christmas elf outfits with the words, "Thinking back to innocent times this Christmas."

Bea seems mostly active on LinkedIn, which is where I find a link to her accountancy business website. Here, much is made of her position at The Woolf, so I assume she gets a lot of business from the school community. I also discover something else through my digital trawl: a legal record dated less than a year ago on the discharge of one Beatrice Pascoe, of an address local to here, of bankruptcy. I think about how she behaved last night at The Woolf. Perhaps Bea's financial difficulties have come back to haunt her. This doesn't come as a particular surprise. In my job, I often see Woolf Mother–types going to the wire with their money: beyond-budget spends on their properties or business investments, overreaches on the kind of lifestyles they expect but can't realistically finance. Having a bit of money can be an expensive business.

My lunch break over, I continue my intelligence gathering, causally asking my colleagues about any contacts they might have had with the five women with the circle pins, without drawing too much attention to my inquiry. The more I find out about these women, the more I want to know. With each new layer of insight, the feeling there's an outside chance I might one day find myself on an equal footing with them seems to grow, whether this is true or not.

Throughout the rest of the day, I spend every spare second I can searching for more clues, becoming sometimes jealous of the lifestyles they lead in my neighborhood, occasionally left disturbed by the contrast between the variously kind, caring, and completely in-control digital versions of the women and the reality I saw at the open night.

I find my little research project comes naturally. I've always had to be one of life's watchers. When I was younger, it was better for me to move about with my head down, staying quiet, alert, unseen, and unheard. It works for me now, too, to lurk outside their world, searching for what I can about the women who make up Amala's clique and what makes them so revered by people around here.

Later that evening, sitting on the sofa next to Pete, not watching the TV but instead clicking my way deeper and deeper through the layers of Amala's and her associates' lives, I stop for a moment and ask myself if my interest is becoming unhealthy. But then, I reason, it's vital to do all the research I can before deciding whether it's right for our family to put The Woolf down as Charlie's first choice. I continue to scroll.

5

A SPRING MORNING AT THE BANK, ONE OF THOSE DAYS WHERE A sudden jolt of the sun's power seems to charge people into doing things they've been putting off for a while. Old folks cash checks they've been sitting on, a woman who doesn't look like she needs the money finally decides today's the day she wants me to find her a loan. Then, there's a man in red trousers and slip-on shoes who appears to be bolting away somewhere nice in a hurry. He orders me to change two thousand pounds to euros and, as I count his notes, proceeds to watch me with a hawkish mistrust I could have predicted. Like most moneyed newcomers to the area, he doesn't bother hiding his belief that people like me are capable of stealing from him right in front of his eyes. I watch him leave without saying thank you and wonder how someone so rude can still think themselves better than the likes of me.

I've been trying to lose myself in my work to distract from my nerves over today—the day I find out about Charlie's school place—but it's no good. I head to the loo for the fifth time that morning to check whether I've secured my first choice for Charlie. I want the moment to myself, so no one can see how much getting this right means to me.

Yes, I chose The Woolf.

No other option could give my family a clean shot at a better life.

When I close the toilet door and take my phone out this time, I see my hands are shaking. I wonder if it's because ever since the open night four months ago, I've lived with a quiet paranoia they'll somehow find a way to leave me and my son out. My body braces for the physical pain of rejection as my fingers fumble to enter my phone's PIN, another kick in my chest when I see the email notification, a final rush of blood to my face when the subject line flashes before my eyes:

The Woolf Academy: accept your first choice

A very specific type of elation ripples through me as I read the short message confirming Charlie's offer. I'm in. Accepted. After everything that's continued to go south since the open night—Jacq's takings at the café, Pete's income, another round of spring promotions in the region that didn't include me, again—Charlie at The Woolf represents the hope we all need.

My stomach churns with adrenaline as I reach the link at the end of the email: "Accept the offer." I'm surprised as I watch my thumb, hovering motionless above the screen, unwilling, it seems, to let itself drop down and accept The Woolf. Some unseen force seems to be stopping me, cautioning me perhaps, that sending my son into that building means risking inviting something unholy into our lives. I think back to Bea's mad warning, then tell myself it came from a place of desperation from the bankruptcy, of her being unable to keep up with the demands of being part of Amala's crew. But still, I can't deny her words have stayed with me. As have Amala Kaur's: *Put my school down as your first choice . . . you won't regret it.*

Amala made me feel so much less than her, and everyone else watching her performance, but she also made it clear she wanted me in her community. She left me with a confusion

I've not been able to process in all these months. Not yet taking the place at Amala's school gives me a sense of control, one I like, particularly as I've barely seen her around town, or coming and going from The Woolf since our meeting last December.

I decide not to tell Pete or Jacq about Charlie's place at The Woolf yet. Instead, I find myself watching TV next to Pete that night, but hardly saying a word or absorbing anything happening on the screen. Behind my eyes, I'm lost in daydreams about what life from September might hold. Over the evening, my imagination pushes deeper into a new version of the future, one where I move among the Woolf Mothers, clutching my own reusable coffee cup, catching up with my new mum friends in the vegan coffee shop over the road from my bank, one of the few places I have managed to observe Amala in since December. More than once she's breezed in to hold court while buying something scrupulously healthy and doubtlessly overpriced to eat, before breezing out again, a trail of women gawping and talking about her in awe in her wake.

The next day, while I still haven't accepted Charlie's offer yet, I find my attention drifting over the road to the coffee shop in every spare moment between customers, watching the Woolf Mothers cluster on the pavement outside. They have no idea that the place where they sip their five-pound infusions was the site of the old funeral home, and where they sit their gym-honed arses the dead used to rest.

It was there I organized Dad's send-off. Back then, the front of the building was a nicotine-yellow office. They told me I'd need a permit to scatter his ashes at the cemetery. I heard my father's voice in my head, telling me to do it his way, illegally. When the time came, I took his ashes to the cemetery at dusk, cleared a patch of undergrowth behind a white marble lion with my hands, and buried a small black granite plaque with his name and dates on it. I shook out his dust on top, wanting, in that moment, to be rid of him once and for all. Now, as I look over at the bare brickwork and industrial piping of the coffee shop from my spot at the bank counter, seeing another landmark of my childhood erased, another piece of my father with it, I decide that I don't mind at all. My son has been offered a place at The Woolf, and I should start living like I deserve to be in our wiped-clean "village," as estate agents now call it.

When it gets to my lunch break, it seems to me it's time I took myself to the coffee shop as it is now. Who knows who I may bump into, what connections I may make. I unpin the name badge from my electric-blue blazer, take a comb through my hair, and apply a fresh coat of tomato-red lipstick, the only one I've ever been able to find that doesn't clash with the ketchup color of my uniform's neckerchief. I feel as ready as I'll ever be. But when I walk past the window to the door and see all the put-together women in short-sleeved boiler suits and floaty dresses, their hair in untidy buns and big white trainers on their feet, the past punctures the present again.

Rotten Rosie, Rotten Rosie.

I open the door and walk inside quickly, willing silence to fill my mind, praying my ghosts don't follow me in. But I know they have, the bullies of my past shape-shifting into the Woolf Mothers. Their eyes are on me, making me feel like a stain, something they want out of their sight.

I take a seat at the smallest table and a young waitress takes my coffee order, tutting when I tell her I'm not eating, just as my phone buzzes with a new email notification.

Subject: The Woolf Academy: Make sure you're prepared

Dear Parent/Carer,

Congratulations on receiving an offer from the country's leading free school. As you prepare your child for their journey into exceptional education and personal development, we advise parents/carers to begin to invest in their child's readiness for school. Our basic uniform consists of:

- Maroon crewneck sweatshirt or cardigan and yellow-gold cotton shirt

- Maroon trousers/shorts or pinafore dress or gingham dress/maroon shorts (summer term)

- Yellow-gold socks (cotton and wool only)

- Brown brogues (no logos, no chrome buckles. All buckles 2.5cm max. in length)

- Maroon-and-gold Woolf Academy book bag, swim bag, gym bag, and crafts bag

- Maroon-and-gold blazer and cap/The Woolf straw boater (summer term)

You are recommended to purchase all items from the <u>shopping section of our website</u> to be confident of compliance to our uniform rules and the quality of the items required.

With kindest regards,

Ms. Amala Kaur

I had no idea Charlie would need this much stuff. Already slightly panicked, I click on the school shop link, and my anxiety explodes when I see the price of each item. Even with a six-month run-up, we won't have the cash for even "the basics."

Do I really know what I'll be getting into if I choose The Woolf for Charlie? I all but throw my phone on the table in frustration, all the while knowing I'll need to collect myself, to show I'm on top of everything before the staff training session this afternoon. Our bank is getting a fresh tranche of money for grants aimed at local independent businesses. I was planning to show a bit more initiative before promotion season rolls around again, but feel almost too flat to bother now. I press the heels of my hands hard into my eyes.

A great waft of fine perfume envelopes me.

The fragrance is woody, like that of the women at The Woolf open evening, but with an additional depth. Jacq's theory is that I have an extra-sensitive sense of smell because I spent my childhood in a heightened state of alert. I usually mouth-breathe when met with an odor so overpowering, but now I find myself sucking in the notes of new leather and rare spice of this scent deep into my lungs.

Amala's perfume.

Was she watching me when I opened her email? Has she been attracted to my table by my own scent, one of distress?

I take my hands away from my eyes and startle when I see a huge cupcake right in front of me, as if it's been put there by magic. Reddish brown like a chocolate sponge soaked in blood, a thick layer of yellow cream on top.

Amala stands over me. "Seems like you might need to reset your day. No need for guilt. We've met before, I believe."

"Excuse me?" I say weakly, cursing myself. I've imagined this moment many, many times. I've rehearsed all the ways I'd sound unintimidated when we came face-to-face again, but now I find I'm looking down, my fingers fluttering the ends of my neckerchief, all decorum and dignity deserting me.

"A red devil's food cake, but dairy-free, gluten-free, guilt-free. It might be just what you need."

I feel a wave of relief breaking across my chest, pride flooding in behind it: Amala has selected me for her gift. I look at her properly for the first time in the light of day. Her hair is like a fine black veil over her shoulders, her face free of any obvious makeup, but her skin still flawless. Not only can I not find the words I've been thinking of all this time, I can hardly think of anything at all. "Um" is all I manage.

She dips even closer to me and flicks a ribbon of charcoal hair behind her ear to better hear me. "Was that a no?" She stands back to examine me anew. "There's no shame in accepting a gift." Her voice, as well as everything else about her, is even richer up close. She says some words almost in an American accent, but it's not this that's thrown me onto my back foot again. It's her invoking the notion of my shame, the thing that runs too close to my surface. My gratitude suddenly spoils into something far less pleasant.

"I'm not . . . ashamed."

"What, so you don't think you deserve a small treat from me?"

Like with Charlie's place at The Woolf, there's something in me that wants to show Amala I don't immediately accept everything unthinkingly. My dad never liked, or trusted, a pushover. I imagine Amala is the same and that holding my position is likely to serve me better in the long run.

"I'm sorry. I have to go."

I get up and start moving to the door, but in my peripheral vision, I catch one perfect eyebrow lifting a degree, as if to ask me, *Where?* As if it's not completely obvious because my machine-washable blazer matches the radioactive blue cardboard window display for personal loans on the other side of the road. I give Amala one of my on-duty smiles as I pass, but decide to stop a moment.

"But I do appreciate the thought," I say, referring to the cake, avoiding saying *Fanks.* "I'm Rose O'Connell, by the way."

She smiles, the apples of her cheeks catching the light in a way that makes me know for certain I look like absolute trash next to her. I stiffen my arms, lest my fingers travel to worry my neckerchief again.

"I know exactly who you are."

I swallow. Everything she says sounds so loaded with intent. I have to get out of here.

"Relax! I know who everyone is." She sighs. "You've been offered a place?"

"Um, yes."

I bet she knows someone in the local authority, someone who gives her special access to the application system I assumed was confidential. I hear my dad, again. *There's no such thing as "confidential," only the confidence to find out whatever you need to know.* He'd recognize Amala Kaur as another person who believes in their ability to jump any protocol they don't like.

"But your place is pending. You haven't accepted it yet."

"I've been a bit busy."

"Only takes a second."

The push and pull of this conversation is making my head spin. I know I'll replay it on a loop later until I decipher the meaning of every word she's said, then rewrite the script so I emerge cool, confident, and on the same level as her. But for now, I'm at the door, desperate to escape Amala's scent and scrutiny. I sense danger around her, something that's only heightened when she calls after me, "You do whatever you need to do, Rose. I'll be waiting for you."

But while my heart clatters, I notice something else from the corner of my eye. A sea of messy buns twitching in my direction. Heads lifting from quinoa bowls, turmeric lattes being lowered from lips. *Her? Why is she on friendly terms with Amala Kaur, why is she being invited personally into The Woolf by Amala?* A fresh wave of pride rushes over my breastbone again as I take in their jealousy. I breathe, and give Amala a wide smile and a wave goodbye, noting how my hand quivers when I do. I need to get better at this.

I just about make it back to the bank in time for my training session. I position myself next to the window so I can keep an eye on Amala as I try to summit the mountain of feelings she's put in my path. She made me feel attacked or, at the very least, railroaded. But simultaneously, and not for the first time, she's made me feel chosen, special. And recalling the way those other women clearly looked at me differently after she spoke to me tastes sweeter than any cake.

I watch them now rushing around Amala, hummingbirds hovering close by so as not to miss a chance to dip their beaks in the orchid. Eventually, she discharges her little fan club and takes the table I abandoned, the cupcake still there where I left it. After a moment, I see her pull it toward her and swipe her finger over the top of it to scoop all the cream into her mouth. She licks her finger with relish. Then, she gets up, walks out of the coffee shop, and throws the rest of the cake in the bin.

What kind of woman can brazenly scoff down the icing off someone's discarded cupcake without fear of judgment? The margin of error for people like me: a cigarette paper. The band of behavior people will tolerate from someone like her: a wide-open plain of acceptance.

Sure enough, the whole scene with Amala and the last image of her taking all the cream and binning the rest of the cake, play over and over in my mind throughout the rest of the day at work. And a warning, too, in my father's voice in my head as I walk home to the flat: *Watch out for this one; this one takes the cream and the hell with the rest.* Nevertheless, the second I get in, I accept The Woolf's offer. Amala will see I've done as she's commanded.

6

I REMEMBER WHEN I WENT TO SCHOOL, RETURNING FROM THE summer break, everyone seemed to have transformed in the space of only a few weeks. Bodies were larger, inching away from childhood in sudden bursts, rapid accelerations that always seemed to pass me by. This summer, characterized by long days without being able to afford doing much else but take Charlie to the park with a bag of sandwiches, I had hoped the sunshine might somehow give him a boost. I've been willing him to be able to start at The Woolf if not transformed, then at least looking more like a boy who might be able to hold his own. But throughout the summer, Charlie has remained adorable, but undeniably small.

He's just about come round to the idea of going to The Woolf with my gentle coaxing and after he got over the fact that all his friends were heading to the average schools down the road, the type Jacq would have doubtless approved of. She's not exactly been disguising her ongoing distrust of the place and it must have rubbed off on me. Because although I've read The Woolf's extensive safeguarding procedures, its "pastoral care offer," and its anti-bullying policy, there's still something inside me that won't be quiet; an idea my son needs extra support to avoid a fate like mine at school. Thinking ahead to the home visits the teachers arrange with new Woolf families before the children start school, I find myself practicing in my head how I'll approach asking Charlie's teacher-to-be, Mrs. Hilsum, to perhaps look out for my son.

Now, toward the end of August, two weeks before Charlie is due to start, I receive an email:

Subject: The Woolf Academy: preschool visit

Dear Parent/Carer of Charlie Jacobs,

This is to confirm your preparatory preschool visit will be held at your home at 6 P.M. on Thursday, September 5th. Mrs. Amala Kaur looks forward to meeting you and your family then. Should you need to change this appointment, please contact the school's office.

At first, I'm baffled. Why on earth is Amala doing the visit and not Charlie's teacher? I've barely laid eyes on her since I accepted Charlie's place, save for a few snatched glances of her gliding into the coffee shop or the new designer boutique that opened just by The Woolf—we may live in the same part of town, but we inhabit different versions of it. But after my initial shock and confusion, another sensation takes over, that of once more being chosen by Amala. Surely, I tell myself, she can't do all sixty home visits for both classes? Having seen so little of her since April, the idea of having a private conversation with her feels like everything else in the orbit of Amala's existence: a luxury.

A week passes, during which I keep noticing all the things I've chosen to ignore for so long about our flat: the tiny amount of floor space we have to eat, sleep, and live in; the towers of white plastic storage boxes poking out from the back of the sofa; the endless guffawing from the self-regarding customers in the shop below. And everything around me looks nowhere near as clean as I want it to, or thought it ever was.

The unmovable darkness of our home feels suddenly so oppressive too. The school blocks out all the light at the front of the flat and very little sun can get into the back because it faces onto the boundary wall of the cemetery, bordered by huge poplars that leave us in their shadows. Charlie's little box room overlooks a patch where broken headstones and headless angels stack up against looming ivy-wrapped Celtic crosses. Because all this terrifies him, I keep his curtains shut day and night. I'd love for us to live somewhere far away from the cemetery, somewhere with our own little garden where he can play, but rents for anywhere bigger have gone the same way as house prices since The Woolf opened, rocketing to places we can't reach. And I can't leave the area. I don't want to. This is the only patch of the world that feels to me like home, for my sins.

And now, after another busy week at work, it's too late to do anything else to make the flat worthy of Amala's positive appraisal, or my own. It's half past five on the day of her preschool visit. I've fed and bathed Charlie already, so at least I know my child is clean and his belly full when she comes. Even though he asked to watch cartoons on Pete's tablet, I've set him up with some new colored pencils and a scrapbook on the little dining table. I wipe the surface around him, while Pete tucks his dumbbells behind our bedroom door, and then hoovers the little patch of carpet they were sitting on.

"You all right? You've not sat down since you got in. No one's coming for another half an hour yet, are they?" Pete breaks into my thoughts.

"I just want everything to go OK, for Charlie's sake."

"It will. He's got you, an amazing mum." He bites his cheek as he looks at his shoes, then rests both palms on the handle of the Hoover as if his limbs are suddenly very heavy.

I throw my cloth into the sink, then rinse and dry my hands

quickly before reaching for his face. "Hey, what's got into you?"

"Nothing." Pete looks to his feet again as if they might give him the words he's searching for, before turning away from me to slot the Hoover back into the slim cupboard between the kitchenette and the living area. "I know this place isn't likely to blow anyone's socks off."

"Where's all this coming from?"

"I've seen the way you've been looking at the flat. I know it's not enough," he tells me, his back still to me.

I follow him and wait for him to face me. When he does, I rest my palms on his chest and he encircles me with his arms, his soapy smell backed by a light musk from the day's efforts drawing me closer. "You're enough for me," I tell him.

It's been so long since we've even kissed, I realize. We've both been plowing through the dreary weeks, some days barely seeing each other. Our mouths find each other, but he pulls away, biting his cheek once more.

"Rose, I won't be around when the visit happens tonight." I'm stunned.

"I'm doing a quote. Landlord job, could lead to loads more work. I don't want to let you down, but we need the money, don't we?"

I breathe, to level my anger and to keep my voice low because I need Charlie to be calm when Amala arrives. "You know they picked up on you not being there on the open night? I thought this evening we could show how you're fully involved with Charlie's life, how we might not own a huge house, but Charlie's home is a good one where it counts."

"It is. You don't need me sitting about here to prove that."

"Why did you only tell me now?"

"I was afraid of upsetting you." He can't look at me, nor I him.

"Go. I'll make up some excuse."

"Tell her the truth. I'm out working for the family I love," he says with unusual force. "What time will she be gone?"

"I'm not sure, by seven, maybe earlier? Please, Pete. I'd really like it if you were here."

"You're not the only one who reads the bills, you know. I can't blow a chance to earn more." What he's saying is true, but why does it have to be now? Why does it sometimes feel like my husband never tries to be in the right place at the right time for me unless I make sure he has absolutely no choice in the matter? Pete guiltily eyes his toolbox by the door. "I'm sorry, OK? Really sorry."

I let Pete kiss me on the cheek before he gives Charlie a cuddle for the night and leaves with a quiet "Bye."

I champ my nails down to nothing waiting for Amala. I pass the minutes rehearsing what I'll say to defend Pete, watching the pavement below in front of The Woolf. I catch Ruby and Tamsin meeting at the gates, each holding large bags with what must be some of the lots for the fundraising auction I know is happening tonight. Ginny, Amala, and Ruby have all been heavily promoting the event, updating their Insta feeds with a constant stream of content on yet another "incredible dona-tion" from one of The Woolf's community. A sample of what's on offer tonight: tennis coaching sessions, a subscription to an upmarket florist's service, designer ceramics, a "financial make-over," five hundred pounds' worth of vouchers for the new boutique, a Japanese knife set.

It gets to ten past six and there's still no sign of Amala, but I do spot Bea, dragging herself to the main gate's keypad and typing in the security code at what seems to be a reluctant snail's pace. She looks to be in a bad way, obviously the weakest link in Amala's chain of mother-helpers.

At quarter to seven, Charlie asks to go to bed. I reason that if he's tired, he should sleep, and besides, I might be able to speak with Amala more candidly with Charlie safely in bed. I tuck him in and go back to the window looking onto the street, wondering if I should call the school to ask where Amala is. The pavement in front of The Woolf is now filled with parents, a thick queue of them, looking over one another's shoulders, a weird anxiety humming through them. I wonder if perhaps Amala has been distracted by final preparations for the event, but then, it strikes me it's probably more her style to let Bea and the rest do the hardest of the work, then waltz in at the last second to fulfill her master of ceremonies duties. So, I sit tight, watching the crowd below swell as my anxiety grows with every minute ticking by.

It's coming up on quarter past seven when the buzzer finally sounds.

"Rose? It's Amala."

Her voice over the intercom doesn't have the apologetic tone I was expecting; in fact, she sounds impatient. My heart rate soars as I imagine her eyes racing over the grimy carpets and walls downstairs. I check myself in the small mirror by the door and try to bring some order to the indiscipline of my hair, noting the color in my cheeks, flushed with nerves, has taken something away from the clarity of my eyes. I wonder if that will be a good thing, given how Amala first reacted to them.

When I open our door, Amala's features are colored, too, a sheen across her cheeks and forehead. When she sees me, she hitches her leather Bottega Veneta bag almost defensively onto her shoulder, revealing a suggestion of sweat on the seam of her taupe blazer.

"Come in. Can I get you a drink? Tea? I'm sorry you won't get to meet Charlie tonight, he was just so tired, so . . ."

While I ramble, something I've tried to coach myself into not doing this evening, Amala brushes the air away with her fingers in a gesture that says, *It's nothing.* I know I should feel less guilty about letting him go to bed now, but she also makes my hackles rise. It's almost as though she's inferring my child is nothing too. It's also clear she's uninterested in where my husband might be.

"Water, please."

"Coming up." I turn to the sink, imagining what a glass of water is like in Amala Kaur's house: a fine, thin glass filled with ice-cold, filtered water from an American-style fridge bigger than our entire kitchen. I feel so worthless as I stick a thick Ikea tumbler under the tap while Amala stands in my usual spot by my window. Her phone trills, but she ignores it, as though momentarily lost in thought. When it rings again, she answers with a reluctant sigh.

"Yes? . . . I don't know where she's got to. I'm in the middle of a home visit . . . Ruby? Would you let me know when you see her next."

Amala turns her back to the window to perform a deliberate survey of our living space. I hear a little laugh through her nose as her huge eyes take in the towers of plastic boxes with all of Charlie's toys trapped inside.

"What is it?" I ask quietly, scared of the answer.

"You can just tell by looking when someone is a good mum. I mean, that's if any of us can tell if we're doing a good job. My Rajvir, his mind can be too skittish, jumping too quickly from thing to thing, hobby to hobby. *Is it my fault?* I ask myself. Is it down to me he can't stick at one thing and be a good example to his peers? Am I doing good enough?"

"So, how can you tell when someone is good enough?" I ask as Amala puts the glass down on the windowsill without taking a sip, as though not even my water is good enough for her.

"How can I tell, did you say? Well, by allowing him to hold on to old playthings, you help your son recognize his own growth. It's good, smart parenting."

At this, I find my heart wants to burst from my chest with raw delight. I make myself speak over the obviousness of my joy at having my skills as a mother complimented by her. "I'd do anything for him if the end result is that he's happy."

"Sorry, what was that? It must be the noise from below, I can hardly hear you." She says it apologetically, but it feels a little too loud, an overplay that I can't help but respond to.

"I'll do whatever it takes to make my son happy." I say this more loudly than I intended too. I don't mean it to, but the way I've spoken almost borders on threat.

She shoots her gaze hard into my eyes. "I'm sure you will."

Unable to bear the sudden intensity, I look away. I know this is an act of submission. Dad always told me if you look away from the eyes of someone first, or speak into a pause they've left for you, they'll know you've cracked and they'll have the upper hand. He told me so much about how to see through what people really want; how to be sure when they're being truthful, or lying. I get the sense, not for the first time, that Amala shares the same kind of insights as my father.

We sit and she begins to take me through a questionnaire on her tablet. She asks about who else is in Charlie's life, who the school should contact in case of an emergency in addition to Pete.

"Jacq, Jacqueline Jacobs, my sister-in-law, my best friend. She was with me at the open evening. She runs the café on the park?"

Amala puts her tablet down. "Oh, yes, I've often thought about popping in there if I feel like something really bad."

"Excuse me?"

"You know, something really bad for me!" She laughs away my defensiveness. "So, what came first for you two, her being sister-in-law or best friend? How did you meet?"

I'm happy to tell her about Jacq, but I'm not fully prepared for the question. "I used to go into her café, back when she'd just taken it over and I'd just lost my dad," I blurt out, then try to slow myself down, put myself in control. "We got talking."

I pause for another second and smile, recalling myself sitting alone in one of the red plastic fixed chairs and tables that line the long galley room of Jacq's greasy spoon, how she started to cut my toast into soldiers for my soup one day, because she'd noticed that's what I always did for myself. A mother hen from the off. Jacq's small acts landed on me so vividly. I liked how she was older than me too. I loved it when she told me what to do with my life. *Move in with me. Apply for a job at the bank. Move in with Pete.* After years of indifference and solitude, someone was finally invested in me enough to show me a path away from my past.

"When I had to leave my family home, she told me I could move in with her, and that was it." I smile to myself, remembering one of our first meals the three of us shared at Jacq's flat. I wanted to cook, have Pete think well of me. I decided it would be impossible to make a mess of a roast chicken, but still managed to bake all moisture from the thing. Pete did his very best, his jaw working overtime to try to swallow a forkful in determined silence until Jacq burst out, "Bloody hell, Rose, what did the poor bird do to you?!," giving us all permission to laugh.

She and I used to laugh so much more back then. When did we stop, when did we find ourselves on different tracks? An image of Jacq's disapproving face at the open night flashes into my imagination.

"Why did you have to leave your family home?" Amala's eyes seem suddenly wide and alert, clearly noting that I've been momentarily lost to reminiscence. She's ready to absorb whatever I tell her next. She smells something interesting, detects something broken. Is she here, I wonder, to search for the defective areas of my life and vet anything that might impact my son's performance, drag down the data that puts her school on the map?

"Oh, stuff to do with my dad." I don't want her to know

who he was, how my ending up practically on the street if it weren't for Jacq was his final act of selfishness. I'd assumed I'd be getting the house when Dad died, but he'd secretly set up some arrangement that gave him money while he lived and the lender our home when he died. My dad had left me homeless. I don't want Amala knowing anything about my crackpot bloodline. It's nothing to do with my son anyway, despite my decision to make Charlie my father's namesake, something I viscerally regret in this moment. Even cursory research by Amala would suggest my father was Charles O'Connell, and Charlie's name would only serve to confirm it. I'd prefer it if Amala never discovered that side of me.

"Sounds complicated."

"It's all in the past now." Only it isn't, because his actions mark every living moment, including this one. "Anyway, I ended up moving in with Jacq, and when Pete moved here from his and Jacq's hometown, we got together, then married, found this place."

"Just like that." Amala clicks her fingers, as if she thinks my life is charmed. She hasn't a clue. "Jacqueline seems a little older than you—is she?"

"I was eighteen when we met, she was twenty-five, but we always fitted together."

"*Fitted*? Not so much now?"

"Yes. I mean no. I didn't mean to say that—"

Amala looks at me sympathetically. "I'm going to take a wild guess your sister-in-law is none too pleased about Charlie coming to The Woolf. Just a hunch, but . . . ?"

I knew it. She *does* know how to read the secrets people try to hide. She's tuned in to the gestures of others, the way we hold our bodies, the language we use, the sentences we can't finish. She knows the ways to sidestep the emotional privacy of others, just as I was schooled to by my father.

"I'm not so sure about that, but even if she did, Jacq and I don't have to agree on everything." I laugh a little while acknowledging the hairline crack that appeared between Jacq and me when I decided on The Woolf. Of course Amala knows to shine a light on it, show the fracture as darker and wider.

"If she's older, maybe she sees herself as something of a mother figure, your sister-in-law?" Amala gives my shoulder a squeeze. "We sometimes need to cut the apron strings in our lives. That's not being disloyal, that's growth. That's finally realizing you've tired of old playthings and saying: *I want something new. I want more.*"

I go to nod, but still the muscles in my neck. To even hint at agreeing with Amala about my needing to loosen my ties to Jacq feels so disloyal as to be disorientating. Jacq's the one person who has been there for me since the day we became friends. She's also the woman who brought me Pete, so ultimately helped make Charlie happen. And if she's still stuck in mothering mode, it's only because it's what I needed her to be all those years ago.

"You should know I'm here for you, to help you get to wherever you want to be. The Woolf takes on not just the child, we get to know every family member, intimately. If we don't understand their successes, their challenges, how can we live up to our *Magis et Magis* proposition? We can't give you 'more and more' of what you need unless we identify what that might be: time, knowledge . . ." She casts her gaze about my home once more. "Other resources. That's why I'm here tonight."

Amala's eyes, intrusively huge and active, scan my face for more clues on my thoughts, on the many things I have less of. She sees, she knows. I *do* want more than my life's given me so far. Jacq wants more, too, that's why she's studying, but my shooting for better things by going for The Woolf doesn't fit her criteria, for some reason. Maybe because it wasn't her idea, perhaps because for once she wasn't in the driving seat of a major decision in my life.

I find myself giving in to the nod in my neck, an odd sense of relief trickling through me. It's OK to say what you have isn't enough and you deserve more. It's not ungrateful; it's normal, healthy ambition, the kind I had before I grew too tired of swimming against the current of low income, low expectations, and my father's indifference that buffeted my every attempt to get upstream. I find I'm suddenly in Amala's side embrace again, but this time I don't mind so much. "You'll have to get used to this," she tells me. "Punjabis like me, we like to hug so we're side by side, shoulder to shoulder."

Shoulder to shoulder. Does Amala see me as her equal? And can I say for sure that Jacq always feels the same about me and her?

Amala's phone ringing makes her jump out of our hold.

"Ruby?" She sits forward, her hair falling like a curtain between us. "No, like I told you, I haven't seen her since early this afternoon . . . I don't know. I've barely stopped all day. I've hardly known whether I'm coming or going. I mean," Amala turns to me, scooping her hair out of the way and looking me square in the face, "I've been at Rose O'Connell's flat since, what time, Rose? Six?"

Her dark irises search mine for agreement. She appears to be daring me to say no. The tension in her eyelids reminds me of my father asking me to do something for him, and I suddenly want to do whatever I can to demonstrate my loyalty.

"Yes. That's when it was scheduled."

I say the "un-lie," something adjacent to the truth but not the reality, from behind the same poker face I presented to anyone who asked me about my dad's scams, especially his last Hurrah. Remembering the way I'd twist the truth at his command should leave me feeling pitch-black, but instead, I find I'm impressed with the speed of my reactions. Amala micro-blinks her approval and I'm reminded of my father's handsome face, never more heroic than when he thought I'd done something right in the middle of doing something very wrong.

"I need to finish up here. I'm sure there's a simple explanation. Have you tried looking outside? . . . Keep me informed." Amala ends the call and I wait for some answers to the many questions running through my brain. But she doesn't give me any. "Well, it's been lovely to get to know a little more about who you are, Rose."

Another seemingly innocent comment loaded with so much more, of that I'm sure. She stands up and I see her to the door, taking a step into the stairway to watch her leave. I see the dirt and the scuff marks tracking all the way down to the street, but find I'm not troubled by them. I watch as Amala pauses, runs her fingers through her hair, and recalibrates her posture with an audible breath. People expect her to look like a model, be the perfect parent to her son —a child she can't allow the room to explore what he likes or doesn't like, giving him only the pressure to perform impeccably at all times—all the while knowing she has to be professionally beyond reproach. Watching her adjust her jacket before I turn the deadlock, I realize that being Amala Kaur requires constant performance. But then, wouldn't most working mothers say the same thing?

I step back inside the flat, buzzing as if I've just come out of an interview, but one that went well, for once. I may not have been 100 percent word-perfect, but I don't think I did badly at all. I wander back to my usual spot by the window, planning to breathe in the brisk evening air to steady my nerves. But what I find outside The Woolf sends another adrenalized surge of blood through my veins.

Because I'm not met with a straggle of well-dressed parents waiting to be let inside for the auction, as I'd expected, but a scene of utter chaos.

Weeping mothers, shocked fathers, faces gasping for air

through bewilderment. An ambulance pulls up onto the wide pavement in the shadow of the *Magis et Magis* sign above the main gate cast by the setting sun. I see Ruby go to meet two paramedics before the three of them rush into the playground.

An accident? My stomach twists. Maybe some older, second-family-type dad got overexcited at the auction and had a heart attack. Then, a flashing blue light fills my vision. A police car pulls up. The sight of the two officers stepping out makes me instinctively duck down, my father's voice without warning shouting in my head, *Don't let them see you!* My guts collapse, and now I'm crouching below the windowsill, sweat forming on my hands and face.

I grab my phone and check Instagram in case I can find anything there. Sure enough, Ruby has already turned tragedy into content. Time-stamped two minutes ago, her post is an image of the sun setting below the city's skyline in the background. The text:

Every sun must set and a new star must rise. Tragic events at The Woolf tonight. One of us has fallen, now we must raise each other up #newbeginnings #resilience #Friendshipforever #BeaForever.

Oh my God.

Bea is dead.

7

AFTER THE SHOCK OF WHAT HAPPENED ON FRIDAY, GETTING every item of Charlie's uniform ready for his first day of school this morning was almost therapeutic, once I'd quashed the queasiness of guilt over borrowing the money from Jacq to pay for it all, that is. The big red minuses hanging over me and Pete threaten to fall on us, or have already dropped between us. We've hardly touched each other all weekend. In my most insecure moments, I wonder if it's because he has someone else. My husband is an attractive man, the kind who turns heads wherever he goes. I've long lived in a state of constant vigilance, no matter how much he reassures me when he knows I'm worried about someone catching his eye.

But I know rationally our lack of intimacy this weekend is mostly down to me and the fallout from Bea's devastating death on my doorstep—which I've kept to myself so as not to spook him or Jacq any further on The Woolf. And our feeling close wasn't exactly helped by the fact Pete has no paid work for the week ahead, coupled with the fresh dump of demands for cash that arrived on Saturday and the hammering of texts telling us we're over the limit for this, about to be charged for that.

It's not too long before it's time to take Charlie over the road to The Woolf for the first time. I stand behind my son, looking at him in the mirror. He's decked out in crisp maroon and gold, standing straight in brogues I've polished to a copper high shine. I let out a sigh as full of satisfaction as it is nerves. The pristine order of his uniform on his tiny, perfect body is a touchstone for calmness among the confusion over Bea and our financial calamities. Everything about my son says he, at least, is going up in the world. I need to believe he could take me with him.

Charlie's been full of questions all weekend: Will his teacher be kind to him, will he make any friends? I am bursting with questions too: What happened to Bea? How and when, precisely, did she die? I've been desperately searching for more information. All I know so far is that the police are investigating, but maddeningly, that seems to have put a stop on any new content on social media, with Ruby posting: "There will be no updates relating to The Woolf until further notice. If you have any queries, please contact the school directly." Neither Ginny nor Tamsin have posted anything all weekend and there's no local news on the death yet either. All I have to go on are the comments that filtered through under Ruby's original post, which was deleted the same day. Many commenters alluded to the "challenges" Bea faced. Some lamented Bea could have been "kinder to herself" and seen "the light in the darkness." The comment that seems to have led to the post being deleted is by Bea's eldest, a daughter, who, I work out, is in her first year at university. She wrote:

None of you knew my mum so stop talking about her like you did. The fact you think she did this to herself proves it. Shame on all of you.

I know firsthand how grief invites us to make heroes of parents who are weaker than we'd ever let ourselves believe. I saw the state of Bea, her deterioration. Amala undeniably co-opted me into her lie about her whereabouts around the time of Bea's death, but I can understand why she might feel inclined to keep her story as straight as possible. Bea seems to have taken her own life somewhere in Amala's school; it's not that she would have had anything to do with this, it's that any deviation from Amala's perfect performance is guaranteed to crank the local rumor mill into action and damage the school's reputation. Why else would she ask me to confirm she was here when the appointment letter said she was, even though she patently wasn't?

Amala, in fact, is the only one of the five of her group to post all weekend. On Sunday afternoon, she shared an image of an empty carpet in a sun-filled classroom, with small spaces marked out for children to sit. The text: "We cannot wait to meet our newest pupils and help them find their place at The Woolf tomorrow." This surely shows she's in strictly business-as-usual mode; it's not the action of a woman with anything to hide or under any shadow of official suspicion.

That said, I can't deny in the dead of night, my mind's slippage into the most paranoid, least likely explanations for what happened between Amala and me. I can't help the word "alibi" from spiking my thoughts all weekend. Not telling either Pete or Jacq about any of it is one way to keep the dramatic theories in check. Also, I don't want them to not enjoy this special day. Jacq's come here to be with me and Pete to see Charlie off on his milestone morning. I lead my son into the living room for the big reveal.

"Oh my word! Who's this smart young man?!" Jacq says first, getting to her feet, the tears in her eyes making me so relieved she can finally see the good in the high standards The Woolf sets.

Charlie strolls over to her shyly. "It's me, Auntie Jacq, Charlie."

"So it is. I am so, *so* proud of you." Jacq drops to her knees now and gives Charlie a hug, but one careful enough not to crease him up before we leave. She grins over my shoulder at me, eyes sodden.

"Pete, take some pics of Charlie while I check the last few bits."

Pete comes over and roughs up Charlie's buzz cut. "Whoa! Who's this big boy we've got ourselves here, then?" He grabs Charlie for a hug, too, and before I can stop him, tips him upside down, which always makes Charlie giggle, but now his shirt's coming out of his trousers and getting creased.

"All right now, that's enough," I say, but I'm not heard.

"Wa–hey!" Pete spins Charlie round so he comes down to the ground, his foot catching a mug on the corner of the table, sending the dregs of Pete's cold coffee flying onto Charlie's jumper. I immediately pull it off and dash to the sink to rinse it out.

Jacq appears behind me, a palm on my hand intended to soothe but that leaves me feeling even more furious. "You'll wear a hole going at it like that," she says. "Here, let me—"

"It's all right, Jacq. I'm sorting it," I snap.

"He'll be filthy by half past anyhow, won't you, mate?" Pete says to us all meekly, to which Charlie nods, but the smile's left his eyes. I can't bear to look at Pete now, or Jacq. The moment to take the picture has passed. I spend the last few minutes before we have to leave blow-drying Charlie's jumper. I could scream when I get it back on him. It's all but ruined, a baggy patch of off-color maroon wool around the golden Woolf Academy badge on his chest. Charlie looks down at it, forlorn.

"It looks brand-new," Jacq tells him.

"It *was*," I say under my breath.

Pete goes to put things as right as he might with Charlie. "I'm so sorry. Daddy's an idiot. You are going to have an amazing first day anyway. I'll be thinking about you all day long. You'll tell Daddy how it all went later?"

Charlie nods and forces a little smile for his father, while his fingers worry the messed-up fabric, making it look worse. He looks like he's about to cry. I stiffen when Pete goes to kiss me.

I don't want to offer him encouragement for this, or sympathy for his parenting fail. Supplies of both are just about dry.

"I'm sorry, all right?" A quiver in Pete's voice as he leaves for another quote meeting that won't go anywhere.

"He is, OK?" Jacq follows up. She gives Charlie one last hug, even more careful than the first. "I will speak to *you,* later. Have the best day ever. Love you, Charlie-beans." She looks to me. "I'll call you tonight, OK?"

"Sure."

Jacq leaves and I take a deep breath, trying not to let Charlie see my rage. I give him one last check, then hug him myself before we head out. Charlie wraps his arms so tight around my neck I can hardly breathe.

THE PLAYGROUND IS packed, swimming with screaming maroon-and-gold children. This, plus the raised vegetable beds, the outdoor ambient instruments, and the designated "Mindfulness Zone" should have transformed the place. But I can't shake the way the shadow of the main building falls on me, how the wind seems to carry ominous whispers from the past.

"Ow, Mum! Too tight!"

"Oh, sorry, darling." It's me who needs to loosen their grip now. I relax my palm on Charlie's hand as we walk.

"What's that?"

Charlie points at a spot where a crowd of bleak-looking parents are standing around. My heart thrashes in my chest. Cordoned-off with police tape in a misshapen rhombus between the outdoor gym equipment, a drainpipe on the main building, and two trees: the site of Bea's death. Instinctively, I look up to the top of the building to see silhouetted streaks of more tape, blowing behind the latticed stone enclosing the roof garden. I trace what Bea's trajectory must have been from the heights of the building, past its five floors, ending in what looks like a lighter, recently cleaned patch on the blackish tar-mac. Her path between life and death.

My stomach squirms as I try to keep my hand relaxed around Charlie's and my breathing level, even though I cannot stop myself from imagining the sensations Bea must have experienced on her last journey. I'm struck by a sympathetic wave of vertigo, my head effervescent.

I focus on the closest cluster of Woolf Mothers standing nearby. They stare at the patch of lighter ground behind the tape, fixated. Two take turns to shake their heads, one of the pair wiping away a tear. Another member of the party looks on impassively. I finally get myself together enough to move me and Charlie past them, as one of them says, "I mean, it can't have been an accident, could it?"

Another replies, "She seemed very troubled, but she adored her children. I knew her a bit, I can't imagine she'd . . . that she'd say goodbye to the three of them like that."

The first voice gasps. "Oh God, what are you saying? The police haven't asked anyone if she had any, you know, *enemies,* have they?"

My face burns. I force myself to breathe through the adrenaline and rationalize what I've just heard. In any ordinary school, the rumor mill would have kicked into action over a tragedy like Bea's, but this is The Woolf, a place used to pumping out epic stories about itself and its people, powered by a super-charged renewable energy: overinvested Woolf Mothers. I will the police investigation to be brief and conclusive about Bea's suicide and usher Charlie out of earshot of them.

"Mum? Why can't the children play there? What were those ladies crying about?"

"There was just an accident. Nothing to worry about," I tell both of us.

As we enter the smaller playground off the main yard, I spot Amala. My relief on seeing her face, clearly weighed down with genuine grief, is immense. A very tall blond man brings her in for a hug and kisses the top of her head. When he pulls away, I can see it's her husband, Darius. I watch him say good-bye, revealing white teeth set firm on a jaw so forceful it threatens an underbite. Looking like an Olympic rower, he's a card-carrying alpha male, reeking of money and of ambitions fulfilled and exceeded. Amala herself looks incredible in a men's-style silk trouser suit in charcoal, almost, but not quite, funereal.

She waves at me, tearfully, as if we're truly bonded after what happened at my flat. As she moves toward me, the gossiping voices seem to quieten, messy buns twitch, glances shoot in my direction from the well-dressed women perhaps wondering why on earth Amala Kaur is acting like a long-lost friend to the only mum in a nasty uniform and name badge dropping off her child. Gratitude surges through me as she strides toward me with open arms.

She walks right past me.

My face boils as her scent drifts by, a memory suddenly surfacing. Soon after I started at AmMidd, the Whichello twins pretended to be my friends. My heart soared when they asked if we could meet in town that Saturday afternoon. Three hours I stood outside Topshop, first in the glaring sun, then in the thundering rain, before quietly weeping all the way home on the bus, imagining how they'd use the whole episode to torture me anew back at school on Monday. I turn my hot head enough to see Amala sideways-embracing Ginny behind me. The pair head toward the front of a line of parents that has formed inside the main building, spilling out into the reception yard.

With Charlie in tow, I move closer to the line. I ask the first woman who lets me catch her eye what everyone is waiting for.

"Clubs. The annual breakfast and after-school application bun fight."

"Oh, we need both. Is there not a place for everyone?" I ask her.

"Ha! First come, first served—unless you're you-know-what." She mimes the drawing of a circle on her lapel and mouths, "On the *inside*."

The bell goes, leaving me no time to ask any more questions before getting Charlie into his classroom. The other boys and girls seem massive. Maybe it's because Charlie's August-born, or perhaps it's because he takes after me, but his classmates look like giants next to him. All of them have such scruffy, uncut hair, boys included. I look at Charlie's buzz cut and compare it with the unbrushed lengths of the other children. It tells the world their parents are so posh it doesn't matter what state they're in: being unkempt is clearly another middle-class badge of honor I could never risk deploying. What's seen as healthy self-expression for their children is, for someone like me, evidence of neglect.

These children also seem so much faster and sharper than Charlie as they zigzag about him, one nearly knocking him clean off his feet. He holds my hand more tightly, before clinging to my leg. Is my son instinctively feeling we don't really belong here, that we're *matter out of place*?

"Can you take me away, please, Mum, please? I don't like the boys here." My worst nightmare: Charlie is beginning to cry.

"Come on, I can't do that, darling." In this moment, part of me dearly wishes I could take him somewhere else, but another wonders why my son isn't more resilient.

"You can! Don't leave me here!" he yells, causing the other parents to look at me and Charlie in unvarnished disgust. They begin to move their children away from us.

Sensing trouble, the teaching assistant comes forward to prize Charlie off me and bundle me out of the door while my son writhes. Some of the children begin to whisper and before I can silence it, I hear it in my mind:

Rotten Charlie.

I manage to turn around to attempt one last goodbye, but am practically shoved out by the woman I assume is Mrs. Hilsum. One final view of my son, sitting at a table all by himself, his head down on the desk. My beautiful boy, losing on day one. The mascara I'd applied so carefully this morning turns wet and silky, tears running off my lashes as I pass the still-snaking queue of parents whom I desperately don't want to see me like this.

I get to the bank at 9:21, six minutes after my contracted start time. My colleague Linda—just one small notch above me in terms of seniority, the most likely to snitch if I'm thirty seconds late, and the leader of a coterie of mums on staff I call The Clockwatchers—will surely round up my start time today to half past. I can imagine their WhatsApp group lighting up: "I've got *three kids* and it doesn't stop *me* from getting in on time." Linda will be complaining to our manager, Marek, in no time if I keep this up, especially because there's no chance of my making up time at the end of the day. After-school clubs don't start until next week and I'm not prepared to pick up my child late on his first day for the sake of getting The Clockwatchers off my back. What was supposed to be a triumphant day for my family, the start of my plans for everything getting better, has slithered into the same crevice where so many days before it have already disappeared: the tight, cold spot between a rock and a hard place.

8

COUNT THE MINUTES UNTIL CAN I COLLECT CHARLIE, IN THE meantime allowing myself to hope that after I left, his day turned around; some boys wanted to play with him, told him it was OK to be nervous, that they were worried too. It's this hope that makes it hurt all the more when it's confirmed at pickup he didn't settle all day. In fact, he's been so anxious, Mrs. Hilsum tells me he hasn't even eaten.

"What was so bad you couldn't eat, Charlie?" I ask him when I know for sure we can't be heard by his teacher or any of the other parents milling about the reception playground attempting to ingratiate themselves with the teacher and each other. "If this is about you trying to get Mummy worried because I didn't send you to where your nursery friends are, then—"

"They kept me on my own all day."

"What do you mean?"

"I was playing nicely, then this lady came into the classroom. Then they made me move all the way on my own at the front of the class."

"Are you sure you weren't maybe making too much noise?"

"I promise, Mum, I was trying my best . . . not to cry." His lip wobbles, tears threatening to spill from his eyes. But maybe he *was* disrupting the class. If he was still crying when the head was doing the rounds, perhaps she suggested it was best if

Charlie sat a bit closer. Charlie's told fibs before, too, just like any child. Not for the first time, I try to convince myself the most likely explanation is the least paranoid. We walk on, Charlie dragging his feet. He's so exhausted, I end up carrying him out of the playground. A notice by the exit catches my attention before we reach the steel gates:

BREAKFAST AND AFTER-SCHOOL CLUBS: APPLICATIONS NOW CLOSED.

I go back to full hours again next week, or I'm supposed to. I was relying on Charlie going to before- and after-school care. Now, I'll have no choice but to burn through what's left of my annual leave. The week after that, I've nothing. I have no idea what I'm supposed to do.

As I'm about to take Charlie through to the street under the twisted *Magis et Magis* sign, I notice a tight cluster of Woolf Mothers. I tune in to their intense conversation.

"I thought I might get breakfast club at the very least."

"Me too."

"Fucked if I know what I'm going to do about my two next week."

It's awful, but hearing some other women, and posh, chummy ones at that, being jammed into exactly the same corner as I am provides some thin satisfaction.

"Yeah, but you must have heard, Amala wants new blood on the inside. Whomever she chooses, they can forget about begging for places."

"What I wouldn't do to make her choose me."

"And you can't ask, can you? You have to wait to be in-vited. Whomever she goes for will only know when they get the *tap on the shoulder*. Whichever lucky fucker Amala thinks has a certain something has got all the good stuff coming her way."

A certain something? What must that be? What must it be like to be the kind of Woolf Mother Amala doesn't only pretend not to know in the schoolyard, but who gets invited into "the inside"? Will she be given one of those golden pins to wear, as well as "all the good stuff," guaranteed childcare places included?

What I wouldn't do to make her choose me. I wonder, what would they do, and is there anything, at this point, I would not consider doing if it meant fixing things by being part of Amala's inner circle? Carrying my spent son up the stairs to our flat, my back and my heart breaking, I begin to imagine nothing is off-limits.

"WHAT ARE WE going to do?" Pete asks me. For a second, I imagine a world where I can turn to him when Plan A has fallen through, knowing he'd know and be inclined to solve another childcare crisis. I think of all those times it's been left to me, locking myself in the loo at work to find some untested childminder to collect Charlie when he's fallen ill at nursery; the many occasions it's automatically assumed it would be me who would call Jacq to plug the hole. "What's the plan now?" he demands, like it's my problem alone. "I mean, what will all the other parents who didn't get places do?"

"I expect they'll share nannies or childminders, pay someone else to pick up their kid and take them to clarinet or French lessons, or Forest School or, I don't know, whatever-is-the-in-thing-that-I-don't-know-about-and-can't-afford-anyway." Pete looks at me like he doesn't know me, but this is the person our situation is turning me into. I'm becoming more cynical, angrier. I continue, "Or, maybe the mums will cut the hours they work to suit school. I could do that, but . . ."

"If we do that, then we'll . . ." He doesn't want to admit the truth lurking in the sentence he's started: I'm the main bread-winner and if my income falls, we're as good as ruined.

"Be bankrupt in a week? Or . . ." I turn back to see his reaction to what I say next, "Maybe you could fill the gaps."

The punch of another truth in my husband's stomach: I'm by far and away Charlie's main carer too. It's me who's on the front row when it comes to everything related to this home and family. Pete is a good man, a father who cares, but still, he never does nearly enough, nothing like the work, the planning, the caring, the remembering of things that goes into keeping us going and that falls, without discussion, on me.

"But you're better at all that sort of thing than me, you're better at everything." This is how he justifies it all to me, and himself. "You'll work out what we need to do, then you'll tell me what you need me to do to help." He looks to me hopefully, as if unpicking the conundrum and issuing orders to get us through it isn't emotional labor in itself.

But I've nothing to say to him. I'm dog-tired of thinking my way round the puzzle of this family's life without any meaningful support from him.

Silence hangs over us as we eat dinner and get our boy ready for bed. At midnight, Charlie wakes up screaming and sweating. I have to hold him so tightly to calm him down. I end up sleeping in his room, setting up a nest of pillows and spare bedding. When the lights are out again, he asks me to pinkie promise I won't make him go back to The Woolf. I tell him, "I swear I won't send you anywhere I don't think you'll be happy to be one day." For once, I'm thankful for the pitch-dark in there. My son can't see my face as I lie to him.

Afterward, I can't seem to drift off, my brain rattling around the same circuits of thought in search of shortcuts, any little loopholes I might be able to slip through, thinking of all the levers I might potentially pull. Maybe the answer is to ask for even more hours at the bank; do a longer day on Friday, Saturday mornings too. That way, I might have the money to pay for a childminder to smooth the troublesome edges of the school day. But if I did that, I'd be even more tired, our lives would be even more chaotic, but more than any of that, I'd see even less of Charlie. Whichever way I cut it, there always seems to be a price to pay that's more punishing than the problem itself.

It's nearly six o'clock in the morning. I can't lie here awake any longer. I decide to take myself off for a walk before the sun comes up, wishing to hear my dad's voice on the empty streets he used to stroll. Today, I'd do anything to hear his advice, however dark it may be.

For the first time in a while, my feet take me to my old road and the house I shared with my father. I've walked here with Charlie many times, pointing to my old room, and lifting him up to the front window once when he was a toddler. The building was empty then, just before the latest owners moved in. We pressed our heads to the glass and I showed him where his grandad would sit and thumb through *Tricks of Confidence*. Charlie asked then, and each time we strolled past the house over the years that followed, whether we could go inside. It pained me to rush us past on the other side of the road, reminding him the house belonged to someone else and we could not let ourselves in; we couldn't even linger where we were, lest I seem like some kind of burglar casing the place for my next job. I stand on the other side of the road to my old home now, like Charlie, struggling to accept I'm not entitled to be inside that house, so desperate am I to pencil my father into the world this morning.

With no one else up and about, I decide to observe the house for a moment. Sadly, our little old place at 43 Bryk Road has suffered the same fate as most of the old terraces hoovered up by the recent newcomers. The front has been sandblasted so the sooty Victorian brickwork has come up clean as an egg, as though the past never happened, as if the generations of ordinary people who once owned my home never existed. From the road, I can see the self-important blue glow of a smart doorbell that tells anyone who cares to know the owners have something worth taking inside. Through the large front window it looks like all the internal walls have been dismantled, and I can tell the back of that poor old building has been pushed right out into what used to be the long, thin garden. The most recent owners have also stolen an extra floor from the ground below and robbed another from the sky above. For good measure, they've even obliterated my home's address. There is no number 43 anymore, only a fancy new house name on a slice of gilded slate screwed to the gatepost.

Instead of the specter of my father in the window, a young boy appears, about seven, in his place. I slip behind a nearby cherry tree to observe him. The boy is a soft-looking child who looks as though he's been crying. My heart falls in my chest for him. I don't want to see his pain, deciding it's time to get back to the flat to return to my own boy's troubles. But just before I go to walk away, a slim, female hand touches the boy's shoulder, prompting him to spin around so he can be picked up. The woman takes him into her arms, her black hair falling about his shoulders. Now it makes perfect sense why the slate screwed into the disfigured brickwork of my home reads *Woolf View*.

Amala.

I gasp as she cradles her son, then tells him something emphatically, repeatedly, something that seems to give him the reassurance he needs. The idea of Amala swanning around the house where I grew up, comforting her son within walls where I should be holding mine, makes me burn. The humiliation of having my birthright pried out of my fingers and ending up in hers, the injustice of it all, fills my stomach. Shouldn't being born in a building give you some entitlement to it? I vow to never let Amala Kaur know she's the cuckoo in my nest.

I trudge back to my tiny, rented stamp of the area my dad once ruled, the truth of the matter worming its way into focus as I consider my situation. I see it more clearly than ever now. The way I'm forced to play the game of my life isn't so much about winning. For someone like me, gaining any control over the things that really matter means deciding what I'm most willing to lose.

9

ON TUESDAY, CHARLIE'S TEACHER GIVES HIM A PERMANENT "special seat" next to her, apparently on the advice of an "independent observer." On Thursday, he's sent home with a letter from the "Pastoral Care Leader":

> Dear Parent or Carer of Charlie Jacobs,
>
> At The Woolf we pride ourselves on the holistic care we provide for pupils and their families.
>
> We've identified your family as one that would benefit from our counseling services for children. These provide a safe space for your child to discuss family challenges and any other worries they may have. We have organized for your child to attend regular sessions beginning next week. However, if you feel you would not like your child to receive the support we believe they need, please notify us and we will suspend the sessions.
>
> Warmest regards,
> The Pastoral Care Leadership Team

I'm stunned. Four days ago, my son was a happy, confident child. Less than a week at The Woolf and he's a nervous wreck who they think needs to see some kind of school shrink. *Family challenges?* I'm torn between rage and despair. Maybe this was always coming. Perhaps it was only a matter of time before my shortcomings as a mum and breadwinner were played out to the point where the whole world could see them all manifesting in my only child. Going to The Woolf has only showed up what has long been lacking sooner than it might have. And if I don't let Charlie have the counseling, it seems they'll mark me as an even worse parent than they already think I am. There's no choice but to let him go to the sessions.

The next morning at drop-off, I calmly ask Mrs. Hilsum why Charlie is in his own special seat, why he's being singled out for counseling. All she can say is, "It's in his best interests," before immediately moving on to speak to another parent. She doesn't look me in the eye and touches her nose while she speaks. It's probably the ongoing lack of sleep making me paranoid, but as I notice her furtive gestures, I think of my dad instructing me on the classic tells of those trying to hide something. I've since seen the touching of the nose plenty of times at the bank, when people try to cash dodgy checks, or access accounts that aren't their own.

When I get home with Charlie, I find yet another maroon letter in his book bag, this one announcing his first school trip next week. They're keeping it local, heading to the cemetery, the place of Charlie's worst fears. I wonder if this week can get any worse, when I turn over the letter and find a handwritten note:

We strongly recommend you attend this trip as a parent volunteer. Charlie has already expressed high levels of anxiety over the excursion. It is in his best interests that a parent takes responsibility for Charlie's emotional needs to prevent disruption to the rest of the class.

The main letter is signed by his teacher, but no one has put a name on the note, which is written in a confident, distinguished, forward-leaning scroll in deep black pigment. Everything about it suggests to me the author of the note: Amala. I bank the knowledge and consider what I must do next.

I GET BACK to the flat after work right before Jacq arrives with Charlie. Since she can't take him out for their usual Friday trips now, she picks him up from school and brings him to the café while I finish at work. After we've bathed Charlie, I get ready to hear about her week.

"Well, my takings at the caff are on the floor, again."

"I'm so sorry, Jacq. I don't know what's happened round here."

"I do." She eyes The Woolf through the window. "I don't know how much longer we can survive, though. Sorry, I know you've got your worries too. Pete told me about his next job."

"Not another one canceling?"

"He's not told you yet, has he? Sorry. I gave him a talking to, but he was pretty distraught when he told me. Don't give him a hard time, will you?"

Clearly keen to end the conversation, Jacq gets out her phone and starts scrolling through the headlines, while Charlie comes to sit on my knee in his towel. He feels unusually heavy, exhausted. How can it be that my son, me, Pete, and Jacq are giving our all to the world and getting nothing back but disappointment and humiliation? Is this ongoing punishment for being born my father's daughter? All I've done since that day of his final Hurrah is try to build a decent life as far away as I could from who my father was. I'm beginning to wonder if I should have bothered.

"Oh my God!" Jacq sits forward on her seat next to me. "Oh my—"

"What's up?"

Jacq holds her phone to me, eager to not show Charlie

whatever she's found. "Isn't that her? The mad one from the open night?"

Bea's death is finally in the public domain. I see a picture of her with her three children dressed as elves alongside the headline: *Tributes paid to tragic mum of three.* I work to keep my demeanor unflappable but naturally disturbed. "It's awful, isn't it? I heard the odd thing on the schoolyard. Did they say how she . . . ?"

Jacq reads: "Police are not treating the death as suspicious, so I guess that means—"

"I suppose it must," I say, realizing how glad I am no one else has been found to be involved.

Jacq shakes her head. "Didn't I tell you she wasn't right?" She lowers her voice. "Didn't I say there was something off about . . ." She cocks her head toward The Woolf outside the window, aware of Charlie half listening to her. I don't need this distraction now. I need Jacq to work with me to kick-start the changes we need.

"Jacq, I really don't want to go over old ground or have us use one woman's problems as a reason for high drama, OK?" Jacq looks taken aback by my uncharacteristic brusqueness with her and goes to speak. I stop her. "I wanted to talk to you about something. There are these local business grants we're administering at work, some for bigger businesses that are struggling, some for smaller businesses that could do with a boost. We've just had a load of new money come through and I've been looking into it." Jacq's expression of annoyance soon turns into confusion, then curiosity, the specter of Bea fading away. "I could make it easy for you, check if the caff is qualified, fast-track your application if you wanted to apply for funding for your business. You could invest in the place, make it over, turn it into something else, give it a new image and a better chance of surviving round here."

Jacq presses her hands together on her knees, before laying one palm on her heart.

"Can I tell you? I've been thinking loads about my dad's family's food lately. I reckon some authentic Caribbean cuisine might fly round here, done the right way. Maybe this is the time to find out?"

Jacq looks emotional remembering her father. Sometimes I consider it a blessing I can't recall even the smallest detail about my mother. In some cases, you can't miss what you never had. But then, there are so many things I want that I've not come close to yet.

"I think the bank releases the cash pretty quickly once you're approved," I tell her. "You could have a new place, somewhere your dad would have loved, in weeks."

"Wow." Jacq looks out of the window, envisioning the transformation, erecting a bridge that links her father and his heritage to her brighter future. Her eyes appear to glow now. A surge of joy over the fact I can help her, a bite of guilt I haven't done so sooner. Maybe I lacked the confidence to get Jacq through the process before, or perhaps it was motivation I was low on, until now.

"I'm going to make this happen for you, Jacq."

She views me side-on. "I've said it before and I'll say it again, you're a dark horse, Rose O'Connell."

I touch my nose. "I don't know what you mean."

10

THE AFTERNOON OF THE CEMETERY TRIP COMES ROUND ON THE Thursday of a second miserable week, full of sleeplessness, Charlie's tears, being late to work, and slipping away on the turn of my last contracted hour. When I knew I had to come on the trip, I realized I'd have to take unpaid leave we sorely can't afford, but some things are more important than a few quid in the bank. With some short-term pain will hopefully come long-term gains. I need to show my face and, perhaps, a little more of the person I am to those I sense might be watching.

I get to Charlie's class and all the other volunteer mums desperately buzz around someone hidden from view. Eventually they part long enough for me to see her: Amala is taking time out of her packed schedule to come on a reception school trip. I can sense the other women know this is unusual. If they, or I, didn't know better, we'd say Amala Kaur is window-shopping for her latest recruit.

Mrs. Hilsum and a teaching assistant wear important-looking high-vis tabards. They request the parent-volunteers to pair up ahead of being given groups of up to five children to supervise. Amala, having failed to even acknowledge me, accepts a plea from the unpleasant, *if I had to explain you wouldn't understand,* mousy-looking woman from the open evening to be her partner. There are also two other classic Woolf Mother–

types who don't seem to know each other, but they blatantly give me the once-over before immediately deciding they'd be better off together. My stomach falls. On my own, I'm left to look after Charlie and another boy, Albert, a skinny, tall thing with reddish-brown hair past his shoulders.

"I don't want to go with him!" Albert cries, causing Charlie's head to drop.

"Come on now, we're going to have a lovely time, aren't we?" I call on my "challenging customer" training.

"I don't want to go with *her*. I want to go with Effie's mum."

Eventually, the teacher decides she'll have to walk Prince Albert down to the cemetery herself, but tells me she'll "hand him back" when we get there. We cross the road, me and Charlie at the back of the pack, on our own, holding hands, standing out for all the wrong reasons. Charlie is silent.

"There's nothing to be afraid of at the cemetery, I promise." I run my thumb along his, willing him to stay calm.

"I don't like dead ghosts," he tells the pavement, his voice quiet but stern.

"Ah, don't be like that. Your grandad, my daddy, he's there. He'll look after us."

The teacher hands Albert back as promised once we're inside the cemetery, along with some bags for the autumn leaves and sticks the boys start collecting. With a task to do, Albert calms down, but not for long. He keeps running off, disappearing down side paths into stretches of broken graves the sun doesn't reach.

"Albert. Come back please!"

He makes his way back and comes in close to Charlie. Before I can stop him, Albert draws his long arm behind him and thumps Charlie hard on his chest.

At first, there's no sound.

I don't move, waiting for Charlie to breathe. The silent pause seems to last forever, until finally, Charlie lets out a terrifying wail. As I try to comfort him through my dread at what damage Albert may have caused to my son, Mrs. Hilsum comes over and asks what's going on. She checks over Charlie for a second, then decrees brusquely, "He'll live," before jerking her head back and forth. "Where's Albert?"

"He was just here. He kept running off."

"You have no idea where one of the two children under your care is?"

"I only turned away for a second to check if my son was still breathing."

I watch her stride to the teaching assistant and say, "We have a situation," looking back to me darkly.

Meanwhile, sobs halt Charlie's breath. I should be focusing on him, but instead, I'm panicking about Albert and how bad it all looks.

What a dreadful woman.

What a terrible mother.

"Is Albert in trouble? Is he dead?" Charlie pleads.

"No, darling, of course not." But what if there's an accident and I get the blame?

I need to join the search. I hand Charlie to the teaching assistant and consider what I've gleaned about Albert, listening to my instincts on where he might go. It seems suddenly obvious to me he would hide himself down the darkest paths he could find. I follow the main walkway, examining the ground beside it, old trails all but overtaken by thick clumps of dark green ivy and head-high knotweed. I find I've reached the site where I scattered Dad's ashes, taking a moment to run my palm over the smooth white paw of the marble lion guarding someone else's memory. I peek at Dad's final resting place behind it, his remembrance happening out of sight, unseen in the soil. Despite everything, I can't but regret to see it so overgrown in the shadow cast by the noble white beast that's nothing to do with my father. I lean down to tug at the ivy that's taken over the patch where I laid his plaque, tearing up the chickweed that's settled there, too, disturbing the soil. Suddenly, I'm taken over by memories of laying my father to rest. I smell the old suit I cremated him in, the remnants of his tar and spice in the fabric. I'm enveloped in it. My father feels near me now, liberated from the ground.

I notice something about the undergrowth nearby, recently snapped stems of knotweed and flattened streaks of ivy, a track of it winding over what looks like a long-forgotten path to a small clearing up ahead. I see a mottled stone sculpture there, a lamb. My dad had told me once that a lamb signified a child's grave. I shiver. It's almost an out-of-body experience as I begin to make my way through the dense ivy and mounds of broken stone, refusing to be deterred by the bones beneath my feet. I can see now that the lamb rests at the helm of a child-size stone chest. I know I'm closing in on Albert.

The lid of the chest has been smashed, leaving jagged marble and a gaping hole at the foot end. A child's cry, muffled, reaches the air from within the stone tomb.

"Albert!"

I climb up to where the stone is still in one piece, then get on my knees, my palms near sliced on the damaged marble as I lower my head to look inside. There the boy is, filthy, with scratches on his face, though otherwise fine. "Don't you worry. I'll get you out of there."

"I don't want *your* help."

But I reach into the tomb anyway, while Albert pushes himself into the darkness of the furthermost corner, kicking dirt into my face, grunting.

"Take . . . my . . . hand." I strain to reach deep inside.

I manage to get hold of his arm. He thrashes about, but not so much I can't pull the top half of him out. I get my arms round him to drag the rest of his body free of the grave.

"Stop it! You're hurting me!"

He's out. I can see three of the other mums spotting us, as they pick their way through the path I've beaten. "He's here!"

I turn back to the boy. "Let me look at you." I hold him gently, my hands on his side; something damp under my fingers.

As the mums close in on us, the boy jabs a little white finger up in the air in front of my heart. "You hurt me!"

I drop my hands from him. "I didn't," I whisper, looking down at him, then watching as the women immediately huddle in around the child, forming a kind of shield against me. It comes out like a breath, as if I don't even believe myself as I notice, to my horror, the slick of Albert's blood on my fingers, which I immediately, almost guiltily, wipe on my trousers.

The boy lifts up his jumper. The mums shriek. Blood darkens the band of his maroon trousers, which he hitches down to reveal a clean cut below his hip bone, fading to a comet's tail of a scrape.

"Oh my GOD! Ambulance!" One of them starts jabbing at her phone. "What did you *do*?"

I try to speak, defend myself, but nothing's coming out. Besides, whatever I say won't be good enough anyway. There's nothing I can ever say or do that will make these people think anything good about me, or my son. They didn't want to be with me and Charlie from the start. They think I'm no better than the muck now on their shoes.

"What this woman has done"—the indulgent English-American twang comes from out of nowhere, while a heady scent smothers the leaking sap and unsettled soil in the damp air—"is save our little runaway."

The other mothers freeze as Amala kneels down next to the crying boy, while I work to contain my delight that, for some reason, she has decided to back me up so emphatically. She tells the child, "Albert, I need you to be strong. You've scraped yourself on the way out of your hidey-hole."

"She did it. She cut me." He points to me.

"What hurt you were your choices. I hope you'll remember this and learn from it."

"I want my mummy."

"We all do, but there are times she can't be there for us and those are the moments we need to find our own power. You show me your power while I clean you up."

Her words work. The boy stands a little straighter as she dabs a glowing white cotton handkerchief on his wound, soaking up the worst of the blood with the gentlest of touches. We all watch, almost hypnotized, and the mood calms.

"I think we can cancel that ambulance now, don't you, ladies?" Amala folds up the blood-stained hankie so that it appears bright white again and puts it into the inside pocket of her Givenchy tote bag.

Albert wanders over to Effie's mum before she starts leading the pack back toward the teachers. "Guys? Aren't we forgetting something?" Amala looks into the air above her, impatient, like, *Do I have to think of everything myself?*

Effie's mum turns around. "What was that, Amala?"

"To thank Rose?"

"Who's Rose?" the mousy woman asks before she can stop herself.

"This is Rose, Rose O'Connell."

The mousy woman's manner transforms. "Of course! I'm Jo. We've actually met a couple of times. Sorry about being so stressy." I offer her no sign she'll claw her way into my good books as she continues, "Thank you, so much, Rose. Great job."

"All right, that's enough." Amala sends her needy sycophant off, and I'm reminded of how she called out Tamsin's dismissiveness when we first met at the open night. Amala turns to me. "Let's get you back to your son." She takes my hand and gives it a little squeeze. "My God, you're shaking! Hey, you're good now." She looks into my eyes, and if there's any piece of her that finds me repellent, it's well buried below something that feels like true understanding, or an accomplished impression of it.

We follow Jo and her familiars back to the main party. Amala walks ahead of me, holding back branches so they don't hit me in the face, warning me to watch my step. "So, how is Charlie settling in then?" she asks me, seemingly out of nowhere.

"Oh, he's fine, fine." I hear my voice crack.

Amala stops to look me over. "Hey, now. What's going on here?" Her hand finds mine once more. "That's it: You. Me. Your son, my son. Playdate at mine tomorrow. Let's discuss this properly."

"Really? That would be amazing. We're actually free today if that's any use." I curse myself for being so obviously keen, worried I've breached some kind of unwritten code on playing it sufficiently cool for her approval.

"Sadly, no." She checks her "preloved" gold Vacheron Constantin watch. "I have somewhere I need to be. I'll come and find you at pickup tomorrow."

I nod, continuing to regret my overeagerness more deeply as I watch her leave the cemetery gates. Waiting for her are her three surviving sidekicks. Ginny is dressed in a dark tailored skirt suit, with the flush on her face of someone who has been crying, drinking, or maybe both. Ruby wears black flared dungarees and a matching slouchy blazer, while Tamsin is in a charcoal satin number that flows all the way down to the ground and a faux fur. Amala takes off the chunky sweater she's been wearing to reveal a black catsuit, then hands Ginny the jumper in exchange for a charcoal trench coat.

They each look variously incredible in their all-black outfits. Then it hits me. The "somewhere to be" is Bea's funeral. I lose a breath at the realization, a woozy type of sickness filling my stomach. I watch Amala encourage Ginny and Ruby to link her arms while Tamsin, head bowed, pulls at her elastic band, tears falling freely. The four of them head in the direction of the crematorium. The last time I saw all of them together in one place was when Bea was there, at the open night. The sight makes me shudder.

As we get back to school, there's something else that renders the image of the foursome's glamorous grief even more nauseating. A poster, encouraging new parents to RSVP to the icebreaker invitation they've received. It's being held on the roof garden, the site of Bea's last, lonely moments. It's as though Amala and the other three are daring people to come after them, to suggest they are somehow implicated in what sent Bea crashing to the tarmac now that the verdict is in. I'm appalled but fascinated at their brazenness, their confidence. Then it strikes me: I have not been invited.

Isolation thuds through me before I remember I have an invite to something even more desirable and exclusive: Amala's home.

11

THAT EVENING, STANDING BY MY WINDOW, I HOLD SOME SMALL hope of seeing Amala and the three others before the day is through. When the street stays empty, I find myself taking out my dad's *Tricks of Confidence*. Thumbing through the pages once more, I try to draw my father from them as he seemed to want to emerge from the ground around me today.

I came along late and accidentally, Dad past fifty by the time I was born. In my imagination I see his face; suave, lined with wisdom. I conjure him in his suit, the cologne he'd wear as he reached the payout day on one of his scams, The Hurrah. He was so persuasive in his appearance as a successful man of business, but if you looked carefully, you'd see underneath the trappings of money-based confidence, he was skint.

It wasn't the knockoff Rolex or the nicotine-stained yellow skin of his fingers that told you he wasn't who he'd have you think he was; it was his shoes. Copper-colored, slim, stiff leather Oxford lace-ups he'd tell people were handmade, which was why he'd repair the thin soles over and over. But anyone who cared to look past his patter would see they were cheap, the shoes of a man who'd rather spend the gains made on betting on some outsider horse at Newmarket than he would on a decent pair of shoes for himself, or his daughter for that matter.

As I read the familiar *Tricks of Confidence* chapters on each stage of the long con, I try to hear his voice again, like I did in the cemetery. But all I summon are hurtful memories of the people I know he targeted and the cruel, charismatic way he relieved them of their money.

The Foundation and The Society were the first stages of Dad's con. This was when he would do his research on his intended victim or "mark." He might zero in on a man who'd carried out some small-scale property development in our neighborhood. He'd ask about, maybe follow them in their daily business for a few days, check the Land Registry and Companies House for what the mark might own and the other businesses they dealt in. Then, he'd recruit a cast of characters to escort the scam through to completion: The Society. An apparently persuasive planner who'd go the extra yard if her palm were greased, a co-investor who seemed plausibly able to chip in funds. Both would be Dad's Society.

Then, The Approach, where Dad would make himself known to the intended victim, usually by stealth. By the time he came to discuss the new lucrative project he was working on with the low-flying property developer, my father would have made it almost seem that partnering-up was their idea. But few people would be ready to go all in yet. That was when The Convincer kicked in. My dad would propose the mark put a little money into some spurious side project. My dad would then wildly overcompensate him, returning the victim's initial investment several times over in a matter of weeks out of his own pocket. The mark wouldn't realize it, but his defense, his ability to stop himself believing in impossible things, had started to break down. But it hadn't perished yet.

That's when my dad would activate The Come In—another person, one of The Society, who would showcase the big prize possible to the mark if only he bet everything on my father's main proposition. In some cases, a totally believable co-investor would happen to be hanging around just as a meeting with the mark was about to happen. In their "accidental" crossover at the building site my father would use as a backdrop to his scams, The Come In would demonstrate his great acumen and stellar success thanks to my father's projects.

Then came The Distraction, something to turn the mark's head, a person or thing with an element of fantasy attached that would absorb the victim's attention when they might have otherwise been fixated on the finer details as the scam reached its critical stage. Depending on the mark, The Distraction could be a beautiful woman who remained just out of reach or, in the case of his last Hurrah, a car dealer contact who apparently held the key to his dream car—something that perfectly matched the person the mark believed he was about to be—at an unbelievable price, a steal, you might say. Because, isn't there a small part of all of us that believes we should have a little more than we're strictly entitled to?

If Dad had done it right, and he mostly did, then the combination of the work of all the previous stages would have softened the mark up nicely for the final part of the con: The Hurrah. It always began with a crisis. Dad told the speculative property developer that an unforeseen issue meant the dodgy planner needed a significant sum to make the problem go away. Dad would offer to put the money in if the mark did, leading him to believe if he didn't throw everything at it now, like my dad and his apparent co-investor appeared willing to, he'd lose not only what he'd already put in, but the tremendous rewards, the unimaginably good life my dad had slowly but surely let him think was about to be his.

The Hurrah would make the mark go all in, against his better judgment, counter to everything he should know about how life works. He'd beg, borrow, steal, anything he could do to get together the sum my dad said was required to make his future real.

There isn't a name, as far as I know, for what happens to the victim after The Hurrah. It should probably be known as The

Crash. From expecting a great triumph and huge financial returns, ice-cold reality would set in. The small-time property developer realizes he was a mark all along. The only thing my father's property investment had generated was his ruin, his complete humiliation.

I close my father's book and shut my eyes hard against the memories banging on the door of my consciousness. I remember having an understanding that most marks skulked away in their shame, not wanting anyone to know they'd been played. A few railed against what my dad had done. But one man was not afraid of shame. He wanted justice, so he confronted my father and threatened to put him away for what he had done. That's where I came into his last Hurrah. The Decoy.

"You spend more time looking at that window, reading that book, than you do me." Pete invades my thoughts. "What have they got that I haven't?" He's trying to make a joke of the distance we both know has been growing between us, not one I'm in the mood to share.

"They do what I need them to," I say, not liking the way I sound at all, but unable to let him off for all the strain I feel I'm carrying on my own, all the plates that will crash to the ground in this family unless I near kill myself keeping them spinning. Charlie runs in and I turn all my attention on him. All Pete can do is watch.

"Guess what? I've got really exciting news," I tell my son.

"Are me, you, and Auntie Jacq going somewhere fun?"

Thankfully, I stop myself from saying, *Better than that.* "You and I are going on a playdate! Tomorrow!"

Charlie perks up, excited, maybe, at the idea he'll be seeing one of his little friends from nursery.

"We're going to the house of a really nice boy who goes to your school."

"Who? There aren't any nice boys at my school." His shoulders and his face fall with disappointment.

"There are and this one is called Rajvir and his mummy is called Amala."

"What? What are you going to her house for?" Pete pipes up, looking oddly stricken.

"She's a new friend. What's the problem?"

Pete doesn't give me an answer before he turns and heads for his bath. I see him chewing his cheek just before I can't see his face anymore. "Nothing."

I refocus on Charlie. "We are going to have so much fun. You'll see, there are good boys, nice people at The Woolf." I take Charlie's hands, stand up from my window seat, and we do a little swaying dance together.

"OK, Mummy. I promise I'll be good," he tells me, breaking my heart. What or who has made him think he isn't? He is; we are. If I've got anything to do with it, soon everyone at The Woolf will be in no doubt we are more than good enough.

"Good is *who* you are." I come down to his level and hold him tight. "And Charlie?"

"Yes, Mummy?"

"I promise to let you choose some new Lego if you promise to keep it secret that Amala's house used to be Mummy and Grandad Charles's home."

12

THE NEXT DAY, JACQ'S GUTTED WHEN I PHONE HER AT LUNCH TO tell her she won't be seeing Charlie as normal, though I'm secretly, and guiltily, glad that we'll have bath time, just the two of us, after our playdate at Amala's. I've craved being solo with Charlie since he started at The Woolf. I long to do that thing that takes time alone and repetition with your child; finding and maintaining a vocabulary that only makes sense to you, one intimate and powerful enough to keep you glued together all the time you're not, all those times your child needs you and you can't be there.

I don't tell Jacq why she can stand down at pickup time today because I can already imagine her reaction to Charlie and me going to Amala's house (*Why do you want to get in with her and that odd lot? Let me know if she mentions why one of her best mates ended herself, won't you?*), and have decided I don't have the energy to defend myself. Instead, I bounce straight into the good news her grant application has been approved. It seems the bank is under pressure to show the scheme's been a success and get the money available to businesses they deem deserving. The funds for Jacq's refurb will be coming through as early as next week.

Jacq's decided to call the new place The Narrow, inspired by The Narrows, the stretch of water that separates the islands of St. Kitts and Nevis, where Jacq and Pete's dad's family is from. It also suits the long, thin room perfectly. Between the playdate and the grant, everything feels like it's heading toward success, as if it were always meant to be.

"Thank you, Rose. I can't believe this is happening."

"Thank *you*. You're helping me in so many ways. You don't even know."

She doesn't, and not only because Marek has started to take more notice of me at work since I led on her grant application. I hear Jacq sigh contentedly at the end of the line, but I still want her to think about aiming even higher—something we should both be doing.

"You know, once the new place is up and running, if it's earning for you, you should hire yourself a replacement, concentrate on your studies, shoot for your MA, your PhD, nothing should stop you."

"Let's see. Baby steps."

"Why go slow, play down your chances? You're the cleverest person I know."

Jacq laughs. "What's gotten into you?"

"Nothing. I just think it's time you and me, and Pete, stopped thinking small, stopped believing the big stuff is for other people."

"And how is my brother doing?"

I wait a beat, banishing from my mind the image of his face as I left the house this morning without speaking to him, let alone kissing him goodbye, before releasing the un-lie from my lips. "He's fine."

I LEAVE WORK a few minutes early so I can go home to change out of my uniform and into my polo neck and jeans before pickup and the playdate. There's no need for me to keep my bright blue jacket and trousers on, so why not be more presentable, relax a little while I'm at Amala's house? It makes sense to do everything I can to keep on top of my nerves.

I get to the playground outside Charlie's class where Amala arranged to meet me as it starts to rain. She emerges from under the veranda, ushers me under her huge maroon-and-gold umbrella, and hugs me hard from the side. I feel as though she's physically shielding me from the judgment of other mums who openly stare at us. I don't bother keeping the smile from my face as Amala tells Mrs. Hilsum to send Charlie out first. Charlie is being chosen for preferential treatment. I wonder if the waiting mums, viewing me in my knackered boots and old jeans, and by her side under her umbrella, are beginning to think the impossible, that I might be the one Amala chooses next. If they are, might I dare think the same?

Together, me, Charlie, and Amala head to find Rajvir, who's two classes above Charlie, before all four of us take the short walk to Bryk Road. On the way, Charlie wants to tell me something, but he can't get it out. He must be so excited to be finally going on a playdate, just as all the other children do on Fridays.

The rain stops before we reach the front gate of my old house. Behind Rajvir and Amala's back, I make a shushing sign at Charlie and mentally prepare myself for what is coming next. I find myself bristling anew at the *Woolf View* signage and at the neat, aggrandizing border of heather and lavender lining the path to my old front door. I walk through the door knowing I need to calm the throb of outrage already reddening my cheeks.

The light coming from the front of the house soothes me immediately. *Home.* I'm back in the place I should never have been made to leave. For a second I'm almost afraid to see my father's face in the shadows as we take off our coats, before I see clearly what I was able to deduce from looking in from the street that morning: this is a completely different home from the one I grew up in. The transformation, the stretching of space, the stealing of light, the money imbued in every object and surface, astounds me.

Charlie follows Rajvir upstairs to play while Amala invites me to follow her into the "main reception," glimpsing back as my eyes suck in every detail, probing the farthest point my vision can reach. My gaze sweeps over the expansive living room and designer kitchen toward the back of the long space with its marble island and enormous, polished concrete dining table. Beyond this, there's a glass extension that seems to house a home office and play area; outside this, a stylish landscaped garden. The only thing disrupting the luxurious interior are a couple of bulky cardboard boxes, wrapped tight in cellophane. One box is half full. I spy files, an old keyboard, a scrunched-up rugby shirt.

"Would you like me to give you the tour?"

It's obvious how much Amala is enjoying my undisguisable awe at her home. Her smile is faint, but her eyes glisten with satisfaction.

"No. Don't trouble yourself." I try to say it lightly, as if I'm not dying to see what else she's managed to do to my house, as though I'm not desperate to absorb each detail I can about the life people like her make possible on the ground on which I was born. "Another time, maybe."

I follow her to her beautiful kitchen. There's not a stretch of Formica or laminate in sight; everything is real, solid wood. The gray marble of her kitchen island is cool under my elbows as I perch on one of the tangerine leather barstools. I feel I'm the only thing making the place look untidy as I watch Amala deftly load a wooden tray with fruit, small, earnest-looking bags of lentil chips, miniboxes of raisins, and two cartons of beetroot and black currant juice, thinking guiltily about the Haribo and hot dogs I usually give Charlie on a Friday.

"Back shortly." She picks up the tray and sashays toward the stairs.

I look around me, hardly able to imagine I ever set foot, let alone lived, in the same bricks and mortar. Frustration begins to accumulate in me, the kind that makes you want to stamp your feet. How has it been Amala's privilege, not mine, to make this house all it could be? Why did she get to eviscerate all traces of my dad? That was supposed to have been my job.

"Now, what will you take?" Amala's return startles me. "Tea? Water? Or I'm fixing a gin. Join me?"

I nod, hearing someone enter the room behind me. "There you are," Amala says turning around. An elderly man, strong and square with a blue turban, thick white beard, and a mustache rolled into neat scrolls that taper to his ears, stands in the doorway. "Your food's coming in a minute, OK?" Amala pours one shot, then another of gin into two balloon glasses.

"What's this? Drinking?"

Amala cuts some fruit on a chopping board. "Budda Daddy, meet Rose. Rose, don't mind him, he still thinks I'm sixteen."

"Very nice to meet you," I tell him.

He offers me a polite nod, shakes his head wearily, and walks out of the room.

"I'll be down in a minute!" Amala calls after her father as he begins his descent to what was the old cellar, which I imagine must be a fully functioning basement dwelling now.

"No matter how old you are, you'll always be a little girl, right?" Amala presents me with my gin. "So, what is it we need to talk about? You seemed so upset at the cemetery yesterday."

I clear my throat. "Quite honestly, I'm not sure Charlie's enjoying school as much as he might. I'm sure it's us, him, *me,* it's not your school." I choose my words carefully, wanting her to understand I'm alert to Charlie's problems but without appearing ungrateful or blaming The Woolf. Being upfront about it is hardly likely to put me in a good position to make things right.

"Let's not minimize Charlie's challenges. Tell me where we've gone wrong."

Charlie's challenges. No indication these issues were nonexistent until he arrived at The Woolf. That pulse of outrage again, which I'm required to breathe over. "Well, I suppose all the singling-out seems to be making things very hard for him."

"And for you too?" Amala leans on her kitchen island so her eyes are now level with mine. She wants to understand exactly how much Charlie's new regime is hurting me. I see no harm in showing her I've reacted to this as any other mother might. "It's hard to know your child has been isolated in class, set aside for being different, being made to see the school counselor. I'd defy any mother to be happy at their child needing all of that."

Amala nods behind her fingers, steepled before her perfect and perfectly composed face. "Rose. What you're talking about are all hugely positive things."

I think of Charlie last night, his hair damp with sweat, as I lay next to him after another nightmare, holding his hand until he fell back to sleep and I could return to my thin nest of bedding on the floor next to him. I don't want to betray his confidence, or the depth of my anger at what The Woolf's treatment so far has done to him, but neither do I want to be guilty of not standing up for him by telling Amala something of what he's going through as a result of all the *hugely positive things.* "My son has hardly slept since he started school."

Amala appears unruffled, unconcerned. "Recognizing where we need a little more help can prove an uncomfortable experience, but these are growing pains. Any extra attention you and your family receive from us is coming from the very best place."

Amala's politician's pivot, converting a tough question into a platform to reassert her achievements, is beginning to make me want to take a crowbar to the slab of marble between us, but I remain focused. "Where we really need extra attention is the after-hours care. I was relying on getting Charlie into breakfast club and after-school. If I'd known these were going to be so hard to get, I would have tried to sort something else out. I suppose it's my fault, but—"

"We're working really hard to make that better for everyone. Our problem is we've been too successful, but we won't compromise quality. If I could wave a magic wand . . ." She wafts her diamond-laden fingers about the air around her. "But we should be doing more for people like you."

"People like me?" My fingers worry the fold of my polo neck.

"Working mums. What else did you think I meant?" She examines my face and tatty, desperately in-need-of-a-cut hair. "What will you do without the after-hours care?"

I tell my drink, "I'll think of something. I always do." I force an optimistic smile before looking back to Amala.

"I'm sure you do." She allows her eyes to rest on mine. I swear I can see her give in to the tiniest shiver before returning her gaze to her hands. My eyes; does she have a problem with them? She dives into the next question before I can dwell on it any longer. "Tell me more about you. I believe you trained in accountancy, but work at the bank."

Is this my chance? Why else would she ask? I have fantasized about this moment and have dreamed up many alternative versions of what I might say next. There's the scenario where I downplay what I'm capable of and hide my background, allowing Amala to discover my past herself, if she cares to. There's the version where I devise an un-lie about what stopped me from being all I might have been. And then there's the situation I gamed where I provide a full-blooded fiction and tell Amala I'm a fully qualified accountant who works in a bank to allow me to focus more of my energy on my family, which impresses her to no end. Ultimately, I choose an account of myself I hope Amala finds both surprising and reassuring: the truth, or at least one iteration of it.

My dad once told me how to retain power when someone wants to use negative information they might have on you: "Put a rosette on yourself." If I get out my perceived secrets before Amala does, stab all the rosettes, all the labels she and others may want to attach to me—criminal's daughter, unqualified failure, lowly bank teller—clean into my skin, this way, I not only get to choose when the pain of the revelations happens, I also rob them of their power to shame me.

"That's right. Despite my early training, I'm a bank cashier and the reason begins and ends with my father, Charles O'Connell." Amala's eyes seem to spark as she prepares to drink in the details of my sordid little life. "He was a career criminal. A confidence trickster, a scammer." I tell her how I was doing all right for myself. Even though I left school at sixteen, I'd been doing work experience at a local firm of accountants and they offered me a junior role and the chance to study for some entry-level exams. By the time I was eighteen, I was studying for the next stage up. My dad was very ill by then, and while he hadn't pulled one of his cons for years, he was still known round here. There were businesses, people who had never forgotten what he'd done to people. A big client my boss wanted to win complained about me being on staff. The owner of the accountancy firm told me my position was no longer tenable because of who my father was. "I got the sack for no other reason than who I'd been born to, and do you know, I didn't fight it? Part of me thought I deserved to have my future taken from me." I can't meet her eye when I say it. *Because I'd taken the future away from another human being,* I add in my head.

"The accountants didn't think you could be trusted, that the apple didn't fall far from the tree?" Amala asks, sounding mesmerized. How entertaining the squalid details of my past must seem to someone like her.

"That was their theory. It's one of the reasons I worked to get my job in the bank, eventually. Pete and I got married and we were trying for Charlie. I wanted to wipe the slate clean on my life. I'd ended up working in the bookies down the road." Ironically, the very same place my father had squandered all the money that ever came his way, but it was all I was confident enough to apply for at the time. "Jacq got to thinking, me getting a job in an institution where money comes in and goes out again just as it should, where you only get employed if you've got a crystal clear record and proven honesty, would help me feel better about myself. Lay to rest how my dad damaged my life."

"And did it?"

"To a point. But there's still so much more I want to do with my life, my brain, all that potential that's not been used yet." I look to her to see if this is the opening I think she might be looking for. She goes to say something, but stops herself as if a fresh idea has sprung to mind. Or perhaps I'm imagining all of it, my paranoia giving way to something potentially more damaging: hope.

"Will you let me cook Charlie some dinner? Stay awhile? They sound so happy up there. Fresh orecchiette with kale pesto OK?" She's already halfway to the kitchen before I can ask what any of that is.

"As long as you're sure." *Please let this be a good sign.*

"Always."

Amala busies herself in the kitchen and retrieves gin and lime, plus various green things for the boys' food from a huge American fridge that is, as predicted, half the size of my entire kitchenette back at the flat. I follow her back to the kitchen to keep our conversation flowing as she collects boiling water in a bright copper pan directly from a designer tap. I've told her plenty about me; it's surely time to see what, if anything, she's willing to share with me. I lean against the kitchen island and deliberately let my eyes rest on the moving boxes and rugby shirt nearby, knowing she'll either have to wilfully ignore my cue, or decide she can trust me. At first she tries the former, smiling overbrightly as she hands me a fresh drink. I dare to probe, see if she can get out of telling me something I don't believe she was planning to.

"Your husband opening a new office somewhere?" I tick my head to the boxes.

Amala pauses, seems to undertake some kind of recalibration. "Darius and I, we're . . . he's moving out."

"Oh dear, I'm sorry to hear that." Amala seems to be attempting to shrug the whole thing off with an unconvincing expression that seems to say, *C'est la vie,* not meeting my eye. But there's no way I want this exchange closed down. "It's amicable, I hope."

She breathes a deep sigh. "We're doing our best for Rajvir, naturally, and keeping up appearances until everything's . . . until such time as we need not to." Amala finishes her sentence and fixes me with a glassy stare, which I take as her silently requesting my discretion.

"Of course I won't say anything to anyone. You know you can trust me on that." After all, I haven't breathed a word about her lying about where she really was when Bea died; I want her to remember she can trust me. She draws her lips together, and I can tell she knows what I'm getting at. We're good at this, me and her, so adept at reading people's signs, especially each other's. It emboldens me to push a little further, as I follow her back to the sofas and take the spot opposite where she sits. "Must be hard, though, with everything else you have on your plate?"

"I'll survive. I always live to fight another day."

"Sounds tough. And expensive." To heat the cavernous space she's carved out of my home must cost a fortune alone. I wonder, why did she have to go so far as to wipe clean any trace of the past, like an occupying force ridding their territory of all native culture? The first flush of gin is beginning to loosen my emotions. The same appears to be true of Amala, who seems to be relishing something only she understands.

Amala leans forward as she tells me, "Nothing I can't afford in the long run." She's almost in my space, face inches from mine. Noticing her own sudden intensity, Amala diverts her attention to her drink, before forcing a change in subject. "Your husband, Peter. Tell me, is he as good a husband on the inside as he looks on the outside?"

I laugh over the weirdness of talking about "Peter" with Amala, and my stomach twists. How does she know what he looks like, and why does she feel entitled to let me know she finds my husband attractive? "He's not perfect, but he tries. Have you seen Pete somewhere?"

"I told you before, when you join The Woolf, we make it our business to discover what we can about the whole family."

We watch each other for a moment.

"Hey, let me quickly plate up the boys' food and attend to *Him Downstairs.*" She gives me a quick pat on the knee and I watch her unfold her incredible frame before me, imagining what Pete might make of the toned lengths of her legs, the narrowness of her waist against the generosity of curves. I consider my own body, slight, but in a small and unimpressive way.

"You know, your dad needn't make himself scarce on my account." I realize he could be a potentially interesting source of insight on Amala, something to let me feel more in control than I do right now.

"Six months of the year he lives with me, and for most of that time, it suits him to stay downstairs," adding, "as it does me," behind the steam of the pan she is draining the contents of. I would dearly love to know what Amala's daddy issues are. There's a dark relief from sensing all is far from happy in her apparently perfect world. But the fact remains that whatever their troubles, even if her husband is leaving, she still has her father with her, only a flight of stairs away if she needs him, not scattered in the soil. The thought provokes a powerful pang of longing followed quickly by an increasingly familiar sense of outrage.

"I deal with grumpy old men all the time at the bank. I don't mind passing the time of day with him." I want to worry the wound, to understand something of the kind of background it takes to create someone like Amala Kaur, the woman with her father in the home that will always be mine and Dad's.

She gives me a tight smile, before angling her face in the direction of the loud giggling from the boys upstairs. Amala comes to stand over me. "My Raj is loving having his little brother over to play. You see, in my culture, we have names for every type of relation on your father's side and your mother's side. But ultimately everyone's a *grandad,* everyone is your *auntie.* Charlie is Rajvir's brother. You and I? We're sisters."

I smile over the ups and downs of her words, the way her pulling me into her world so intimately makes me feel at once accepted, and threatened. If there is one person who understands how perilous being family to a person can be, it's me.

Amala adds the finishing touches to the two plates of ear-shaped fresh pasta with green sauce she seems to have whipped up out of nowhere and ferries it upstairs. When she returns to the kitchen, she produces another plate for us and piles it with piping hot samosas and chutney, which I somehow didn't even notice her preparing. It would have taken me hours to deliver the food she has for us, the boys, her father, and the results would have been dreadful. For Amala, everything she touches seems to turn into something wonderful. When it strikes me that she is blessed with her Midas touch, I wonder, does that make me somehow cursed?

Another drink settles into my bloodstream and the chat between us becomes less intense, more relaxed. Over the deliciously spicy samosas, we talk about what our boys like, discuss how much we each love the area, or our alternative versions of the same place. As I grow accustomed to Amala's huge sofa of patterned black velvet adorned with mustard-colored honeysuckle, words want to spill out of me. I'm in danger of forgetting myself and why I'm here.

"Charlie and I should get going, leave you in peace."

"Please, stay," Amala tells me as she gathers another pair of empty glasses to take back to the kitchen. "I'm not done with you yet."

My heart bounces behind my ribs. I'll stay as long as she asks, as long as it looks like I'm still in with the chance of what those other mothers would kill for. Do I give in to my now gin-fueled hope and believe in impossible things?

Charlie wanders into the living room. He leans into me and whispers in my ear, "Can we go home soon? For bath time, just with you?" He rubs his tired little eyes. I check my mobile. It's gone seven. I can't believe how quickly the time here with Amala has passed. "Give Mummy five more minutes. Go on and play, good boy." I send him away.

I know I promised him some one-on-one time, but there are things I've promised myself, too, improvements to all our lives that have a chance of beginning tonight. One day, I hope he'll understand how not putting him first in this moment was about meeting his needs in the longer term. My logic right now is the same that requires mothers to go against their every instinct to place their own oxygen masks over their mouths before their child's as the plane plummets to the earth.

Amala returns and takes the seat right next to me. She sets

down a tray with a steel pot of tea and matching beakers. She fills my cup and a soft steam of warm milk, sugar, and spice fills the air.

"I'm assuming you have some understanding of The Circle?"

There they are, the words you're not supposed to say. Amala and her associates: *The Circle.* It's happening.

Dehydrated from the alcohol I'm not used to drinking, I thirstily take a sip of the tea. It immediately burns my tongue. I nod to Amala's last question and disguise my pain.

"And you know all about Bea."

"What do you mean?"

The samosas, the gin, and hot milk, all of it suddenly curdles inside me. In none of my daydream scenarios do we talk about Bea. I don't want to have to talk about that poor woman, her death, or my backing up Amala on her whereabouts the night she died. I need to maintain my grip on the plausible deniability over there being anything remotely suspicious about the un-lie I was brought into.

"You know that, very sadly, she died." Amala's eyes are lost into the middle distance, her features tight with pain. "It's awful. The whole thing."

I don't say anything, only watch out for any tic or twinge of facial muscle, the movement of her hands, wrapped protectively around her cup for now, any gesture or pause that might tell me if she is speaking the truth to me about Bea.

"She'd been making mistakes, and her attitude was bringing me, all of us, down. But I stuck with her. I thought I'd given her every chance, everything she needed to succeed and be happy, all that I could do for her." Amala turns her glistening eyes to me. "Sometimes, no matter what we do, our best isn't good enough, is it?"

I shake my head, still assessing whether I might be convinced by this, admittedly persuasive, performance.

"I still can't believe she's gone." A swollen tear falls almost into Amala's chai.

"I'm so sorry for your loss. It must be incredibly hard for all of you."

Amala nods, uses the back of one elegant finger to remove the remains of her single tear from her cheek, before clearing her throat and looking directly at me. Suddenly, she's switched to business-as-usual mode. "You're aware Bea helped out on the financial side of things at The Woolf as a member of The Circle?"

"I had heard something along those lines."

She nods, in a way that says, *Of course you have.* "The Circle makes The Woolf all that it is. Naturally, there are certain rewards for being part of the team that makes this happen, which I'm confident you're aware of, though we do try to be understandably discreet about these."

"I've picked up the odd thing here and there."

"I'm sure." She holds my gaze unblinkingly. "I've been wondering, Rose, whether you're prepared to give that *little bit more* to The Woolf."

I wait for the words and draw a breath deep into my lungs. They seem to take forever to arrive, but surely, they are coming.

An image of me sitting in the toilets at work the day of the school place offer.

My thumb hanging over "Accept the offer" but refusing to go through with it. That sense of innate resistance feels vivid again. I feel words forming in my throat.

"Rose O'Connell," Amala says it loudly, firmly, like a judge about to hand down the sentence for the convicted, her hands reaching toward my neck. I have to stop my natural instinct to bat her fingers away.

Wait—

"Welcome inside The Circle."

Stop—

A sharp scratch.

The pin of the Circle brooch punctures the skin on my throat.

I find myself suddenly wondering if it is a brand-new pin, if Amala keeps a ready stock of them. Or, I can't stop myself from thinking, is this the very same one that belonged to Bea? Has it found its way from the blood-soaked collar of a dead woman's clothes to mine?

I keep my face still over the discomfort of the jab and the disgust at this last notion as Amala tucks the pin into its catch. "Come to my office on Monday morning before school. I'm going to make it so you realize everything your family's life should be."

And with these words, this promise, I immediately forget about the scratch on my neck, disregard the many ways I've been cautioned about Amala Kaur, and put all thoughts of Bea out of mind too. In this moment of anointed victory, I even forget my son is there, startling when I hear his voice.

"Too tired for bath. Bedtime. *Please,* Mummy."

Guilt wants to seed in my chest, but I harden against it, instead saying to Amala, "Thank you. I will show you I'm capable of so much more than you might think."

Because some things are more important than missing a single ritual of motherhood; there are moments in your life when you have to ignore the voice that seeks to keep you small. Smallness might be easier when it comes to protecting yourself from danger and remaining unseen, but it costs you the chance to be more than you might. What I've just achieved is going to transform my life, and Charlie's. This is what I need to believe now.

A blur of bag-gathering, gloves lost and found, hugs and good wishes, and Charlie and I are ready to go.

"Good night, Rose, Charlie." Amala views us with what

seems to be a curious fulfillment as she closes her door. I beam back at her, tipsier than I can remember being since my wedding day, so much so, I've forgotten to do up Charlie's coat against the autumn air before we left. I kneel down on the front path, fingers fudgy with alcohol.

"Mum?"

"Give me a chance, Charlie. I'm doing my best." I pull the zip into its catch.

"The thing I wanted to tell you before, can I tell you now?"

"Go for it."

"It was her."

"Who?"

"Amala. She's the lady who told my teacher to sit me on my own."

"Amala? Oh, she was looking out for you. She was making sure you had the help she could see you needed." I project with the confidence of an overemoting drunk person, compensating for the lack of truth they suspect is in their words with the strength of how they express them.

I hold his hand too tight all the way home, my head light and sickly; the sensation of being too high in the sky, struggling to find my oxygen mask, anticipating the terrifying drop to the ground.

Part Two

INSIDE THE CIRCLE

THE PLANNING HAS BEEN JUDICIOUS: THE SETTING OF HER ALIBI; all the care taken to avoid cameras that might have otherwise captured her vehicle as it moved toward its target; the actions to limit the transfer of paint and glass to clothes and skin. So long as she accelerates only at the last minute and avoids traceable internet searches and telltale returns to the scene of the crime, she is almost confident her capture will be avoided.

What she does not evade are the sounds of the diabolical act. After the initial thud, as the body met the metal of her bonnet, came the crack of a skull smacking into her windscreen. Then all was quiet; a snatch of silence as the impact granted her victim temporary flight before her car's tires squealed her getaway. So much like the first time.

As she speeds away, she imagines the scene she left behind; breaths losing volume and frequency with each exhalation, with each throb of blood onto the road's indifferent surface. A body shattered by physical trauma, not even able to feel the rain falling. The desperate summoning of final thoughts.

As she parks the murder weapon in its usual spot, she imagines the blackness creeping in around the edges of her victim's vision. She checks behind her to see that no one is watching, giving the orange streetlight illuminating her an accusing glare. She can't help wondering if all the victim's eyes can see now is a tangerine smear of brightness, becoming smaller; the thought makes her woozy. But if it isn't already, it will surely be over very soon.

As she lies in bed, wired, awake, sleep refusing to arrive, something inside her knows it is finally done. Death. She can feel it.

This is when it starts.

Thud. Crack. Silence.

Thud. Crack. Silence.

A horrific replay on a loop in her mind.

Later that night, the sequence still playing on repeat, half-delirious, sleep-deprived fantasies take over. She imagines the sensation of absolute darkness that swept her victim through to death's oblivion. Their pain is over, but hers will endure. And for a moment, at least, she wishes they could swap places.

13

GET BACK FROM AMALA'S HOUSE AFTER THE PLAYDATE FEELING nauseous. Pete is finishing up his workout with the TV on. "Bit late? You doing OK, big guy?" Charlie waves and yawns his way to his room. I follow.

"We got chatting," I mumble.

"Oh yeah. What about?" Pete calls after me.

"Later. Need to get this one to bed." I try to speak without betraying my drunkenness.

In Charlie's room, I pull off his uniform and scoop his PJs from the floor.

"Are you sleeping in my room too? I don't mind if you don't. It's OK if you want to sleep in yours and Daddy's room." Charlie can see things aren't right between me and Pete and the realization makes my heart break.

"Don't you worry about me, Daddy, or anything. Daddy likes having a big bed for himself and I like sleeping here with you." Charlie begins to nibble the inside of his cheek. Guilt. I cannot have him believing the problems with me and Pete have anything to do with him. "But I'll be sleeping in my room with Daddy tonight, OK?"

"Yep." His expression lightens immediately, as does my heart. "No nightmares for me," he says, lying back, halfway to sleep already, and yawning. "I had the best . . . time . . . ever."

Eager to feel like a better mother than I know I've been

today, I take his tiny hands in mine and make him an oath I feel confident about keeping.

"Charlie, I promise you, today's just the start of it."

I hear a slur in my voice I don't like. My presence here is polluting my perfect boy. I avoid breathing fumes over him and leave him on the verge of sleep to near-stagger to my bedroom.

Pete follows me in and puts a glass of water and two paracetamol on my bedside table before sitting awkwardly on the end of the bed, watching me pull off my clothes. "So, you had a big chat with that Amala then?"

"Can we talk tomorrow?" I down the pills with a big gulp of water. "I ended up having a couple of drinks."

"Yeah, I can see that. So long as everything's all right; you're OK?"

I nod, not able to get my head to the pillow quickly enough. I crash into our bed and a dark sleep overcomes me. I dream of my dad. His face and voice fade in and out of my mind.

Do this for me.

When have I ever let you down?

He asks me it over and over, as he always did. Unlike the compliant silence of the lonely, craven child I was, I tell him the truth: "You let me down all the time, Dad, all the time." But, oh, when I see that face of his again. Those gleaming green eyes, the soft lines of his wicked smile reaching across worlds to me, I believe, for the thousandth time, he is alive again. My pain melts away, my heart fills, my mind lost in the heart notes of his day-to-day scent: Benson & Hedges, a suit jacket in need of a dry clean, the mineral traces of cement on his shoes. The possibility of his affection feels so immediate, because my father has chosen *my* dream to attend and now he holds me in a way that never happened in my real life, no matter how I longed for it. But when I pull away, I see it isn't my father's embrace I've lost myself in. It's Amala Kaur's.

The mutation of my father into Amala is so disturbing as to sober me into overheated wakefulness. I sit up, sickened, still half asleep, unsure where I am. Pete wakes up and rubs my back.

"You're safe. You're here."

I make myself imagine that the fresh cold water Pete brings me is cleaning my body, and conjure the calming feel of my son on my lap after the bath I'll give him in the morning to cleanse my mind. I drift off again.

When I wake up after hours of oblivion, despite my dry, acrid mouth and light head, I feel rested for the first time in months. It's as though I've wiped out my sleep debt. I remember I might now have a shot at erasing our financial dues too. A dizzy kind of euphoria begins to fizz in my mind. Because while I know there are things I am yet to understand, factors I need to work out, I remain certain too that life is finally going to change. *I am inside The Circle. The messy buns and white trainers won't believe it on the playground: Rose O'Connell is The One.* I imagine the glares, alive with envy; Jo and all those other stuck-up mums on the cemetery trip, gobsmacked. Before the weekend is through, I'll polish my Circle brooch. I don't want anyone to miss it on the lapel of my uniform. I can barely wait for Monday morning, when all the Woolf Mothers will finally look at me differently.

It strikes me the last time I felt this good was when me and Pete first got together. My life before Jacq had made me a loner in every aspect of my existence. I was still very nervous around men, around most people, in fact. But when she introduced me to Pete, when he came here to live with Jacq, six years into my knowing her, I noticed something different about him that persuaded me to get past my inhibitions.

When Pete came into the café, women's jaws would loosen. They wouldn't be able to finish the sentence they were in the middle of; the friend they were with would disappear, their children too. I watched their eyes scamper over his face, his neck, his arms, his chest, down to his flat abdomen and below. When he passed, I could see them try to cram every patch of his face into their memory, their mouths watering at the symmetry of his lips, the unthreatening beauty of his hazel eyes, the flawlessness of his skin. I watched with fascination when Pete happened to catch the women's eyes. I'd marvel at how their faces would open and bloom. I grew fond, too, of his struggle not to blush when this happened, and appreciated the sight of his whole body clenching against the attention. There have been hundreds, maybe thousands, of attempts to turn Pete's head, and they did not end after we got together.

It was easy to see that, for any woman, Pete would be her absolute prize. Back when I first knew him, I remember daring to imagine how it might feel to walk down the high street with Pete holding my hand. I played out how bulletproof I'd feel with him as my boyfriend if I were to ever bump into the Whichello twins again. If I had this beautiful man on my arm, there would be no denying who had won. I would be almost untouchable. And Pete wasn't just drop-dead gorgeous, so much so I could hardly believe he would want me, he was obviously such a sweet man too: sound, uncomplicated, easy to be around.

At twenty-four, I'd still never slept with anyone. Jacq gently encouraged me to let my guard down while no longer bringing up the embarrassing stories from when they were kids, or having a go at him for anything and everything. She wanted to elevate him, to make sure he was my "one." Because Pete and me as a long-term couple was the ideal solution for Jacq. With us together, she'd not lose either of us to anyone else. She'd get to keep us both and maybe more; the idea of the baby that would be Charlie emerging from the stars above us all that summer, as the three of us talked about what our futures might hold.

"Mummy! Daddy! Guess who's a-w-a-aaake?!" Charlie sings out from his room.

"Wow. He's been out like a light for twelve hours straight," Pete says, smiling, happy to know Charlie is properly rested, and clearly thrilled to see me next to him in bed once more. "Be with you in a minute, buddy!" he calls out, but goes to nestle into me in a way that sends a surge of heat through me. I feel suddenly conscious of the alcohol I know I'm radiating.

"Sorry, I smell like the barmaid's apron."

"Think I care?"

I shake my head and let my hands find the back of his neck, smooth and warm. It's enough to encourage Pete to slide his torso onto me and he dares to kiss me deeply. His lips feel brand-new, or maybe it's my own mouth that's different somehow. I feel very drunk again. I run my hands over the hardness of his shoulder muscles, down his silken back, pressing my nails into his skin as I draw his weight onto me.

I stop to wriggle out from under him, then take his phone and hurry into Charlie's room. I give my son a quick cuddle, and find a cartoon for him. "You watch this awhile, then we'll have a lovely breakfast together and a nice bath."

He nods, his face unnaturally illuminated by the screen.

When I get back to bed, I want Pete to see I'm different, a new me. This morning, sex isn't the usual semi-functional, get-it-done act, something else on the to-do list after signing consent forms and polishing my boots; it's me appreciating every gorgeous inch of my husband and every pretty piece of me.

We're done just in time, still panting and naked below the duvet when Charlie bursts in. "Finished!" He jumps onto our bed and Pete and I both laugh, together.

"Right, let's get you some toast, little man. And a cup of tea in bed for you, miss? What did you say your name was again?"

"*Dad-dy!*"

"I'm Rose. Rose O'Connell and you'd better not forget it."

Pete salutes. "Back in a mo, Ms. O'Connell." Now it's his palm on the back of my neck. He brings my forehead to his. "I've missed you. I know I'm far from perfect, but I love you, Rose."

I dip my head lower, as if trying to look into his eyes, though my lids are closed. He leaves the bed to get dressed. I watch Pete pulling on his tracksuit bottoms, admiring the slither of lateral muscles across his back as they tense and release. He turns to show me the flesh, taut and sinewed across his stomach, and the definition of the obliques on either side, the lines of shadow directing anyone's vision downward. Pete, my prize, my secret weapon against those women who'd want to imagine they were better than me. Did he really choose to stay faithful to me forever? Do I really believe I'm good enough to have that as long as we both shall live?

"Stop staring at me, woman!"

"I do love you, too, Pete. Don't ever forget that, will you?"

"Why would I do that?" He laughs, following Charlie into the living room.

Alone, I lie back and replay the key moments from last night again and again. I need to process everything I learned about Amala and what she makes of me before I see her again on Monday morning at my first meeting of The Circle.

"Here's your tea. No, don't get up, you chill as long as you like."

"Pete, sit down a minute. There's something I need to tell you."

He falls to sit on the end of the bed, the smile on his face dropping too. "What's up?"

"Nothing's *up!* I've got good news."

I grab my polo neck from the pile of clothes on the carpet where I left it and turn the pin toward him.

"What's that?"

"There's a group of well-thought-of mums who support The Woolf's work: fundraising, PR, legal affairs, and the finances. Everybody wants to be part of it and, as of last night, I am. No one actually calls it by the name, but it's called The Circle."

"That's what you and her were talking about?" Pete searches my face.

"*Her*, Amala? Yes. I'm going to start helping them out on the financial side of things. What else?" I hunt his expression in return.

"So, you're going to do work for that Amala for nothing?"

"No! Why would you assume the worst? They're not all bad, the new people round here. They might have money, but that doesn't make them a different species to us."

"You've changed your tune." Pete doesn't contain his confusion, given my intermittent moaning over the years as yet another piece of the neighborhood is flattened, jet-washed, or reformed.

"That's because I can see now that we're just like them really, or we could be if we let ourselves. As of Monday, life is going to get a whole lot easier, so much better for all of us. Charlie's going to get the best sort of attention from his teachers; he'll get everything he needs to make the very best start he can."

"Shouldn't he have been getting that anyway? Isn't that why we sent him to that school?"

"Life's not like that, Pete."

"Not at The Woolf, it isn't." There's a tightness in his neck now; he wants to shake his head, but knows better not to. "So, what exactly is it you'll be doing?"

"I'll be helping out with the accounts, like Bea did."

"You're the new dead woman, then?"

"*Pete*. I don't know why you're being so negative. Someone

had to do something to make things the better for us." Why does my husband always have to be the barrier to the good things, not the bridge that helps us get there? I can't change our lives for the better if he's not willing to come with me. If he doesn't do something toward the effort to give Charlie a brighter life, quite honestly, I'll be perfectly within my rights to drag him kicking and screaming to it.

"And you didn't trust me to be the one who could change things?" He says it quietly, inviting a sympathy I don't feel inclined to dispense.

"We couldn't wait that long."

He takes a huge section of cheek into his teeth. Deep guilt, but no evidence to suggest what I've just said is unreasonable. "Pete, you need to trust me. What happens next will be for the good of all of us."

He lets out a deep breath that says, *We'll see.* It's good enough for now. He goes to kiss me before getting back to Charlie, but stops suddenly before his lips reach me.

"What the hell happened there, on your neck?"

My fingers go to cover up the bloody scratch on my throat.

"It's nothing. I did it to myself."

14

ALL WEEKEND, ESPECIALLY LAST NIGHT AS I PREPARED MYSELF
for my first meeting with the rest of The Circle this morning, I've heard so many of my father's platitudes returning to
me. Now that I'm on the precipice of actively being on the
inside, I feel as if his words won't leave me alone, particularly
his advice: "Put a rosette on yourself."

In fact, ever since Friday night, after being back at my old
house where I secured Amala's endorsement, I've felt my connection to him deepening. Seeking Amala's approval seems to
be rebooting my factory settings, my need to do anything I can
to have my father applaud me. It's why I lied over and over for
him, it's why I did what I did for him on the building site
when I was eleven, his last Hurrah. It's why I never asked for
any help from my dad with my bullies. I wanted him to think
I could take the pain, or fix what hurt me all on my own. Until
the day I snapped and he issued his "rosette" pearl of wisdom,
the one rattling round my head as I make my way to The Circle
meeting.

It was the day before my very last at AmMidd High. The
Whichellos had gone to the trouble of stealing my jumper. I
found it eventually, right where I'd left it, under my desk. I
pulled it on to leave for the day and realized the snorts and
sniggers that echoed about me were louder than usual, crash-

ing into my chest, sending sweat down my back, my pulse banging in my temples. And it happened: I'd reached the limit of what I could take.

I ran home not quietly, not inconspicuously, but sobbing, not caring about who would see me. We were breaking up for our exams the next day and I knew there was no chance my results would reflect what I was capable of. How was it fair to expect me to memorize the events of war, recall the structure of cell walls, critique the thoughts of others, or master the languages of French or maths, when so much of my energy went on simply keeping myself safe? I realized I'd never show my true potential because I was primed for invisibility or flight from peril, not only at school, but also at home, where I lived in fear of the police taking me away, or Dad, or both of us. The years where I was supposed to grow had made me smaller.

I pulled my jumper off before I got to our front gate. Seeing what was on the back of it, I let out a cry that was more like a roar. The Whichello twins had ironed a string of brown transfer letters on the back, for everyone to see as I fled school:

ROTTEN ROSIE.

I stormed into the house and threw my jumper at my father through the local paper he was reading in his armchair. I wanted to shock him into comforting me for once, do something that a normal father might when faced with a distraught teenager. Instead, he thumbed the dung-colored letters on my sweater and spoke to me with the same coolness I'd heard him use on his marks.

"In life, there will always be people who want to take your power off you. But every one of them will only ever be as powerful as you let them."

"How do *I* let *them* be powerful?!" I yelled. I was so demor-

alized, so enraged, as I attempted to draw from a much-needed
well of parental care, only to discover it dry.

"Do you think they'd still come after you if they thought
you wouldn't cry? Put a damned rosette on yourself. Claim as
your own the thing about you they want to use against you.
Get there first. Oldest trick in the book."

On the last day of high school, we were allowed to wear
whatever we wanted. I'd badgered Dad for some money to buy
a dress for the seniors prom, even though there was no way I'd
be going, and chosen a cheap red satin-like, knee-length A-line
dress, with string straps, cut on the bias. It fitted my petite
frame well, and it suddenly seemed a shame it wouldn't see the
light of day. So, with the help of Dad's advice and my sewing
box, I "pinned a rosette" on myself. I was going to claim the
bullies' power back for myself, for one day only, at least. I stayed
up all night preparing my outfit, my fingers shaking, and, by
the time the sun came up, covered in spots of blood.

The next morning, small white plasters on half my fingers,
I walked into school, deliberately choosing the entrance where
I knew the Whichellos and their consorts would be waiting.
Oh, their faces when they saw me. On the front of my dress,
I'd sewn raggedy letters that covered my chest and stomach:

ROTTEN ROSIE.

With these words emblazoned across the front of me, I didn't
need to wait to hear it spoken behind my back, pinned on me
by someone else; I'd taken ownership of that name. I had no
new shoes to go with my dress, so I decided to wear the battered
trainers I had for PE. I'd even taken possession of my shit shoes.

It was both the hardest and the easiest day of my whole time
at high school. I was talked about everywhere I went; my red
dress, my punkish lettering, my untouchable attitude, even my

trainers, drawing a buzz of admiration, not the repulsion I was used to. The Whichellos and the lesser bullies watched me, but they did not speak. They did not dare appear out of step with the tide of opinion that had turned in my favor.

When I got home, Dad asked me how my day had been. I didn't want to tell him his advice had proved brilliant. He wasn't entitled to share my win. I may have dodged the physical and mental blows for one day, but the scar tissue I'd accumulated because of him would last and last. But of course I didn't need to tell him the tactic he'd suggested had been effective. He knew people and he knew me better than any of them. Later that night, he came into my room as if to check on me, something he never did. Was he here to deliver some soft words, ask how I was, to pull me into an embrace finally? No. My father had come to take a bow, to steal a circuit of my victory lap.

"Never forget what I've taught you today. When someone wants to control you, their power to do so begins and ends in you. It's yours for the taking. You know I'm right. When have I ever let you down?"

The battle between recognizing the trauma my father had inflicted on me and my longing—to be with him, to be more like him—feels more vivid than ever. As I climb the stairs to Amala Kaur's inner sanctum and a whole new era of my life, I feel my father's presence all about me.

15

MY BRIGHT BLUE CASHIER'S UNIFORM AND KETCHUP-COLORED neckerchief feel even more lurid than usual against the wood paneling outside Amala's office. Her secretary eyes me from behind her computer screen, before telling me to take a seat. I'm distracted by the large glass cabinet dominating the wall next to her.

"I'm fine standing, thanks."

I move to the cabinet, my eyes rushing over the bricks of glass and abstract platinum forms set on mahogany within the cabinet, keen to see what Amala seeks to showcase to those about to enter her office. Some of the awards are for the school, but most are for Amala herself. Educational pioneering, inspirational leadership, female figure-heading, it's all here. Framed photos of her with business gurus, the local MP, a recent education minister, the mayor. More images of her meeting various officials in New York, Bali, Hawaii, and at some kind of alpine retreat, none appearing in doubt of her brilliance, no corner of the globe seemingly untouched by it either.

There are framed shots of Amala with the other women of The Circle too. Here she is at the side of a pensive-looking Tamsin. They stand in front of a foreboding chrome sign for The McCandless Foundation, Tamsin looking uneasy as Amala delivers some kind of speech to an assembled crowd of people who all look rather like Tamsin—clear skin, slightly horsey teeth, white and pink faces, no traces of hardship to rob them of dentine or collagen. A caption confirming the foundation was an early and significant donor to The Woolf Enterprise when the school was first established.

In another photo, Amala hugs Ruby as she accepts a digital PR award for a Woolf social media campaign, #ExcellentYou. There's an accompanying plaque with some words about how every child maximizing their potential "helped frame Woolf values in the mainstream educational narrative." Ruby and Amala flank a well-known blogger and charity campaigner who, I believe, was recently made a dame. I wonder if Amala imagines she, too, will one day be ennobled.

Then, there's an image of Amala breaking ground with a bright silver spade. *Our Mindfulness Zone. Every journey begins with the smallest action,* a white card of text reads, also revealing the "Zone" was paid for by a thirty-thousand-pound grant secured by the lone figure at her side. Bea. In this photo, I can see the woman Bea used to be. She wears the blouse she wore at the open night, but it's pristine and creaseless. Her hair is bright, her eyes full of vivacity.

A waft of lilac, the clink of metal. The secretary is at my side with a key to unlock the glass cabinet. She ignores me as she retrieves the photo of Bea and the text card, then relocks the cabinet and turns to drop the card in her wastepaper basket. She then climbs onto a stool to place Bea's picture in a high cupboard that appears to be filled with toppled cylindrical cardboard tubes and dusty box files, confirming Bea is now as useful as this detritus. I watch, agog. Bea is being erased from The Woolf's history before my very eyes. But I also wonder, how did the school manage to spend thirty grand on what's little more than a wooden deck with some awning?

"Rose! Come in."

Amala stands in the doorway of her office, leggy in tailored dark gray leather trousers paired with a baby-pink, pussy-bow silk blouse. "The others will be here shortly. I wanted to grab you on my own for a few moments beforehand. Can we get you a tea, coffee?"

"Just some water, thanks."

Amala nods at her secretary, who returns the gesture less happily than she might. I give her an on-duty smile, before following Amala.

I've been in this office before, sat stony-faced while the headmaster sought answers on my lateness to class, split lip, ripped jumper. But my dad trained me to never snitch to any authority, no matter what help I might have desperately needed. Regardless of the urge to confess all, I always left this room having given nothing away. I'm hoping I can do the same today. That feeling of having a shot at an equal footing by getting to know more about the women of The Circle is only likely to grow if I know more about them than they do me.

Amala lowers herself into a huge maroon leather swivel chair, which waits behind a stately wooden desk. The desk is inlaid with gilt and has a soft, maroon leather covering: bespoke, expensive. At Amala's back is a large pane of darkened glass that wasn't there when this place was AmMidd High. This no doubt specially commissioned addition provides Amala with a bird's-eye view of the school hall, a high point from which to observe her empire discreetly. This must have been from where she first appraised me at the open night. I don't know that I was imagining that spotlight after all. I *have* been watched by her from the off. My dad's voice tells me to stay calm to try to maintain control, now that I am beginning to get a flavor of the efforts Amala goes to in order to keep one step ahead of the likes of me.

Amala steeples her elegant fingers and flashes a quick smile as she crosses her legs behind her desk. "So," she utters, then immediately pauses to examine my reaction. There's a real sense of her enjoying this moment, where I swear I can almost hear her saying to herself, *Now, just what am I going to do to you?* I bite my lips to stop myself speaking into the pause. I won't submit at the first opportunity, as much as I'm dying to say something, perhaps a reference to her hospitality on Friday, anything to make her as warm and friendly as she was then.

"Actually, would you excuse me for just a moment?"

She leaves. I think I see an almost undetectable turn of her head to witness my reaction, but my anxiety is so high now, I can't tell whether or not I'm being ridiculous. I breathe and take a fresh look about the place before my eyes come to rest on her desk. The stack of papers nearest to me faces my way. If this were confidential correspondence, then surely Amala would have put it out of sight. I slide the top sheet closer to me for inspection:

THE WOOLF ACADEMY SENIOR SCHOOL

STRATEGIC DEVELOPMENT PLAN

Amala Kaur and Virginia Kirkbride

I let my fingers shift the cover note to one side.

> Since its establishment just three years ago, The Woolf Academy has transformed the lives of hundreds of children and revitalized a once-deprived community. We now seek to build on our vision that every child we teach between the ages of four and eleven can exceed their expectations, to older children. The Woolf Academy Senior School is envisioned to be a state-of-the-art, leading edge institution for those aged eleven to eighteen.

"Oh, you've found my secret plan."

I jump and replace the top sheet as Amala hands me a long

twist of clear glass, two diamonds of ice clinking within. I was right when I guessed she could transform even a glass of water into an expression of opulence.

"Sorry, I didn't mean to pry. I shouldn't have looked."

"You'll be brought into the plans anyway. I'm delighted to see you expressing an early interest." Her eyes glisten. I feel as if I've walked straight into her trap. She wanted to establish whether I'm prone to snooping, and now she knows I am. I curse my sloppiness.

"You wanted to discuss something before the others arrive? Was it about how I might take over Bea's workload? I just saw your secretary putting her picture away. It's really all so sad, isn't it?"

We both watch each other for a second. I can tell Amala realizes I'm trying to steer the conversation in my favor. My efforts are immediately dismissed.

"Rose, I need to be honest. I've experienced a spot of friction among the group in light of inviting you inside. It seems there are some people who think they can do a better job than I can when it comes to selecting the perfect candidate to join us, to replace our dear Bea, as you referenced."

The perfect candidate. Me. That sense of being chosen ripples pleasantly across my chest again. Resistance from the likes of Ginny comes as little surprise to me, but Amala defending me so strongly does.

"Rose, are you listening?"

"I am. What do you think I might do to make things a bit smoother?"

"I think the best course of action is simply for you to be," she leans forward and takes a beat, "exactly who you are."

This seems like more code I'm unsure how to crack. I feel suddenly vulnerable, more nervous than ever about meeting with the rest of the women.

"It's time." The secretary is standing in the doorway, and I can see the others have arrived. Tamsin comes in and sits herself next to me, but without acknowledging I'm there. Ruby files in next, raising a civil palm that belies the utter bewilderment held in her pout. Ginny arrives on a cloud of heavy sandalwood that does little to disguise the petrol-sweetness of barely metabolized alcohol. She views me with open distaste and appears reluctant to take the final seat, the one next to me.

"Come, sit, Ginny, join us," Amala instructs.

Ginny throws herself down in the manner of a petulant teenager. I notice now how we've been arranged before Amala in a tight, obedient little semicircle.

"Rose?" Amala begins. "I'm assuming you'd like to say a few words about who you are, what your role will be within The Circle?"

I had naturally expected Amala to lead on the former, and most definitely the latter, but of course, I was wrong. I should have known my induction would begin with a test. Ginny glares, Ruby glances up from her phone for a nanosecond, and Tamsin looks on with a sympathetic smile that makes it clear I'm unlikely to clear the low bar she's setting for me.

"Um."

Put a damned rosette on yourself. Claim the thing they want to use against you as your own. Take their power away.

"Well, as you all know, my name's Rose O'Connell."

"Can't really hear you. What are you saying?" The skin on Ginny's knuckles strains blue as she grips her chair. Amala shoots her a look, eyes glowing, not in the way of a warning, but something that feels far more disturbing. As I falter and Ginny smells blood, Amala Kaur is entertained.

I swallow and straighten myself on my seat. "As you might know, or can certainly tell by what I'm wearing, I'm a cashier in the bank. I know I'm not your friend Bea." All eyes cast downward, except for Amala's. "You might not even see me as a friend at all yet"—I sense at least two sets of eyes now rolling in their skulls—"but I'm very good with numbers, extremely accurate."

"So am I; so are most intelligent people." Ginny looks to the ceiling in affected, agitated boredom. "So please, do share with your new group of friends, what would you say your USP is?"

I look at her, confused.

"Unique selling point," Ruby utters, stifling an irritated yawn.

Amala's eyes twinkle. She, at least, seems to be having a great morning.

I venture an answer to Ginny's question. "Well, compared to many other women you might have chosen to join you, I was born and raised round here, which gives me very strong local connections."

"Can't imagine why that would ever prove useful, but there you go," Ginny says to her hands, which I notice are shaking, before glaring right at me.

"And I have excellent attention to detail . . ." I look her straight back in the eye, before letting my gaze travel over her thin wrists and the hands quivering on them. She quickly folds her arms across her chest and looks away, an act of defense and submission. "Which means I can bookkeep, make sure we're on top of our invoices, reconcile all of your brilliant fundraising efforts." I nod in Tamsin's direction, and she accepts the gesture with a trace of pride. "And I can support our profile with the right guidance too." Ruby nods, though does not smile. "I will, of course, ensure everything I do is executed efficiently, legally, compliantly, and hope I make a big contribution to The Woolf, The Circle, and to its future endeavors." I keep my expression open, my eyes free of intensity that might increase their potentially disarming greenness. In return, I see the other women's faces strongly suggest they each have somewhere better to be than in any room listening to me.

I look now to Amala for guidance. Have I said enough yet? Her perfect lips purse in consideration as she allows my last statement to hang in the air. I don't want to keep talking and seem nervous and keen to impress, but I also don't want to come off as cocky. "Well, that's just about me!" I shrug, clasping my hands together to show I don't think too much of myself as I await their judgment.

"And doubtless, if you receive any intelligence via your position at the bank, anything that might be to the benefit of The Woolf, we'll be the first to know?" Amala asks me, though her gaze moves across the group.

"Oh, I'm only a cashier, like I said; they don't bring me in on anything important."

"But if there were opportunities you would share them with us?"

I think of Bea, so hopeful, perhaps, that all that money she sourced for The Woolf might have been spent on something that might help the children cope with the many and high expectations their parents and school have of them. I wonder how she felt when she saw the disconnect between her efforts and how thinly they looked to have been deployed. What would Amala claim she would do with any money I might secure, and how will I respond? But I can't worry about that yet. For now, all I need to do is toe the line.

"If I were to come across any kind of opportunity that's right for The Woolf, then, I would look into it, of course." I glance at Amala, then the rest of the women, for a sign of approval that doesn't arrive. More fool me for expecting any notion of praise for following orders. On the inside, I'm beginning to see this is just what we do.

"Tamsin, how are plans coming along for the icebreaker next Friday?"

I'm relieved it's someone else's turn, but know I'm going to have to pretend I'm not even slightly hurt to be one of the only parents not invited.

"All the invites to the list we discussed went out a fortnight ago, nearly one hundred percent attendance of one or both parents." Tamsin's gaze grazes me momentarily, confirming she's party to my exclusion. "Amala, I heard what you said to make the roof garden unrecognizable after . . ." The room almost seems to cool for a second, as though Bea's spirit has entered the silence. "Anyway, that's all in hand. It's going to look magical and we're odds on to make ten thou plus."

I nod at Tamsin's progress report, but I feel my lips hardening at my being left out before I can stop them.

"Everything all right, Rose?"

Of course, Amala sees me struggling. I almost hear Bea now: *You should know by now, nothing gets past Herself.*

"My invite must have gotten lost." I think of the dozens of house parties, sleepovers, shopping trips, and bored Saturday afternoon hangouts in the park I was never invited to, not as a teenager and not now either. I do all I can to keep my face neutral as I await Amala's defense, because surely it was she who ultimately signed off on any attendee list, even if one of the other women might have put it together first.

"If you don't have an invite, then I suppose it must have been misplaced. It goes without saying, you're invited, Rose. Ruby. What do you have for me?" That's it. No apologies, no further questions.

"I'll be leveraging the icebreaker for content and messaging, sensitively acknowledging the recent *events* on the roof garden." *Events?* A woman, Ruby's friend, supposedly, *died* there less than three weeks ago. "But reminding everyone endings are beginnings, for the new parents at The Woolf and for the next lot. Same messaging should hold for the next open evening in a couple of months too."

I watch Amala nodding approvingly while a wave of nausea breaks on my stomach. Bea was buried only the day before I replaced her. My feelings must be clear for Amala to see. "Moving on, Rose, isn't easy for any of us." Amala looks to the others for buy-in. "But it's what we have to do. If we fall, collapse under the weight of grief, what good will that do for the school, its children, the parents who look to us to bring excellence to their lives, this neighborhood? We move forward for the good of everyone. Isn't that right?" A chorus of clear "Yeahs" that still somehow sounds hollow arises from the others.

Unhappy that any attention has been diverted to responding to my questions, Ginny abruptly kicks off her update. "So, I've had the weekly Freedom of Information ask from Mrs. Angry."

"A disgruntled parent with an axe to grind because she recognized this wasn't the place for her child," Amala chimes in for my benefit. "This one submits a request to establish the costs involved each time I give my time up for a vital overseas fact-finding mission, or sees any kind of expenses she doesn't like for some reason. Now she's trying to cause trouble over poor Bea."

"Anyway," Ginny continues, "I'm chucking this one out on a Section Fourteen. It's a repeated claim and vexatious. The only big worry remains whether she intends to go to the press with her so-called suspicions. She tried to threaten it again last week; I walked her through the probable costs of libel if she were to make her unfounded theories public. The family may claim it couldn't possibly be suicide, but the police have made their conclusions, and I pointed her toward those and the likely outcome of the coroner's inquest. Hopefully, that'll calm her down, that and the Pascoes leaving town." Ginny seems barely able to keep the irritation from her voice, as she dismisses Bea's family having to move away, perhaps because they don't want to be in a neighborhood that maintains their mother, their wife, their daughter left the world of her own volition. Ginny acts as though batting away people like Bea's family, now on the outside, and "Mrs. Angry" is little more than supremely tiresome: these furious and insistent flies, desperate to defile her perfect plate.

I feel horrified for a moment, imagining myself as the mother on the outside, but then my chest swells with self-regard when I realize I am now one of those people others are bitterly jealous of. I've earned myself a seat at the highest table. I don't have to worry about being like "Mrs. Angry."

"I mean, I do wish these people who realize they don't have any place being here would simply take the hint"—as she says this, Ginny looks at me and me alone—"and just fuck off."

My lungs deflate and a blush rises through my neck. I can see Ruby smirk and Tamsin make a meal of holding her expression still, the social equivalent of abstaining from a vote, as a finger finds its way under her band to give it three flicks in quick succession.

As the meeting comes to a close, I steal a look at each of the women in turn. I'm overwhelmed by the feeling that while I'm on the coveted inside of The Circle, I have absolutely no friends within it.

16

THE MEETING WRAPPED UP, I MOVE TO LEAVE AMALA'S OFFICE
alone and start the slow walk to work, the sound of Ruby,
Ginny, and Tamsin's conspiratorial laughter reverberating off
the walls behind me. My legs feel as heavy as my heart.

"Where are you going?" I hear Tamsin say, assuming she's
speaking to one of the others. "*Rose*. I'm talking to you. Do
you need to be somewhere?"

"Oh," I turn back to her, "I was heading to work."

"We need to on board you. This way."

Not a polite request, but a haughty order I find myself unable to challenge. I drag my leaden body into a small meeting
room on the same corridor as Amala's office. It's dominated by
a wall-length window with a view over the reception yard.
Something welcoming in its familiarity catches my eye.

"There's my Charlie!"

He's with a teaching assistant. I immediately panic over
what might happen now as the TA leads my son over to a cluster of chummy-looking, unfeasibly tall children. As she kneels
down to speak to their little group, my fingernails dig into my
palms. Is Charlie being made to apologize for something he's
not done? But when the TA leaves, the group of children
opens up to include Charlie and immediately turns into a
jumping cluster of maroon-and-gold caps. That change in our
world, it's just happened to Charlie right before my very eyes.

In fact, my son's blended in so easily, I can't pick him out anymore.

"Oh, I've lost him."

"Jolly good." Not listening, Tamsin has sat down behind me with a maroon box file on her lap. She appears to be looking at some notes. I take the seat opposite and watch her elastic band flex as she riffles through various documents; I feel obliged to ask her about it.

"Tamsin, would you mind if I ask you a personal question?"

She smooths one hand over her belly, which I only see now is swollen, and gives me an *Aren't I awful*–type smile. "Yes, it *is* a baby bump. Twenty-two weeks. A third girl to add to the other two, plus the boys. Only just weaned the youngest, but thank God for nannies, right?" She sets aside her papers while I struggle to comprehend being the kind of woman who can have as many babies as she pleases because there's always someone they can pay to do the hard yards.

"I was actually going to ask you about your band." I make sure it doesn't come out as spikily as I mean it.

"This?" She pulls the red stretch of elastic taut and lets go, flinching as the snap reddens her wrist while seemingly trying to show me it didn't hurt at all. She turns her extravagant features to me. "It's a release, when I feel like I need it." I don't try to hide my confusion. "I'm working through some things." She forces a smile. "I find it's best not to judge."

I feel told off, my outrage already simmering, when she turns the file to reveal the gilt text on its spine:

CHARLIE JACOBS

A stab of dread seeing my son's name on Tamsin's lap. She rests her hands above it, as if Charlie somehow belongs to her now.

"Charlie's file. Everything about him in one place." This

must be part of what being in The Circle does for the members' children, but this service feels, in this moment, like a threat. "Amala's way of making sure your child gets what they deserve."

Your child, as in everyone's, or *your child* as in mine and mine alone?

Tamsin pulls some leaves of stapled paper from the file. "*This* is to confirm his place at breakfast club and after-school, which I'm told you require. If you'd just like to sign here, here, and here."

She hands me a pen. Just like that. It's done; fixed. I see a line of dates; Charlie has a place in after-school club from tonight and starts at breakfast club tomorrow. Numb with the shock of the ease of it all, I watch my hand sign next to the crosses. There's no reason not to commit to the answer to my prayers, the wraparound care my family simply cannot function without, but I know I'm not out of the woods yet.

"How do I settle up for this?" I hope and pray the fees are subsidized for members of The Circle. I need the hours, but paying for them might mean my job is costing me money.

"We don't cover the cost by direct debit," she says, an unspoken *stupid* at the end of the sentence. "It comes from the work." Tamsin sighs at my naivety.

"So, it's free?"

"Paid for by exchange."

She blinks, then smiles, her insincerity glimmering through. "And what extracurricular sessions have you an interest in? He can do these alongside breakfast and after-school."

"Are those . . . do I pay for those through exchange too?"

A faint huff of impatience. "What's Charlie into? Rugby? Computer programming? Piano?" She hands me a tick list and a timetable from Charlie's file. "Let me know ASAP."

I view the exhaustive list. "Thank you, Tamsin."

She stands up and I feel obliged to do the same. Dropping her creamy palm, heavy and presumptuous, on my shoulder, she tells me, "We don't really do *please* and *thank you* round here. Amala's idea. If you have to say thank you, it means you didn't believe someone would do something for you, so it's actually quite rude. Oh"—Tamsin's thumb and finger reach for her nose; whatever she is about to say to me is either embarrassing or not wholly sincere—"I've been having a bit of a clear-out at home. Wondering if you'd want to step in."

"Step in?"

"Save me a trip to the charity shop. Some of them might fit you with a few alterations." She gestures to three stiff, rectangular card bags peeking out from behind the door, as though shy. Each bag has long cord handles and is emblazoned with the name of a designer I'm not familiar with. I'm almost speechless.

"I'm . . . I'm not a charity case—"

"Sorry, what? Charity shops? Yah, I always do a major rationalization before each term. I know I should stop buying things, I *do* know that, you know." Her eyes dart to the door and back, as if she's having a conversation with an invisible person while her thumb now finds its way under the band on her wrist.

"OK," I feel I have to say.

"You were the first person I thought of."

My cheeks flush with shame at this seemingly well-intentioned comment. Women like Tamsin have no idea how they sound to women like me; charity doesn't always feel like something good and pure, not when you're the one on the receiving end.

"Rubes!" she calls out, while packing away my son's file. "She's all yours."

Clearly I'm also the kind of woman that women like her are

used to ordering about. My consent, my feelings, are not so much inconsequential as things she can barely imagine existing at all.

Tamsin leaves without saying goodbye as Ruby enters, staring at her phone. "Hey," she says quickly before launching into a mini-monologue: "I've just pinged you our brand values and social media guidelines. Everyone on the inside is expected to do their bit, mostly on Insta, ideally. We need to all put ourselves out there, not look like we're hiding away. But, obviously, with my profile, I'm our key social media presence; I set the tone, lead from the front." She finally drags her eyes off her phone, but only so she, too, can take in my problematic hair, face, uniform, and knackered boots. "I can direct you. Tamsin's helping you, yeah?" Ruby sucks in her lips ever so slightly in a way that displays she's a woman whose seconds are too precious to waste on hopeless cases. She looks at me blankly, as if she's composing her next post behind her eyes. I find myself giving in to the desire to make her pay me the courtesy of her full attention, and maybe dig a little deeper into the woman behind the self-made brand.

"Must be a lot."

"What?" Her eyes are drawn back to her phone screen.

"Being @RubyWins all the time, having to look as amazing as you do, be as upbeat, showing you're making the absolute best out of absolutely everything."

"I've made my choices." She says it calmly, but I see she's lost some control over her selfie-ready expression. In fact, underneath the lip gloss, designer dungarees, and statement accessories, Ruby may be fraying a little around the edges, just like the rest of us. I can't resist tugging on the thread of her insecurity, but I don't want her sensing the twitch of the tension.

"We have to, don't we, make the choices we feel are best for our families?"

She cocks her head at me, defensive, curious. "Yeah, we do. And I've made some good ones; recently, anyway. Not so great ones in the past, I'll give you that, like when I married my ex only for her to leave me eight weeks after our son was born. That wasn't my best work, for sure." She says it all without smiling, plainly, as if she has nothing to hide. "I understand why some people feel they need to judge me for putting my life, and my son, out there. They might even argue I invite the world to have an opinion on us for the sake of what they might assume is easy money." Ruby is rattling her words off now as though reading from a post she's composed and repurposed many times. "But if anyone thinks what I do is easy, that's because I do a good job of making it look that way. People like me, who people look to for inspiration for better lives, we work hard."

"I should think it's exhausting." I smile as I would to a tearful customer, inviting her to keep going, concealing how I'm dying to hear more about the pain and disappointment in her life, so I might have the smallest chance of feeling, for a moment, less alone in my own.

"Whatever people say about me and my son, doing what we do, it's worth it. I get paid to wear someone's trainers, recommend some earbuds, have a meal with my son at the latest opening. Every single post is a brick in the life I'm building, and the bigger and stronger it gets, it puts me another step further away from ever being *That Mum* again."

"That Mum?"

Ruby finally throws her phone onto the table between us and leans toward me. I feel she may be about to tell me something fresh and real, an insight, perhaps, she isn't able to mine for content. "*That Mum* who drops her child off in the morning somewhere she's not one hundred percent sure about and walks into her work every single day feeling like an open wound. *That Mum* who returns to work after having a baby, clutching to the distant possibility her request for flexible hours won't be shut down so she can say good night to her child just once in between weekends. *That Mum* who realizes two things too late: no matter how hard she works, how much smarter she is than the next guy, she'll never be promoted again because she's found herself in a career where 'part-timer' is thrown around like a mortal insult and a second pregnancy is sure to be met with guaranteed redundancy."

There's such a dark comfort to hear the strains another woman is under, ones that sound so close to my own, it loosens my tongue. "I might not have a high profile or anything like you have, but there's been too many times I've been *That Mum*. What you're talking about, that's my life, too, Ruby."

She looks me dead in the eyes. "Was my life, *was*. Not anymore. Never again."

She snatches her phone from the table, leans back, and checks it while resetting herself. It's as if she worried that even being in proximity to someone who's clearly still *That Mum* might somehow taint her.

"I think you're done for now."

So much for all that "kindness" I've seen her secreting online. Ruby seems to sense my witnessing the disconnect between the brand and the woman.

"Listen, don't think me an arsehole. I mean, I can be a bit of a dick sometimes, but that's just who I am. I know myself now and I don't change that for anyone I don't have to. I may as well warn you now, if you feel this is too much change, if you can't cope at any point, do yourself, and us, a favor—admit defeat, throw in the towel. This"—she points at the Circle brooch on one of the straps of today's oversize dungarees—"trust me, it isn't for everyone."

I'm dismissed. I get up and walk away from Ruby without saying anything further. She thumbs at her phone, too preoccupied to realize how small she's made me feel. Right now, part of me wants to become even tinier, reduce the size of the target for The Circle's snipes, their dark sport, their high-handed instructions.

I make my way through the corridors as quickly as I can, remaining on high alert even when I'm all but out into the air of the playground. I know all too well that when you begin to think you are safe is the moment you are most likely to be subjected to an assault.

"Hey! Stop!"

And there she is, someone who is going to exert her power over me, despite the fact she has no right to. My insides pop and squirm as I turn to see Ginny standing in the middle of the corridor behind me, her arms folded tightly across her chest as they were before.

"Let me be clear. If anyone's taking over here when Amala leaves for the senior school, don't get any ideas it's going to be you."

"I wouldn't think—"

"Two things. One: you are nowhere near to having what it takes. Two: I have given up far too much to have that taken away from me. Understand?"

Ginny struggles to articulate "understand" without slurring. Perhaps it's the drink that's skewing her perspective so much that she's threatened by what she thinks Amala can see in me. But if I'm unable to make an ally of her at this stage, quietly maintaining Ginny's sense of jeopardy about me is probably the next best alternative.

"I understand you perfectly." I turn to leave.

"Oh, the icebreaker. Shame you didn't seem to have made the first cut. Now you're coming, be there at eight." I glance behind me to see her smirking. "Make sure you're there bang on time. Amala can't abide tardiness. On the inside, you can't put a foot wrong."

Something I'm beginning to understand all too powerfully.

17

CHARLIE IS EXHAUSTED BUT HAPPY AFTER HIS LONG DAY AT school. This time, he doesn't emerge from The Woolf like a candle about to go out, but a great beacon of smiles and excitement. He tells me he was moved from his "special seat" and back with the rest of the children on the carpet. And, at after-school club, the other boys asked him to play.

Though the fact he was ever separated from the class tugs at me, I see little benefit from kicking the hornet's nest. Why risk his newfound privileges by asking why he was moved or by whom, or why they might think he needs his counseling sessions? Instead, I focus on counting our many blessings as Charlie comes alive over dinner that night, chatting away about all he's done with his day. It's finally like I imagined it would be with him at The Woolf. As he talks so animatedly and confidently, I feel my boy blossoming before my eyes.

Just as we've nearly finished clearing the table, Pete and I find ourselves watching as Charlie builds a Lego tower that's taller than him, the highest he's ever built.

"Look, Pete. Charlie's thinking bigger, growing into everything he could be. Maybe we could let ourselves do the same?" I move to Pete and lay my hands on his chest. He holds me tight.

"If you say so."

"Why, don't you believe things are getting better already?"

I wish my husband could let himself be unambiguously positive for once. If he doesn't feel he can do any more for this family than he already does, then the least he can do is improve his attitude about all the extra effort I'm putting in.

"I don't know. It all feels like too much drama: Charlie starting off so badly, so upset, now he's on top of the world. It's not how school should be, it's not— Charlie, careful!" Pete shoots over to him, just as the tower collapses and Charlie cowers under a shower of sharp-cornered bricks.

"You all right, mate?" Pete holds Charlie and checks the side of his head where one of the bigger bits seems to have caught him. Charlie nods, lets go of Pete, and starts to build again, unafraid.

"Here, let Daddy help you. Maybe not so high this time, eh?" Charlie scrunches his face, unhappy with Pete's suggestion.

I come over to join them. "Why don't you let Mummy do the last tallest bit and you can stand well back?"

"Deal?" Pete asks Charlie. He nods, handing Pete a stack of bricks for him to add to the already growing structure.

I tell myself that no matter what happens, Pete, Charlie, and I are a team, one that's set to win in the end, even if Pete might not always appreciate my path to victory, or what bumps we may encounter along the way.

I LET PETE give Charlie a quick bath so I can get going on my social media profile, beginning by taking inspiration from Amala herself. Her Instagram gives me a clear window into how she likes to live her life, and she is far from shy of posting the rewards of her success. Her latest post shows her posing next to an Amazonian-looking life coach she's recently hired to "continue to test the limits of her potential." Ruby's posted about her excitement over the (free) meal out she and Elvis will be enjoying tonight, and Tamsin has a picture of one of her girls on a horse at the city farm, the nanny just out of frame.

Ginny posts as I'm about to click away. In the image, she is clearly in the midst of crying, even though it's blurred.

Can't do tis on my onnwn anymore. Work, father in law w dementia, my kids. LIFE!!! It shouldn't be thsis fucking hard.

The post disappears almost as soon as I've finished reading it. I swipe down to refresh the screen in case it might reappear, but it's nowhere to be found. Did Ginny regret showing the side of her usually hidden from view? Or was she told to delete it?

Ginny is at almost ten thousand followers now, Tamsin has reached just over seven thousand, and Ruby is now breaching a staggering nine hundred thousand. How will I develop a following to keep pace with at least Ginny and Tamsin's? I decide the type of woman we're looking to attract needs to see something of themselves but slightly better, something nearly real, close enough to be attainable, but still out of reach. I need to show people something of myself, but a heavily edited version of that reality.

I form a relatively simple idea in my mind, but one I think could work for me and within Ruby's guidelines, which state, among other "brand values," that everything we stand for, everything we post or publish in the name of The Woolf, should be *Aspirational, Realistic, Uncompromising.*

I take a white sheet from my drawer and lay it over the top of Charlie's Spider-Man duvet and pillows to create a clean backdrop for the photo. I want to suggest a sophistication and self-care people wouldn't expect from the poor mum in the radioactive blue polyester. I change into one of Pete's jumpers and let my shoulder hang out, just a little, before touching up my hair and makeup. Next, I head to the kitchen to find a decent-looking mug. I realize all of them are chipped, cheap, and nasty. None will do. I look at my bowls, deciding they will look chic, designer even, if I shoot them from dead above.

I need to create a bright, healthy-looking hot drink to go in the bowl, but I can only find Ribena, which anyone will recognize a mile off. I want to look like I'm drinking something only I know about, the secret elixir to my health, happiness, and success. I spot what I need—Charlie's little craft box: glue, pipe cleaners, little pots of paint. I click the kettle on to boil, splotch some red and yellow in the bottom of the bowl, and pour on the hot water. Satisfied with my for-display-purposes-only concoction, I return to Charlie's room with a carrier bag, into which I swoop all of the toys and bits on his bedside table. I use a tissue to clean off the dust, so on camera it will appear spotless. I place my steaming bowl down to fetch the pièce de résistance, a vintage book covered in fraying claret fabric.

I lounge on the bed, looking into my phone's camera, *Tricks of Confidence* lying on my heart, and attempt to appear tired, but in a satisfied, *I earned this moment* way. I take a few trial shots, reassuring myself the book's title is barely legible from the angle I'm shooting. I'm quite enjoying myself, putting to use my eye for detail on how people hold themselves, the little symbols we give others through every tiny choice we make. I look at the results so far and see something is missing. The magic ingredient that will make this picture fly.

"Charlie!"

He comes to me at first with a huge smile, fresh from the bath, but his face falls when he sees what I've done to his room.

"Where's all my stuff?"

"Never mind for now. I'll put it all back. Come here and give us a cuddle."

He jumps right on top of me and comforts himself by playing with my hair. "Leave off, Charlie. I just did that. Come on, shuffle down a bit, give me some space."

Charlie slides down and holds me round my waist. I can't get him in the shot with my other props unless I hold my phone out farther away.

"Here, like this." I move Charlie's body where it needs to be. "Don't look at the camera. That's right, put your head there, let your arm drop to the side."

"Why are you being weird?"

My arm is starting to ache from holding the phone above us. "Please, Charlie, do *one* little thing for me." I ignore the harshness of my own voice as I manage to get the shot I want and not a second too soon. Charlie climbs off me, trying with all his might not to cry in his confusion.

I do feel guilty about Charlie being upset, but no one understands the pressure I'm under, everything I'm trying to do for this family. So, I spend the next minutes in his room, setting up my profile with the name I've been thinking about for a while: @Rose_Between.

How many times did I hear that stupid saying when I was sitting between my male former colleagues at the bookies' counters. "A rose between two thorns, eh?" they'd say, slipping me their stakes and creased betting slips under my window. Now I feel like a Rose between two phases of her life. The next section might well prove thorny, too, but at least I'm moving away from the same old pains and disappointments. I need these to change, even if it's only a new kind of agony I give myself before I get to the better times. I am changing; a Rose between.

I follow all the people who've commented on the most recent posts by Ginny, Ruby, and Tamsin and get ready for my inaugural post as not only a Woolf Mother, but also one who's breached the hard outer casing of The Circle, against the odds.

@Rose_Between Important announcement: This is what hope looks like. A knackered mum flopped on her child's bed at the end of the day, thinking about all we can get and all we can give our tomorrow. Since he's started at an exceptional school, I can see a future for my son that neither of us could ever have imagined was possible. #achieve #attain #aspire #TheWoolf #happymum

I can hear Charlie weeping now, his dad asking him what's the matter, so I give the caption just a couple more reads before posting it. I find Charlie trying to bury himself in Pete's chest.

"Charlie, don't cry. Mummy didn't mean to—"

My phone buzzes. I don't finish my sentence. My post already has ten likes.

18

O N FRIDAY AFTERNOON, AT THE END OF WHAT HAS BEEN A standout week at work for me—no late starts, no sneaking off on the turn of the hour—I get a call from Amala. I dare to take it, ignoring Linda's resentful glare.

"Rose. Unforeseen circumstances. There's no after-school activities for Charlie today."

"Oh, I . . . I'm not due out of here until six today."

"I've organized a Plan B for you."

Of course she has, this is what it's like on the inside. The normal turbulence of daily life is smoothed over so much you barely feel the blows. "Really? Thanks so much, Amala." At the sound of her name, I can see Marek take note of whom I'm speaking to, and I bank this for future reference. Everyone round here with any interest in The Woolf knows and hero-worships Amala Kaur; why should my boss be any different?

Amala continues, "Charlie's at Ginny's house. She's just taken him home with her two."

My stomach falls. My beautiful boy with her? I can't imagine her being anything but nasty and cold, never mind likely too inebriated to notice if he was in any kind of trouble. Naturally, Amala picks up on my silence and instantly decodes its meaning.

"There's nothing to worry about. You and Ginny may not see eye to eye, but Charlie's in good hands, I promise. She's had to lay off the other stuff today, too, something to do with her father-in-law. She isn't expecting you until after six. I'll text you the address. Finish your work, everything's fine."

I release the breath I've been holding. I'm learning that one of the strongest planks of Amala's charisma is to make you feel completely relaxed, grateful in fact, for something diametrically opposed to your better judgment. Another quality she shares with my father.

I tell myself Charlie will be fine. Ginny is many things, but she's also a mum; she wouldn't harm a child. I try to get on with serving customers as I would normally, but I make mistakes. My mind's not in it. All I can see is Ginny's skinny face atop her folded arms, looking at my son as she looks at me, like a person who shouldn't be anywhere near her; matter out of place. After half an hour, I give in.

"Marek, I'm so sorry. I need to make a quick call."

I don't wait for his sign-off, or to pay any notice to the *Here we go again* glances from Linda. I pull down the blind at my station before the next customer can approach.

My fingers find the speed dial. "Jacq, can't talk long. I'm in a fix. Is there any way you could pick up Charlie? He's at a mum's house round the corner from the café."

"No probs. We're dead here anyway. I'll close up in a bit and get him. What's going on?"

"Issues with the after-school club. I'll text you the address. Thanks, Jacq. I'll come and get him from yours as soon as I finish here."

"It's OK, no rush. Charlie's at a schoolmate's house, right? Just you calm down and I'll be on my way in a bit, OK?"

I breathe, so grateful, and wanting to believe in my heart that she's right about him being OK. "Jacq, you're a lifesaver."

I get back to my counter and I see there's still more than an hour and a half left until I can leave. My fingers worry my neckerchief in between the next two customers, my on-duty smile blatantly fake. I know, rationally, that no harm is likely to come to Charlie at Ginny's house, but still, I feel a primal urge to know my son is safe.

"Rose, if you need to go, please go."

I barely register Marek talking to me. "Sorry?"

"I assume this is about your son. You've had a great week. If you need to fetch him, go do that, OK?"

I'm already grabbing my things as I speak. "Thank you so much, Marek. I'll make it up, I promise."

He waves my apology away. "I heard you were talking with Amala? Ms. Kaur? Well, I'm sure she's doing the best by your son." He gives an assured nod, then does a funny sort of salute as I pass.

I'm momentarily puzzled at this seeming newfound respect. It's only a temporary release from my panic. I run down the high street. If I pass by the café, I can quickly let Jacq know I'll collect Charlie, without wasting time calling her now. Like a woman possessed, I barrel past the school and toward the park, reaching Jacq's café just as she's pulling down the metal shutters.

"Whoa, mate! What happened to you?" Jacq takes in my panting form.

"Nothing. You can stand down. My manager let me go early to get Charlie."

"I'll come with. I've hardly seen him since you've gotten him into all these fancy-pants extra classes."

I allow my body to tip over into a post-run recovery position, hands on knees, so Jacq can't see my face as I work out how to dissuade her from coming with me to Ginny's. I've not had a chance to let her know about my being inside The Circle yet, what it all means for me and Charlie. She hasn't yet noticed my golden brooch and put two and two together from seeing them on Bea and co. on the open night. I've been looking for the right way to frame the news; bringing her along to Ginny's house isn't it.

"It's all right, Jacq. You go home, put your feet up. Let's take him to the park together in the morning."

"Don't sweat it. I'm dying to see him and besides, I hardly had anyone in today. I'm not even slightly knackered, more's the pity."

"The thing is . . . This school mum, Ginny, she's kind of like a leading light in this new sort-of team I'm part of at school . . ."

"Right," she says slowly, instinctively wary.

"It's less of a matey kind of relationship, more professional, if that makes sense?"

"Not really." She puts her bundle of keys in her bag and looks at me anew.

The longer I stand here and explain myself to Jacq, the longer it will be before I can extract Charlie from Ginny's house. Jacq clearly has her sights set on coming with me, so while we walk, I tell her a potted, and persuasive, version of what's happened to my life since the playdate at Amala's last week.

"Wow, sounds like you've got a bit of a golden ticket there, I suppose," Jacq surmises after I give her my story.

"You only suppose?"

"I don't know, I've always been told there's no such thing as a free lunch."

"It's not free. I told you, I'll be helping out on the finances." I realize I sound defensive.

"As long as you know what you're doing."

"The fact you've had to even say that tells me you don't think I do."

"Don't be like that, I'm just looking out for you."

I wish I could tell her that sometimes I don't want her to look quite so closely at everything I do for my family. Sometimes I don't need her protection, or her forensic scrutiny.

"Is this the place?" Jacq says into my silence, staring up at a foreboding four-story Georgian terrace. This whole row was completely dilapidated a few years back, home only to vagrants and rodents. Now, the likes of Ginny find themselves in one of the most desirable addresses in the neighborhood, having hewn luxury and "lateral space" from the weary grandeur of the homes where the area's long-dead luminaries once lived; those wool merchants and landowners now replaced by corporate lawyers and management consultants. I'm about to ask Jacq to wait outside when she speaks again. "Look at the size of it. I've always wanted to see what they've done with the insides of these things."

I press the bell, Jacq right behind me, obviously not going anywhere but inside Ginny's home. A church-like "bong" reverberates through the expansive hall behind the door. No one comes; not a sound after the echo dies. A lurch of fresh anxiety in my stomach, which I can't manage to dismiss as paranoia. Charlie is in there. My Charlie is trapped in Ginny's house and now, no one's coming to the door. I know it's ridiculous, but images flash through my brain: Ginny slumped in a corner, Charlie hurt, crying. What have I done, leaving him with someone I didn't trust?

Jacq takes control, reaching for the huge lion's head knocker and giving it a resounding bang. "Come on, mate," she mutters, stepping back.

Eventually, I hear what must be Ginny's twins barging past each other, screaming in their plummy accents. The door is heaved open to reveal two girls, scrawny blond things like their mother.

"Hello. Is Charlie here? Where's your mum?" I'm completely ignored. Instead, they fall over each other to race up the stairs. Still no Charlie. Still no Ginny. Jacq shrugs. I step inside.

"Hello?" I call out, walking nervously down the hallway ahead of Jacq. The corridor is bright matte white, with a ceiling reaching up at least twelve feet. The walls are covered in pictures of Ginny in her younger days: graduating from col-

lege; standing with her husband on a wooden bridge somewhere steamy and foreign; at the top of a mountain; holding
her newborn twins. She's smiling in all of them, bright and
sincere. I realize I've never seen her like this before. The best
I've seen Ginny manage is a smirk. Even though her face and
frame are so much fuller in the pictures than they are today, she
looks altogether lighter.

I walk on, sucking in every detail I can, and spot a storage
space under the grand stairs. Peering into it, I see it's packed
full of pale blue plastic bricks. I read the writing on the side of
one: *Stay-Dry Adult Incontinence Pads*. The products couldn't be
more incongruous among the scale and elegance of Ginny's
perfect home. I remember the hastily deleted Instagram post
that mentioned her father-in-law.

"Hello? It's Rose here!"

Still no sound. I walk down a short staircase, just a few steps
before the floor opens up into a spectacular room with a huge
glass table and chairs, a light fixture composed of long strands
of crystal at the very top of the ceiling turning their way to the
center of the table. A double-height, floor-to-ceiling transpar-
ent wall separates the room from the garden outside.

I hear Jacq utter a quiet "*Wow*" as I finally spot Ginny, leaning against the large window in the corner of the room, gazing
out into a seemingly endless garden of grand, mature trees and
shrubs.

Her arms are folded across her as usual, one hand cradling a
huge glass almost full to the brim with white wine. Behind
her, at the far end of the glass table, is my Charlie, coloring,
oblivious.

"Ginny?"

"Shit! I mean, you know. *Shoot*. Didn't hear you creeping
up."

Ginny's voice is tired but clear. Her goblet seems to be the
first she's had today. Amala wasn't lying about that.

"Mummy!" Charlie gets off his seat and runs to hug my legs. "Idabelle and Xanthe have got a *massive* playroom, and they've got a slide in it and a tepee and games and a swingy seat and everything! I had the best time ever!"

Ginny gives a little smile over her shoulder, and I'm surprised to see it looks real, like the expression in those dated images, but then she stiffens up and seems to cool, turning her gaze outside once more. She hasn't even noticed Jacq is here. "Ruby wants to speak to you. Unsurprisingly, she's not pleased about you posting without authorization."

I want to challenge her tone, or at least do something to acknowledge how she's just issued instructions to me like some kind of servant, but no good can come of my butting up against Ginny now. I only hope Jacq doesn't say anything, now or later when we're out of here. Besides, hasn't Ginny taken good care of my son for the best part of three hours? "OK, thanks for the heads-up. And thanks ever so much for this afternoon."

"No thanks. You know that. See you soon, Charlie," Ginny says, angling her head back in his direction, which prompts him to leave me to give her a sweet little hug round her legs. She instinctively raises her arms out of the way and lets out a gasp, but then allows a hand to relax on Charlie's back, her eyes closing in what seems to be a tiny moment of serenity.

"I really liked chatting. You're really nice," he tells her.

"Oh, that's nice. What was it you were chatting about?" I ask, trying to mask my panic at the idea of Ginny worming her way around his life, and mine.

"Rain forests! And Ginny's favorite animals!"

Ginny's face flushes as she snaps her head in the opposite direction of Charlie. If I didn't know better I would say my kind, well-mannered son has just made Ginny cry.

"Come on, you," I say, and he grabs my hand, his grip so much firmer than I've noticed it ever being.

Walking home, Jacq and I let Charlie chatter on about his

day, and all the while I hope the change in him, the way he's brimming with such clear confidence and energy, will discharge Jacq of her need to take me to task about Ginny being so blatantly dismissive. These hopes are soon dashed.

"They all like that at The Woolf?" Jacq eventually asks in one of Charlie's quieter moments as we reach home.

"Like what?" I figure it's worth trying to make out like she's misinterpreted the situation.

"They all talk to you like dirt?"

"God, Jacq. She's just stressed out."

"Really? And someone else wants to bollock you about something you've put up on Instagram or whatever? Who do they think they are? Can't imagine they speak to each other that way."

I say nothing, not wanting to give the slightest hint that what Jacq has said is deadly accurate, but unable to lie to her either.

"Well, I hope it's worth it."

"Jacq. Take a look at your nephew. Tell me he's not doing good."

We watch him, skipping on ahead, singing a little tune, such a change from his being defeated and listless when he first started, when I wasn't on the inside.

"Well, in that case, I just hope you still know what you're doing."

"So do I," I tell the chill twilight air at an even lower volume than my normal speaking voice.

19

THE NIGHT OF THE ICEBREAKER, MY MIND TURNS OVER AND over on what the Woolf Mothers will make of Pete. I coach myself to remain strong when one of them doubtlessly laughs a little too loudly at something he's said, lets her eyes unabashedly race over all of him, tries to put a hand on him and leave it there. Pete's never given me any reason to believe he'd ever do anything to respond to all the attention he might get, but I can't help my insecurities from taking my mind to dark places sometimes, especially times like tonight when we're going to be surrounded by legions of tall, well-groomed women, none of whom ever moan at Pete or ask him to be more or better than who he's inclined to be. I try to put these thoughts aside, focus on the positives of the situation, and, indeed, the task at hand.

While I'm sure it is widely known that it was me who turned out to be "the chosen one," tonight feels like it will become official, a coming-out parade where I might show I'm worthy of my newly bestowed rank. I know I'll be watched; I expect to be tested. I desperately want me and Pete to pass, to blend in among the typical newcomers who make up the wider Woolf community. I'm full of nerves, but there's also a part of me that can't wait to get over there and stand proudly in my rightful place with Amala and the rest of The Circle.

The exquisite thought of this being my first night living my life as "a someone" rushes through me as I smooth down the outfit I've chosen: a white silk dress, pleated and belted, with a striking navy trim on its high collar. It looks preppy but nevertheless glamorous, like something from the 1940s with a sophisticated, modern overhaul. The label says Rodarte and when I googled it, I discovered it would cost more than a thousand pounds to buy new, which, with the original tag still attached, it's as good as. Thankfully, though Tamsin is taller than I am, the dress looks fine worn longer and needs minimal adjustments. I set the belt on the tightest notch, which accentuates my waist and makes me appreciate my slightness in a way I can't remember ever doing before. I attach my Circle pin with pride.

Pete comes up behind me.

"You look amazing."

"So do you," I say, taking him all in, my pride soaring, my fears about the other women there tonight too.

Pete seems to pick up on my conflicted feelings. "Are you sure it needs both of us there? You know I'm no good at this sort of thing."

I feel as if I've been thrown to the ground. "*Pete.* No! You're coming. No arguments." The roughness of my tone shocks him and I immediately see it risks making him want to stay home even more. I can't have that, even if I do feel fearful about having to watch a bunch of posh mums salivate over, and try to turn the head of, my husband. "I don't know why you're so worried," I tell him as softly as I can manage.

"*You* seem to be," he counters, and I put down the lipstick I'm holding before I can reapply it. "We've both seen the types who send their kids over there."

"So, don't you want to know more about those families, see what we're getting into?"

I regret my choice of words immediately. *What we're getting into* sounds risky, dangerous. You "get into" things you should know better not to; you "get in" too deep. I try to reset my sentence. "You know, what we're lucky enough to be a part of."

Pete ignores my attempt to pedal back. "Whatever that place and those people are like, it's *you* who's got us into it." It comes out tightly, as if he didn't want to say it like he had, but he's nevertheless happy to remind me of the truth. "You didn't exactly give me, or Charlie, any say."

In the mirror, I see hurt mottling Pete's brow.

"We always agreed I'd do the heavy lifting on finding him a school place and that's what I did. Please, let's put a smile on our faces and show The Woolf what we're made of."

I move to him. He immediately expects me to place my palms on his chest and I don't disappoint, laying my hands on his heart and allowing his arms to encircle me. If Pete can feel as though he's shielding me from something, the ravages of a changing world on our doorstep that's tried to leave us behind, or the pain from my childhood, I know my husband will feel better about himself. So, I have him take me into him, like a twitch snare, but one where the animal knowingly triggers her capture.

"Rose, will you promise me something? If you see any Woolf Mother–type trying to . . . Get too much with me, you know what I mean." I do, of course. "If I look like I need rescuing, do it, OK?"

I nod, and while Pete smiles, a frown lingers on his forehead. For some reason, I don't think he quite believes me.

When Jacq arrives to babysit, I rush us out of the house before he can entertain the idea of dropping out a second longer, and ahead of Jacq having the chance of bringing up the oddness at Ginny's house. It's a relief to leave the flat as Pete and I make the short journey over the road to The Woolf in good time for the eight o'clock start.

I type in the key code to the main entrance, another privi-

lege those of us on the inside enjoy; we don't need anyone else
to buzz us in and out, or tell us where, when, and how we can
access the school. Pete, meanwhile, has the look of a man
awaiting the hangman's drop. He gazes above us, as if expecting
the gallows. Instead, he finds the showy, meter-high letters
spelling out the school's motto in twisted steel.

Pete's mood threatens to seep into mine. My thoughts are
swallowed by the idea of Bea before she headed to the roof
garden that night. How much, how long had she planned
doing what she did? Did Bea absolutely know, did she truly
have certainty she was in the final hours of her life? Pete sees
my sudden gloom.

"Let's get up there!" I tell him overcheerfully, as the gate
closes behind us with an ominous sound of metal on metal. A
sense of being captured as I glance up to the roof garden and
an image of Bea forces its way into my mind again. A woman
trapped by what she felt her life had become, silhouetted
against a dusky sky, mentally broken and seconds from physically shattering on the black tarmac we're now treading on.

Pete and I don't speak as we trudge up flights and flights of
stairs. Finally, we're on a larger landing with the inky void of
the stairwell below us. Ahead is a door edged with light and
emitting muffled laughter, the rise and fall of raucous, over-
confident conversation, self-satisfied guffaws.

Blinding light.

I raise my hands to my eyes. Someone is holding open the
door for us, telling us to step inside. I blink through the throbs
of dazzling yellow before it subsides and a lilac haze fills my
vision, accompanied by the unmistakable fine wood and musk
of Amala Kaur. By the time my pupils adjust, the first thing I
can make out is her head over Pete's shoulder as he dips to her
level. It almost looks like the long, black twine of her hair
might wrap itself around him as she goes in for a double air-
kiss on his cheeks. His arm instinctively comes up to touch her

elbow as she leans into him. The two of them are framed by the dreamlike purple lights that are hanging everywhere, alongside garlands of blue and white flowers. The whole place looks like a fantasy, heady florals fighting it out with the challenging rareness of Amala's scent. I realize I've barely let myself breathe since I've entered her airspace.

Amala turns to me. Her lithe arms are draped in the gray silk of a high-necked, Gothic-inspired dress, which fits the drama of the roof garden perfectly. The thick golden circle is pinned to the fabric at the center of her throat. Amala's eyes rush over me as she approaches through the ephemeral violet glow. When she reaches me, I don't get the face-on air-kiss she gave Pete, but one of her sideways hugs. Though she's at least five inches taller than me, even in my heels, she's just as narrow, though there's a hardness I notice in her arms and body, likely a product of her thousand-pound-a-month celebrity trainer. Her strength surprises me as it has before, the way she brings my frame firmly into her body space without consent, her fingers so rigid around my upper arm that I flinch at their grip. I'll be marked with her scent for days now, too, I can tell. So will Pete.

"Why are you so late? You should have been here at six."

"Six?!" I've broken one of the golden rules at the first opportunity. Looking around, I realize the loud chatter is down not only to that signature confidence of the Woolf Mothers and Fathers, but is being super-charged by two hours of alcohol consumption.

"Ginny said I should come at eight," I tell Amala almost in a whisper, the scar tissue from my years of bullying rubbed open again.

Amala shoots a dark look Ginny's way as we watch her drain a large glass of wine. Turning to me, and looking right into my eyes, Amala tells me, "Well, now you're here, I'm *ridiculously* pleased to see you. You look great, by the way. I doubt very much whether Tamsin could have carried that dress off like you are. You look just the part."

I find I'm repeating the somewhat loaded compliment in my head before she's even finished uttering the words, a swell of pride in my chest. While clearly the "part" I'm playing is in opposition to my standard status, and she's reminded me that my designer dress is not quite mine, Amala is still letting me know I'm right where I should be. This surge of endorsement is heightened as she takes me by the arm and leads me out into the clusters of Woolf Mothers. In among the dreamy violet lamps, the lilies and orchids, and the sea of expensive jumpsuits and blinding-white trainers, any image in my head of Bea on the precipice dissolves. All I can see, for one bright moment, is the future.

A group of well-put-together parents prepares to break to include me and Amala. I seem to drift in on a waft of her scent. "Everyone, I'd like you to meet Rose O'Connell, a new Woolf parent who's become an integral part of our fundraising and governance endeavors. You're good here, Rose?"

Amala disappears the moment she deposits me, a gleam of amusement about her features as she leaves me. If this is some kind of initiation ritual to see whether I might sink or swim socially, I must not allow myself to drown. Then, I remember it again: *Put a rosette on yourself.* Well, I already have one, an actual insignia of success. I glance down to the bright gold of my Circle pin, breathe, and in the most relaxed, self-assured way I can, I take in a considered panorama of the rooftop, as if appraising the work of my associates. Let them all know who I am, then come to me.

"Give us the boy."

A very tall blond man dominates the space in front of me suddenly, handing me a flute of champagne. Darius, Amala's husband, doing his part, it seems, to keep up those vital public appearances despite their split.

"I'm sorry?"

"Let us take your boy and we will give you a man." His black eyes bear down on me. "Darius. The boss's support act."

"Lovely to meet you." I look up to him, trying my best to appear as if what he's telling me is new information. But he's not concerned with me, his eyes stalk Amala as she snakes through the new Woolf Mothers and Fathers, accepting fresh hits of admiration at every turn. His jaw hardens in what looks to me like almost violent desire. To my own shock, a scene plunges into my imagination: Darius hoisting Amala onto him on the enormous black velvet sofa that sits in what was my old living room, her hair tangled in his fingers, their perfect bodies wrapped around each other, minds lost to how incredible they must look.

My attention drifts back to Amala in the here and now as she moves toward Pete, lurking on the margins of our group. She pulls him into conversation. I expect to see him indulge her in a moment of small talk before looking to me to save him. Instead, he dips his head low again, so it's right next to hers as she says something I can't hear. Amala turns her back to me, her curtain of black hair blocking any sight of my husband's face. She throws her head back in a burst of sudden, silent laughter at something Pete's said. I see him take a swig from a bottle of beer while his vision seems to settle on the momentarily exposed skin of her neck.

"O-K! How many can we put you all down for?"

Ruby has found her way into the center of attention, directly blocking my path to Pete and Amala, commanding the scene in pale blue, parachute silk dungarees, the small gold circle pinned to the left strap, a long-sleeved white crop top underneath. Everyone in a two-meter radius moves for their handbags or reaches for their wallets. The slippery flutter of twenty-pound notes and threatening flash of red fifties catch in the lavender light. Ruby begins to swiftly swap the notes for small maroon booklets, working her way round to me. I let my fingers play with the clasp of my clutch bag to keep them away from my neck as she closes in on me. Out of the corner of my eye, I watch Amala step ever closer to my husband.

"How many for you? I'm sure you'll want to tell your growing number of followers how generous you've been to-night." Ruby gives my new look the once-over.

"Ruby, I've been meaning to talk to you about that." Truth be told, I've been ignoring the request to seek her out and take my telling-off. Why would I voluntarily turn myself in?

"This isn't the time or the place to dwell on it, just don't do it again. I'd rather not have to speak to Amala about whether you can be trusted to act as a brand ambassador at all. Don't make me the arsehole, OK?"

I think of what Jacq might do, part of me wishing she was here right now to give Ruby the dressing-down I'm not able to. I switch the subject. "What are those?" I gesture at the booklets.

"You didn't read the invite?" *I never actually received one, which is why I'm late and clueless.* "They're Woolf Lottery tickets. The winner gets twenty-five percent of the prize pot, which is shaping up to be huge. I don't know how Tamsin does it," Ruby says, somewhat slyly. I follow her gaze to see Tamsin draped over not one but two dads, both clearly well-oiled with tonight's open bar. Red-faced, they appear enthralled by the magnificent creature between them, the swell of her baby bump somehow only adding to her aura of wanton extravagance. She whispers into each of their ears in turn, causing them to scan the roof garden shiftily.

"I'll take"—I spot the wedges of flapping paper being stashed away by the parents around me—"two, no, three."

"That's seventy-five. Cash, ideally, to keep our transaction costs down."

"*Seventy-five?*" It comes out too loud, with the strangle of incredulity. The snap of what feels like hundreds of heads in my direction follows.

"It's for a good cause!" Ruby makes a short laugh that stops as soon as it starts.

"I'm so sorry. I don't have the cash on me." I think I hear a tut from the group, but when I look for the source of the noise, it's just one of the dads, smacking his lips around the top of a beer bottle before leaning into Tamsin's ear. "We've come out without anything on us tonight."

"That's not a problem." It's Amala, thank God. She's broken up her one-on-one with Pete and seems to be letting me off the hook. "We take all major debit and credit cards. No Amex," she says conspiratorially, leaning in close so I'm assaulted by the dark zest of her fragrance. A fresh pump of adrenalized shame hits my veins with the realization Amala is here to see if she might heighten my humiliation, not lessen it.

"Oh. Great." I begin to fumble with my clutch, determined to hold my ground.

"Three books, was it?" Amala signals to Ruby to hand her a brick of maroon paper from her brown satchel, the gilt on the tickets and the gold of Amala's brooch both winking at me.

I dig around and find the one credit card I might possibly have seventy-five quid on, as she turns around to hook Pete onto her arm. I see him watching with barely hidden anguish as I spend our food budget for the rest of the month on strips of paper.

"Oh, everyone, meet Peter." Amala introduces my husband as if he were her own.

A ripple of uninterested "hellos" is released into the evening at Pete's entry into the crowd. That is until, of course, the eyes of the women nearby catch full sight of him. The booze clearly has lessened their ability to hide the shock of immediate desire. I sense that even Ruby can see my husband is a thing of beauty, as I catch her looking him up and down. Given the rapture bubbling through the air, I can't hide my pride as Pete slides over to me with a humble smile and places an arm around my shoulder. Still, I can't shake the underlying feeling I'm little more than a stump in a forest of tall, perfect women.

"What do you need?" Darius has emerged to mash himself into Amala's space, as though he senses something like competition. A hand finds the small of Amala's back as he demonstrates he's ready to do her bidding, despite whatever is troubling their relationship.

"Did you see where Tamsin went?" she asks him quietly.

"Slipped away to apologize to Howard for yet another *marital mishap*? I dunno."

"Darling, *please*." She takes Darius's hand from her back and squeezes it, which you could read as *Oh, you are awful* or *Shut the hell up.*

"Let me track her down." Darius takes a decisive sip of his drink.

"No. Best if I go."

"Have it your way." He says this with intention, too, something hard but weary about it. Is this how it always is between them, that she tells him what to do and he has to like it? Might this be why he moved out? But seeing him with her now, it's hard to imagine any of it was his idea. The chemistry between them doesn't speak of a man whose marriage is ending. To see them now, anyone would struggle to believe they've really split up.

"What would I do without you?" Amala brings her perfect face to his heroic jaw and kisses his cheek. I see her eyes flick to me as she does, revealing she knows I've been watching this exchange. Nevertheless, I can't help but keep my eyes on Amala as she heads to the doorway that leads downstairs, halted, as usual, by yet another mother who wants to ingratiate herself. Ruby moves on to another set of parents waving their notes in the breeze. Pete and I find ourselves alone.

"What were you and Amala chatting about?" I say it as lightly as I can manage.

Pete smiles at me, but his eyes dart warily over the rooftop as if to check for who might be listening. "Oh, her? Work stuff."

I watch for his tell, the shadow to emerge on his cheek. Nothing. "Work stuff?"

"She was asking for some advice on sinks."

I look quizzically at him.

"Yeah, I'm something of an expert, if you can remember that far back."

And the look he gives me isn't a guilty one, it's not over-bright, something to compensate for what he shouldn't have said or done with her. It's Pete, in his own way, letting me know he's sorry about how little paid work he's had lately and what that's done to us.

"I remember." I take his hand in apology.

Pete pulls his collar away from his neck. "That Amala. She's a bit . . . full-on. If it happens again, if I end up alone with her, promise you'll—"

"I'll rescue you."

I watch Amala untangle herself from yet another mum who stopped her in her path before finally disappearing down the stairs alone. The night I followed Bea and Ginny into the school hall last December springs into my mind. This is a fresh opportunity to gather what could be valuable insights on the other spokes in The Circle, one too good to miss.

"Pete, just hold my glass a minute."

"Where are you going?"

"I need to catch up with Tamsin about something. You'll be fine for a sec."

"But—"

I follow Amala down the stairs, stopping my descent at the

sound of a raised female voice bouncing off the fourth-floor corridor. I tentatively open the doors into the walkway in time to see one of the dads who was all over Tamsin staggering out of the girls' loos at the far end. He looks flushed and flustered, doing up his zipper as he walks in my direction. Panicked, I edge back, but can't resist continuing to watch. The first dad is rapidly followed by the other, pulling his jumper back on. As they turn to look at each other, they seem to decide there are no words for a beat until one of them speaks through gritted teeth, his hands on his head.

"Fuck . . . Fuck . . . Fuuuuck." He stops, turns back on himself, and heads to the boys' toilets, I assume to clean himself up and work out what he'll be telling his wife. I hear the other father clattering down the stairs, clearly barely able to stay upright, either in shock, inebriation, or both. For all their airs and graces, these pillars of the community, members of higher society, the gentrifying forces driving the cleansing of my neighborhood are as sordid as my dad and his crew ever were.

Once alone, I walk carefully toward the girls' toilets. I'm a couple of meters from the door when I hear Amala's voice bouncing off the tiles.

"There's only so much I can do to protect you, Tam. You've done brilliantly with the prizes tonight, and I know you're working some more family contacts, too, which is all well and good, but God, Tamsin, those fathers have only been here five minutes. Let's both hope my gentle warning is enough to keep their mouths shut."

I hear a mumbled response from Tamsin. And a sob.

"*Your mother did this, didn't do that. Your father set you up with Howard and if he finds out none of the kids are actually his, then goodbye allowance.* Think you're the only one with family issues?"

Silence interspersed by sobbing, before I hear Amala again.

"If another pregnancy isn't enough to stop you *losing control, needing a release,* or whatever, then, I don't know, scale up the therapy, or the retail therapy; get yourself a thicker wrist band, whatever it takes. Either get in control of yourself or boost what you're bringing in because I don't do relationships that leave me in debt . . . Or maybe it's time someone alerted your father to the true state of your affairs. Maybe that's the wake-up call you need."

A cry now from Tamsin. "Please. Amala, don't talk like that."

"There comes a point when it's healthier to take the bandage off, let the air get to the wound."

Something inaudible from Tamsin.

"The school is at a threshold. With the right kind of people, with Rose, we can go all the way. I cannot carry deadweight."

With Rose, we can go all the way.

My palm flies to my chest: an unambiguous compliment from Amala, and her assuredness of my positive contribution to the school. A powerful rush of vindication takes me over. I've heard enough; in fact, I've heard exactly what I want to hear. I retreat from the corridor and back up the stairs. My breath is quick and hot, my mind divided as I climb back to the roof garden. Tonight feels dangerous, as though I'm dancing on a knife's edge of something startling in its potential. Despite overhearing the barely veiled threats to Tamsin, I find my chest puffing outward as I repeat in my mind: *With Rose, we can go all the way.* Amala is seeing me exactly as I hoped she might, as I've dreamed she would.

When I get back to the roof garden, and a grouping of three random Woolf Mothers move to chat to me, I feel I definitely *should* be there. I'm in no way matter out of place. I can't wait to tell Jacq how no one here tonight has seen me as dirt, but someone worth talking to. I politely but assuredly give the women the slip so I can find Pete, who's making pleasantries with a couple of nondescript, standard-issue Woolf dads. I take hold of his hand and we make more than tolerable small talk with another couple for a while before others join them. People seem to *want* to talk to us.

Amala returns to the scene and I consider my response. My father was an avid but unsuccessful gambler. Watching him lose is how I know when to quit while I'm ahead, and this is that point. I've made my mind up before Amala saunters over to us.

"We were just saying we'd better head off now, hadn't we?" I look to Pete. "Your Jacq needs to get to that thing, doesn't she?"

"Yeah. The thing." Pete's knuckle finds the tip of his nose, ensuring that anyone with half a brain will know he's lying.

Amala tuts. "Nooo. Leaving so soon? But we've only just got started."

I hold firm. "Thank you for a lovely evening. It's been so nice to get to know some of the other parents."

"I can't wait for everyone to know you much better. Can you make it to my office before eight on Monday? I'd say we're ready for the next phase."

Whatever that might be, I've now passed Amala's threshold for readiness. I am also prepared. And after what I overheard before, I don't hear Amala's ask as an order, but a request for the time of someone she knows could prove indispensable.

"Of course. I won't be late."

Me and Pete walk back down the stairs in silence. Passing under the contorted metal *Magis et Magis,* an important night now behind me, I can't wait to replay the events of the evening again, maybe post something on Instagram: an image of the school rooftop silhouetted against the purple light still beaming out of it. I turn to take a final glance at the monumental building.

"There's *definitely* something not right about the whole set-up here." Pete undoes my moment.

"I think there are just some things we're not used to yet, but we will be soon." I squeeze his hand, wanting so much for him to come along on this journey with me, but somewhere knowing that whatever Pete may be able to contribute to this next phase of our lives, it may not always be given willingly. Pete doesn't speak for a moment, gathering the words in his mind to say what he wants to say with care.

"Rose, you have to see it: that place, the bloody lottery tickets you spent all that money on, those people! Is it too late to get Charlie in somewhere else this term? I mean, I know what you said about the grades and everything, but Jacq reckons kids transfer all the time. She says the whole operation is a bit off after she saw you with that Ginny when you went to get Charlie, that clique thing you're in, and now that I've seen how it is—"

"*That clique thing?* I'm part of the school's fundraising and governance team. How can you *still* believe your sister is better-placed than me to make the right call for our son?"

"No, it's just . . ."

I raise my eyebrows at him, daring him to keep challenging me, continue to come after all I do, knowing everything I can throw in his face about how little he's doing to keep our family afloat.

Pete changes tack. "If nothing else, can we never go to one of those nights again? You left me up there on my own like bloody bait for ages."

"I'm really sorry you feel it was that bad tonight, but we're going to have to cope with certain things if we want our lives to move on."

Pete huffs, unhappy, but unable to argue with the fact something needs to change.

We let ourselves in, finding Jacq at the dining table with a stack of books and her laptop. "That was quick! What happened?"

"Nothing. We did what we needed to do and came home. That's all," I tell her sharply.

"Is it?" Pete says under his breath.

"What's going on with you two?" Jacq asks her brother.

"Rose let them rinse us for seventy-five quid we don't have."

Jacq starts to pack her things. "What for?!"

"Dunno, maybe someone needs their diamond shoes polished," Pete tells the coatrack as he hangs his jacket.

"What's he going on about?" Jacq asks me.

"Tonight was a fundraiser. They were trying to *raise funds.*"

"Yeah, at twenty-five quid a pop for a book of raffle tickets."

"That's a bit much." Jacq zips up her bag.

"Oh yeah? And how many kids have you put through an elite free school, or any other, recently?" I regret my words as soon as they come out. Pete's face registers their hurtfulness as Jacq bites her cheek. There's nothing she would love more than to have kids; it just hasn't happened for her yet. She's never found the right person, maybe never will. "I'm sorry, Jacq, I only wish you'd both have a bit more faith."

"It's fine, Rose. It's done. You've made your choice. Seems like you're deep into it." She says it like she's sure it's a bad thing, one I'm too dense to see I'm "getting into."

"Because of what I'm 'deep into,' Charlie's getting amazing care, before and after school, special one-on-one support, and incredible opportunities to learn the sort of skills that sets a boy apart. So, if we're asked for a little more than we might at a regular school and we're getting so much more back, I don't see why that's so surprising."

"Whatever you say, Rose." Jacq opens the door before saying to Pete only, "See you."

"Bye, sis. Thanks for tonight."

I don't need to see Pete's despairing look to tell me I have some making up to do with Jacq, but I can't think about that now. There's too much else I have to think about, too much else I need to prioritize before I see Amala again.

20

DESPITE MY PRIDE AT WHAT AMALA SAID ABOUT ME, I CAN'T help but stress over what she's going to want from me, exactly what "the next phase" will entail. I end up barely sleeping on Sunday night, gaming through how the meeting might go. Surely, she wants to get me started on The Woolf business, tell me how I might take over at least some of Bea's work, but I get a strong feeling I should be prepared for anything.

At least this time round I'm used to Amala's unsmiling secretary, who all but winces at my uniform when I arrive at five minutes to eight on Monday morning, after handing Charlie over to one of the office staff who promised they'd get him to breakfast club. I realize I was so rushed I'm still holding Charlie's lunch box, its turquoise plastic clashing terribly with my royal blue uniform. Thankfully, the secretary barely looks at me, instead waving me straight in. But when I step inside her office, Amala isn't there.

Alone, I place Charlie's lunch on a side table and walk slowly around the office. I run my palm over the invitingly tender leather of her desk, then move behind her chair and view the main hall below through the darkened pane of what I've assumed to be blackout glass, which I now see extends into a thin gallery, accessible through a slim door near to Amala's chair. I can see what looks like a lighting and sound deck, doubtless intended for use at school productions. Seems I was right about the spotlight I felt on my head at open night after all. My disquiet grows as I look down into the hall where older children are learning to fence. The sight of them in their unsettling white masks, being encouraged to stab each other, makes me shudder.

I turn away and lay my hands on the sumptuous maroon leather of Amala's chair. It screams quality, shouts status. I wonder how comfortable this deep, spinning hammock of a seat is. With another long day serving other people at the bank ahead of me, Amala's chair seems to beg me to sink into it. There's still no sign of her, so I turn the chair toward me, eye it wantonly, and ready my knees to bend, about to slip into the throne of molded leather.

"Rose? Come here, would you!"

I jump, seeing the swish of Amala's hair disappearing back into another side room I didn't notice. I follow her guiltily, wondering if she saw me about to take her seat. I find her in a surprisingly large shower room. Of course she would have some kind of en suite; Amala Kaur couldn't possibly be expected to use the same facilities as the teaching staff. I scan the bathroom, noting a bale of maroon towels with gold piping as the trim and a discreet stack of loo rolls, half expecting these to be maroon and gold too.

"What do you think?" Amala's hands are on her hips. She's looking at her toilet, asking me to do the same.

I don't know what to tell her. She continues regardless, "It's a little . . . tired. This whole suite could do with an update, wouldn't you say?"

"It all looks fine to me." It's true, there's nothing obviously wrong with it.

"Peter, he's good at this sort of thing?"

I bristle when she says his name, her lips shaping themselves around the "P" and stretching out the syllables to a full and unfamiliar "Peter," but I do not let it show. It's a gesture of trying to somehow make him her own again, just as she did at the icebreaker. I won't show her how instinctively rageful that makes me feel, not now.

"My husband fits bathrooms." I immediately regret the obviously possessive "my husband," but the way she tucks a strip of black hair behind her ears tells me it hasn't necessarily registered. I notice her lobe sparkles, studded with diamonds arranged into discreet letters on a diagonal slant: *MetM. Magis et Magis.*

"Rose, I really think it's time you consider projecting yourself a little more. On the inside, we're not to be meek or hide who we are, we must be—"

"Aspirational, realistic, and uncompromising."

Her huge eyes shine. "You've already memorized our brand values?" What fun it must be for her to see me trying so hard to impress her.

"I have a very good memory."

"Me too. It's a gift, isn't it?"

"It can be," I say, unsure if she's complimenting herself or me, but taking it for myself regardless.

"So, Peter. I'd like you to send him to me."

I swallow, steeling myself to respond to her demand. "Oh, he's quite busy. I'll need to—"

She plows on, untroubled by my protest. "Ask him to pop by tomorrow morning."

"I don't know what he's supposed to be doing tomorrow."

"Yes you do." Her eyes take on another level of liquid vivacity, the kind I've seen before when I haven't done exactly as she asked immediately. "He's coming here. He can prioritize my job because I'm paying him upfront. Go on." She waggles her inverted fingers in the air to shoo me toward the task. "You can generate the invoice now and I'll move the money over. I'd say five thousand gets us off the blocks?"

Five grand.

It's happening. The rewards. I imagine the money flowing into the empty void of my bank account and escort my bristling anger to a quiet place deep inside me, somewhere Amala cannot penetrate.

"Follow me."

I do.

Amala leads me out of the bathroom and produces a thin laptop from her desk drawer. She enters the password and hands it to me. "I've created a new login for you and prepared a template for the invoice. All you have to do is enter the appropriate bank details and sign it off wearing your new Accounts Assistant hat."

"Won't that look a bit . . . dodgy?" I want to show her again I don't take the easy way through a situation. I need her to see my resistance, my tendency to consider things carefully before committing, is part of my makeup, no matter how eager for her approval I know I must appear.

Amala sighs. "Rose, this is The Woolf. We don't do *dodgy*. We do trust and efficiency. That's why I keep it close. I'm sure you've gathered, for example, that Darius runs the IT here." She peers at me to check my reaction. "Ruby and Tamsin accept percentage points on the funds raised for the school and consultancy fees, respectively. Ginny, too, and her legal practice has more work from The Woolf and our community than she can handle."

I'd like to show Amala I can halt the juggernaut of her instructions if I so desire. "I suppose the same was true for Bea and her accountancy clients? Do you suppose maybe she couldn't keep on top of all her work? I keep thinking about her, wondering how she got to the stage she did, I suppose."

"Don't." Amala's tone is not gilded with any kind of gentleness. "Bea is gone. You didn't know her. She wasn't your friend." She forces her voice to lighten. "What I mean to say is exactly as I've said before: Focus on the future." Amala watches me for a moment. "Your husband can help me with something the school needs. Now why, when I don't need to, would I look outside our Circle family?"

"I suppose it's only because it involves me signing off an invoice to my family. I just wonder how it would look to the outside world should the likes of your Mrs. Angry, school inspectors, auditors, the press, whoever, decide to investigate."

"We're a free school, permitted to give onerous red tape the slip and spend our budget how we choose: wisely."

"But—"

Amala's face turns as she struggles to hide her growing impatience. "Let's not waste any more time." She angles the laptop to me. "All you have to do is add the finishing touches." I can tell Amala notes the worry I've allowed to linger about my expression. "Rose, this is what we do on the inside, but if you'd rather . . ."

A threat. Not fully spoken, but there it is. Now I understand for certain: it's her rules, or else.

"No, of course not."

So, under Amala's watchful eye, I begin to tap in Pete's trading name, our address, then the sort code and account number to our joint account.

"All done? Very good." Amala takes the computer from me, prints off the invoice, and presents it to me. I take a deep breath as I see the figures dance in front of my eyes.

"Send Peter to me at eight sharp."

"OK." I feel my nails dig into my palms. "Is there anything else?"

"That's enough for one day, isn't it?" She laughs, believing, I think, that I'm asking for even more. Perhaps that's the sort of trick she would have pulled in my shoes.

"I'm ready to do whatever work's needed to support the school, prove to you and the others I should be here." I correct Amala's assumption.

"I know that. It's one of the reasons I chose you." Amala watches me behind steepled fingers in a way that makes me want to get out of her office as quickly as I can. Something about her expression puts me a whisper away from the knife's edge once more.

"I'll be off then." I retrieve the lunch box from where I left it. "I don't suppose you know where they took Charlie?"

"He's in the hall," she says, with a stillness to her face that suggests a certain savor.

"Down there?" I can't stop myself from racing to Amala's dark window, all the while feeling her watching me. Yet another test, yet more entertainment for her as I fail it.

"Yes. I saw you didn't manage to return your extracurricular activities form to Tamsin yet, so took the liberty of enrolling him into fencing with Rajvir. I mean they say you should wait until they're at least seven, but, when you believe in a child's potential . . ."

I notice, in among the strong white frames of older boys below, a very small child. I can't see his face, but I know behind his netted mask he must be terrified. I watch a much larger child advance toward him in two aggressive leaps, his weapon pointed straight at the boy's heart. That can't be right, terrorizing little ones like that. Just before the tall child looks about to pierce the boy's tiny rib cage, the little one struggles to pull his head gear off, stopping the older child from coming any closer.

It's Charlie.

I silence the cry in my throat when I see his face, soaked in sweat, his jaw hard, as if he's determined not to wail after the attack by the other boy. He doesn't want to be their plaything, their target practice. The crisp whites Charlie wears look far too large, like a man's clothes, boxy on his narrow shoulders, the trousers gathering about the knee. It all gives him the appearance of some kind of child soldier. I have to fight the urge to run out of Amala's office and swoop him into my arms.

"No need to thank me, Rose. I think you know my rules on that by now."

JUST BEFORE I put him to bed, when he's usually most relaxed, I plan to ask Charlie if he'd like me to take him out of fencing without making him anxious. But when I see him practicing his little moves with an imaginary foil in the living room, I hold back. Maybe it is the sort of thing he needs to boost his physical confidence. Perhaps Amala was right to push him more than I might be inclined? I'm about to tell Charlie to brush his teeth and prepare myself to broach the subject of Pete's job tomorrow at The Woolf once Charlie's in bed, when a text pings from our bank.

"What's going on here?!" Pete holds his phone out to me.

"What's the matter?"

"This: our joint account balance. They must have made some kind of mistake. We've been paid a massive amount by . . . The Woolf Enterprise?" He looks at me, almost accusingly.

"No mistake. You've got some work there. Tomorrow. You're doing Amala a new shower room and loo, for her office. You're to go and see her in the morning. That money is your upfront payment." I speak quickly and as firmly as I can manage, knowing as well as he does how strange the arrangement sounds.

"Just like that? I've not even seen the job, quoted on it, nothing. Who pays for work upfront like that without so much as a quote? I don't—"

"You don't what? Like being this far back from our overdraft limit? OK, I'll cancel the job, give back the money." I don't say it unkindly, doing my best to make it sound light and jokey. I want to give him permission to enjoy this moment, believe that some things aren't too good to be true. I go to him, place my palms on his chest, let him feel like the bigger one of us. "Go along tomorrow and if you still feel the same, we'll walk away, OK? But, personally, I think this is life going our way for once. This is what happens when you're on the inside. All the other women's bank balances are benefiting. What's the problem if ours does too?"

He sighs. "That's the difference, right there, about how you're seeing it and how I do. You're thinking: *Everyone else has been picked out to dip their beaks in, why shouldn't we?* What I want to know, what you want to be asking, Rose, isn't *Why not?* The real question is, *Why us? Why you?*"

Why can Amala see my potential, but my husband can't?

At that moment, Charlie side-jumps in front of us, slashing the air with the invisible saber in his hand.

"Pete, I am more than you seem to think I am." Pete goes to defend himself, but I stop him. "You can't see how we don't have to be the people we were. We can be better than *us*. We can follow Charlie's example and believe we're good enough to be like *them*."

By now, Charlie has taken the remote control and is using it to stab one of the big cushions on the sofa as if it were the older boy terrorizing him this morning. It's suddenly disturbing to witness. Charlie, not normally an aggressive boy, jabs at the cushion over and over before abandoning the remote to pummel his target directly with his fists. I go to him.

"That's enough now, Charlie."

"Good enough to be like them?" says Pete behind me. "Who says any of them are good in the first place?"

21

WANT PETE TO MAKE A GOOD IMPRESSION THIS MORNING WHEN
he goes over to The Woolf and Amala, so I encourage him to
wear his best jeans and a decent T-shirt under the Boden
sweater I splurged on at Christmas after seeing what the Woolf
dads wore at the open night. It's now a good shade lighter than
when I stuck it on our credit card last year, but still the nicest
thing he owns.

"Why've you laid out my Saturday gear?"

"Just trying to help. You're not likely to be getting your
hands dirty today. You'll mostly be measuring up, taking her
through the trade catalogs for suites and tiles. You want to look
smart and professional, don't you?" He closes his eyes for a
second and sighs, as if to say, *If you say so,* before pulling his
T-shirt over his abs; I find myself wondering what Amala will
make of Pete when she has a proper chance to scrutinize him.
Will she notice his body is even harder and leaner than Darius's
apparently Peloton-toughened physique? (I've noticed he's fond
of showcasing both—the body and the bike—on Instagram.) I
wonder, too, if Darius has fully moved out yet. Amala must feel
lonely in her huge home, with only her and Rajvir to fill it
now.

Since I've been inside The Circle, time in the mornings
seems to have stretched. I have minutes where there were none

before, a calmness about the start of the day I've not known since before I had Charlie. We have some time before we need to leave for Charlie's first school choir session, which I signed him up for last night to stop Amala from booking all his activities as she saw fit, reasoning choir has to be the perfect counter to the aggression the fencing seems to inspire in my son. I have enough time to update my growing numbers of followers on Instagram.

I've not posted anything since my first successful attempts. I know from studying Ruby's profile that to build followers, you need to keep giving them something. It seems to help generate both content and empathy if you have some kind of enemy, be it a real person, or just fear and negativity. And if you can create an ongoing drama from which you emerge stronger and morally victorious, even better.

I thumb through Instagram again, clicking over to @RubyWins. Today, she's marking her one-year anniversary of winning her running battle with an "anti-fan" troll posting under the name @ThroughTheLookingGlass. It was a skirmish Ruby escaped by heading to the moral high ground, propelled by her much-boosted following. Typically, @ThroughTheLookingGlass would have a pop at Ruby for things like "pimping out her vulnerable son for coin" and for "preaching humility in Fendi trainers that cost a month's wages for normal mums."

As I scroll through the comments on the original posts, I see how Ruby's increasingly enraged and enlarged band of followers immediately piled on, unloading even darker insults onto @ThroughTheLookingGlass: "Karma's gonna find you and any child you have and it ain't going to be quick and painless" and "Ruby is a role model. I can only imagine what kind of joyless bigot you must be if you've got nothing better to do with your pathetic excuse of a life than take down a strong, independent mother."

I click over to one of Ruby's most famous and well-liked posts, the dignified and impassioned plea for kindness and understanding toward @ThroughTheLookingGlass she posted a year ago. It was apparently enough to silence the anti-fan, and got more than half a million likes. Ruby magnanimously forgave them, even writing: "I believe in the good of everyone, even you" and wishing them "love and peace and a better day for you and whoever your family might be."

The statement made huge ripples in Ruby's influencer world, even spilling over into newspaper columns, breakfast TV, all commentators lauding Ruby's dignity, holding her up as an inspiration for modern mum influencers. Her follower count, and presumably how much she could charge for sponsored content, skyrocketed. For all the pain @ThroughTheLookingGlass apparently inflicted on Ruby, it seemed in the end, her most avid hater proved valuable grist to the mill. I'm intrigued and inspired by Ruby's trajectory as I consider my next post. I decide I'm going to take a selfie before I get my uniform on.

First, I try on one of the beautiful dresses from Tamsin's throwaways. Like many of the items she gifted me, the dress is both expensive and, as far as I can tell, unworn, the label still attached, a symptom, it seems, of the "retail therapy" Amala alluded to at the party. This "piece" is a silk ruffle maxi dress with a beautifully dark floral print, and the label reads: The Vampire's Wife. I slip it on and while it's far too long and broad for my frame, it feels wonderful to have something of such exquisite quality against my skin.

I step into Charlie's bedroom and open the curtains to reveal the view onto the cemetery he remains terrified of. I lean on the windowsill and bunch the loose silk of the dress in my fist behind my back to create the illusion of a garment that fits me perfectly, take a selfie, and compose the accompanying text quickly and instinctively:

@Rose_Between Shadows chase us every day, from the shadow of the grave to the shade of those who would criticize our ambitions. Every day on this earth is an opportunity to find your own light #achieve #attain #aspire #TheWoolf

At drop-off, I mean to take one last look at Pete before he heads up to Amala, but as soon as we get into the school's main building, we bump into the choirmaster, who immediately recognizes me and welcomes us warmly. I don't even get to kiss Pete goodbye before he climbs up the stairs to where Amala will be waiting for him.

I tell myself I can't think about it too much, or too long; there's only so much I can control. I make myself instead focus on Charlie, whose eyes are half-closed. "Come on, sleepyhead. It's time you get those lungs working." I give him a little tickle, but he doesn't laugh, only wanders over to his designated spot at the center of the front row obediently, a position where I can tell he'll get extra attention. A couple of older girls in the back look at each other and bristle. Doubtless, they'll report back to their mothers that Charlie is receiving "more and more." I content myself by imagining him getting a solo in the next performance, no matter how exhausted he may seem now.

Some messy buns come my way as I head off to leave via the main gate. I brace myself as their eyes sweep over my face, then my uniform. *Rotten Rosie. Rotten R—*

"Good morning." One of the mums smiles, and deferentially so.

"Rose! How are you?" Jo, the mousy mum, overtakes her friend to be at my side, delighted to be able to make a show of being on first-name terms with me.

"Gorgeous pic this morning." The one whose name I don't know speaks nervously. "That dress fits you like a glove. I can never find anything that fits me like that!" She allows herself a small, nervous laugh. "It was me asking how you did it, in the. comments?" she asks hopefully, wanting to know the name of my secret personal stylist or tailor, perhaps.

"Oh, I have my ways," I say far louder than I might normally, swishing past them.

Fakery.

As I get to the main gate, where I greet another bank of beaming, ingratiating faces lining my exit, I take in the *Magis et Magis* above me, but this time I feel as if the words are just for me. More and more approval, more and more respect, more and more opportunities for me, and my family. I push the gate's release button so I can start my walk to work. I'll get there before I'm due to start, and I feel as if I'm truly getting a bounce on my day, accelerating my entire life.

"Rose."

Ruby is at my side looking as agitated as she sounds. I can guess what she's about to say to me, but buoyed by my day so far, I don't ready myself for a blow, but instead prepare to repel a punch.

"Oh, hi, Ruby, lovely morning, isn't it?" I keep my voice breezily innocent.

"I let it go once, put it down to you being not used to how things are done, but post without my approval again and there'll be consequences, OK?"

"I'm sorry. I was in a terrible rush."

She turns to her phone while continuing to reprimand me. "You need to make time for the proper checks. I can't have anyone posting whatever they want when they want, least of all . . ." *You.* "Least of all a new member."

I pause, waiting for her to look at me. "It seemed to go down very well."

"You must have been getting lucky." She looks me up and down, noting the new Porte & Paire ballet flats I have on today, barely worn by Tamsin, now mine. They're clearly a little too big for me, even with the extra pair of socks I'm wearing, but equally far better than any of the other knackered shoes I might have otherwise worn this morning. "I'd prefer it if we didn't rely on luck. You ever heard of a trust exercise called The Circle?"

I shake my head.

"It was the inspiration for how Amala runs the school with us. A group of people stand in a circle and bend to sit on each other's laps at the same time. Everyone gets to sit if they all bend in the same way in the same moment. If one of them doesn't bend correctly, if they don't do exactly as they're told when they're instructed, then they all fall. Understand?"

Of course, I comprehend how the women of The Circle are bound by the disturbingly uncomfortable pressure they put one another under.

"I understand," I tell her. Ruby gets back to her phone with a faint nod and starts walking away from me. "I'm glad you stopped me this morning actually, Ruby. I'd love to grow my followers. Maybe one day you can tell me more about what really boosted your numbers. There must be something you did to grab people's attention . . . something you did completely off your own bat?"

Ruby looks momentarily stunned at my cool boldness, then flustered as she tries to choose the right words. "Want my advice? Don't try to get ahead of yourself."

"Or anyone else for that matter!" I say it with a little laugh and wait for her reaction.

She looks at me with eyes narrowed. "I have to go." Ruby moves to return to the school building before thinking again. "Maybe you'd like to think about that old saying about being discreet on the way up, because you never know who you'll meet on the way down." She turns, but her head does not tilt down to the phone, but to the sky above, a gesture of someone who feels they need to gather strength from some higher power. Not an act of submission, exactly, but it emboldens me to call after her with my correction.

"It's not *Be discreet,* it's *Be careful:* Be careful how you treat people on the way up because you never know who you're going to meet on the way down."

22

AT WORK, TODAY IS THE DAY WHERE THINGS START TO FEEL
distinctly different, as if I really am a changed person to
everyone else, everyone who isn't on the inside, that is. Marek
seems so pleased with my sorting out Jacq's application for her
business grant, along with my timekeeping, that he comes to
find me on my lunch hour. Before he even speaks I know this
conversation is going to be good for me; the way his eyes scoot
to my brooch and back furtively tells me so.

"I noticed . . ." He doesn't finish the sentence but draws an
invisible circle on his chest.

"I suppose at The Woolf, *they*," I, too, gesture toward my
brooch like he did, without uttering the name of my affilia-
tion, "can see I'm someone willing to give more to get more."

Marek nods to the floor. "I'm going to set up a meeting
with Linda. She's overloaded with the medium- and large-
sized grants side of things. You should be working on this too."

"I'd love to, Marek. I'm capable of more than maybe you've
assumed."

He shakes his head, as if to dismiss what he's clearly thought
of me these last six years since I've been working here. "You
know, I wanted our eldest to go to The Woolf. We went to an
open evening there, but my wife didn't like how we were
treated. She didn't bother applying there when the time came.

We're looking for the right place to send our middle daughter soon and—"

"Let me see what I can do about changing your wife's mind about The Woolf. They've welcomed my family with open arms; I can make sure your wife will feel exactly the same."

I expect I'll be involved in the open evening this year. I can invite Marek and his wife personally, make sure they arrive early, escort them myself into the room of favored parents, so they can be charmed by Amala's charisma.

"I'd like that. I'll get Linda to find some time for you later. Thank you, Rose."

"No need for thanks," I say, taking a leaf out of Amala's book.

Just before lunch, I give in to what's been at the back of my mind all day and text Pete to ask how it went with Amala that morning. He replies, saying he's still there and will be all day. I tell myself this is a good sign, but my mind buzzes for the rest of the afternoon, wondering how Amala is getting on with my husband, what they're talking about, what he's making of her, and she of him.

I'm grateful for some respite from my imagination, which is beginning to run away with me, when I step into my meeting with Linda. In fact, I forget all about Pete with Amala when I immediately note a tension in Linda's lips and the over-generosity of a smile that never quite reaches her eyes, confirming she's as angry as I anticipated at my relieving her of some of her responsibilities. I must admit, it feels almost as sweet as the fawning "Hellos" and "Gorgeous pics" at school this morning.

After an hour of "being shown the ropes" by Linda and an informal catch-up with Marek, my day at the bank is over. I head to the school, with a nervousness in my stomach, but still feeling bold enough to go up to Amala's office first to find Pete under the guise that it would be nice if he and I picked up Charlie together today. As I approach the antechamber, I see the secretary is away from her post. I linger outside Amala's closed door for a moment.

I can hear the tone of Pete's voice, but not what he's saying. I can't make out any of Amala's words either, but I hear her laugh. Once, twice, three times; irrepressible, as if Pete is the most joyfully hilarious man in the world. After each laugh, she talks a little more and I wait a little longer. Turmoil blooms in my guts.

It's been quiet now for perhaps a minute, maybe less. Time is warping and stretching. I tell myself to stay strong, stay calm, no matter what, beg myself to believe it would be ridiculous for Pete to fall so easily under Amala's spell, or that she would display such unabashed cruelty to me.

Still, after I knock I find I don't go in immediately. I call out, just in case I need to give them time to adjust themselves and spare me seeing things I can't unsee. My mind has gone to its dark place, where the inevitable has finally happened: Pete has given in to the attention of a woman who is better than me.

"Hello." It comes out as little more than a whisper at first. "Hello?" I say again, waiting a beat or two before I allow myself to knock at the door again.

"Come in!" Amala calls.

A rush of relief when I see her sitting hidden behind her computer screen, hammering at her keyboard. Pete is nowhere to be seen. "Good. I wanted to speak with you. I've been reading again in the local press about business grants your bank's overseeing. Anything you think is right for us?"

The release of my paranoid tension is short-lived. I'm shocked by her frankness, the total absence of any attempt to dress it up as anything more than what she's just put out there: an outright demand for me to bring her money. In the face of her unexpected candidness, I do all I can to remain firm and unemotive. "I've actually just been given some extra responsibility around these, so I'll be in a good position to know if there's anything The Woolf might qualify for—"

"I know you can make it happen." A hard, businesslike brusqueness about her and no indication she's impressed by my effective promotion at the bank.

"I'll do my best, of course, but it's not the sort of thing I can guarantee."

"There are no guarantees for anything in this life," she says, almost to herself.

"Is my husband here?"

She doesn't look up when she tells me, with what sounds like distinct relish, "He's in the shower." She lets the statement rest there for half a beat before adding, "Still working away."

At this point, Amala decides to stop typing and emerge from behind her desk. This reveals to me she's wearing a white camisole with two slight strands of silk barely containing her breasts, her arms and shoulders bare. The camisole is tucked into the tightest of pencil skirts. Her waist is a narrow band, her hips stunningly, but stylishly, generous in comparison. She turns to collect a piece of paper from her desk and, in doing so, bends over to showcase the split at the back of her skirt, which stops just shy of utter immodesty. The whole look is stomach-turningly, obviously sexual. A part of me prays my husband's triggers for temptation aren't so predictable. Despite feeling as drab and unenticing as I ever have, I have a sudden urge to show Amala I'm not even slightly worried about my husband spending all day with her looking as irresistible as she does.

"If you like, I can send Pete round to yours this weekend."

Her eyes seem to spark. "Really, why?"

"In case you had anything you need another body for, what with Darius gone. My husband's very handy if there's anything you need help with." I breathe over the adrenaline surging through my chest, determined not to show her how much my show of strength is paining me.

"Ha! I'm sure he is." She watches me for a moment. "You really wouldn't mind me borrowing him?"

I leave the question hanging for a beat.

"Of course not."

Amala regards me, a trace of uncertainty on her unlined brow that confirms I've managed a move she wasn't expecting. My disquiet is nudged aside by a deep satisfaction.

"Hello. Thought I heard you." Pete comes out of the bathroom, taking his work gloves off and wiping his hands on his good jeans, oblivious to any charge in the atmosphere between Amala and me. He is breathless, sweating lightly through the close-fitting T-shirt I chose for him to wear under the Boden sweater. Amala seems to find the look impossible to ignore, judging by the way her eyes dance over each inch of him. I'm torn between hardly being able to look at her greedy gaze and wanting to observe every lascivious detail of her eyes as they crisscross my husband's form.

Pete goes to kiss me, remembering Amala is in the room only when I step away. "Good day?" I ask him.

Pete looks to Amala hopefully, waiting for her to answer, his subservience making me reassured and appalled simultaneously. He needs to keep her happy, but the way he is seeking her approval is heating my blood once more.

"You've made a great start. Why don't you get yourself cleaned up and I'll bring Rose up to speed."

I breathe now through the hot discomfort of Amala ordering my husband to "get himself cleaned up" as Pete disappears back into the shower room once more.

"Oh, Pete," I call, my eyes on Amala, "hope it's OK, but can you pop over to Amala's at some point this weekend? She's got some things she could use a hand with."

"Whatever you say!"

Amala moves to perch on the edge of her desk, the tension required to hold her body firm to it seeming to accentuate every bit of her to the point of scandal. "I'm in need of someone steady. A monthly maintenance contract to look over all the plumbing and washrooms across the school and any future school."

"OK." I keep my voice level.

"I'm going to put Peter on a retainer." Pete emerges from the bathroom to stand next to me. "He's shown himself to be just perfect today."

"He definitely has his moments." I smile up to him. *Think of the money, Rose. Think of all of it,* echoes my father's voice as I try to quell my fear.

"We'll have a much better arrangement than we do with our current contractors. We're putting them on notice, aren't we, Peter?"

"Like I said, it's your choice. I'll happily do the work if it's there." Pete sounds hopeful, but also wary, as though worried he might be the butt of a highly orchestrated joke.

She retrieves the laptop I usually work on and presents it to me. "I took the liberty of setting everything up. Just print this contract off, take it home, read it over, and, assuming you sign it, you'll be our named contractor from that moment on."

Her eyes zip back and forth over mine, clearly searching for signs I'm either overwhelmed or preparing to resist her will. Determined to show neither, I scan the contract onscreen as quickly as I can. I spy the retainer amount in bold. Before I can stop it, an involuntary gasp leaves my throat. Ten thousand pounds a month. This could prove life-changing.

"The amount is the standard retainer for looking after every sink, tap, and toilet."

Pete peeks over my shoulder, and his eyes, too, are immediately drawn to the huge number at the top of the document.

"How much? You must be joking! I'd never charge any-thing like that!"

"*Pete,*" I say at the same time Amala breathes, "Peter," softly, like a spider inviting a fly to inspect the prettiness of her web. Amala takes over. "Peter, I don't want to bore you with the finer points of punitive private finance initiatives that would want to charge us the same for less. I trust you to provide very good value."

"Rose and I will need to discuss it, won't we—?"

I cut him off before he talks us out of the opportunity. "If it's what the school budget already allocates for, then there's nothing we need to worry about. We'll take a read tonight and bring it back signed for you tomorrow."

Amala nods at me, happy to see I've found a way to position it to myself so it feels justifiable, defendable. I will Pete to agree, to let down his guard and get used to accepting what's being offered by Amala.

She gets up and walks slowly back to her maroon throne. "Peter, you should follow your wife's lead. Think about saying yes more than you say no." She does read minds, just as I do.

"Shall we go get Charlie?" Pete asks me, clearly keen to get away.

"Actually, Rose, there's one more thing I wanted to speak to you about."

"I'll leave you two to it and see you down there." Pete leaves, watched by Amala. I ready myself for whatever else she has for me.

Amala smiles, while her eyes seem to appraise me. "I was thinking you and Peter might like to celebrate our new ar-rangement. It seems the perfect opportunity to show you're living your life a little more visibly now."

"OK." Concern over where this is going fights it out with a miniburst of self-regard.

"Have you heard of The Nutmeg?"

Is this another test? Do I lie? "Should I have?"

The tiniest moment of patient sympathy before she speaks. "They're about to go from two to three Michelin stars. There are no tables until summer, but I happen to know the head chef."

A pause.

"I've booked a table for tomorrow night for you and Peter. I'm assuming your sister-in-law can babysit. Time to live our values, Rose. Build your profile, your brand."

"I don't know what to say. I want to say thanks, but—"

Amala closes her eyes and puts her palms in the air by her head to block my gratitude. "Just say you'll go. Oh, and Neres, that's the chef, said he'd take extra care of you and Peter. Would you repay his kindness by perhaps sharing an update on Insta?"

"Of course."

She smiles, her work with me for today complete. I nod my goodbye, but she's not quite done yet.

"I also wanted to say, I know sometimes it may seem like I'm testing you."

I don't agree with her, but I don't say no either.

"The truth is I am." She looks for a moment very serious and I immediately prepare myself for the fact she might be about to criticize or expose me in some way.

"That's because I can see the skills you have others may not, and that's no bad thing, is it?" A fresh smile moves through the fullness of her lips and past her cheekbones to her enormous eyes.

I return a modest smile. "No, I don't think it's bad at all."

23

THE NEXT DAY, I GET UP EARLY TO SPEND SOME TIME GOING through Tamsin's gifted clothes in search of the perfect outfit. I read up on The Nutmeg as soon as I got home yesterday. It turns out to be yet another element of the transformation of our neighborhood that has, until now, completely passed me by. In a basement, on a road just off the high street, the most demanding and discerning foodies from miles around congregate to enjoy an exclusive fine-dining experience that matches their need for ever-more extraordinary things to put in their mouths in stunning surroundings. There is only one option for all guests: the tasting menu, a parade of seven courses, along with the accompanying "wine flight." On the website, the descriptions of the courses—"Bird," "Root," "Leaf," "Jam"—are as opaque as the pricing, but while I realize the bill will be astronomical, there's no way I'm turning it down. Amala has found me a table people would kill for and, besides, within one hour of my handing in Pete's signed retainer contract this morning, an incredible ten thousand pounds cleared in our account. The sensation of transitioning so rapidly from red to black is almost dizzying.

I'm in the bathroom, experimenting with gel to slick back my hair away from my face. My hair looks suddenly modern and confident compared to the half-grown-out pixie cut into which it would normally fall. I slip on my chosen dress for the night. It's in a similar royal blue as my bank uniform, but this dress, by Reem Acra, retails at more than fourteen hundred pounds and consists of the most luxurious floor-length, textured fabric with voluminous bell sleeves. It didn't take me long to shorten the hem, though I did feel a prickle of guilt as I stitched, thinking of Tamsin trying to spend away her worries. I blank out, too, Amala's threatening words to Tamsin at the icebreaker, making my mind pivot back to the fact that I am in Amala's favor: I am the one she thinks can take The Woolf all the way to where it needs to go; I'm the one about to waltz into the most sought-after reservation in town because she chose me for it. That's all that matters to me for now.

"You look . . . Wow," Pete says, when I leave the bathroom.

"You look like a queen, Mummy," Charlie follows up.

And I have to say, I feel it.

When the buzzer goes, it abruptly ends my moment of feeling imperial. What will Jacq say when she sees me: Will she approve of me, or immediately note I'm wearing clothes that have no place being on my back?

"Bloody hell, is that you, Rose?" she says, the second she claps eyes on me.

"It is. Do you like it?"

"You look so . . . different." She stares at me almost mystified. Apparently unsure what to do with her emotions at seeing me almost unrecognizable, she focuses instead on something she does understand. "I want to know everything about the food tonight, OK? I've got to think of places like The Nutmeg as The Narrow's competition now. Will you come and see the works soon?" she asks, sounding uncharacteristically needy, like she doesn't know or trust the new me well enough to care about her world anymore.

"Definitely. I can't wait."

I wish I could tell her that what she sees in me now is just as much me as the Rose she knew before The Woolf and The

Circle. I was only ever waiting for the opportunity to change, not the ability to do so.

It's a few minutes' walk to The Nutmeg's address, the glossy ocher door to our destination marked only by a silver plate with an engraving of a nutmeg above an intercom.

"Hello?" I say into the speaker, determined to overcome my nerves. "This is Rose O'Connell. I—"

Before I can finish, the door opens into a stairwell, alive with mossy plants fed by banks of UV lights. The whole feel is immediately otherworldly.

"Whoa," I hear Pete say behind me.

At the bottom of the stairwell we are greeted by a young woman in a black suit with a wide smile and a French accent so thick, I feel as though I may have left the country. "Good evening. Welcome to our supper club. In a moment, I will take you to your table, but we would like you to begin your experience this way. May I first take your coats?"

We swap our coats for a varnished nutmeg with "Table 10" painted onto it and follow her into a square pink room. It's just as magical as the staircase, with a small, silver-fronted bar at its heart, every available space around it also given over to plants. My olfactory sense is bombarded: citrus, herbs, floral notes of every kind, sandalwood too. Lining the room are chaise longues with small tables where pairs of beautiful people have already begun their "culinary journey." We're seated at one next to two men I recognize. Pete turns and mouths, "Isn't that them from—," a thrilled look in his eye.

I nod, my mouth open in the overawing specialness of every little thing about this room, not just the film actors next to us. "It is!"

We are presented with some kind of fizzing aperitif and a selection of fine wafers standing in a rich-looking yellow mousse. Neither Pete nor I have any idea what we are eating, but for once, we don't hold back; we allow ourselves to be taken to somewhere new. The wafers taste variously of the sea and the sky, the aniseed in the drink escorting our taste buds to heights they've never known before. We find ourselves repeating "Wow" and grinning at each other, our minds blown.

This continues when we're taken to the main dining room. Seven plates of food that seem to make my brain spark and my stomach delight are presented, Pete and I marveling at the imagination of the plating—on hay and stones, even on a minilawn of micro herbs—and the sheer magic of the tastes and textures on our tongues. Just when we think it can't get any better, and we could not eat another bite, something even more beautiful and intriguing than the last dish comes our way until finally, an affable-looking man in chef's whites brings over a collection of petits fours not advertised on the main menu. This must be Neres.

"You enjoyed everything?" He deftly places the sweets on tiny earthenware plates with thin wooden tongs.

"Mate, your food is incredible," Pete tells him.

"We're totally blown away," I say, prompting the lauded chef's knowing smile. "Could you possibly take a selfie with us?"

Neres walks round the back of the table for the picture while the rest of the diners, including the two film actors, look on, intrigued as to whom we might be to warrant the star chef's special attention. When Neres leaves, Pete and I watch each other, still beaming. I wonder if we'll ever stop smiling, ever want to eat anything "normal" again, or if I'll ever come down from where I am right now. I want to come to places like this every day, to have people see me and know I belong here.

"I feel like we've been on holiday or something," Pete tells me.

"Me too. I'm so full, but completely refreshed, like I've woken up from a long sleep."

Pete shakes his head in gleeful disbelief.

The bill arrives, encased in a large silver nutmeg, split at its seam to reveal a curl of paper. I reach for it first.

"No, don't. Let me." Pete takes the bill from its holder.

"I warn you, Pete. It's going to be massive."

"It's OK. We can afford it, can't we?"

I nod.

Pete deals with the bill without so much as a flinch, but when he nips off to the bathroom, I check the amount: nearly seven hundred pounds. An unthinkable amount of money. And yet I can't help but feel it was completely worth it. My sense of justification grows when I see our selfie with Neres is already my best-liked post yet. When we leave, when there's nothing more they can possibly do to lift our night any higher, no further extension to The Nutmeg's hospitality, they present us with a ceramic dish of homemade smoked butter and a "signature sourdough" to take home with us for the morning. At this level of existence, it seems you always get more than you expect.

IN FACT, THAT night at The Nutmeg a couple of weeks ago was just the beginning. The life that was stained miserable with debt demands, broken incomes, and a child who seemed to be drowning before my eyes is starting to feel like the distant past. Because my neighborhood's great wave of gentrification has finally collected my family into its barrel and is sweeping us to a golden shore.

By far and away the most important feature of this new territory is that my son is no longer being left behind. Charlie is becoming stronger, quicker, smarter, and more resilient each day. He even looks different, as though he's grown an inch or two. I've been letting his hair grow out too; the beginnings of soft, dark brown curls now framing a face that looks a little sharper, but no less beautiful. More so, in fact. Although we don't really have the room to store them, I've bought Charlie a top-of-the-range bicycle, scooter, and skateboard. He looks, and is becoming, a child with Woolf strength, with the *Woolf polish*.

Every moment, everywhere I look, everywhere I turn, I am bathed in approval. At work, where Marek's de facto promotion is in full swing, and at the schoolyard, where all the Woolf Mothers seek me out to share their admiration and acceptance, this real-life experience transferring online too. Things are going even better than ever with Amala. For now at least, she seems to be giving me some breathing space regarding the grant situation and, in the meantime, bringing me into work to establish the new senior school. I am beginning to feel indispensable.

This morning, I drop Charlie off at fencing, collect some paperwork from Amala's office, and seem to float across the yard on the crisp October air and the chorus of approving "Hello, Rose," and "Amazing photo you posted," and "You look great," from the Woolf Mothers.

I'm about to release the steel gate and make my way to work early when a thin, bony finger pokes firmly into my shoulder, bringing with it a moment of primal terror. I turn around, half expecting to see the Whichello twins.

"You might be wearing Tamsin's clothes to look like one of us."

It's Ginny, her face flushed, features loose, her gaze falling to my ballet flats secretly held fast by my extra socks.

"You may be aping Ruby to gain popularity among . . ." She gestures vaguely to the mums behind her in the playground. "You may have somehow gotten your husband's feet under Amala's table, and you may, for whatever reason, even though Bea had more qualifications in her little finger than you have in your entire body"—she views my diminutive frame—

"find yourself suddenly front and center of planning the growth of the Woolf network."

Ah, I see. Looks like Ginny has learned of my latest additional responsibilities, which accounts perhaps for both her rage and the fact that she's already on her way to being drunk.

"But just so you're clear, *we* haven't changed our minds. No one on the inside really thinks this is where you should be." Her lips flail, as if guiding her next words to them from the air. "Or where you'll stay."

Old me would have quaked and cowered. New me sees just how far Ginny is threatened, which empowers me to say what I say next.

"No one on the inside thinks I should be here? *No one?* What about the most important person, Amala? And what about everyone on the outside?" I raise my hand to a cluster of passing messy buns, who immediately wave back enthusiastically. "They seem to think I'm right where I should be."

"We'll see. You might not know it yet, but you," a finger jabs the air in front of my heart, "*you* are on borrowed time."

I turn away from Ginny, realizing my breathing is calm, my blood pumping with controlled regularity. It's different from the last time Ginny tried to put me in my place after my first awful meeting with The Circle.

"Have a nice day, Ginny." I return to releasing the exit. "You might want to start it with a lie-down." The metal gate separates us with a resounding clang.

24

LATER THAT DAY, ON MY LUNCH BREAK, AN HOUR I ACTUALLY feel entitled to take these days, I head to Jacq's café—now her restaurant, The Narrow. I feel a little guilty that I haven't been there yet, despite my promise to Jacq that I couldn't wait to see it. But I've been too busy with things at The Woolf and at the bank, especially with Pete working so late as he has been this last week. Amala has also requested Pete's skills at her home at least once these last couple of weekends since the first time I offered his services. I don't enjoy the way she commands my husband's time in this way, but I don't stop it either. It's clear for different reasons: Pete and I are becoming invaluable to Amala.

When I get to The Narrow, I see why Jacq has been dying for me to see the transformation. I'm astounded by the change. The site where I first met Jacq, the place where the possibility of Charlie ever began, has now, like the rest of the neighborhood, become unrecognizable. I let myself inside with a pang of something melancholy, tempering my pride in Jacq's new venture and myself for getting her there. Even Jacq looks different, her hair down, a great fan of curls around her head. Everything about her is renewed and enlivened.

"Wow, Jacq."

"I know. Told you you'd like it." A tinge of *What took you so long* in her tone I choose not to dwell on.

"Look at you. Look at this place." I survey the blond wood booths, the tastefully neutral walls, and the works by local artists that dot them.

"I know. I can't bloody believe it. It's like a dream."

"It's not a dream, Jacq. It's all real and it's all down to you and your vision."

Jacq makes an *Oh, you* face before reaching behind the newly installed bar area to retrieve something. She holds out a wedge of stiff envelopes. "Invites for your lot at the school, Amala and co. They must be doing something right given what's happened to you and Pete since you've been in their gang. Who knows if you'd have thought about my grant if you hadn't got carried away with The Woolf."

My head falls, and I feel caught out by her. I eye the envelopes in her hands, one with Ginny's name on top.

"Hey. It's OK, I meant it in a good way. Take these off me, would you?"

I hesitate a beat before doing so. I'm more than happy for Amala to see the transformation of Jacq's place from the outside, but she, Ginny, Ruby, or Tamsin cannot be let inside The Narrow or any sphere Jacq and I share. The Circle and my life with Jacq are two separate things. There's no benefit in crossing the two, but there could be much pain.

"Rose, did you hear what I said? If people see Amala and the rest of the crew here, we'll be winning, won't we?"

For once, it's me who doesn't hear Jacq the first time. "I'll see if any of them can come. With or without them here, don't you think we're already on top?"

"You might be right there. I mean, who could look at us two now, my brother, too, and say we aren't winning?" Jacq smiles with a burst of pride extending to me that I suddenly find difficult to accept, given how much I'm keeping from her about The Circle.

"Oh, look who it is," Jacq says, gazing over my shoulder to

the street. I turn to witness none other than Amala on the pavement outside, appraising the new signage, and then, the metamorphosis within.

"What are you waiting for? Invite her in." Jacq physically nudges me.

"I'll probably see her tomorrow. I can give her the invites then." I can't bear the idea of my two worlds colliding, now or at the opening. I don't want Jacq to pick up on the essential master/servant basis of my relationship with Amala, and I don't want Amala to glean any deeper, therefore potentially useful, insights about me from Jacq. I may be riding high, but I'm doing so on the knife's edge I've been teetering on since this all started. If I don't proceed with the greatest precision and caution, I will get cut.

It's too late now. My pulse soars, my feet sweat within my double layers of socks as Amala lets herself into the café, no pause, even as her eyes rest on the sign on the door: CLOSED. To her, it's clearly another protocol to which other people find themselves compelled to comply, not her.

The combination of her skin and the baby-pink satin suit she wears looks perfect against the fresh yellows and taupes around us. No one could help but feel overwhelmed by her presence, particularly on seeing her in such close proximity for the first time, as Jacq is.

"Hello there," Jacq says with a deference that's as irksome as it is uncharacteristic.

"Amala, this is my sister-in-law, Jacq."

She nods in Jacq's general direction, her eyes themselves too busy absorbing every detail of the old greasy spoon's evisceration around her, rather than Jacq herself. "This place looks incredible."

"Thanks very much. Actually, we were hoping to invite you and your colleagues at school to my launch night." Jacq signals at me to hand over the invites.

Amala ignores her and runs a long finger over the nearest leather booth. "New kitchen, new interiors, new everything."

"It's all down to Rose and the bank—"

"I had nothing to do with it, really," I interject, with as much modesty as I can convey.

"But Rose, it was all—"

Amala's eyes shoot back and forth between Jacq and me.

"Here, I'm sure you're all very busy on a school night, but these are invites for yourself, Ginny, Ruby, and Tamsin." I hand Amala the cards. "Anyway, we don't want to keep you . . ."

Amala smiles, satisfied, self-assured as always, completely unhurried. She looks at Jacq directly for the first time, leans into her space, her back to me. "You know, I'll often say this about your sister-in-law: Rose is a wonder and she's far too modest about it."

Jacq smiles widely and so innocently. "Couldn't agree more."

Amala goes to ask Jacq another question, but I jump in again. "I'm so sorry, Amala, we've got a few things to be getting on with before I have to get back to work, so I'd best be seeing you tomorrow."

It's too quick, far too firm for Amala not to know I'm desperate for her to leave now. Her lips remain poised mid-interrogation for a second before she straightens her expression into something coolly neutral. Amala smiles at Jacq as she waves the deck of invite cards at her and turns for the door. Jacq waves back enthusiastically, then grabs another handful of invites and envelopes and starts stuffing one into the other, giving a small shrug.

"Amala: she didn't say thank you for the invitations."

"Oh, she's got a thing about it. We're not really allowed to thank her for anything," I explain. "I think she reckons if you say thank you, it's like you're not close. Saying thanks implies you never expected she'd ever do something for you."

"And you won't necessarily expect to be asked to do things for her. Interesting. Like balanced reciprocity. You only ever give because you expect more in return. In fact, as soon as you receive something, you're in debt to the other party. You may even be facing a loss."

Am I in the process of simply reducing my financial debts while accruing ever deeper obligations to Amala?

Jacq emits a satisfied sigh. "Anyway, Rose, what Amala Kaur says about you, it's true. You are a wonder. It's like you've become someone completely new."

"That's not true."

"Say again, Rose?"

I speak louder. "I said, what I am now, it's not a different me. It's who I was all along."

25

THE NEXT MORNING, I WAKE UP NATURALLY BEFORE THE ALARM. I open my eyes to see Pete looking at something on his phone; a strange intensity about his face that I can't place and don't like. I watch him for a moment longer as he remains absorbed in his screen.

"Morning."

Pete startles, immediately locks his phone, then places it on the bedside table, taking half a second to ensure it's screen-side down.

"Morning, you." He stretches over to kiss me.

"Everything OK?"

"What?" Pete appears innocently confused.

"Whatever you were looking at on your phone. Looked pretty distracting."

He yawns, cupping his hands over his mouth before running his finger and thumb down the bridge of his nose. "I was just reading the headlines."

He's lying, but what about? He was working late again yesterday and ran straight to the bath, as if he wanted to avoid me. Unsure if I'm being completely paranoid or not, I nevertheless make sure I head to Amala's office this morning, tracking Pete up there while I check for the signs as he interacts with her. What would tell me they are having an affair? Overfriendliness? A studied, overplayed professionalism? In the event, I see nothing conclusive. Pete gives Amala a cheery "Good morning" and gets to work straightaway. She, meanwhile, watches Pete as he removes his jacket, apparently taking in every fascinating movement as he slips it off his shoulders and hooks it onto her hat stand before getting to work on the finishing touches to her bathroom. There is clearly interest on her part, as there has been since the very start, but it does not seem to be returned, at least for now.

Amala then makes a point of watching me, her lips still and thoughtful behind her sparkling, steepled fingers.

"We could get a grant through your bank, a significant source of funding. Why haven't you already started to look into it?"

I find myself taken aback by the sudden baldness of her demand. "I'm sorry, I suppose I've just been so busy with—"

"Your followers? Enjoying the finer things in life? They're not criticisms, by the way." And yet the way she's said these words cuts through me.

"I've been a bit preoccupied with work, for The Woolf, at the bank."

Her mouth is an unimpressed pout now. "If there are opportunities to support us, I shouldn't have to ask you to bring them to me."

"You're right. I should have thought of it sooner. There are funds for special projects. I'll look into it today, but I think all we'd need to do is demonstrate the plans for spending it for the wider benefit of the school."

"Say, if we can show how we'd allocate funds for an extension of the Mindfulness Zone, they'll give us the same amount." How quickly her mind pivots into a plan when money is involved, like she's blinded to any other matter.

"That's about the size of it."

"Do get onto it, please," she continues. "It feels like we may have already wasted too much time."

"I'm s—"

"Please. I'm not mad on apologies. I'd rather people show they're sorry by the things they do."

I can't help but feel stung by her disappointment in me, her harsh tone, but she doesn't notice. Her attention appears to be taken by Pete once more, specifically his muscled forearms as he drags a sack of tile adhesive across the floor.

"The renaissance of your sister-in-law's place suggests they must be giving it away."

I bristle at her belittling of Jacq's restaurant, not that she sees this either. "I wouldn't say that, but let me see what I can do." I vow to get on it immediately.

"I'll see you later," I hear Pete call, just as I close the door on them.

I PRIORITIZE MAKING sure Amala knows my worth, generating a business case and working with Pete to create some rough but persuasive plans for extending the Mindfulness Zone. Amala signs off on this, as expected, without a word of thanks for my swift work.

A few days later, before I leave for The Woolf in the morning, I see ten thousand pounds has cleared in one of The Woolf's many accounts because of my efforts. I allow myself a smile as I sip my tea, viewing the school through my window, the wintry morning's sun yet to melt the frost clinging to the brick of the northern side of the main building. This is what taking some control feels like.

My moment of satisfaction, however, is short-lived.

Pete wanders into the living room from the bathroom, phone in hand, smiling tenderly into the screen before realizing he's being watched. When he looks up and sees me observing him, he abruptly adjusts his expression. He worked late again last night, and the night before.

I can't look at him. Charlie comes up and hugs his dad's legs while Pete's hands clasp the back of his shoulders. They do a little swaying dance together in the kitchenette in a way that would usually melt my heart.

"You got another long day at The Woolf again?"

He breathes out. I can hear the nerves in his chest from my window seat. "Actually, I've asked Jacq to pick Charlie up later. I've booked somewhere for dinner. Thought it was time we had a good talk."

"OK."

Perhaps the moment is nearly upon us. It seems Pete may want to confess in a public place where there is less chance of me exploding. The move has all the hallmarks of being someone else's idea.

26

ALONE WITH HER IN HER OFFICE, I NOTICE AMALA FAILS TO PICK up on my coolness and expects me to act, as always, like her dutiful servant. Is this how she would behave if she were sleeping with my husband, expecting me to do everything she requires, perhaps just as he performs to order? I work through the throbs of rage that threaten to take me over. I have my suspicions but no grounds yet, so I must bide my time, and continue to do as instructed. Still, I sense a distinct change in the atmosphere today, so I need to be ready to hold my ground.

"These invoices need paying."

Amala hands me a loose pile of paper, fragrant with traces of pine and coconut oil. I'm right in thinking these invoices smell of other places. They variously originate from tradespeople, a building materials supplier, plus a wine merchant, all based in the South of France, Provence. With her in her leather throne and me in my usual spot at a small table toward the entrance to the office, I discreetly google the address of the property the bills are related to and am far from surprised to learn it is Amala's converted eighteenth-century farmhouse in the foothills of Mont Ventoux. I recall seeing its views into the vineyards and the Rhône valley, its two gîtes, and an infinity swimming pool from many of Amala's Insta posts.

"Just for our records," I begin as neutrally as I can, "could you explain how these expenses are related to The Woolf?"

She doesn't so much as flinch. "More than once I've used stays in the gîtes to reward staff and for fundraising, receptions, and the like."

"And there's a register of these uses?"

"Yes. Somewhere, I suppose, if anyone should ever have their suspicions—which they shouldn't and they won't." Her tone hardens the deeper into the sentence she reaches. "Just crack on, Rose. Nothing bad is going to happen because of it."

I breathe, knowing I'm going to be met by Amala's further frustration, but this morning, deciding to push on anyway. "Amala. This spending, some people might say it looks a bit . . . it might be seen from the outside as a little questionable."

"Things only become questionable when they are questioned." She reminds me so much of my father in this moment, as though her skewed perspective on things is the most natural, the most intuitively correct, position any person could take.

"Well, there are some things that beg the question."

The second the words leave my careless mouth, I regret them. From the other side of the room, Amala is steepling her fingers again, watching me from behind them. After a moment, she produces her invite to Jacq's opening night party from her drawer and starts to fan herself with it, as if it were a vital piece of evidence in a trial she's about to reveal.

"I can't get how much you've helped your sister-in-law out of my mind." She flicks the card with the hardness of her nail, sending a clean thwack into the corners of her office. "That was all your work, wasn't it?"

"I wouldn't say that. It was Jacq's plans, her—"

Amala takes an audible inhalation over my words. "Ten thousand cleared in our accounts today."

"That's great. I was hoping it would." I know by now it serves me better to always let her feel as though she's one step ahead of me, telling me something I don't know.

"*Just* ten thousand. It seems to me, you're prepared to stick your neck out for her, not so for me."

I bite my lip, sensing the escalation to come.

"Sorry, Rose, I can see I've made you uncomfortable and that makes me unhappy. Because I feel like we've become so close in the short time you've been on the inside. I really feel I'm your *behenji,* your sister."

"That's so nice to hear." And it would be. It would be such an immense comfort if what Amala is saying to me came from a place of full sincerity. Having her close to me, another woman who I knew for sure shared not only my kind of ambition, but also my ability to read people, might have given me someone I could be wholly myself with; the same for her. A true and equal friendship between me and Amala might prove something quite special. Is there a parallel universe where we bond, where she might genuinely like me better than I believe she does?

"So we're sisters. And sisters do anything for each other, just as you have for Jacqueline."

"Amala, there's no more money I can get for you."

"I'm sorry?"

"There are only grants left for businesses with significant assets, much greater than—"

"Half a million."

"Right. You know?"

Of course she's made it her business to know, to put herself that crucial one step before me on any track I attempt to follow.

"Well, you'll also know, then, that The Woolf doesn't qualify. To get the big grants you need to be able to match them pound for pound. The enterprise isn't anywhere near half a million. Even if I could somehow get the application through compliance—"

"But you *could* though, couldn't you?" There's a certain prickle of pride across my chest, even as I know what she's asking, the position she's prepared to bully me into. "Rose, I think you know by now the others want you out; I'm giving you the chance to show them they're wrong about you, providing you with the opportunity to justify my supporting your privileges and the personal brand you appear to be building. I hear from Ruby you're becoming something of a major hit on Insta."

I try to get ahead of the fact I've broken another one of The Circle's rules, in addition to not instantly finding ways to provide Amala with *More and More.* "I thought I was doing the right thing. I won't post without Ruby's sign-off again if that's what you want."

Amala's expression doesn't alter. "I think you probably understand by now, if you need to seek permission from anyone, it's from me. And from what Ruby has told me, it seems you may have stumbled upon the specific and delicate secret to her success. You've seen Through the Looking Glass?"

My heartbeat picks up a little. Is Amala confirming my suspicions about Ruby?

Ever since my sleuthing on her profile and my mild agitation of Ruby at the school gates, I've started to wonder if she herself was behind @ThroughTheLookingGlass. The anti-fan's posts were all geotagged in locations close to wherever Ruby was, and while their writing was full of bile, there was something similar about their sentence patterns when compared to Ruby's posts. I could almost hear her voice in my head as I read them. Now it does indeed seem that all that time it was Ruby tearing herself and her son to pieces for the delectation of an online audience. It was Ruby inciting her followers to defend her—against herself—in order to ingrain @RubyWins into the online consciousness and grow her cost per sponsored post. What a price to pay for avoiding being *That Mum.*

Amala talks calmly, her voice unwavering. "I untangled the roots of Ruby's exponential growth and I understood her motivations. She wants more, she wants to do it her way. I suggested she'd be perfect for The Circle and assured her that if she allowed me to leverage @RubyWins for the greater good of The Woolf, then I would do everything in my power to ensure her unusual strategy was never understood by the wider world."

"You're protecting Ruby."

Amala sends a short breath of laughter through her nostrils. "Rose. I protect all of you."

The only way to get inside The Circle is to never ask.

Amala asking me to bring in money confirmed the blatantly transactional nature of The Circle, but now I know it's more than this; it's what I'm sure Jacq would say is feudal. We pay our dues, our homage to our overmistress and, in return, she "protects us" under the umbrella of her all-powerful matronage. Amala shields Ruby from the possibility of being outed as her own anti-fan while leveraging the profile for the gain of The Woolf. She promises Tamsin she won't encourage her family to disinherit her so long as she can divert more and more of their philanthropy to her empire. Ginny, while being vital in the efforts to bat away the Mrs. Angrys and defending The Woolf against wider scrutiny, is also a desperate alcoholic barely clinging to family life, making her seemingly even more pliable and therefore useful to Amala.

As for Bea, she was bankrupt; her finances, not to mention her social standing, would be in peril once more if she stepped out of line. What did she say to Ginny on the open night? Was what Amala asked of her toward the end so dangerous she was willing to throw in the towel rather than do it? Showing she was prepared to walk, ready to live outside Amala's protection, made Bea a risk, undeniably the weak link in The Circle's bond.

This is why you never get invited in if you ask.

The women of The Circle are chosen by Amala less be-cause they can prove to her they are the richest, most stylish, most successful, or skilled. They find themselves on the inside because they have the most to lose. Bea showed Amala she wasn't afraid of losing the strings-attached gifts being in The Circle gave her. She'd made her own decision about how far she was willing to go, not Amala. And then she died. Now, it's not pride I sense rising in my chest, it's a hard chill.

"So, Rose, the question is, do you want me to protect everything that's good about your life now?"

I want to tell her I had a life before she came into it—it's not she who determines the success or happiness of my entire family—but I'm suddenly too afraid to show my defiance. I allow my fingers to travel to my neckerchief, eyeing the clock on the wall, which is nudging toward nine o'clock. "I really should be getting to work now."

Amala's eyes come alive with outrage at my stubbornness. "It's time you delivered more, Rose."

She looks to have me over a barrel. Dare I say enough is enough now, just as Bea did? "Amala, what I think you're talk-ing about me getting into, I could lose my job, and more be-sides."

She doesn't react. It's time to show her a different tack, one I think might better appeal to who Amala Kaur is deep down.

"It's too high risk for The Woolf and for you," I continue. "What if I did end up helping you? What if you got the money, then you invested it, spent it? Then, what if they found out we'd cooked the books to get the money and they wanted it back? They won't do that quietly. They'd make an example of this place and of you. The Woolf's reputation would be ruined. Everything you've built would go down the drain."

She presses her index fingers to her lips, which are pursed in amusement. What else might I throw at her, what other levers might I pull that make me look as though I'm focused on her needs first, not my own?

"You've helped me and my family so much, it's down to *me* to protect *you* from making this mistake," I finish and await Amala's reaction.

"Protect me?" Amala feigns an eye-rolling ennui. "You know, poor old Bea tried that line. Of course, we now know the one person Bea needed to focus on protecting was herself and her poor decision-making. Maybe the same is true for you? Like you, Bea could have continued to have it as good as Ruby, Tamsin, and Ginny, but made her mind up to not go the extra yard. She made her choice but clearly couldn't handle the consequences."

"You asked Bea to apply for a big grant, but she wouldn't or she couldn't?" I dare to ask.

"An element of both." Amala confirms what I've suspected.

"And when she didn't, you—"

"Had no choice but to tell her she was on the outside and, for whatever reason, she sadly found that impossible to handle. It seems to me that with your income stream, new image, new legions of fans, that perhaps you can understand how she felt."

I feel less afraid of Amala now, just a fool. *This* is why she encouraged me to build up my social media following; not because I was somehow naturally better at it than Ruby, not because she admired how well I appeared to be living The Woolf's "brand values," but because she knew how easily I'd become addicted to the validation.

"Now you see why, despite everything Ginny and the others think about whether you belong on the inside, it had to be you."

"Why's that, Amala?" I want to hear her say something truthful to me, so I might know exactly where I stand with her from now on.

"Because I know, unlike Bea, you can do what I'm asking, and that you will."

And now something else is startlingly clear: There was nothing else Amala liked about me except for my uniform. She wasn't, as I'd begun to hope, looking beyond it and to the person I am when she invited me into The Circle. She was excited by the smell of my desperation, and my job at the bank was the one thing about me she believed had any value at all. I can feel it, a sad shard of longing inside me. It stabs at my need for approval, and at my humiliation for ever letting myself believe I might have ever had it from her. How could I have ever let myself entertain the notion that someone like her could see me as anything more than a servant?

"It's so much more than the money for you, isn't it?"

I redden. I can hear the blood thudding in my ears.

"Relax, Rose, I'm with all your followers and fans; so far you look to be doing a stand-up job of supporting The Woolf. But there will be those who will question why you, the volunteer finance assistant, are signing off your own family's invoices, accepting significant monthly payments which you yourself organize. It might, depending on how it was revealed, look to your followers as though you were attempting to skim off what should have gone to educating the children of this fine community. I mean, how else could you afford your designer wardrobe and supper at The Nutmeg?"

Amala has worked to trap me with my own vanity, the fact I let myself believe I belonged in those dresses, in that restaurant, in this gilded version of my life. My heart pounds.

"Just as you've been watching me, Rose, I've been monitoring you." I turn my gaze away from her before I can stop myself from committing this act of submission, one that confirms her suspicions of my watchfulness are correct. "Goodness, I don't think I've ever seen one of our brooches shine so brightly on anyone." She leans forward to squint at the Circle pin on my lapel. "God, do you . . . do you actually *polish* it?"

I try to answer, but Amala waves away my reply with a mixture of distaste and disinterest.

I wonder what might happen if right now, I removed my brooch and left it on the table, if I gave Tamsin her clothes back, deleted my Insta, took Pete off the payroll and told him never to see Amala again, pulled Charlie out of all his classes and clubs, and walked the three of us back to our little home above the shop. I fantasize about it for a split second, but this option is no longer available to me.

I stand there for a moment longer, not saying anything for as long as I can bear, one final show of resistance.

"OK, Amala. I will work to create evidence of assets or income to the level you require. But the amounts we're dealing with means it won't be easy."

"Achieving the best outcomes rarely, if ever, is." She says it with a sneer, baring her teeth with an unattractive bitterness. For the briefest of seconds, I wonder what made Amala Kaur's soul so ugly inside.

"Come back here later. You have work to do."

"I can't tonight. I have somewhere I need to be."

"Ah yes," she smiles knowingly, "dinner with Peter."

I stop myself from asking her how she knows, but she's already ahead of me.

"We've been spending a lot of time together recently. I know what he has in store for you."

I can take no more of her today. I don't say another word and I leave, sensing her watching my every step as I exit her office in a heady daze.

Today, Amala Kaur has shown me what it really means to be inside The Circle.

She's also made it abundantly clear what she thinks she can get from me.

But as I take myself away from her office the real question is this: When I suspect she may already have my husband in her sights, when I have no real money of my own, no celebrity, no business, no inheritance to retain, why else was I chosen by her for The Circle? What else, exactly, does Amala think I have to lose?

27

TODAY IS A DARK DAY ABOUT TO BECOME SIGNIFICANTLY blacker. I should have told Pete he didn't need to take me out to tell me whatever he's going to, and especially not at the place he's chosen. Because opposite the restaurant where Pete has requested I meet him used to be the brownfield square of land my dad would use for his property development scams. He'd organize to meet his mark there, often bringing with him some of his Society. It was the site of his last Hurrah and the end of any hope I might have had of having a good and decent life. I can't bear to be in this part of the neighborhood, then or now. Because today, there's a block of flats on the plot that represents everything wrong with what's happened round here.

At the top of the block is a handful of luxury penthouses, complete with bamboo-sheltered outside spaces, with water features and giant porch swings. A sign advertises a gym and swimming pool for those residents, and at street level, there's a wide and shining glass door, manned by a porter. Sandwiched between the penthouses and the gym, a sop to the town planners who sought assurances the development would include "affordable and social housing," there is a stack of mean flats for the resident poor, accessible only by a grubby door on the street, all amenities strictly out of bounds. The whole thing turns my stomach, as does this restaurant, which used to be my dad's preferred boozer and now serves up not mere food and drink, but a "dining concept," "Tel Avivian gastro sharing plates." Every bit of me wishes I could be somewhere else.

The maître d' points me toward our table where Pete awaits. I walk slowly toward my husband, watching him for a moment before he realizes I'm approaching. He kneads his hands together, then rubs the back of his neck once, twice, three times. Something is clearly making him very nervous. Can he really be here to tell me it's over, that he's realized he could do so much better than me, that Amala Kaur is the woman who finally and emphatically succeeded in turning his head?

"Hello," he says like a stranger, as if we're meeting for business. I half expect him to shake my hand, but instead, he gives me a soft kiss on the cheek, his hands reaching for mine, holding them both close to the wrists while I remain stiff.

"How was your day? You've been so busy lately. You ready for a drink?" He looks about for the waitress, who I see is on the other side of the room laughing with a bunch of Woolf Mother–types.

"This is fine." I sit down and pour myself a small glass of water from the jug on the table.

Pete's face falls. "What's the matter? Something happen?"

"You tell me." I feel suddenly very tired now. I wonder, for a moment, if I can do any of this.

A waiter stops near our table. He places a wet silver bucket in a stand directly behind Pete, doubtless getting ready for the arrival of more guests like the women the waitress is buttering up over the way, laughing loudly as if in on an exclusive in-joke.

"What's going on in that beautiful head of yours, Rose O'Connell? I can't get near you these days." Pete's voice cracks through my thoughts.

"I've had a tough day." I turn to look him clean in the eye. "I'm so tired of feeling how I do, too small, too low, no matter what I do and doing all that I have to do on my own."

"I hate hearing you speak like that. You don't need to, Rose. You never did."

Pete peers at me with a woundedness I can't fathom while I let myself stare across the road to the nasty block of flats. The lower-rent inhabitants have stingy little balconies, and I can see kids' bikes tied to the railings, along with a couple of sun-bleached plastic rocking horses, and brave if defeated attempts to create minigardens from gaudy plants that accentuate the cheapness of their setting. It strikes me that poor people aren't allowed to pasture their children on actual soil, only tiny patches of concrete hanging perilously over one another's heads.

Some days, like today, I truly hate everything that's happened round here, everything that starts and ends with Amala Kaur and The Woolf, all the sacrifices and trade-offs families like mine are required to make in the name of "progress," the many ways we have to give way to those richer than us, and show we're thankful for jobs that allow us to serve them: at the bank, cleaning their homes, serving their food, delivering their parcels, driving their taxis. The least they could give our children is sunlight and grass. Even the organic cattle served in this restaurant get these things.

"*Rose!*"

"What?"

"Do you like those flats? You're staring at them. You didn't hear me."

I look at Pete again. The sun might not be finding those unfortunate tenants' terraces, but it is bouncing off the road and settling on my husband's face. The curve of his lips, the perfect slides of cheekbone, the purity of his eyes as they ask me to tune in to him make me wish things could be different, but what's done is done, or will be soon.

The waiter puts a flute in front of me, then Pete.

The pop of the cork makes me jump in my seat.

I'm poured a glass of sparkling wine, then Pete. I look to the waiter for answers, but he concentrates only on wrapping a white napkin around the bottle before walking away. Pete's hand reaches for mine across the table. He is shaking. He dips his gaze low and turns his head toward the block of flats across the street.

"Start from the bottom, count up three. Now, count five windows over and stop at the one second to last before the end."

I move my eyes, confused. The fifth balcony along is by far the saddest. The occupants have lined their tiny stamp of out-side space with some kind of tatty rattan screen. Behind it, I spy a hammock in Hawaiian print and a glitter ball, accessories that all cry, *Hey, we're broke, but we make our own fun here!* But how much enjoyment could anyone honestly extract from such a measly space? At least whoever lives there doesn't look like they have children.

"That's going to be ours soon. That's our new home, Rose."

Sickness wells up inside me. Pete keeps talking.

"Shared ownership. I've put our name down. It's ours, we've done it. Finally, a home of our own, somewhere for Charlie to grow and play and call his own, too, somewhere away from the cemetery, the sound of people in that stupid shop below us. I know I wasn't so sure about that school, The Circle thing, it all seems a bit . . . it's made you . . . well, any-way, it's my work at the school that's paying for it," Pete con-tinues, spilling words out over my undisguised shock. "It's three bedrooms, well, technically two, the third bedroom's more of a box room or study-type space. Hey, maybe it can be Charlie's Lego room."

Pete gazes out the window in wonder while I watch his face, lost in imagining the life waiting for us up in that slice of cement and breeze block. "The kitchen's not massive, but we could get a little table in there, I reckon, and the living room's at least as big as what we have now. Oh, I can't *wait* to show you! Best of all, check out that balcony. Me and you, sitting out in the evening, watching the sun go down, talking, making memories, getting to know each other all over again.

"I've missed you, you know, since you've gotten involved in The Circle. I hardly see you and even when you're with me, it feels like you're not really there. If I'm honest, Rose, what I've been feeling is alone. I'm lonely." I bring my lower incisors so hard into my upper lip that I wince. "Oh, Rose, I'm sorry, I didn't mean to make you upset. This is supposed to be a happy moment!"

He lets out a little nervous laugh, while I attempt to compose myself. It gives me no pleasure to hurt my husband when he is so open and raw, but there's something inside me that simply won't allow me to sugarcoat what I say next. If this is the best he thinks he can do for me, then a big part of me feels he thoroughly deserves everything that happens from here.

"Pete. It's awful. I hate it."

He opens his mouth. Nothing comes out but a half-strangled croak.

"It's tiny, it's tacky, it's cheap. And we won't be escaping noise; we'll be moving to a place where we're sandwiched between the racket of four other skint families shouting at each other, above us, below us, every which side we turn."

"I thought you'd be . . . I couldn't wait to see your smile when I told you." Pete's tone is dead with shock. Mystified, he stares into his drink, a sign of the celebration that's never happening. He's stunned, trying to conjure the magic of the alternative universe where he presented a new home that matches the lowly dreams he assumes, like him, I hold.

But I don't dream small. I dream bigger and better. I aim for so much more.

He swallows the tears aching to escape. "I thought I'd be

making you so happy," he repeats. "I thought you might actually be proud of me."

"Proud of you? What, for locking ourselves into scraping along the bottom. I mean, don't *you* want more than *that*?" I gesture toward the block, unable to stand the sight of it, almost able to see my own face up there, staring desperately back at me over the traffic, Charlie moaning in the background, dead geraniums swinging about my head in park-bench green plastic containers.

Pete twists his flute. "No. No, I don't. I've got everything I want. I thought I had."

"You can go and get Charlie. I'm going for a walk." I get up to leave.

"Looks like I was right about the school, your little clique, and what it's done to you, after all."

I pause.

"You've always had this thing inside you, this drive. I admired it, once, the way you focused on getting your job at the bank, the way you did your best with the flat, how you try to keep up with things changing round here, but that bit of you, what you're doing at The Woolf, has taken it too far. It's made that good piece of you—"

"Go on." I glare at him, inviting him to say the awful thing I believe he wants to.

"It's turned something good into something rotten."

IT GETS LATE, but I don't go home. Pete calls again and again, then Jacq, repeatedly, but I don't answer. The longer I walk, the stronger I hope I'll feel. It strikes me I haven't been on my own for any amount of time for so long. I begin to see that who I am is a loner who's pretending not to be. Living as I did with my father, with us both operating in bubbles that bumped into each other from time to time, this feels like my natural state. Self-reliant, self-sufficient. There's a reason I didn't take Pete's name. I was never his. I thought it was because I was my father's; now I think it's because I've only ever belonged to myself. I must have defaulted to this nature once I'd worked out no one wanted me as their own. That's why I can't blame myself for any of this.

It's very dark now. With my phone off, I don't even know what time it is. As I walk by the park's railings, some guilt, some contrition finds its way into me. I can't get Pete's wound-edness out of my mind, but neither can I block that image I had of myself trapped forever by his misguided attempt at improving our lot. The disappointment is deep and sends me spiraling back down into anger. My husband thinks I am rotten now. But don't things need to break down, so new and better things can grow?

A voice calls my name. "Rose! What the hell happened to you? Pete's in bits."

I barely realized I was passing The Narrow. Jacq brings down the metal shutter over the front door and locks it.

"What are you doing here so late?"

"I've got loads to do before we launch. Where've you been, Rose? What are you playing at?"

"Just walking, Jacq. Is that allowed?"

"You could have just told Pete, *No, thanks,* or *Well done for trying, but it's not going to work.*"

"What?"

"The flat? He was so excited. It's lovely inside, you know."

"You've seen it?"

"Yeah. A few times. Where do you think he's been when he's been working his 'extra hours'?"

"So, let me get this straight: Pete decides where we should live based on what you say, on what *Jacq* thinks is the right thing for us, not what I want?"

"He wanted to surprise you. I thought it would be so good if he could get himself in the driving seat for once."

"Ah, OK, now I see it. Let me guess, was this your idea?"

Jacq bites her cheek. "I thought I was helping you. After everything you'd done for me, I thought giving Pete a nudge to take the reins for once would be good for all of you."

"Only it wasn't him driving it, it was you. You wanted to engineer the whole next bit of my life so I'm kept in a place I don't want to be."

"What are you talking about? That flat's great, you should have given it a chance."

I don't want to raise my voice at Jacq, but I don't think she'll ever see or hear what I really feel unless I shout. "I don't want to give some crappy little flat a chance! I don't want to be the sort of person who lives somewhere like that and I don't want you controlling my life anymore!"

"Oh, and what kind of life would that have been if I'd never come into it? At least you've got a family now!"

"Yeah, well, maybe it's time you stopped focusing on the one I've made and get one of your own."

I feel it. I've jumped over the line and into somewhere new and cold, gone too far into the zone of the unsayable, the things you can never retrieve. But all I feel in this black second is freedom, the total liberation of delivering the truth to someone in a way you know they cannot ignore and can never be undone.

Jacq stops dead and I know she's finally, truly listening to me for the first time in a long time. Her curls are down, but her face doesn't look light with optimism anymore; in the streetlight, I can see it's weighed down with wounded dread. It doesn't matter that she's created a beautiful restaurant, or carved out a potentially wonderful new existence for herself; with her family in crisis, none of this matters. It pains me, too, but she'll see in the end I was only ever shooting for the long-term good of this family, that I'm right to do things my way.

"And all the people inside looked at her red shoes."

I send out a gust of hot air from my lungs, turning it into steam around me, as Jacq begins one of her anthropological parables I've never felt less in the mood to hear.

"And all the figures gazed at the shoes as they made her dance. And when she put the golden goblet to her mouth, she thought only of the red shoes. And she could not stop dancing."

"What are you going on about?"

"And she became very frightened." Tears come into Jacq's voice now as she walks away from me and down a side road to her flat.

"Jacq?"

"'The Red Shoes,' Hans Christian Andersen."

"Some kind of fairy tale?"

Jacq keeps moving away from me. "She wanted to stop dancing and she wanted to throw the red shoes away," she calls the words out into the air, "but the shoes had grown fast to her feet. She couldn't take the red shoes off." I can just about make out her choked words in the night air. "Less of a fairy tale, Rose, more like a nightmare."

WHEN I GET home, Pete and Charlie are in bed. I doubt either of them will want to see me, so I settle in for the night alone on the sofa with only a throw and my coat for warmth.

My bones ache, but still I can't sleep. Faces emerge from the darkness behind my eyelids over and over. What Charlie's anxious face must have looked like when I didn't come home; Pete, when I told him I hated the life he saw for us in that flat; Jacq, as my cruelty hit her; my own face in that flat window, pleading with me in the here and now to hold the line, to stay true to who I am and what I want. Why shouldn't I? Why should it be me who gives way?

I google "The Red Shoes," despite myself. A peasant girl is taken on by a rich woman who gives her shiny red shoes "fit for a princess." The girl loves the shoes too much; she won't even take them off for church when she should be wearing her humble black boots. The red shoes become cursed. They don't let the girl ever stop dancing, her eternal and damned performance serving to warn all the other vain girls who put their desire to be admired above their love of anything else. No matter how hard she tries, the red shoes would not stop the girl from dancing and they would not come off her feet.

How could the girl ever be rid of the devil's red shoes? Why, she had to chop her own legs off.

28

'VE HARDLY SPOKEN TO PETE SINCE LAST WEEK, AND I'VE TAKEN to sleeping on the sofa every night now, telling Charlie it's because Daddy started to snore so much because he's working such long, hard hours at The Woolf. Pete keeps trying to start conversations with me, find a way back, but I push him away again and again. Even though I now know there's nothing going on between him and Amala, his stock remains low after what he did with the flat and what he said to me afterward. The same is true of Jacq, who's been bombarding me with texts I don't know how to return. Because I can't change my feelings about the vision of the future Pete has for us, enabled by his sister, and I can't unwind the bind I'm in with Amala now.

Because if I were to expose Amala's wrongdoings, then I would surely reveal we, too, are feathering our own nest via The Woolf. The only real difference between us and Amala is that our income pays for debt repayments and life's basics, while Amala's skimmings fund the kind of lifestyle most can only dream of. I'm not sure which truth would look grubbier if exposed to the wider world.

Then, there's the whole question of *the alibi* that has never left my mind. The police investigation over Bea's death may have concluded, but "Mrs. Angry" has sent us another letter, this one darkly implying that justice will be served one day "for what Amala Kaur did to Beatrice Pascoe." Worse, Bea's mother and eldest daughter continue to campaign on social media for the coroner to at least record an open verdict in their inquest. They cannot believe the woman they knew and loved would choose to leave them as she did. The question is, now that I know more of how Amala Kaur really operates, do I?

I've spent most evenings in the working week in her office, saying as little as possible, even when she goaded me last week about the flat.

"So, how did you like your dream home? Pete showed me the brochure. He was so excited to show you."

"It's not quite right for us."

"What was that, Rose? You don't think it's right for you? I would have thought that sort of place would have suited you down to the ground."

I work to make the grant application as watertight as I can, in a state of constant high alert. The archived expenses and accounts confirm my suspicions: Amala has been hiding eye-popping expenditures in plain sight since The Woolf was first established. Almost half of the initial government grant to set up the school was diverted to the enterprise and then was spent spuriously: a thousand pounds on "branding," though at a prestigious jewelers—I deduce this is the payment for the diamond "MetM" earrings; the purchase of Darius's Bentley using Woolf money. The funds were significantly boosted along the way via the generosity of The McCandless Foundation.

I also understand now how someone working in education and without Tamsin's allowance affords her impressive wardrobe. I wonder how parents would feel if they knew every donation of more and more money, time, goods, services, and traybakes, often generated after working hours so long some of them barely see their children between weekends, are as likely to pay for a Birkin bag, satin Alexander McQueen blazer, or the wages of a Provençal pool boy as they are on resources for their offspring.

For some time, I've been aware of the ebb and flow of monies into and out of this company creating confused streams and extremely blurred lines between The Woolf's fundraising instrument and the limited liability company from which Amala pays her own salary and extracts her generous expenses. No matter what I do, I still can't make any of it add to the level needed. I'm frowning at the screen detailing another quarter's worth of the same complex web of income and extractions that ultimately shows up a shortfall that cannot be accounted away. It's all I can do to sigh at what I see.

"What's the matter? We must be nearly there by now."

"We're still looking at a big gap."

"You're smart, Rose. You'll find a way."

It's time I make the situation as plain as I can for her. "Amala, I've tried and tried. This isn't about me or anyone else not being smart enough, not Bea, no one. You need a magician, not an accountant or bank employee." I put my hands over my face so she can't see into my eyes and I cannot see hers when I tell her, "On this occasion, you need to accept what you want cannot happen."

I wait a moment, letting the news sink in before taking my hands off my face. Amala paces around the office as if hunting down the solution. I wonder if perhaps what I'm witnessing is the true difference between her and me, the very thing that's kept me in the financial and social hinterlands all my adult life. Because when I've had my many knockbacks and taken my wrong turns, I've taken them into my stomach, where they have stayed. Amala doesn't allow the issues facing her to ulcerate; she gives them the slip and skips onto the very next strategy to get her where she wants to be. Again, my father comes to mind. How adept he was at finding ways through tight spots, even bringing his child into play if it meant getting past those who would stop him. Nothing was out of bounds if it meant securing what he'd set out to gain.

Amala now halts in front of me. "You should know by now, I don't believe in magic or trickery." I look up to see her huge dark eyes, seeming to want to search my soul in this moment, which suddenly feels even bigger than it might. "I *do* believe in taking appropriate risk where you can, where it allows you to shoot for—"

"More and more?" I interrupt, moving my eyes away from hers, my voice quiet but loaded with an exhaustion, and defeat.

"Precisely. You've finally caught on." She walks away toward the great window on the school hall before snapping back round to her office. "The house. It's perfect."

She approaches me again, her eyes shimmering, not unlike Bea's that night she tried to warn me to steer clear of Amala. She continues, almost feverishly, "It's all in my name, Dudda Daddy's idea when we bought it the same time we set up The Woolf."

"The house in Provence?"

"No. Too complicated. Our house, my home, here."

"Amala, I really wouldn't—"

But she isn't listening to me. Instead Amala is warming to the madness of bringing into play the very roof over her head. "Now, if I transfer it to The Woolf Enterprise, even temporarily, we'll have more than enough, correct?"

"Technically, yes, but—"

"Perfect. I'll get Ginny onto it straightaway. I'll let you know when it's done and you can get this over the line."

I leave my seat. Now I want her to look me in the eye and hear me tell her she is going too far. "You don't want to do this. Trust me, you don't want your home, your child's home, to get mixed up in this. The home you bring your family up in is one thing that should be outside any business of yours, of anyone's." Imagine if she knew where my words were truly coming from, how much deeper she would be able to twist the knife, but I can't think about myself now. I have to focus on what I might say to dissuade Amala from her insane strategy. I add, "With you and Darius apart, you can't risk taking anything else away from your son, believe me."

Amala falters for less than a beat, her hard stare dropping from my eyes for an almost imperceptible moment. "Despite your trying to watch our every move," she gives an involuntary shudder, "you know nothing about how my marriage operates. Being in it for the long term is why we're not together right now. I wouldn't expect you to understand."

"The separation isn't real?" Are any of the relationships that comprise Amala's life true—her connection to her "friends," her spouse, even her father, authentic?

Amala brings her lips together forcibly as though stopping her from saying too much. But the words, and the gesture, have been heard and seen. And now I know something about her she didn't want me to. She speaks over her own carelessness. "We're doing this. Starting tomorrow. You have no choice."

Still, I can't argue with her now. Despite her little slip, the fact is, she's right.

AT WORK THE next day, my heart feels heavy and my head pounds. I don't post anything on Instagram, save for a moodily lit shot of me: "Friday feelings. Pushing through the burnout to a fun-filled weekend. #Pusharder #Aimhigher #Woolf-Mother." It ticks up to two hundred and fifty likes by lunchtime. I wonder what Ruby will make of this.

At least that's one part of my life that feels completely under control, the curated and creatively shot version of my life, one that crops out my distressed husband and my exhausted son.

I gaze out of the window, remembering the day Amala strong-armed me, or so she would have believed, into choosing The Woolf at the coffee shop over the road. I imagine myself sitting at the table then, Amala looming over me, offering me her toxic wares. Nothing could have ever prepared me for how I feel now. On paper and online, my life shines like the gold trim on a Woolf blazer, but up close, all the gloss is gone. I'm lost in thought, in all the things I still don't know about myself yet, when Amala walks into the bank.

I brace myself while behind me Marek straightens up. I hear him clear his throat and in the corner of my eye, see him pulling his shirt over his potbelly and ensuring his tie is sitting straight on it. Meanwhile, I'm plunged into a fresh pool of self-hate. The idea of Amala seeing me here, a radioactive bluebird in my plexiglass cage, makes my whole body clench. I hope she's here to maybe cash a check, get some currency for some upcoming "fact-finding" mission to the Caribbean, and be on her way. Of course I know that nothing is that quick, or simple, with Amala. She approaches my counter and as Marek observes me, I do all I can to keep my expression set at friendly and professional.

"Great news!" She slaps two diamond and gold hands on the counter with a metallic clank that makes me jump. "I've spoken to my mortgage lender and Ginny. Looks like moving the house over to The Woolf Enterprise is a cinch, a relatively straightforward deed transfer." Amala flicks her glance behind me to my manager. "Hello? It's Marek, isn't it? Rose mentioned you were considering The Woolf for your daughter. You *will* come to our next open evening in a couple of months, won't you?"

Marek nods, dumbfounded at his personal invite from

Amala Kaur, but also by the physical presence of the woman herself, the skin with a light behind it, the hair from heaven, the oversize oatmeal blazer that serves to make her frame tinier and enhance the drape of snowy silk dipping below her neck, inviting the eye to follow. It's that flawless beauty, that sense of total perfection, that robs you first of a breath, then of any idea you wouldn't do as she asks.

"Would you mind if I booked some time with Ms. O'Connell here? It's strictly business. I'm applying for a significant grant through your branch on behalf of what I hope will be your child's school."

"Of course. Take the consultation room."

"But isn't Linda supposed to be busy in there with—"

"Now good?" Amala cuts me off.

My manager nods and moves to unlock the door to the consultation room, while, without any choice in the matter, I bring the blind down on my counter and obediently follow my mistress. There's a small circular table and two bobbly blue chairs that match my jacket and trousers. Every bit of me wishes I had someone else's life right now and equally, every part of me knows that feeling is about to get markedly worse. Amala has trouble written all over her face, her eyes dancing over the mélange of blue polyester before her with a sickeningly sweet expectation.

"Do take a seat," she tells me, as if this, too, my place of work for years, is her domain. But when you're her, it's as good as true, the whole world belongs to you. Doors fly off their hinges before you touch them, people fall to their knees in worship and do your bidding without question.

"Amala, I'm really busy today, so if we can get to whatever you need as quickly as possible." I remain standing. Amala smiles down at my Porte & Paire ballet flats. They're slightly scuffed, likely because of the difficulties I have walking in them since they don't quite fit. A realization throbs through me: I've spent my whole life wearing shit shoes. I'm done with it. As I make a silent vow that very soon I will never wear cheap, secondhand, broken shoes on my feet again, Amala's gaze returns to mine.

"I'm going to sleep with your husband."

29

MY JAW DROPS. A THRUST OF FRESH ADRENALINE IN MY VEINS. Amala surely cannot have seriously said what I think I just heard.

"What did you say?"

"I'm going to sleep with your husband. And you're going to make it happen. Now, please, sit down."

I don't take my seat out of obedience to her. I fall into it.

"It was actually you who gave me the idea when you seemed less than convinced about my separation from Darius, so let's discuss what you're going to do."

"What?" I breathe, but Amala is not listening to my questions. She has only commands.

"Ideally, I'd like to get going this weekend. Darius has moved out, but you made me realize I need more to stand up the story we're no longer together. We all make sacrifices for the things we really want in life, don't we? But honestly, sleeping with Peter won't be the hardest thing I've ever done in the name of preserving what's mine. In fact, I can't wait." She runs her tongue over her top lip, delighting in my speechless reaction. "Darius is taking Rajvir to his mother's on Sunday, Daddy's gone for his customary six months in Canada with my cousins, so it's the perfect opportunity."

"Why would your husband—"

"My husband, and this should come as little surprise to you, does as he is told. I've got both of us this far and I have plans that will guarantee we'll fly even higher. Once we get the grant and the senior school gets off the ground and we weather any inspection of our assets, we can reunite stronger than ever and with all the rewards due to us. Our split, Peter as my prop, is all an insurance policy to ring-fence what we have should the worst happen"—she looks hard into my eyes—"should questions be begged."

In among the raw horror of how Amala dares to make my husband an attractive pawn in her long-term game of apparently endless acquisition, I realize I know who Amala Kaur really is. She's the crazed girl in the red shoes, so entranced with her own self-image and the luxuries she represents, she's strapped them to her legs until they are stuck fast. As long as she keeps dancing, lives her dream of performative wealth and success, she doesn't care what it does to her, or anyone else.

"I know from experience he's a tough nut to crack. That's why I need your support here." She waits for me to ask for an explanation, clearly enjoying the seconds stretching before she continues.

"I had him over to my house, for a quote, about a year ago. I'd seen him around. I mean, a man like that is hard to miss. He has something of a reputation. You must be aware you're married to *The Hot Plumber*? I know, sounds so . . . pornographic, doesn't it?" She scrunches her features up in a way to suggest she just uttered something deliciously naughty. My stomach turns. "It's sad but true; he turned me down when I offered. I mean, who could resist that body, that face? And made all the more moreish because of his unwavering devotion to the *missus*. You know how much I love a challenge when something I want catches my eye."

"My husband is more than a face, a body, a *challenge*!" Amala views me with an arched eyebrow. "He's a good man with a good soul. He's not like an Uber or a Deliveroo you can order whenever you fancy!" I'm shouting now. I don't want to give her the satisfaction of losing my cool at work, but Amala must still see my rage. Through gritted teeth I tell her quietly, "Why the hell would I help you sleep with him?"

She sighs, bored. "Ever wonder why all those jobs kept canceling? Why his work ground into the sand?"

As my mind works its way to the truth of Amala's destructive impact on my family, her eyebrows raise in a *You've finally caught up* fashion, an assuredness I would like to smash into the blue walls around us. She's been bad-mouthing my husband around town. She's taken us to the brink, ruined a good man's business.

Amala affects another sigh. "Rose, when I talk, people listen. It's a gift, I suppose. They listen whenever I've talked about Pete's unbecoming conduct and shoddy workmanship. And they'll listen should I need to put you outside because of your unseemly fraud, the way you allowed your husband to use my school as a personal cashpoint. He's even more implicated than you are at this stage."

"If *anyone* is going down for being corrupt, it's you."

"Please. I'm not that stupid, careless, or poor. You come at me, I come back at you with a team of lawyers who'll have you, and your husband and your son, on the streets before you can say Hashtag Mum Goals!" She lobs the words from one of my recent Instagram posts back at me like a javelin.

I find I'm shaking suddenly, recalling the image of Pete's face when I rejected the flat he'd found for us. *Poor Pete. I'm so sorry.* I take my head in my hands, knowing she is watching every gesture. "This isn't happening."

Amala stands, looks out of the small window into the street, starts to speak again as if dictating a purchase order. "Peter. Make sure he showers, of course, and that he wears some decent boxers. I prefer the classic white Calvin Kleins I see poking out of his jeans some days. I know, so nineties, but if it ain't broke, right?

"And don't bother sending him round in that faded Boden thing you're so proud of. Don't let him shave in the morning. Oh, and I need to know you've abstained for at least forty-eight hours so he's"—she turns and winks—"really ready to go." There were depths I'd suspected Amala Kaur would be willing to sink to, but the savor she displays when talking about my husband proves the most nauseating.

"This has to stop."

She hitches her Birkin bag onto her slim shoulder, her business here complete. "You already know things stop only when I say they do."

I LEAVE WORK, my body heavy, my mind moving like it's in treacle, trying to game how the various moving parts between Amala and me might work, everything she has on me, all the levers she could pull to stretch me this way and that, leave me variously imprisoned, homeless, divorced, disgraced, alone. My fingers itch to pick up my phone, call Jacq, invite her into my rage, have her engineer this situation for me, fix it so it's all over. But even if she was returning my calls, this isn't something I can tell her, or anyone. I'm in too deep, and about to go deeper. Because whichever way I play the thing out, anyone would see there's no choice.

That night at home, while Pete's distracted playing with Charlie, I pull his oldest T-shirt from the dryer, then take his other shirts, including his Boden top, now a faded shade of gray, and all but two pairs of white Calvin Kleins, and put them back into the laundry bin. While I'm in the bathroom, I hide his razor. I bed down for the night on the sofa, but I have one more thing to do before I turn out the lights.

"Pete?" I call.

"Rose?" He comes to stand hopefully in the doorframe, but I don't look at him. If I do, I risk telling him everything. "Just come to bed, please. I hate this."

"Aren't you still disappointed in me, Pete? And what's the point anyway if you think I'm rotten." It hurts to say his words, but this pain suits my purpose.

"I don't know what I feel, but I know I don't want this, me and you apart."

"You're going to have to get used to it." I try to quash the cry in my throat.

"What are you saying?"

"You never hear me, Pete. It's part of the problem." This, at least, is entirely true.

"I heard you, all right, but I can't believe what I think you're trying to say."

I brace myself against the words I have to say to my husband. "What we want, it's too different. We've been going this way for a while. You need to start thinking about making a life away from me. We don't fit anymore." I tell the patch of sofa to my left, not wanting Pete to see how difficult this is proving.

"I don't believe you. At least look at me when you're telling me you want us to be over."

I sit up, look him coolly in his perfect face, and I tell my husband, "I don't want to be your wife, not for now, maybe not forever. We need a circuit breaker. In time, you'll come to see this was the right thing. For the time being, you should consider yourself a free man."

He rubs his hand across his forehead as if that might reveal the answer under the layers of his mind. "You say I don't know you. If you think being free of you is what I want, even for a moment, then you know *me* even less."

Pete turns and closes our bedroom door. Behind it, I hear

muffled but unambiguous sobs. I message Amala, my heart like lead:

Let him talk. Let him cry. Make him feel like you're a team. Make him feel good about all of him. Delete this message. If he sees this, it will never happen.

Pete. My first and only love, the father of my son, the limb I must sever.

30

DON'T SLEEP ALL NIGHT, KNOWING THAT SATURDAY IS COMING and Amala plans to message Pete. The text arrives in the afternoon. Pete's pushing Charlie on the swings when it happens. We've headed to the park together, so Charlie can imagine everything's fine between his parents. Pete gives him a quick tickle on the neck every time he swings back, making Charlie squeal with delight, which only makes everything so much worse. Pete tuts when he sees the message.

"What's the matter?"

"It's Amala. Something else needs fixing urgently at hers." Pete puts his phone back in his pocket and continues to push Charlie. "It's Saturday. She can wait."

I look at Pete, my hands finding my hips. "Please, Pete. It's important we stay in her good books. You should do as she's asked, and not take your time over it." He has to go. I walk over to the swings and move to take Pete's spot behind Charlie.

Pete huffs. "Fine." He catches the swing in his hands one last time. Charlie tips his head back, so their beautiful faces are next to each other. Pete gives Charlie the most tender of kisses on his forehead.

I try not to think where Pete's mouth will be next.

. . .

PETE RETURNS THREE hours later. I tell him there's a pizza in the oven and stay by Charlie's side at bathtime before setting up my nest of bedding to sleep in his room tonight. I need to do everything I can to avoid Pete, especially as I notice the stench of Amala all over him.

How easily my husband fell once given the slightest of nudges. I can only imagine the performance of understanding and comfort Amala must have laid on to get him where she wanted him, though I do my best not to.

On Sunday, I say my first and only words of the day to Pete.

"I know what you're doing."

"Oh, Rose. I don't—"

"And I don't care."

"*Rose.*"

"Two rules. We're not telling Charlie, or Jacq, and you sleep here, not there. Understood?"

Pete, his hazel eyes wet, his perfect lips trembling, nods his weary agreement. He is hurting and he is regretful. He should be both. And I have no place in persuading him otherwise.

"I can't be around you today," I tell him. I leave Pete with Charlie and spend the day freezing and alone by the marble lion near my father's ashes. A light snow falls and I welcome it. There's an icy comfort in the idea of it cloaking me and him together, uniting us under the same still, white shroud. What I wouldn't do to be with him again and never see Amala Kaur for as long as I live.

The next morning, I can't face Amala or the other women at our usual meeting. I only hope Amala has enough humanity in her to appreciate why it would be unbearable for me to see her so soon after what she has done with my husband. So, I take my body to work, my soul remaining with my father, part of me now wishing I could share the cool, settled earth with him, not having to worry about how I'm going to get through this day, or any other. Just before I raise the blind on my counter, I draw a deep breath from the air. I feel as if I need to show my father, and myself, how strong I can be when fortune looks to be leaving me.

With the snap of the blind, there she is.

Amala waits for me, her obscenely glossy lips held in a sickeningly satisfied smile. I startle, then quickly regroup. If she's here to bundle me into the consultation room to gloat, I will make sure she's disappointed. Anything she does to me now must happen in full public view.

"What do you want?" I ask with the minimum volume possible.

Linda and The Clockwatchers are suddenly interested; Marek, too, who clearly let Amala in ahead of official opening time. I can sense his *Everything all right here?* waiting in the atmosphere.

"What was that? *What do I want?* Only to tell you how I've done exactly what I set out to do."

"I don't want to know anything about it." I say the words quietly, but in a voice powered by a spurt of hate. Amala blinks her surprise, the previous bubbling of mischief in her eyes now replaced by a vigorous simmer of rage.

"Everything all—" Marek steps over to the counter.

"Yes, everything's fine, thanks. Ms. Kaur was just leaving."

"But not before I give you this." She forces a thick, rolled envelope of papers through my counter's metal trough. "It's everything you need to get our funding application through its final stage. You'll see to it that Ms. O'Connell is able to prioritize processing it swiftly?" Amala speaks to Marek over my head.

"She'll get on it right away." He gives me a quick, grave nod, the air of a man watching a subordinate being pressed for the combination to the vaults while Amala holds a gun to both our heads.

"Unless there's something worrying you about the state of our application as you understand it? Concerns?" Amala flicks a glance to Linda, who quickly shifts her gaze away, but will patently not stop listening to the exchange unfolding.

She leans in so close to my window that I can smell not only her dark and complex scent, but I'm sure I can detect the sweet and simple note of Pete's deodorant too. I need her gone.

"Yes. Or. No. Tell us nice and clearly."

"I can see no reason why this application will prove problematic." I say it robotically and loud enough for Marek to hear.

"Wonderful." She beams, mask affixed once more. "What was it you said when you first crossed my colleagues' paths at the open night?" She leans away from the window now and brings her hands together as if in prayer, then opens her mouth to affect a cruel whisper-voiced and exaggeratedly high-pitched impression of me: "The key skills for any cashier are numeracy, accuracy, but above all, honesty." A silent laugh at her own joke.

I'm thankful for the thick plexiglass between me and her face. She should be too.

TWO TERRIBLE WEEKS pass before Jacq's big opening this evening. Over the last fortnight, I've not seen or heard anything of Jacq, and Pete and I have avoided each other as much as we possibly can. I leave the room when he plays with Charlie, who's become simultaneously more forlorn, but more stoic somehow in a way that tears at my heart.

Pete doesn't look like Pete anymore. He no longer works out, doesn't seem to eat much either. This whole affair is making him smaller and all I can do is sit by and try not to watch. I focus my energies on doing what I can to keep Charlie's spirits up and hope we can hold off telling him anything permanent has changed. But of course Charlie knows things aren't well with his family. He is his mother's son, his grandfather's boy, after all.

I've done everything I can to reduce the friction in our household, putting myself into a state of shutdown. It's a familiar kind of emotional stillness, something I have done all my life out of necessity. My childhood taught me to recognize when something hurt emotionally, then face it down with the mental strength to not let myself get lost in the suffering that might normally follow. I learned how to acknowledge and accommodate pain without fully living it. It's a skill I started to hone when I realized I didn't have a mother and everyone else did, finessed when my father left for hours or even days, and finally perfected when he brought me into his last Hurrah.

Pete is apparently "working late." The sitter I've booked has arrived and the second I'm ready, in one of Tamsin's dresses, a Nanushka belted satin midi in copper, I decide to leave the house before my darker thoughts overpower me. I take a shot or two for my followers on my way out, knowing the comments about how the metallic tones alight my eyes will do something to power me through the evening.

"Kiss?"

Charlie blocks my way out. I flatten the pang of regret at the sight of his ankles, visible below the hems of his pajamas. He really has become taller and leaner these last couple of months. I'd normally be the one who notices and gets him the new clothes he needs. It's a shock to realize I haven't.

"Of course, darling. I'd never forget to kiss you before I say goodbye."

"You would."

I pull away from him, holding him gently by the shoulders. "Why would you say something like that?"

"You forgot this morning and yesterday and the day before and the day before and—"

Is it true? Does shutting down on Pete and Amala mean I've shut down on Charlie too? Shame floods me.

"But it's OK, Mum. I'm a strong boy. I know I need to be strong, especially when things change."

"What are you talking about, sweetheart? Has Daddy said something?"

"Not Daddy. Rajvir's mummy. She tells me lots of clever things."

I feel as if I'm falling, but try to keep my voice steady. "When does she say this stuff?"

"When I have my Wednesday time. After lunch. Rajvir's mummy is so, so kind."

Amala is the one who's been counseling Charlie.

Her alone with my child, walking around his mind, my marriage, my soul. It's not enough she's made me give her my husband, she's forced me to sign off my son too. What does she want with him? Why? How can she even think about bringing a child, *my* child, into her game? Even if I withdraw consent for the sessions immediately, whatever balance I thought I've managed on that knife's edge has just been taken away from me anyway.

I may, in fact, never have had it.

31

I DON'T SO MUCH WALK TO JACQ'S OPEN NIGHT AS STOMP. THE thought of Amala alone in a room with my son, extracting his innermost thoughts and feelings, is a million times worse than imagining what she does with Pete. I need to protect him above all things. I consider the moving parts in my high-stakes situation. I need to get a clear read of where I am, how I got here, and how the hell I'm going to get my family out in one piece.

Jacq.

She might have a way; she might have the angle I've missed. She's twice as smart as me and knows herself better than I could ever dream of. She doesn't let herself get hung up on people's perceptions of her; she doesn't live her past every day, stewing in what losing their dad did to her and Pete. She's taken ownership of her life, her heritage; she puts a rosette on herself for real. I need to be more like Jacq, appreciating what I already am and all I already have, and less like Amala, forever chasing her *More and More* into the darkest of places. I can't alter what my dad made me do or change that I was ever his. All I can do is work with the people who truly love me to find a way to live the truth of it, my way.

I get to The Narrow as the final preparations are being made. When I find Jacq she looks focused, if not a little stressed, as she gathers jam jars with a tastefully messy arrangement of wildflowers for each of the tables. I realize how badly I've missed her these past weeks. I should have been on the front row in the run-up to her big night, I should have been here to help her set up tonight. I feel a deep thrust of pride as I watch her move about her new world, but a thud of regret. We've exchanged no words since I said those unsayable things to her. As far as I know, she's not spoken to Pete either.

Jacq sees me walk in, but doesn't speak. Neither do I. I simply go to the counter, pick up what's left of the jars, and start distributing them among the tables. Amid the clatter of pans, the chef's yelled demands, and the clink of glasses being arranged and filled on trays, Jacq hands me a lighter before placing candles in rustic ceramic cups on each table. I follow her, lighting each wick in her wake. When we're finished, she looks to me and nods at the switch on the wall near me. I kill the lights and the whole place sparkles, including Jacq. Her eyes wet, their sudden beauty, so much like Pete's, rips through me.

I go to speak. I want to tell her how sorry I am for the damage I've caused, plead for some understanding, given all she's achieving in the slipstream of my plan to change things for myself. Or maybe I want to tell her that no matter what's in the past, and what's going on now, I will always be grateful to her; for giving me her care when I needed it more than I'd ever want to admit, and for introducing me to a kind, if flawed, man and thus bringing me my son. She *is* my family.

I open my mouth, but just as I do, the door opens and half a dozen people file in. Jacq and I share the shortest of laughs, her shooing the tears from her eyes with the back of her fingers. Whatever else Amala throws at me, whatever harm she tries to put in my way, I have Jacq. I have more than Amala could ever dream of.

The room fills. I busy myself taking shots of the wildflowers and selfies with the mason jars of "seasonal blackberry shrub" Jacq's laid on. Someone taps me on the shoulder. I turn around to see two women who look eerily similar, pale-skinned, short black bobs, black cherry lipstick to match their dark eyes. Something so familiar about them, but they're not old friends. I don't have any of those.

"You're Charles O'Connell's daughter, aren't you? Rosie?" says one with the veneer of politeness that's undermined by the hard line of her mouth.

"Do you remember us?" the other woman chimes in.

I snatch a breath from the air. I want to fall into the seat nearest me, I want to shout for Jacq, I want my father to get here and tell me how to get the better of this situation.

"Gaby. Emma." Their names leave me in a strangled exhalation.

Jacq is on the other side of the room, so she doesn't see my peril. I'm crushed by the sudden feeling of being profoundly alone, so utterly small. Here I am, cornered by my past, unable to move forward because blocking me in the here and now are the Whichello twins.

"I remember." My words emerge in a high-pitched whisper. The pair look at each other conspiratorially. I feel as if I might actually faint. I try to summon my father to me, will him to come to my aid now, tonight, the days to follow. *Put a damned rosette on yourself. Don't let them take your power, take theirs off them.*

"My dad . . ." I clear my throat. The Whichellos appear to be oddly ready to hang on my every word. I start again. "My father's cons followed the same pattern." My voice falters, but on I push; what other choice do I have? "It would have been the same for the scam your family got caught up in." One twin glances at the other, but she is looking only at the ground, an act of submission that serves to power me forward. "The structure my father used was as old as the hills and just as hard to miss if you weren't fooled easily, or inclined to believe in things obviously too good to be true. There's nothing particularly clever about any of it. It only takes time and knowing people's true nature. I'm sorry your uncle or whoever didn't see through him, but it was plain to see if you didn't let yourself be blinded."

I wonder if the Whichello twins have heard the crack in my voice, or noticed the sheen developing across my brow as I've spoken.

"That's OK," they say, almost in unison.

"Sorry?" I'm floored by their out-of-character magnanimousness.

"*We're* sorry," the one I believe is Gaby says. "We saw you and we wanted to take our chance to apologize after all these years. We know we made your life hell at school. The jumper? *Rotten Rosie*? But we're not bad people, we just got caught up in our family's stuff. We didn't know how awful your home life was."

"It wasn't . . . what do you know about my home life?"

The one who I believe to be Emma looks to the floor, but Gaby is bolder. "We heard your dad didn't look after you properly."

"I . . . I never went hungry."

When the words leave my mouth, I realize, the truth is, he barely cleared this, the lowest possible parenting bar. I lived on tins of tomato soup and burnt oven chips; it's why I know nothing about food, can't cook, don't care about it like most people seem to. Is that what made me so physically small? Have I, blinded by the love of my father, forgotten to pin to myself the most meaningful of labels: *neglected child*?

"We heard he barely took care of you *and* he got you mixed up in his world. It must have been so scary for you."

"We actually heard he made you watch a man die. Is that true? We're just so, so sorry."

"*Gaby.*" Emma nudges her sister, who looks embarrassed as she realizes she may have said too much.

But I see him now, bursting free of my memory into the now.

The falling man.

I step forward to the edge of the scaffold. I want to grab the plummeting man in a suit back to safety, even as he flies to the broken ground below. He reaches for me each and every day, because no matter what I felt in my heart, I didn't save him; I sent him to his death. I did exactly what my dad told me to.

I knew it was big. It felt huge in the buildup to The Hurrah, in the moment itself, and in the mess of the aftermath as it reverberated through my father's life and mine. And I did it all in the hope it might be enough to meet Dad's approval, for him to perhaps tell me I was loved. But I didn't get this, the thing I wanted above all things. All I received was a lifetime of guilt and years of bullying for being his daughter that destroyed all the chances I could have otherwise had. Far worse than my father's lack of care that kept my adult body small is the damage that confined my entire life to a lesser place than it ever should have been.

My breathing shallow, I spy Jacq closer now, and on her own for a moment, relighting a candle that's been extinguished.

"I have to speak to my sister, excuse me." I leave the twins and race over to her, my heart's rhythm feeling altered in my chest. I can't ever own my past. Because I never wanted to. The best I can hope for is to trap it, so it may never escape, or at least outrun it more successfully.

"Jacq, I need to talk to you, right now." It doesn't matter that the Whichello twins are already turning to leave, one of them offering me a meek palm raised in farewell; this is bigger than the bullies of my history.

"OK." She searches my face, forces calm over the concern that's made her jaw tighten. "Come with me." Her hand takes mine. She leads me into a storeroom, the air within it sweetly warm, alive with cloves and powdered bell peppers.

"What's going on?"

"I'm in trouble. I thought I had it all under control, but now—"

"Rose, slow down. Start at the beginning."

I tell her how I let Amala involve me and Pete in fraud at The Woolf, and how she's about to get me in deeper with the grant application. And then, the shocking news I learned today, that Charlie's counseling sessions at school, the ones I thought would give him a safe space to speak to a trusted grown-up, were with Amala all along. Saying everything out loud feels in part like a purge of all the dark and rotten things that I've been keeping from Jacq, but now that I've laid it out for us both, I can see what an utter mess I'm in and I haven't even gotten to what might seem to Jacq like the very worst part.

Jacq looks stricken. "Oh my God. Is Charlie OK? Does Pete know?"

"Pete." I can barely bring myself to say it, but we're here now, at the point of the conversation with Jacq when I can't shy away from the awful, tawdry truth of it. "Pete is sleeping with Amala. He's not with me for the time being; he's with her."

Jacq slumps back onto the wall. "I'll bloody kill him."

"No. I mean, yes, it's pathetic, but I told him we were over for a while first. It's on me, not him, so don't give him a hard time, OK?"

The nails on Jacq's splayed fingers push into her forehead.

"Jacq, I need your help."

"Damn straight you do." Her hands find her hips while her eyes examine the floor for any signs of sense, some small indication that life as she knows it with me, Pete, and Charlie isn't the disaster I've told her it is. She puffs out her cheeks and looks at me. "This is all seriously messed-up, properly screwed. She does not get to do this to us."

There's so much else I want to tell her, but at least this is a start. "What do you think we should do?"

"I don't know yet. I need some time. I need to speak to Pete, find out what he's playing at. I need to get my bloody head round all of this."

"I'm so sorry, Jacq. This was supposed to be your special night."

She chews her cheek and shrugs.

"Jacq? Would it be OK if I gave you a hug?"

She snorts a laugh, turns her face to the ceiling with fresh tears in her eyes, and holds her arms open to me. I slip mine under hers and bring her to me. We hold each other for a moment without either of us speaking. I hug her more tightly as relief at telling her and anguish about all that might come alternately roll through me.

"Come on now. That Amala's not going to get the better of us. Not if I've got anything to do with it."

A sob escapes from my chest, as if it's been waiting there, captive for years. "Love you, Jacq."

"What was that?" she says, her head over my shoulder.

"I said—"

She laughs and sets me away from her, her hands firm and warm on the sides of my arms. "I heard you the first time."

She kisses my head.

My sister. My protector.

I wonder if I'll ever stop crying again now that I've properly started. Jacq hands me a stiff white napkin. "I need to get out there. You get yourself together in here."

Jacq watches me as I take the napkin off her and the odd relief of crying in front of someone I truly love seeps into every tiny muscle in my face and neck. I find I have to lower myself, knees bent, back pressing against the wall until I'm sitting on the floor. I could curl up inside this clove-sweet cocoon and never come out to face the bind I'm in. Jacq, who has been shaking her head to herself, readying herself to greet her guests, sees my body registering just how feeble and outplayed I feel in this moment.

"It's going to be OK, all right?"

And in that moment, I believe her.

"I'll see you in a sec."

When I make it out of the storeroom, all is quiet except for Jacq, who's tapping the back of a knife gently against the yellow label on a bottle of Carib beer, making a speech to the crowd rapt at the sight and sound of her; a woman coming into the height of her powers.

"I said I wasn't going to do this, but sometimes, you've gotta do what you've gotta do." She looks to me and gives me the tiniest nod. "I hope you've all been enjoying some samples from the new menu. I didn't get to know my dad too well, but this was the sort of stuff his mum might have cooked him, but with my little twist on it all. Cook-ups, stews 'n' droppers, and, my personal favorite"—she picks up a small white plate with a triangle of tart, a full yellow heart on it in an ocean of white icing sugar—"the cake I'm told was his favorite too: Tourment d'Amour, The Agony of Love. It's believed the sugar and almonds fortified those who ate it with courage, and who doesn't need a bit of that now and then?"

Her eyes find mine again before Pete coming through the door catches her attention. I see the familiar twist in her cheek. I dread to think what she'll unleash on her brother when she gets to him. I almost feel sorry for him.

"Welcome and thanks to my little brother, Pete, for all the plumbing advice and a lot more besides. But the person I want to thank from the bottom of my heart, for everything she's done for me, for everything she is and all she thinks I can be, is my sister-in-law, my business adviser, and my best friend. This new place is about rediscovering my old family, the family of my father, but Rose, you've become my family; you've made a new family, one that means just as much to me as the one I came from. So, I'd like to officially dedicate The Narrow to my father, Derek Jacobs, and also to you, Rose O'Connell. My sister."

Jacq sounds choked as she says my name and tips her bottle in my direction. I try not to let the memory of Amala saying she and I were like sisters enter my mind and ruin the moment, but it's too late. Amala, flanked by Ginny, Ruby, and Tamsin, is now striding into the restaurant. I didn't think she'd dare show her face, but I should have known better. She wouldn't miss out on the chance to flex her social muscles and demonstrate her total infiltration of my family.

"Well, that's your lot. Cheers." Jacq hurries down from her chair, not waiting a beat to absorb the warm applause filling the room. Instead, she all but crashes through the crowd to Amala. I follow her.

"Jacqueline, before you begin, it seems as though someone's updated you about myself and your brother and while I should imagine you don't exactly approve of me—" Amala starts, but Jacq's not hearing it.

"I don't know what you think you're doing, but you should be a lot more careful."

Amala takes a bite of air, unused to anyone not showing anything but servitude and obedience in her presence. The only person I ever saw or heard take her on properly was Bea, and look what happened to her. The thought of it sends ice down my spine.

"I know your game. Rose told me everything. This is where things change for you."

Amala gulps again, but has no words to share yet as she struggles to respond to Jacq's bald honesty.

"Don't like it when the shoe's on the other foot? Bullies never do. Get out of here and take your cronies with you."

Amala looks to Pete to fight her corner, but all he can do is chew his cheek, unable or unwilling to stand up for Amala against his sister.

"And you can leave my brother well out of it. If he's not realized his mistake already, it won't be long now. I can guarantee you and him won't last. And that bent stuff you've got my sister into, rest assured I'll see you get what's coming for it. I know exactly where your bodies are buried." Jacq seems to be shining with purpose: protecting me, Pete, and Charlie, making sure Amala will one day soon face her comeuppance.

Amala's face hardens as she grasps how far I've broken The Circle's unspoken oath of silence. Tamsin, looking horrified, pulls her band so hard it must surely be about to break her skin. Ginny, meanwhile, watches the whole exchange over the top of the cocktail glass she's tipping into her mouth, a dribble escaping onto the khaki silk of her jumpsuit. Ruby has distanced herself from the group to offer an onlooker a selfie.

"Jacq. Tonight's about you, not me, not them." I touch her arm and can almost feel the pulses of adrenaline below her skin. I see Amala visibly relaxing now that I've called Jacq off. Her sudden assuredness boils my blood. "Pete. Want to know who's been screwing you over after you turned her down the first time round?"

Pete's mouth opens as the penny drops. He looks to Amala. "Correct."

I tell Pete how she did her best to make sure no one hired him again after he rejected her advances, how she maligned him to any newcomers who'd listen, which was all of them. And finally, how she forced me to send Pete to her, under threat of seeing us prosecuted for stealing from The Woolf. "I'm sorry, Pete," I finish triumphantly, as Amala looks to the street outside now, perhaps wishing she were there.

It's hard to know whether she's more uncomfortable about Pete understanding that she's been bad-mouthing him to the point of ruin, or the fact that now everyone knows a man, my husband, has said no to her. Amala's momentary loss of power seems to turbocharge mine. "She's the reason we ended up sitting ducks for The Circle and she's only using you to prop up her sham split with her husband to protect all the money she's diverted from the school into her own pocket."

Pete goes to speak, but Amala halts him. "We're not discussing any of this now. Do not say a word." Pete shakes his head, his fingers reaching for his skull, his thumbs rubbing his temples. What has she done to my husband?

I catch Ruby and Tamsin eyeing the door, clearly dying to exit the scene. Ginny looks on with an expression I can't put my finger on; a trace of grudging respect for me having come out fighting? Pete, in the meantime, continues to seem bewildered and bereft.

"Let's get out of here. Amala?" Ruby is halfway out of the door, always conscious of the image she and The Circle are projecting to the community. She's clearly agitated that people nearby have caught on to the ugliness unfolding and are watching, hungry for more.

"I don't get thrown out of anywhere, least of all, places like this." Bitterness powers Amala's glance as she casts it about Jacq's beautiful new restaurant with obviously misplaced disgust. There she is for all to see: the real Amala Kaur.

"Well done, sis." Pete has stepped forward, though he is unable to meet Jacq's eyes. "I'm proud of you. I'm sorry I've not done anything to deserve you feeling the same about me."

"We'll talk tomorrow, OK?" Jacq doesn't move her gaze from the floor, only raising her head when she senses Pete leaving.

"May as well stay with her tonight," I tell the back of him. "You two have a lot to talk about."

Jacq and I watch Pete go outside, his head bent in shame. He stands by a lamppost on the street, looking right at me through the window, seeming to beg for my understanding through the glass separating us. He's been played and now he knows it. A thrust of regret in my stomach seeing him so floored. All Pete wanted was a simple life: a home, a woman, some kids, enough money to get by. Despite what he's done, I hope he can still get what he's always wanted one day.

Amala and the others finally leave too. I watch them walking down the road, Pete shuffling at the back of the pack, Amala leading from the front. After a moment, I see Amala dropping back to speak with Ginny, then side-hugging her subordinate hard, so much so she's rocked almost off her feet.

I realize Amala, like me, doesn't have any real friends. I thought I was bad at friendships, but she's even worse. She only has people who are in her thrall, or who live in fear of her. An overwhelmed lover and some cowering associates—not allies, not friends, not partners at all. Even if I don't have many friends, I have a true sister and I don't have to take on Amala alone anymore. Jacq and me united means there can be only one loser at the end of whatever game Amala believes she's been playing: her.

I feel some innate shame lift, some pride blooming inside me. Not the kind of pride you ask other people to give you, by fawning over you at the school gates, or on Instagram; something authentic, a sense of pride that comes from who I really am.

AFTER ALL THE other guests leave, I text the sitter, asking her to stay on later so Jacq and I can have a drink on our own.

She and I talk. And we laugh. And we cry. Then we laugh until we cry again. We cover everything, from the first day we met, to the last fight we had, every angle I can tolerate on where it might have gone wrong with Pete. I can't help but tantalize her with the possibility it isn't over between me and him, regifting her the unit of me, him, and Charlie, and her. I feel lighter somehow, being with her in this building as we once were. It's like we're at the very start of us again. I was in a hard spot then, no family, no home, no nothing. Jacq made it all better. Here I am again, my back against the wall, and her ready to find a way to peel me off it.

It's racing toward midnight when a hard, cleansing rain begins to beat against the window. We both listen to it fall for a moment.

"I'd better go, Jacq. Walk you home?"

"I might just have one more. Wait for the storm to pass." Jacq puts her feet up on one of the brand-new booth seats, crosses her legs at the ankles, and leans back. She absorbs the dying candles reflecting off the walls, basking in the light and the vision of the future that, despite the troubles with Amala and Pete, started here tonight.

"Do that. Take your moment. You deserve it."

"Enough." She bats away my unusual sentimentality with a sideways two-handed swipe at the air. "I'll call you tomorrow. We *will* get this sorted, one way or another. OK?"

"Yeah, we will. Night, Jacq."

Jacq, her cheeks flushed with the last of our tears, eyes soft with the final burst of our laughter, looks as she did that first time she cut my toast for me, sat down at my table, and asked me who I was.

"Bye, Rose."

THAT NIGHT, I can't sleep. The cold rain pounds my window, alcohol encouraging wakefulness and the grinding of my mind. I think about my next moves and go over what missteps I might have taken up to now, wondering, panicking if I should have been so upfront with Jacq after all. It's getting on for three in the morning when I hear the key in the door.

"Pete?"

Have tonight's revelations or his sister's disappointment been enough to dislodge him from Amala's grip yet? A cold disbelief takes me over: surely Amala would simply wriggle free of the accusations, put them down to jealousy. I know Pete's so often blind to the truth and Amala will see this too. It's not my husband's tread I can hear moving across the living room.

I sit up in my bed, panic taking over. I look around the room for something I might use as a weapon and quickly realize I am completely defenseless.

Charlie.

Please, let him be safe.

For all the mistakes I've made to get me to this point of what feels like mortal danger, I silently beg that my boy will be spared. A raw terror shakes me, but I must be strong enough for whatever happens next.

A creak of floorboards just beyond my door.

A black crucifix now in the doorframe of my bedroom. A dark scent fills my room.

"Rose."

"What are you doing here? How dare you let yourself into my home."

Amala drops her arms by her side and steps into my bedroom, casually, proprietorially, her presence barely distinguishable from the charged gloom around us. I have felt threatened by Amala before, I have felt shocked and sickened and intimidated. I have never felt scared of her. Not until now.

"I want you gone. Right now!" I whisper it forcefully, but I'm hardly able to get the words past my airless lungs, to sound as if I have any strength at all.

She sits on my bed. I pull my duvet closer to me, gathering it up under my chin, as though it might offer me some protection.

"I've left Peter sleeping. He doesn't believe what you told him tonight."

I knew it.

"But that's not why I'm here. He was going to call you in

the morning. He's exhausted from being with the police. I thought you should know—"

"The police? Know what?"

Has Jacq's move tonight made Amala strong-arm Pete to back up her story that I'm guilty of embezzlement? Has she managed to persuade my husband to set me up? My mind races as I do everything in my power to show Amala I'm not afraid of defending myself against whatever she thinks she can use Pete to frame me for.

"Jacq's been involved in a road traffic collision. A hit-and-run."

Now my breath is truly gone.

Fear rips through me in a way that snatches me back to my father's final Hurrah, the sort of terror that transforms you in the next beat of your heart. Amala says nothing, but breathes the air in my room calmly.

"Please. Please tell me. Is she—"

"Jacqueline is dead."

PART THREE

THE CENTER OF THE CIRCLE

THE THICK CANVAS OF THE DEAD WOMAN'S DESIGNER JUMPSUIT does well to contain her shattered bones. Unlike the first body on the tarmac by the outdoor gym equipment, this time, there is no visible blood. But there must be a rupture inside, veins and organs opened by slivers of broken bone.

That's about right, Jo, the Woolf Mother who discovers the body this time, silently whispers to herself, once the initial shock subsides. Looking at the dead woman and thinking about it, Jo finds it somehow appropriate that something inside of the woman herself dealt the fatal injury.

Another body on the playground. Jo is seriously beginning to question her judgment. Were the darkest, maddest rumors about Bea Pascoe correct? Suicide or not, did The Circle have a hand in her death? Has Jo, in her quest for excellence for daughter Effie, now found herself entwined with something sinister, something no longer covetable? Might the school with the most hotly contested places soon become—whisper it—*undersubscribed*? In her horror, she imagines a zombie institution, surrounded by once-thriving families now staring down negative equity, the mortgage debt accepted to breach The Woolf's tight catchment zone now far higher than the value anyone is willing to pay to have their child walk under the twisted *Magis et Magis.*

Jo regards the dead woman's body as coolly as she can, shaking her head in regret. The problem was that she'd allowed herself to have too great an idea of what she was capable of. Even Jo could see she was beginning to overreach. The woman had forgotten her place.

Jo goes to call the emergency services, then changes her mind. Here is an opportunity to score precious points. Jo knows she and the rest of the community will have to round on the dead woman, declare her yet another single bruised apple fallen from the tree, rather than allow the notion of institutional decay to fester. Starting from now, she can boost her chances to fill the newest vacancy on the inside. Her first call, then, is not to the authorities, but to one of the members of The Circle.

Jo tells herself that the dead woman's story is really nothing to do with her own. *She* just wants what's best for her child. She would never let that noble intention turn into something that rots from within.

32

ALWAYS KNEW I WAS A MISTAKE. NO ONE TRIED TO HIDE IT FROM me. Associates of my dad, people who didn't know me, they would all joke without reservation about the twelve years between me and my next sibling. Some kinder people said I was my mother's last gift to the world, arriving two years before she died, but most older people left me with the clear understanding I should not be here. When the bullies made it obvious they didn't think I deserved to be in their world, it only affirmed what I'd been made to feel from the day I was born: someone who shouldn't be here.

This was why whenever my dad asked me to do or say anything for him, I mostly did it. I constantly chased the feeling I did belong, that it could be perfectly right that I was born, that maybe I'd come into the world to be wherever he was and to be his. For all the pain he caused me, I loved my father, or I at least lived with a dependent ache for him, that deep pull for his approval that felt like love. Did he love me back, did I ever do enough to earn that? Maybe.

He was extremely weak toward the end, just after I turned eighteen. I finished feeding him one day and he surprised me when his hand dropped on mine. He was never prone to signs of physical affection, or much in the way of contact at all, another area where I have found myself my father's daughter.

"Something you need, Dad?"

His eyes told me no, but his hand, squeezing mine with what little power he could summon, told me he had something important to say. I could tell he knew he didn't have long.

This was it.

Was he finally ready to say he was sorry for all the potential that being the con artist's daughter had wasted, the happiness and friends I might have otherwise had? Would he apologize for getting me wrapped up in his last Hurrah and give me some peace before leaving me forever? Or might he just possibly tell me for the first and perhaps last time that I was wanted, that I was loved.

"Oh, Dad."

I lifted his limp hand and shaped it in mine, cupping my face, the anticipation of relief from his words rushing through me as I looked into the sparkling green of his eyes. I could still perceive the suaveness of his features under the thin bluish leather of his skin. I remember closing my eyes and relishing the scent of his fingers, the tea leaf and tar of his Benson & Hedges cigarettes. When I opened mine, his eyes were not resting on me, but had landed instead on the bookcase, his old red *Tricks of Confidence* book on top.

He wanted it in his hands again.

I went to pick it up and all but threw it at him before turning away. He could have his damned book near him as he approached his dying day, but there was no way I was going to sit there and read it to him. I was done with doing as I was told so that I might earn a tiny scrap of his approval; I was over leaving myself vulnerable to the torture of disappointment, the agony of loving someone who only ever wanted you for what you could do for them.

But then he let out a painful grunt that made me sink to the floor beside him. He took a deep breath that made his chest rattle in a way the doctors told me would happen as he reached the end. I didn't want to hear it.

"Don't hurt yourself. Don't speak."

He dropped his hand on the book and slid it toward me. "Rose. You."

What was he saying to me? Accept who he was: A beautiful but broken thing, like his antiquarian book with its ragged binding and wicked truths? Or was he saying accept who *I* was, his favorite child, the only one who deserved to receive his precious book? Sometimes, I find myself believing it's because my father felt genuinely closer to me, saw the most of himself in me, but when I consider what this says about me, I shut that thought right down.

Those two words he spoke to me that day were his last. And now all I have left of him is a guidebook to ripping people off and the one-sided conversations I have with him every day.

From this moment on, I must start a new conversation with someone I love and who is gone, a person with whom there was still so much left unsaid.

Jacq is dead.

How? How could she have been taken away from me at the moment I need her most?

After Amala exploded the truth of Jacq's death in my face, she left me alone in the darkness. The second I hear the front door close behind her, I dial Pete.

As the line rings, I realize I'm calling him with some hope in my heart. It doesn't feel real until I speak of her with someone who loved her as much as I did. Maybe it's all a sick joke. "Pete? Is it true? What Amala's just told me?"

"I didn't know she'd . . . I was going to let you sleep, let you have one last night without . . ." Pete's voice is oddly calm, but only for a moment. "She's gone. She's really gone. It's . . . I can't believe it!" Hearing the rawness of Pete's pain crash through his numb serenity takes my breath away.

"What happened?"

"Some stupid drunk." Pete gulps a damp breath into his

lungs to get the words, any word, out. "Right after she'd locked up for the night."

"I'd just said goodbye to her! I should have walked her home . . . Oh God, Pete. What are we going to do?"

He and I cry quietly for a minute or so without saying much, the reality of Jacq being gone opening up like a black hole in our lives, one that can't be filled with words or tears, a great chasm we'll have to accommodate somehow without allowing ourselves to be sucked in. In this moment, I feel absolutely together with my husband. I take a deep breath and before I can stop myself, ask, "Do you want to come home, Pete? You don't really want to be there, do you? You know she's lied and lied to you."

I hear a door opening, then closing in the background of the room Pete's in. Amala is home.

"I have to go," he tells me, but I don't want him to leave me alone with myself.

"What'll I tell Charlie?"

"No, Rose. You don't have to tell him. You don't have to deal with everything, you never did. I want to. I want to hold him and hug him and tell him everything's going to be all right."

"But it's not all right, Pete, is it? You can't be making promises to him you can't keep."

A pause on the other side of the line. "This isn't about us, Rose; this isn't about you."

I hang up, unsure that it isn't.

THE NEXT MORNING, Charlie sees that I'm a mess the minute he wakes up, and forces my hand. I tell him he won't be going to school today, and Pete and I will be off work.

"Why? Are we doing something fun together, all three of us? Can Auntie Jacq come too?" His beautiful face brightens at the prospect of a happy reunion, just the four of us, making what follows even more brutal.

"Something very upsetting has happened to your auntie." Now his face floods with darkness and fear. It's already one of the worst things I have ever seen and today has barely begun. "Your auntie got caught up in a car accident last night."

"Is she OK?"

"No, darling, she was hurt, very badly hurt."

"But she's going to get better."

"No, my sweet." Charlie's hazel eyes fill with tears and bafflement. He doesn't grasp what I need to say next, why would he? He doesn't know how unfair and cruel the world is yet, but I am going to be the one who lets him know, in this next, dreadful second. "Very sadly, your Auntie Jacq was so badly hurt that the people in the ambulance couldn't help her. I'm so sorry, darling."

I hold my breath for a moment knowing with stomach-churning certainty that what I say next will be burned on his soul forever, that his life will always be divided by the seconds before he learns what I tell him and after them. "Auntie Jacq died, darling."

And now, he wails. Charlie howls and he screams. The people in the shop downstairs, the Woolf Mothers bustling past below to the breakfast club, will all wonder what cruelty my son is suffering up here. I hold him tight to my chest to comfort him, and to silence his cries. We stay like that for a while. I rock back and forth with Charlie on my lap, on autopilot, lulling his heart back into a rhythm recognizable and me into a determined, focused beat. Each sway lasts as long as my mind says to itself:

She won't get away with it.
She won't get away with it.
She won't get away with it.

Charlie and I get to The Narrow just after nine, when I've arranged to meet Pete. I texted him to say I couldn't hold off telling Charlie and got the sense he was relieved I'd taken matters into my own hands. When we get to Jacq's place, Pete gathers me into his hug with Charlie. We stay like this for a while, Charlie's form feeling like it's shaking with each tear of his heart, Pete's diminished body slack with grief. I hold them to me with all my strength, wishing myself bigger than I am.

"Oh, Pete," is all I can say when we finally separate.

"I don't know how I'm going to get through this."

"But you will. We all will. We're all going to have to be stronger than we feel right now." Some old instincts kicking in again, my dad's words from that dreaded day finding their way to me.

You need to find a way to be stronger than you feel and do as I say. No one saw you, I swear. When have I ever let you down?

Pete holds Charlie's wet little face in his hands and looks into his eyes before breaking down and crumpling his upper body around his son. I can't bear to see it.

"I'll make us a tea. Charlie, would you like some of—" I gulp. "Would you like a piece of Auntie Jacq's special cake?" He shakes his head. I nod and get myself away as fast as I can, falling into the storeroom where I set my own sobs free. I try to imagine I can smell her once more. Her hair wax, the warm, bready smell she'd held in her clothes if she'd been testing recipes in the kitchen, the faint medicine of cloves. I try to make her alive again through my own acute senses, but when I inhale, all I take from the air is the scent of Amala.

By the time I come out of the kitchen with our hot drinks, she has arrived. How dare she insert herself into this scene, enter Jacq's space again? How dare she use my family's tragedy to build up the appearance of a real relationship with my husband? I see Amala is talking to a man in a brown suit, who introduces himself as the police sergeant on the case. He turns to me now.

"I'm told you were likely the last person to speak with Ms. Jacobs?"

I look at Amala, attempting to contain my anger. Is she going to try to pin this on me somehow?

"I must have been. We were sitting, just there." I point to the booth where we put our worlds right. "Chatting, laughing. It started to rain, I offered to walk her home, but she said she wanted to stay and have a beer by herself. I think she was planning on just sitting there a few minutes, taking it all in."

"And what time was this?"

"It was gone eleven, half past?"

"And you'd been drinking?"

"We'd had a couple."

"Two, three, four? More than that?"

I can't help myself from bristling. "Jacq isn't dead because she'd sunk a few beers."

"*Rose.*" Pete shakes his head, glancing down at Charlie, who starts crying afresh.

"Maybe we'd be best taking your statement down at the station."

"Statement? If anyone needs to give you a statement it's . . ."

I look at Amala, whose head tilts behind the sergeant, daring me to tell him about her row with Jacq. But then, what might she tell him about my activities at The Woolf? Where might it lead if I start telling tales right now?

"It's surely the people who found her . . . Who did find her?"

"The owner of the residential property next door."

I'll bet their lined curtains twitched at the sound of trouble. Next door is another strip of Victorian terraces that used to house cabbies and nurses and have now been scooped out by lawyers and brand consultants.

"And did they . . . Was Jacq able to tell that person what she saw, any idea who did this to her?"

I clutch my stomach and look away, as if diverting my eyes from the sight of Jacq, crushed, stunned in the rain, which comes to me like a sword through my chest. Did she cry for help? What went through her mind as she lay there, dying?

"I'm afraid not. It's likely she didn't know what hit her."

I sink to the seat where Jacq and I were together just a few hours ago, but in a different version of my life.

She didn't know what hit her. Jacq didn't know, but it's my mission now to make sure I do.

33

THE WEEK THAT FOLLOWS IS LOST TO PLANNING JACQ'S FU-
neral. I beg Pete not to let Amala come out of respect for
his sister. Besides the fact I know Amala is almost certainly
involved somehow in what happened to Jacq after what she
said to her at The Narrow, there's also Jacq openly despising
her at the last. But when we speak on the phone the morning
of the funeral, Pete informs me Amala has to be there.

"She wants to go, pay her respects." Something unnatural
about the way he speaks, as if he's parroting what he's been told
to say.

"If you really think her being there is what Jacq would have
wanted, Pete—"

"Please, Rose. Drop it. Let's not fight. She would have
hated it."

She would have hated too how I can't do anything to bring
the person I think is responsible to justice, not yet. I didn't lie
to the police, exactly, but I did give the sergeant an un-lie,
driven by the fact I can't fully articulate the depth of Jacq's
vitriol toward Amala, or retell Jacq's *I know where your bodies are
buried* comment in the way it was meant. Too many others
heard her to leave it out of my statement entirely, but I present
it as some kind of female drama, powered by liquor. It's a story
that appears plausible enough to go with. It will have to do, for
now. Of course, I feel the cold prod of guilt in not immediately

seeking to incriminate Amala, but there are so many moving parts here, plates spinning precariously on their spikes. I will Jacq's spirit to understand my motivations.

For their part, the police have begun to get some things right, like the fact the vehicle in question not showing up on any of the cameras on the area's main arteries suggests a local person who traveled only by ancillary roads. And this wasn't some rogue joyrider or standard criminal Jacq was unfortunate enough to cross paths with. There is no telltale burned-out stolen vehicle to be found to suggest it's a known felon emphatically destroying the evidence that would otherwise incriminate them.

The autopsy of Jacq's poor body also revealed something strange. Even with the rain, which would have washed away some of the vital evidence, there are no traces of paint or glass anywhere on her, extremely unusual given the impact of the car. It strikes me there is something about the way Jacq's "accident" has played out. I'm reminded of that saying: *If you want something done well, ask a busy woman.* Jacq's slaying feels distinctly female.

The investigation could do with the attention of a busy woman too. I can already sense it running into the sand, with no obvious lines of inquiry, no evidence to suggest anything more suspicious than a drunk driving hit-and-run without intent, and the police's full caseload. I can't have that. I need to find some way to secure justice for my sister. Every night, I dream of Jacq. Her wax, singed cotton, and clove scent fills me, and she's there by my side in all her vivacity and heart. But she's angry, not at rest, because justice is not being served. I know I have to do something.

After the heartbreak of Jacq's funeral, I walk to the places that meant the most to her: round the lake at the park where we first hatched a plan for us both to take a chance on each other and move in together; across the stretch near the playground where Jacq left me and Pete alone for some spurious reason, giving us the space for something more to grow between us. By going where her feet walked maybe I can find a path to bringing her killer to justice. I need to feel close to her to do this, and not attend her wake, where people will speak of her only in the past tense.

My phone rings. It's Amala. She is the very last person I want to speak to, but I know if I don't talk to her now, she'll come after me all day with whatever it is she wants to hurt me with, when all I want is for my thoughts to be on Jacq. Reluctantly, I accept her call.

"Rose!"

"What do you want?"

"I thought on this saddest of days, you might want to hear the good news. The grant's come through. When are you coming back so we can deal with the lump sum together? You should get some kind of reward, don't you think?"

Almost incredible to believe Amala thinks I would be so stupid as to voluntarily tighten her hold on me by accepting another cash bribe. "I want nothing more from you and no further part in anything else you may have planned."

A near-silent snort of laughter down the line. "You know that's not up to you. You don't put yourself on the outside."

I'm reaching my breaking point now, running out of what it takes to stay ahead of her, if I ever had in the first place. "You've taken my husband from me, you've tried to get close to my son, you've already threatened my reputation, my freedom, and more besides. Do you honestly think I'm going to expose me or Charlie to any more of you than I have to?"

"You're thinking of removing Charlie from The Woolf?"

My silence appears to confirm I've been researching transferring him to another school. What else would she expect someone in my position to do?

"You want to cause him upset and disruption by extracting

him from an exceptional setting because of his father's new relationship?"

I imagine her irises have never looked larger or brighter as she says these words to me, as though she is the one with my son's best interests in her heart. Just like my father, never more herself when she's scooping out someone else's life. A parasite so beautiful the host realizes too late they've invited death into their cavity.

"Please, just for today, find a shred of decency inside you and leave me in peace." I move to hang up.

"That anyone could take a lecture in morality from *you*." Amala's voice has shifted. It seems to come from her stomach, bass replacing breathiness. A pause betrays her own shock at spitting the depth of her hate down the line. She forces a switch back again to her self-aggrandizing, semi-transatlantic tone. "I'll be seeing you on Monday, then? That's when Peter says your compassionate leave ends at the bank? Oh, and I wouldn't recommend keeping Charlie away from school, if that's what you were thinking. We wouldn't want you to be responsible for any unauthorized absence; have people thinking you're the kind of person who thinks they're above the law, would we?"

"Me above the law? Amala, I might be the daughter of a trickster, but I'm the innocent party."

An unexpected silence down the line.

"I'm the one who's been had and you're more of a con artist than my father ever was . . ."

Amala ends the call.

I say to the cold air around me, "A trickster: from Foundation to Hurrah."

It's true. It hits me now.

All the steps she's taken to get me to the point I'm at now, how closely she has mirrored my father's tried and tested process.

In Amala's Foundation, she scours the school community

for a certain type of woman on the edge, before digging around in their lives until she finds the perfect combination of skills and needs. The chosen ones must reveal themselves to be as desperate as they are useful. Bea, Ginny, Ruby, Tamsin, and now me, all offer valuable services to Amala, but also hold secrets that guarantee we'll do whatever is asked of us when she gets to asking.

The Circle is both Amala's mark *and* her Society.

The women of The Circle are the victims Amala relieves of their time, energy, and loyalty in order to maintain the level of income she requires for her lifestyle, *and* the people she grooms to execute the grander scams, like the one she tried to make Bea lead and has now brought me into. It strikes me suddenly how my father would have surely approved of this as a stroke of dark genius; the unique way The Circle provides continued bites of the stolen cherry.

Amala was more thorough in her Foundation than Charles O'Connell ever was. She must have spent time researching my history, my father, then made it so she came to my flat to see the depth of my deprivation when compared to her life. She even organized it so she could poke around in my son's mind to understand all she could about me, my many weaknesses.

Her Approach began at the open evening, followed up by that day at the coffee shop when she tried to give me her red devil's food cake and get me to accept Charlie's school place. She also made sure we were both at the trip to the cemetery to ensure our paths crossed and she had a chance to invite me to her home and then into The Circle.

Her Convincer was multilayered: the immediate and emphatic end to my childcare and financial quandaries, the very best of The Woolf for Charlie the minute I was on the inside, the first lump of money she made me pay Pete. The Come In are the rewards she and the women of The Circle skim from The Woolf. If everyone else was doing it, why shouldn't Pete and I join the ranks of Circle members, partners, and families milking the school's funds month in, month out?

Amala's Hurrah: she's not only looked to have bagged my husband, but a grant worth half a million. The crises Amala called on to make sure it happened were a series of threats, first to throw me out of The Circle, then to incriminate both Pete and me for apparently creaming-off unauthorized thousands from the school coffers.

But what would I say was her Distraction, the thing she used to turn my head when I might have been looking more closely to avoid being set up?

It hits me with a thud of shame.

It was myself.

She weaponized my craving for approval, the deep-seated need I carry to be accepted and liked, even if this is by means of a two-dimensional online version of myself. She egged me on into an ever-more absorbing life on Instagram, where I might harvest the adoration of women who would otherwise view me as matter distinctly out of place.

She played me. Amala Kaur played me good.

Is this why I've been so drawn to her? Was it less about seeking her endorsement, the life-changing care for Charlie, the transformative money and status to which she provided me access, the wider adoration she facilitated?

Was this the real reason I couldn't get Amala Kaur out of my mind since that cold night in December last year? Because she is the one person in the entire world who most powerfully reminds me of my father?

34

CONTINUE TO WALK IN JACQ'S FOOTSTEPS, FINDING MYSELF
across the road from The Narrow now. Jacq's restaurant looks
heartbreakingly new from here, matching the pristine row of
sandblasted, hollowed-out terraces next to it. I run my gaze
along them, noticing a few have name plaques, just like Amala's new version of my home. As I cross the road, I can see the
house directly next to The Narrow fancies itself as *Park Towers*.
I allow myself a bitter laugh as I take it in along with the pre-
dictably smug smart doorbell, its passive-aggressive blue glow
apparently enough to warn the bad guys not to bother darken-
ing their pressure-washed front doors.

A pedigree cat, with lush gray fur and a self-satisfied,
snubbed face, sits atop a bike storage box to one side of the
door before leaping to the wall opposite. The doorbell alights,
its recording sensor triggered by the motion. A well-kept
woman in her fifties opens the door and shoos the cat inside.
Perhaps she's the one who called the ambulance and was with
Jacq in her last moments.

"Hello."

"Hi. Can I help you?" she says, not unkindly.

"I'm so sorry to disturb you. I believe you may have looked
after Jacqueline Jacobs from The Narrow after . . . when she
had her accident."

"Yes," she bites her lip, "that was me. Are you her friend, family?"

"Family," I tell her, and it feels so bittersweet to be able to say that out loud to someone. "I wondered, could I have a very quick chat with you? I wouldn't take up too much of your time, but—"

"I'm Seraphina. Would you like to come inside?"

We walk into her home, another old building pushed to its limits, but the procedure here has been done with some care, a little respect. I spy a vintage fireplace, not an ornate Victorian one, but a plain enamel surround that the owners in the sixties might have installed. The whole place smells like chamomile tea, which is what Seraphina offers me, as well as a seat at a rough-hewn oak kitchen table.

"How long have you lived next door to the café?"

"A little over two years," she says with what seems like embarrassment. "I'm afraid I never went into Jacqueline's café in all that time, but I liked what she'd done with the place." She meets my eyes with a kind smile. "I had a reservation there this evening, as it happens. In another world . . ."

Seraphina is very much part of the problem I see around here. She's one of the drivers for Jacq's place needing to ditch the fry-ups and mugs of tea for a "dining concept." But, I reason, that's just who she is. Her tastes, her money, her background are no more her fault than my background is down to me. After all these years of resenting people like her, I realize with a jolting relief this woman did right by Jacq when it mattered. I vow to do my best to at least keep my mind open about her.

"Would you mind if I asked you about what she was like when you found her?"

Seraphina nods gravely. "She was obviously catastrophically injured. I couldn't really hear her breathing."

My mouth feels suddenly very heavy, these details making what happened to Jacq more real, even more painful.

"But she was . . . I can tell you that her hand was warm, and I held it until the ambulance arrived. I told her . . . whether it was right or wrong, I told her everything was going to be OK and she said something back to me, just before . . . I believe it may have been the last thing she said before—"

"What did she say?" My pulse quickens, hope for a clue rushing into my chest.

"A man's name, her boyfriend or partner, perhaps? *Charlie*?"

My throat is now fat with a new type of agony. "My son. Her nephew. Charlie," I manage to say.

We leave his name to settle for a moment while I draw a deep breath from the herbed air around us. I must get back to the task at hand.

"And you didn't see any car speeding off?"

"No, but I heard it. That's what made me come to the window. The bang, the collision, then the rev of the engine, it woke me up, tore me out of my sleep. Horrendous." Her eyes disappear into the middle distance. "I told the police everything I could, anything I thought might be helpful while I was still on the scene and everything was fresh in my memory."

I nod my thanks once more and another swollen tear falls from my face. The cat leaps onto my lap with a resonant purr. Its furry face seeks mine. I stroke its head and allow myself a little laugh when the purrs become thunderous.

"I saw this one set off your doorbell. Must drive you mad."

"Oh, it does. It's triggered by close motion, but that's her favorite spot out there, day and night." She smiles, before her eyes widen. "Wait, do you think there's a chance—"

My hand reaches my mouth as Seraphina grabs her phone and feverishly swipes and scrolls. I know there will be something there for me. I can feel it, a vibration of approval in the air from another energy. I close my eyes and try to feel Jacq around me, but underneath the soft chamomile, all I detect is the sour musk of my father.

They won't get one over on the likes of us, the likes of you, my girl.

It doesn't take long before Seraphina finds the video from the night in question. She pauses and looks guiltily at the screen. "Do you think you could check? I don't think I can . . . I can't face seeing it, hearing it again. I'm so sorry." She passes me the phone, her hand trembling. Mine shakes, too, as I nod and begin to scan through the footage.

The streak of the cat across the camera, once, twice, with nothing else going on behind it as the evening progresses. Then, at the third leap, the cat moves just before a car speeds by behind her. I hit pause and reverse pinch with my finger and thumb, enlarging the view through the driver's window.

Her grim face behind the wheel, illuminated by dirty streetlight.

I try to remain calm, quickly sending the video to myself.

"Are you OK? Did you find something?"

I look at the screen for a moment.

No one will see you.

"No."

Seraphina looks on apologetically before her wary gaze reaches her phone.

"Why don't you let me delete everything from that night? Just for your own reassurance, so you won't stumble on anything you don't want to see, or hear, ever again."

Gratitude takes over her face as I remove from her phone all evidence of Jacq's murder.

35

MONDAY MORNING. I CAN TELL CHARLIE IS READY TO GET BACK to The Woolf. He's craving any sort of normality after the week we've had. His beloved auntie is gone and he's worked out there's something going on with me and Pete, even though we've told him his dad's staying at Jacq's place while he sorts out her affairs. My poor boy's world is in pieces; no wonder The Woolf feels like a safer place than home to him.

I have no choice but to send him in, plus I still need The Woolf's breakfast and after-school activities until I can sort things out. Before Jacq's death, Marek had been talking about giving me even more responsibilities, and right now work is the one thing in my life I might be in full control of. I can't bring myself to do anything else but to keep my career's upward trajectory going. I'm not so lacking in self-awareness to believe this or anything else I'm into is exactly what Jacq would have wanted, but I can't imagine she'd be happy with me throwing away everything I've gained recently in the name of grief. This includes my social media profile, which is serving to boost my confidence in the face of Amala's assault on my life and my mourning Jacq.

I have posted less recently and when I do, it's mostly about my grief. One of my best-liked posts was a photo of me in the designer black boiler suit I wore to the funeral and don't want to take off, like a modern-day Victorian. I've felt so alone since she died that the likes and kind comments were enough to get me out of the door and face another day. Some people may judge me for that, and perhaps I would have done the same to someone in my position until I got here myself. I might know people, understand how to read them, but I've not always been so good on the empathy front. That was more Jacq's strength. Throughout my life, so few people have been willing to walk a mile in my shoes, why would I waste my energy imagining the pain of theirs?

The only person I do that for is Charlie. Naturally, I've withdrawn my consent for the counseling sessions and, as far as I know, Amala has known better than to override it. Even the most cursory checks and balances would show how totally inappropriate this would be given what's happening with her and Pete. But the overall problem remains, Amala has been counseling my son without my knowledge and like so many things when it comes to how The Woolf operates, it happened in the vacuum of proper oversight. Amala or one of The Circle always mark their own homework.

When I get to the bank, I sit down with Marek for a "return to work" interview before we open, ostensibly to check whether I was really ready to come back after everything that has happened. But as we wrap up, he looks gravely serious, a switch from the earlier avuncular care.

"No time now, but we need to discuss a particular matter. We'll be sitting down again for a discussion before you leave today. I wanted to let you know. I want you to know it's coming, OK?"

Oh God.

Does Marek know what I've done with the grant for The Woolf? Does head office? Is this how everything ends?

Given how I've helped him with Amala, perhaps this is Marek giving me a head start, a chance to escape the pack of bloodhounds coming to track me down. But there's nothing I can do to get ahead of any investigation now. I've come too far already. There's no going back, no undoing what I've done, or trying to change the story now. All I can do is wait, both for Marek's next move and for something else that's carving my insides with each passing minute.

After work, I am going to face Jacq's killer.

I'm scared and sickened at presenting her with the truth. But there's a small part of me, too, that cannot wait to show her that while she has thought so very little of me, a stain on her perfect world, she was stupid to assume she'd get one over on me. Despite my fear, I'm almost giddy at the idea of it, coming at her knowing how unprepared she will be to see me as I really am.

My late meeting with Marek does nothing to stop me from leaving the bank quaking with adrenaline.

I'm heading to The Woolf.

As I punch in the passcode to the main gate, I hear my name spoken, quietly at first, but as I walk across the yard, under the shadow of the school, it grows louder. By the time I walk into the school hall, it seems to scream, then comes roaring at me from the dark corners.

Rotten Rosie.

But I don't clench and brace myself, I absorb the cruel chant, syllable by syllable. I can no longer let these memories weaken me; they must galvanize my spirit in the face of Jacq's killer. I head up the stairs.

I reach Amala's office. The secretary is locking the glass cabinet. She looks at me ominously as she withdraws the key and returns to her post. As she retreats to her desk, she watches me all the while, seeming to invite me to observe whatever she's been attending to. I approach the cabinet with caution, instinctively knowing I won't like what I see.

In the void left by the framed image of Bea at the ground-breaking ceremony for the Mindfulness Zone is an image of an unlikely Woolf Mother, a reportage shot. She stands alone in the dreamlike purple light, surrounded by floral arrangements that strike me now as almost funereal.

It is me.

The blinding light I stepped into on the roof garden at the icebreaker was a camera's flash, capturing me without my knowledge or consent. I read the accompanying caption: "Rose O'Connell, esteemed member of The Woolf Community who single-handedly raised a grand total of £260,000 for The Woolf Academy." It's a clear move to ensure my responsibility for the new tranche of funding is there for all to see. I feel as if I've been enshrined in a tomb.

I've seen enough. I don't wait for the secretary's permission to enter Amala's office.

"If you were hoping to talk to me, I'm afraid I'm about to leave. Takeout night."

Amala shrugs her shoulders close to her frame, as if in anticipation of all the cozy affection she's expecting from my husband, before grabbing her bag and keys and preparing to dismiss me. But I can't go anywhere yet.

"You need to hear what I have to say."

She stares at me, Birkin bag on her shoulder, prepared to give me a second, perhaps finally sensing some danger about me.

"It's over, Amala."

36

THE BAG DROPS FROM AMALA'S SHOULDER, HER HEAD TILTS TO
one side. She comes out from behind the fortress of her
desk to perch on the front of it, arms folded.

"Goodness, Rose. I am intrigued."

"This isn't a joke. I've just been told by my manager there's
about to be an audit of all the grants we've given away."

"*And?*"

"Head office is on the lookout for fraud. It's been rampant
with these grants, apparently. The audit will focus on the recipients' company history, the assets and liabilities, unusual activities leading up to the application, and take a fine-tooth
comb through the plans for spending it. Your grant will fall
apart on every single criterion." I brace myself for Amala's reaction to this, because so far, she's taken everything I've said in
her stride.

"And is Marek still looking forward to his guided tour in
December?"

"This is way above him. He's as worried as I am, as you
should be. He approved it all, waved it through, because of
who you are and what you promised."

"Not unlike yourself, then?"

"He was as naive as I was. But now, it doesn't matter what
you say. There's only one way this ends, and that's with you
outed for what you are."

She sighs, determined, as usual, to show me how unruffled my revelations have left her. "So what, exactly, are we going to do about this to get me off whatever hook you think I'm on, which, surely, you're on too?"

"Do? There's nothing *to* do. You transferred your residential home to a business of which you are chief executive. You did this to falsely inflate its assets in order to access monies you were never entitled to so you could pay for your next piece of designer furniture or jewelry, your next five-star *fact-finding* mission to Bali, or the golden towel rail in your château." I almost laugh at myself as I call out the vulgarity of her spending, framing it exactly how it should be seen: unseemly and immoral, not "aspirational" in the slightest.

Amala doesn't flinch. "But you made the application."

"And I could lose my job over it, but it's you who benefits. I'm out. I'll get what's coming to me anyway, now. You've lost all the power you ever had over me." I turn to leave the room, forcing my shoulders to relax, making my lungs slow. I am in control now. I can finally feel it.

"Where do you think you're going?"

"There's someone else I have to see tonight."

A shadow streaks outside Amala's office. The secretary pokes her head in.

"I was just leaving," I say, but Amala waves my words aside.

"Rose was about to close the door, but if you'd do the honors . . ."

The secretary retreats with a nod, pulling the door shut in a resounding and final clunk. I'm not going anywhere until Amala says I am.

She paces about the room, her fingers coming to a steeple that rests on her lips, before getting out her phone and issuing an instruction to someone else she knows will do as they're told. "Get here, now."

I hold myself in silence while Amala stalks about her office waiting for whomever she's summoned. It's not too long before Ginny arrives. "What's going on?"

"Could we temporarily transfer the assets in the enterprise to Rose? Make her chief executive?"

"Her? You're serious? After everything I've done for you." Ginny looks at me, stricken, her words spat through loose features.

"This isn't about rewarding her, for God's sake. This is about dodging a bullet." Amala looks to me. "When is this audit likely to happen?"

"I won't do it. You need my consent, my—" I say, but Amala doesn't want to hear me.

"*When?*"

I breathe through my rising outrage at how easily Amala believes she can force me to do her exact bidding. "As early as next week, so even if you could do this, there's no time."

"Ginny will give you everything you need. Tonight."

Amala cannot believe I'd willingly go along with her plan. "This is too much, too far." When the words leave my mouth, I recall Bea saying something strikingly similar to Ginny less than a year ago. A cold pressure makes itself known on my chest.

Amala, who has been acting as if I was no longer there, suddenly stomps up to me, her eyes on fire, enraged by my uncharacteristic volume and clarity. "You! . . . *You* . . . you will do exactly as you are told!" She steps back, appearing shocked at her visceral reaction, before returning to her desk where she taps away. A moment later, my phone buzzes with an email notification.

The subject line: *Rose O'Connell: financial irregularity concerns log.* There's an attachment, a spreadsheet. I click on it and the screen fills with forensic detail of the monies Pete and I have received, a breakdown of the market cost of the goods or services, and the massively inflated costs we've accepted for these.

There it is, all ready to go at the push of a button: my family's corruption, our complete ruin in one neat file.

"I've not sent it anywhere. Yet."

Amala's faux-sympathetic, assured smile sends my fists into tight balls. She picks up her bag again. For her, there is nothing further to discuss. Part of me would like to give in to the crippling insecurity inside me. But I won't. It's not in my nature. My father is long dead, but he never left me.

I watch Amala pull the door behind her on Ginny and me and listen until I hear the sound of her heels fade to silence down the corridor.

I turn to Ginny, knowing that when I speak next it will be in a voice with a resonance and confidence she will not have heard from me before. I probably sound like a different person.

"From now on, you're not going to do what Amala asks you to do."

Ginny observes me, mild confusion on her face, which she soon dismisses with a snort. "Oh, really. And whose orders am I to follow instead? *Yours?*"

She gets her laptop out of her bag and all but throws it down onto a low table in front of Amala's magisterial desk. "Let's stop messing around and just get on with it, shall we? I don't want to be here with you any longer than you do me."

"You'll do as I ask from this point onward."

Ginny rolls her eyes and crosses her arms across her chest with a resentful clunk of her bangles. It sounds as though she is trying to lock a door.

"You're going to do everything I want because I know you killed Jacq."

37

GINNY FLUSTERS, TUTS, PUFFS OUT HER CHEEKS, SENDING A faint gust of alcohol into the air between us. "If you think for one second I . . ."

"Take a look at this."

I turn my phone's screen to Ginny. I watch her absorb the reality of what she's looking at. When the video of her mowing down Jacq finishes, she finally turns to me, gathering her thin mouth to the left side of her face in a moment of thought before she rises from her seat. She moves casually now behind Amala's desk, over to the long sideboard below the mirror. She seems to count three doors along, then stoops down to retrieve a dusty bottle of red wine and a high tech–looking black corkscrew device that has the thing opened in one slick movement. She grabs the nearest vessel to her, what looks like an unwashed mug, and pours a long glug into it. She takes a sip, then another, then one final gulp before she speaks.

"How did you . . . it doesn't matter." Another long sip. "You haven't told the police?"

"Not yet."

Ginny tips her mug in my direction. "You know, I always thought there was something more to you than you were letting on. Amala saw it, too, clearly. It always seemed like she had something in mind for you." She looks to the floor next to her feet. "She always knows much more about us than we first realize. She knew Bea, facing bankruptcy again; she could see Tamsin and the specter of disinheritance; Ruby's lies—"

"And what about you?"

Ginny appears almost oblivious to my being in the room now. "I'll say one thing for her, Amala did everything she could to protect me—or should I say, her. Reconnaissance to establish there were no traffic cameras that might have caught me between my place and the road; strict instructions to stay within the speed limit, and only accelerate at the last; my alibi, that I'd tell my husband the twins were unsettled so I'd stay in their room that night. She even took the keys to my car and did something to it, covered the front in a layer of cellophane so not even a minute trace of my car would transfer to the scene or to . . . the body. She got lucky too. The rain would have washed any further evidence away. Yes, Amala's always been lucky in life, hasn't she? Not so me."

"Amala wanted Jacq dead because she threatened her empire, her reputation, her freedom. I can almost understand this—as much as I'll ever get what makes someone like her think it's acceptable to take another life to protect the quality of theirs—but, Ginny, how, why did you let Amala make *you* a killer?"

Ginny's tears start to fall, but without any visible emotion from her. They pour down her red-gray cheeks to her scrawny décolletage below.

"I already was. I killed a child. A boy."

I gasp.

Ginny turns to me and lifts her chin, as if asking me to judge her. Ruby, Tamsin, and Bea's secrets, the sources of their desperation, feel trivial now.

"Seven years ago. Shortly after the twins were born." She turns away again now. "I had . . . I was very, very down. I drank. I drove. It was midnight. The boy was fourteen. I mean, what kind of mother lets her teenager out on a school night at that time?"

How outrageously typical for someone like Ginny to seek some way to blame another mother for her own crimes. "What kind of mother gets behind the wheel drunk and kills another woman's child?"

"Touché . . . Of course, I wanted to stop, I wanted to help him, but I thought of my children, my family."

"Yourself?"

"That too."

"And you left him there to die."

She concedes the truth with a nod. "I didn't tell anyone. Just let it eat me up while I read about the appeal for witnesses, the scenes at his funeral. The press covered it. He was a would-be musician; talented, it would appear. It was the hardest thing. That's when I started to try to drown it all out, when I stopped knowing how to get by without a drink. I encouraged my husband to work away for months so he didn't have to be with me. I couldn't keep hold of my clients, my marriage was in pieces, God knows what damage I've done to my children. I took on caring for my father-in-law as punishment; penance, I suppose."

"And Amala swooped in like your new best friend, looked like she could fix it all."

"The Woolf, The Circle, her. I had something bigger and better and stronger than myself; this incredible safety net to catch me before I fell to the ground and smashed into a million pieces."

"But it wasn't a safety net."

"She recorded me telling her everything when I'd had a drink one night. It was a trap."

"A spider's web. Amala never chose you for The Circle because you're clever, beautiful, moneyed, or influential; the reason you got invited in is because you looked the most likely to let yourself get caught."

Ginny shrugs. "It's not as though you're any better than me in this respect. She's got you right where she wants you."

"For now, maybe." I watch her for a moment, assessing how best to get Ginny where I need her. "I have evidence, Ginny, but you could make your life easier by telling the police you were acting under duress, under *her* orders."

"What? And potentially double my sentence when she tells them what else I've done? If I only got found out for what I did to your sister-in-law, there's still a chance I could be out before the twins hit their teens if all goes well."

"*If all goes well*. My sister-in-law, my best friend, is dead. You killed her and you drove off like it was nothing."

"I'm sorry. I am! I wish things were different, but we all have our secrets. You know Ruby's and Tamsin's, now you know mine and it's by far and away the worst. This isn't who I am. I try to do the right thing by people. That's why I'm looking after my father-in-law, even though it's killing me."

Tears continue to drop from her eyes. It's as if some part of her brain still has the appropriate wiring, but a good part of her has shut down. I suddenly feel a creep of sympathy, of empathy. Because I, too, know what it is to be forced to do something terrible, then quarantine a part of yourself so you can function, all to not lose your mind while you live and relive your terrible choice every damned day of your life.

"If it's any consolation, I've ruined my own life, not just the loved ones of your Jacqueline and," Ginny swallows, then coughs her way to the next word, "Jayden. The boy I . . ." Her voice disappears to nothing behind a sob. There's something about Ginny's desperation I understand; something I can also use.

"Will you hand yourself in?"

"Of course not. I'll wait for the knock at the door I've been expecting for years already." She looks me up and down. "And anyway, maybe your evidence on what happened with your sister-in-law won't stand up. I mean, that could be anyone on that video, you can't make out the registration, I have my alibi and there's no forensic evidence. They might not believe anything coming from someone like you with an axe to grind and a lengthening track record of cooking the books here. So, don't think you can bribe me with your threats. You're not anywhere near as good as you think you are, or need to be."

"Not nearly as good as Amala?"

Ginny swallows another mouthful of wine. "You said it."

LATER, WHEN GINNY and I are finished at the office, I collect my son and head home. When I lock up for the night, I make sure to put the chain across my door. Amala may have tried to steal my husband and the keys to my home, and she may have thrown my liberty into her wicked game, but when she comes for me again, she will not find it half as easy.

38

I'T'S MONDAY. THERE'S AN IN-SERVICE DAY AT SCHOOL. PETE'S taken Charlie to the park and is dropping him back to me before I make dinner and he returns to Amala. Now that Jacq's funeral has passed, Charlie is hardly buying that his dad is staying there anymore. The story won't hold much longer. Something has to give.

I'm terrified of what the hours ahead might bring, but when I look at myself in the mirror, I see my eyes have never looked more vividly green. I look exactly like my father on one of his giddy Hurrah mornings. Although my whole life as I know it seems to be hanging in the balance, oddly, I feel exactly like myself.

Pete lets himself in, chewing his cheek, head bowed as is his way these days, eyes sunken pockets, as though he's not slept for weeks. His arms lack the tone and volume they had before our troubles; he seems so burdened and ill-equipped to carry the load on his back, as though he cannot take any more.

I give Charlie a hug. "Straight into the bath for you, OK?"

"But I already had one this morning."

"Do as your mum says, please." Pete knows me well enough to understand I can't stand it when he comes in smelling of Amala, her scent transferred to my son through his father. "And make sure you put those clothes in the laundry bin while you're at it," he calls after Charlie. Might Pete be ready to cleanse himself too?

"You want to stay on for a cuppa? Some food?"

"You making it?"

"Um, no. Frozen lasagna."

"If that's the case, then . . ." he says with a faint smile, one I recognize. Pete always seemed to actively enjoy the fact I can't cook. Perhaps he enjoys how it's the one thing he has any idea he might be better at than me.

"So, how's it going?" I say, as neutrally as I can muster as I set up another place at our table.

"You know—"

"No. I don't know a thing about your life right now." I allow a tear into my voice.

"I miss her, Rose. I miss my sister so, so much. I see her everywhere." Pete struggles to stay ahead of the sob in his chest. "I miss *you.*" He reaches for my hand, a jolt of something stunning in its familiarity passes between us.

"So?" I dare to touch his face, and he leans into it like a cat who hasn't had a stroke for too long. "What are we going to do about it? What do you think you've been playing at?"

He looks through the window, over at The Woolf, as if it might be listening. "I don't know if I should say anything, Rose. I'm so confused. I don't know what's the right or wrong thing to do anymore."

I watch my husband, his brow mottled with sorrow. I won't make this harder for him than it needs to be. "Do you actually care about her?" I ask, though I dread the answer.

Pete rubs his eyes, as if they are full of scales he must be rid of, and shakes his head.

"So, what is she? Just a warm bed? Don't tell me you don't think she's beautiful."

"*You're* beautiful. You're all I want! She treats me like I'm nothing."

"And you let Amala do that?" I could kill her right now, but my greatest rage is reserved for Pete. He's the one who made the promises to me and then leaped into her bed at her bidding. "Why are you with her, Pete? When you know she's just using you?" It's time Pete was made to really face the truth.

He holds his head in his hands, either in shame or sheer exhaustion, which I can't yet tell. "You're normally so good at reading me, Rose. But you've been too distracted this time. Me and Amala: Haven't you worked out what's really going on by now?"

39

THAT EVENING, I WALK DOWN FAMILIAR STREETS. THE ROADS
follow the same patterns, the houses still squashed up together as they ever were, but now, instead of looking like
homes in their plots, they seem to me like rows of overly proud
women, heaving their chests outward, fighting each other for
space.

It feels as though Jacq wants to speak to me now as I walk
the neighborhood alone. But I'm not ready to hear her, even
though I sense her reaching for me, warning me about what
I'm about to do, begging me to rethink my next move. She
asks me to think of her, reconsider what I could be sacrificing.
I chase her voice away. I can't have her worrying the edges of
my conscience. She'll never truly understand how I've never
lived in a world where I get to do it all right. I have to let some
things go. I wish it weren't so, but for people like me, it always
is, ever was.

I'm here.

Number 43 Bryk Road. *Woolf View.*

I bang on the door in the way I know the police do, three
forceful knocks that seem to make the house, and the bones of
those within it, shake.

It's time.

Somebody saw.

They know what I did.

I hear these words now, spoken in the voice of my eleven-year-old self, as my knocks echo behind the new front door of my old home. But I am not that girl anymore; I am not the one cowering within the walls of my father's home. I am the one on the outside, safe and in control.

Amala answers the door and immediately tries to appear unmoved by my presence. She won't look that way for much longer.

"Pete told me everything."

"Has he now." She steps away from the door, inviting me to follow. "Good. You've come to collect his things. Do it. He has nothing I really needed anyway." She allows me through to the hall, as if she has nothing to fear from me, like there is no way I could hurt her whatsoever. "I mean, it would have been nice enough in the event, but your husband is no Darius."

"But it still hurt when he said no to you, when he had no intention of ever touching you, when you had to use the threat of me in jail for my supposed wrongdoings to convince him to make like you two were a thing."

Even though I have never believed I truly deserved being on the receiving end of it—even less so now—I have been made to realize that being faithful to me, protecting me, is Pete's true nature. People can judge him as wrongheaded, but he went along with Amala's performance of their affair to keep me safe. That game is now up. It's time I put my family's world back in the order it deserves to be in. This, including the unfailing love of my husband, is what *I* am entitled to.

Amala snorts her silent laugh. "Your husband is nothing more than an attractive side dish, but he's by no means the main event. As long as you felt you'd lost him, then . . ." She brings her lips together to stop herself midflow, as if there's more to say she does not want to declare. "Your husband has fulfilled his purpose. The bank's audit will clear me of any wrongdoing, not so you, and it will silence those who would like to bring me down. Meanwhile, Darius will be back when I choose him to be."

"You sure about that? He looks to be getting pretty cozy with that life coach of his." His recent Insta posts have been filled with inspirational platitudes next to shots of him enjoying quality time with his "personal change guru."

"Don't you have anything better to do than stalk us?"

I hate the tone she's using with me, the one that says I'm dirt. But today I feel fully charged against it. I wonder if my eyes are lit purest green now like my father's and whether Amala can see it yet.

"I do, as a matter of fact."

The moment has come.

My veins pump with delicious anticipation. I hand Amala a large brown envelope.

"Here."

She looks at it like something infected, holding it away from her body. "What's this?"

"An eviction notice. You're illegally occupying my property. There's a termination letter in there, too, relieving you of any duties you may once have held at The Woolf." I struggle to keep the smile from my face, but then abandon my efforts. Why shouldn't my mark see that her fall has sent me skyward?

"You can't do that." She laughs, looks me up and down, almost pitifully.

"I can. I have."

Now she looks mystified.

"You're a confidence trickster, Amala. You've taken me through all the stages of your scam with The Circle. But your long con has fallen apart. Mine, on the other hand, has just come together."

40

AMALA'S HANDS FIND THE WALL BEHIND HER, WHILE HER IRISES zip left and right in the clean whites of her eyes, searching for some notion the world is exactly how she believed it was. She can't yet grasp the truth that it really isn't.

"The start: The Approach. Your Approach wasn't when you came up to me in the coffee shop with that horrible cake that day, or even when you tried to humiliate me at your open evening. It all begins with The Foundation and The Society."

"The *Approach, Foundation, Society.* Where are you getting all this from?"

"My father. His book, *Tricks of Confidence;* his ways."

"So, the rotten apple didn't fall far from the tree."

I stare at her, daring her to hold the expression of repulsion her mouth has curdled into. She should learn to adjust how she speaks to me from here on in. I launch into the sentences I've been rehearsing, louder and firmer than she's ever heard me speak.

"The Foundation: Do your research and find the right mark. Yes, I've been watching you, and Bea, Ginny, Ruby, and Tamsin much longer and more closely than you could ever imagine."

Amala's cheeks flush with indignation, while she works to appear unaffected by my words. "No, I can imagine your voyeurism over my life perfectly well."

I ignore her and the sting of her evident repulsion and continue. "I found out all I could about their lives and the ways you operate. After the open night, me and Bea had a little chat, you might say. I did my research online and on social. I also discovered Bea had made some initial inquiries into the grants with Marek. She stopped short of going for the big money, seeing that even if it *could* be done, it shouldn't. That was the 'shit' you kept on asking her to pull. Endlessly. Relentlessly. Before Charlie started at school, before I'd even accepted his place, I started working out how I could appear to meet your brief. I needed to look useful to you as well as badly in need of help to get my life on track. And when Charlie started school, I got better and better at being who you needed me to be and at seeing what I could get if I succeeded."

Amala scoffs, her cheeks coloring as she struggles to keep ahead of the shock and outrage blistering through her. "Come on, Rose. Let's have the whole truth here; you wanted to be near me, like a kicked puppy looking for a new mistress. You'd have done anything to get on the inside, be part of my world, and feel better about yourself. If you looked desperate, it's because you very much are."

I bristle. There is truth to what she says, but I can't blame myself for it. Being my father's daughter isn't the only thing hardwired into me, it's the need to feel accepted too. The irresistible draw of approval from people who seem to count, the ones who do not dish out their care for me easily, like my father, like Amala. It's not something I want to dwell on, not here, not ever again.

"The only important thing to remember is that you didn't choose me. I chose you." My mind flashes back to the day I decided I would work to make myself impossible to ignore; the first time I went into the coffee shop, bracing myself, knowing I'd stick out, hoping I'd be able to make my initial Approach to Amala if I kept going in there. I didn't hide my desperation, which was, of course, real, and I played up my bank uniform, making sure I wore it there and at school drop-off and pickup every day even though, *because* in fact, it made me different from the other Woolf Mothers. My radioactive blue polyester made me impossible to write off as without purpose. I made it so Amala couldn't *not* put me inside The Circle. When I knew that there was no other way I could fix the mess of my family's life and when I discovered that Amala had my family's home, it galvanized me into getting in as deep as I could, despite what happened to Bea, in fact *because* of the corruption I knew I could turn to my advantage, if I could only play the long game right.

"Once I'd worked out what I was going to do, then came my Approach: that day at the coffee shop. I wanted you to start thinking about me at work and seeing me on my knees. I planned to keep going in there until you came to me. I didn't have to wait long at all. And when you made sure you were on the cemetery trip, I did too. Then, you invited me into your home and all the way into The Circle. I was on my way."

"Go on, Rose. Do keep going, I'm all ears. Tell me, have you been working with someone on the inside?" Her words are thick with patronizing sarcasm that sends a hot pulse of rage through me.

"Tamsin, Ruby, and Ginny? Don't be stupid," I almost spit. "They're your Society, the people you've groomed to facilitate *your* con." I calm my tone so the next thing I tell her lands as hard as I hope it might. "Mine was Jacq. Not that she knew."

Amala takes a gulp of air. I must say, I wasn't prepared for how much I would enjoy seeing her so taken aback, but I do. Little wonder my dad was so effervescent those mornings. I could see how this feeling could be quite addictive, risking more to get more.

"Jacq was my co-conspirator, my Come In, the thing that

made you determined to get every penny you might through me; that was after I'd thrown you a Convincer."

Amala gives me a hopelessly bewildered look. What sport it is to see her struggle to keep pace with me. "My Convincer was the first ten grand, which I'd actually sourced from The Woolf Enterprise only to gift it back, but so muddy are the lines between what's yours and what's The Woolf's, you didn't notice. Jacq's restaurant was *my* Come In, the perfect way to show you how big I could score."

A ripple of resentment seems to build to a tsunami of disgust, and comes crashing down on Amala's face. I can tell she's never been played before. In that moment, I wish Jacq were here right now, watching me sock it to Amala over The Narrow. But then I realize it's not Jacq I want as my audience; it's my dad I wish could witness the reveal of my most audacious and risky play yet.

"In many an effective long con, of course, you sometimes need to call on The Distraction, something to turn your mark's head while you get going on setting up The Hurrah, the crunch point where it all pays out."

She lifts her chin defiantly and views my unimpressive frame. "Enlighten me, what exactly do you believe is your so-called Distraction?"

I let myself enjoy a short, silent laugh, the kind she herself has previously deployed to accentuate my humiliation at not understanding.

"My husband."

I dare Amala to judge me as she looks down at me from where she stands in her heels. "You think you made me gift him to you to support your sham split story? No. It was going to happen anyway. I was lending him to you knowingly."

If he couldn't, or would not, shoot as high as I was aiming for our family, my husband needed to do something to facilitate all the work I was prepared to do to get us there. I never enjoyed throwing him into play, but I had so few tools at my disposal, in the end, I felt I couldn't not use his most obvious assets.

"It was so obvious you wanted to sleep with him, with or without your sham separation. I've seen how women like you look at him. All I'd have to do is set it up, send him to you, make it easy. I assumed he'd give in to you, but I made the wrong call. He loves me more than I ever understood."

"I could have turned him," she tells me coolly, "with a little more time. Regardless of what did or didn't happen with him, I still won: You still hated seeing him with me."

I harden. "He hated the idea of being with you, as we both now know." I try to control myself once more. "I took a chance because, let's just say, after everything I've done to keep my family life on track, he owed me one."

Amala shakes her head again, but not in disbelief, in bewilderment. "Do you know, I thought it was bad enough you willingly handed him over to me when I asked, but the fact you wanted it to happen . . . I mean, do you have any kind of respect for the man at all?"

"How respected did your husband feel when you told him you had to take mine, all for some scam to protect your wealth?" I'm sure I look quite ugly now, the anger frothing out of me. I take a breath. "Anyway, what I might have done isn't a patch on what you have."

Amala raises her eyebrow, encouraging me to continue. I'm disturbed at the peculiar calmness that seems to have descended on her. Perhaps she'll lose her composure again when I explain how I'm about to claim my family home back.

"Let's talk about The Hurrah, the payoff."

"Wait, let me get to the spoiler," she says with a forced ennui. "There is no audit of the grant."

I stumble over my words, only for half a beat, but still,

Amala sees me falter. "The more I protested against you setting me up in your place, the more I knew you'd be convinced it was the only way to go. Honestly, there have been times when this has been almost too easy." I swallow. *"Oh, Amala! It's over! If they look into our grant, you're finished! Please, don't set me up as the beneficiary! Don't make me the stooge, the one who'll go down, you wouldn't do that! Please!"* I mimic her high-pitched affectation of my voice. "I did have a big meeting with Marek, but it was to confirm my promotion," I tell her, not bothering to address the smugness that's crept into my tone.

Amala sighs. "This is all rectified very easily, from my point of view. I'll just get Ginny to reverse whatever she did to put your name on everything. You haven't banked on the level of loyalty that binds each woman inside The Circle to me, Ginny in particular. She knows better than to not do whatever I ask of her."

"Ginny works for me now."

"What?" It comes out of Amala's mouth almost as a whisper.

"I know she killed a boy in a hit-and-run *and* she killed Jacq. I have hard evidence. But I'm not using this to keep Ginny on a choke chain like you did. She wants to get better; be better. I've promised her she's free as long as she lets me help get her the support she needs, with her drinking, her father-in-law, whatever it takes. Sometimes the carrot is more powerful than the stick." This sounds like one of my father's wisdoms, or perhaps one of Jacq's anthropological parables, but it's all mine.

Amala tries to speak.

"And, of course, I know killing Jacq was your idea."

"Don't be ridiculous."

"Ginny confessed to me, Amala. You were afraid of Jacq. You didn't bank on me telling her what I'd gotten into with you and you completely underestimated who she was. That's the real difference between me and the others. They don't have a Jacq in their lives and I do. I did." Amala looks on, feigning the fact she remains unimpressed by me or my brilliant sister-in-law. "You could feel things beginning to crumble, you could see Jacq's bravery, her potential to finally undo the racket of your life. But it can't be her now, it has to be me. And I'm not going anywhere."

Amala smiles quizzically. Her mind must be short-circuiting as she tries to imagine she's still in control, a world where she hasn't been outmaneuvered by me. She pulls herself away from the wall and takes a step in my direction while I keep talking.

"You didn't know that all this time, you've been the cuckoo in my old family home. This place was never *Woolf View,* it's 43 Bryk Road. It's mine, always was, always will be."

A pause.

Amala steps around me. She's behind me now in the manner of a huntress assessing her prey. I turn, tracking her as she circles me, the beginning of something like panic budding in my chest as I realize she's nothing like as scared as I hoped she would be.

"So, sweet, innocent, humble Rose O'Connell is putting her own quest for social acceptance, for more than she's earned in her life, more than she'd ever deserve, over what others might suppose would be justice for her apparently beloved sister-in-law?"

"It's not—"

"You are somehow claiming the moral high ground after loaning your husband and selling out the memory of your supposed best friend for this place . . ." She wafts her hands and eyes around the hollow atrium of the hallway. "And for what you think will be the admiration of a community who otherwise see you for what you really are, a lowborn, rotten stain on the neighborhood."

"Lowborn? Who do you think you are?"

"Who do you suppose *you* are, Rose O'Connell?"

A sigh of satisfaction from Amala, almost like someone on the brink of their own Hurrah. "Of course I know this place was yours."

Now it's me gasping for air. Where did I go wrong? What would my father have done to ensure he'd never be put in this position? The fact I've just been blindsided by Amala is proof I'm not exactly like him; I'm not half as good at this as him. Or her.

"And because I know this and so much more about you, including the very worst of who you are, it's me who isn't going anywhere." Amala is right in front of me now, but I know whichever way I step, she will block my way.

"Your eyes," her voice is characteristically quiet, gone is the faux breathiness, the rise and fall of haughtiness and odd trans-atlantic intonation, "they terrify me. They always did. They're his eyes too. Your father's."

41

AMALA'S VOICE TAKES ON AN ALMOST CHILDLIKE QUALITY, AS IF she's returning to a time when she was very much smaller. "I was always afraid of him. I've always had good instincts about people and had a sixth sense about him: He would not be good for my family. I knew it, the second I saw him." She pauses to observe my reaction. "You look shocked, Rose. I know you didn't think you were the only one who knows how to see inside people."

"I . . . I'm sorry if my father hurt yours. He seems fine now," I say hopefully, desperately.

Amala nods in sarcastic agreement before continuing. "Whenever your father would come round, I'd run to my room. I couldn't bear those repellent snake eyes you both have. But I wanted to know what he was doing with my family. I asked my mother one day and she told me he and Daddy were going into business together: the Anglo-Asian Hotelier Kings of Town! We were going to be rich. We'd move out of our flat above the butchers on the high street and into a house with a garden and our own front door just in time for my sixteenth birthday. Everything my father had worked for, all the sacrifices he'd made plowing his money into his unsuccessful property developments, and my whole miserable childhood with no money, nothing nice to wear, no holidays, no space, it was all going to be worth it. There would have been a reason for every horrid day." Amala talks into the middle distance, as if she has her own Whichellos in the room to hear her sorrowful fury.

How funny that in all this time of trying to understand Amala, I didn't see the most obvious thing: both of us have been running away from poverty and shame. Both of us have been working to insulate our self-esteem and our children's lives against them. The key difference is that Amala has been so much more successful than me in doing so.

"I grew up round here, too, and I grew up poor. I went to AmMidd too. I left the year before you started, I believe. And, yes, your father went through all those classic moves you know so well with mine. From The Foundation, as you called it, to The Hurrah. But when your father manufactured a crisis that would relieve my father of his life's savings, Budda Daddy, Big Daddy, who had the better head for business than his younger brother, had gotten wise to your father."

"The man I met in your kitchen? He isn't your dad?"

"In a way, Budda Daddy, the oldest brother of my father, is my father now. He naturally took in my mother, brother, and me after your father killed mine. Your father and you, of course."

He's reaching for me again, bursting free of the place I've quarantined him in my mind.

A hand clawing for mine in the air, across the years between that awful day and now. The falling man.

An Asian man in his fifties. Gray suit. Full lips, it strikes me now, the same as Amala's. Her father plummets to the ground, his eyes asking the child on the scaffold: Why? I'm back on the very edge of the planks, nearly falling myself as my arms reach instinctively but pointlessly to bring the falling man back to safety, even as he flies to the ground below. It's too late for him to ever be safe again. Is it too late for me?

"Budda Daddy sent my father down to the so-called build-ing site to face your father. I believe it was little more than a set he would use again and again, wasn't it? It had rickety scaffold-ing up a stack of breeze block. My father had let yours know he was onto him and would come to find him on-site. He couldn't find him, but you were up there, waiting precariously on the edge of the scaffolding. You looked to be alone. My father wanted to bring you to safety, protect you in a way your father never would."

I feel a blast of cold, as freezing as the wind through the broken soles of my shoes on the edge of the scaffold that day. How I shook, just as I am shaking now. I didn't want to get up there, didn't want to do any of it.

"How do you know anything about what really happened that day? There were no witnesses. Dad told me."

"I was there. I saw you. I watched you distract my father before yours sprang forward to push him to his death."

"But Dad said he'd made sure no one was looking. He wouldn't let me down." I say this very quietly, but Amala hears me, then looks at me with something like pity.

Another lie from my father.

I understand now how it has really been.

I've been living my whole life on borrowed time.

My father must have never cared for me at all.

Something inside me seems to break. The jagged joint be-tween him and me snapped.

"I was eleven, only a child. I've been so ashamed my whole life, ever since that day." And the child I was made to be from then on ruined the woman I became, and all of that has led me here.

"You talk about shame as if it belongs only to you." Amala shakes her head, which is turned to the floor. "I let Budda Daddy talk me out of going to the police. He didn't want any-one to know his own brother had been so gullible and told my mother he wouldn't help us if I talked. So, we let the verdict of suicide stand and I let you and your father get away with his murder." She brings her huge eyes to mine now. "You stole every chance my family had, then you took my father's life, and my pride with it. This life I've built"—she sends her eyes around the space she's created inside my old home—"this is my way of righting the wrongs. I'm living the life we should have had then, now. I've made for myself the kind of life my father deserved. I even bought my husband the Bentley your father promised mine once the deal was done, part of his Distraction, you might say? In fact, I've created a lifestyle for my family that's almost unimaginable to the bereft, homeless sixteen-year-old you made me."

I want to tell her it wasn't me, it wasn't my fault. That being forced to do what I did made a part of me dead, too, damaged my every interaction since, even with the people I came to love.

"Me and my mum and younger brother had to go and live with Budda Daddy on the other side of town. We were forever indebted to him, which is why I take care of him for half of the year now. This, I can live with, but what I've never been able to get over is how you and your father stole *my* father from me and continued about your normal home life."

She doesn't know about the loneliness, the guilt, how my home life—while I had no choice but to grow used to it—was by no means *normal*. "Do you know, when it happened, it was just before I started at AmMidd. They started calling me Rotten Rosie from day one and do you know, I felt it, I lived it."

My words tumble out of me, a hot gush of lava glad of the cracks in the rock that might let it burst out. But Amala doesn't want to hear about my agonies; she only wants to make them much worse so as to exonerate herself in the process.

"I converted my fear of trusting others into my fuel, my power. I taught myself to assume the very worst of people and to treat them accordingly, to my own ends. Unlike you, I also got myself an education, had a great career in advertising, then found a brilliant husband with money, too, had a baby, but still something was missing. I wasn't healing. I couldn't see the world as I wanted it to be anywhere."

"So you came back here to remake the neighborhood in your image?"

"So, I returned and I bought the house of the green-eyed devils who killed my father. I gutted it and made it my own, transformed it into the very best it could be. But still, it wasn't enough. I couldn't scrub history off me, couldn't wipe it clean off this house, these streets. It began to consume me, the bitterness you internalize when you've been cheated out of something you were sure would be yours."

I wonder how she can say that, even as she stands in my house, the building where I was born, one that was confiscated from me.

"I started something with the power to change all of that. A school so exceptional, I might mold the entire neighborhood to my exact liking, claim the whole damned thing for myself, where no one like you could touch it. And why shouldn't I be rewarded for helping the area become all it could be, for finding a way to rid itself of the likes of you."

It doesn't come as a surprise and yet I experience Amala's words like a slap. Her intent wounds me, how it isn't only me she wants to cleanse the area of, but anyone else like me, every working poor family still clinging on to the postcode. But what would an entire neighborhood of people like her, families she deems good enough for The Woolf, look like?

"Amala, if you succeed, think about it. Who'll cash your dodgy checks, who'll clean your house, fix your cappuccinos, field your calls, pluck your eyebrows? People like me aren't only good enough to be part of this neighborhood, we're essential. I've as much right for my child to go to The Woolf as anyone."

She scoffs. "You are so far below the standard for families I encourage into the school community, that's what I saw clearly at the open night. That's why I first gave the signal to send you the message that you are not the kind of person we seek. But then, I heard your name, saw those eyes in the spotlight, and my heart, my soul, was dragged back to that day at the fake building site. You had to be his. And aren't you just that?"

"I'm nothing like him." The words leave me, but I don't know if I believe them. And now that I'm being taken to the edge again, do I even want them to be true?

"You're every bit his child. A liar, like him." She peers at me, seeking my reaction to what she'll say next. "And just as your father did to mine, I plan to destroy your family."

42

A WAVE OF COLD PRESSURE ON MY CHEST. I'M AFRAID OF AMALA now, as I was when she invaded my home.

The next thing she won't ask for, she'll take.

She turns to a bureau in the hallway and from it retrieves a maroon-and-gold box. I know what it is before I even read the name on the side.

"I'm begging you. Leave him out of this."

Amala drops Charlie's file from a height and onto the bureau's surface with a slap. "It wasn't me who brought your son into this. It was you."

I want to argue with her, but how? What she's saying is mortifyingly true. My son was my Trojan horse that got me into position for my con in the very first instance.

"I've logged all of my concerns, everything I've gleaned from my counseling sessions with Charlie, and more. A litany of failures and grave concerns. Then, there's what happened on your watch to poor little Albert that day at the cemetery."

I recall that afternoon, how darkly in control I felt, how like my dad. I remember, too, how good it was to be suddenly under Amala's patronage. Only a matter of weeks ago, but it feels like a lifetime. A time when Jacq was still here, a time when I was convinced I could pull off my plan.

"Jo and the others are chomping at the bit to tell their version of events. Sadistically leading a child to a tomb to hurt him, just because you felt he'd slighted you? Then, there's what Ginny will log, retrospectively of course, after his impromptu playdate and their little chat."

"Charlie will never back you up." I'm sure of it.

"As head of The Woolf's Pastoral Care Team and Safeguarding Task Force, I'm the voice Child Protective Services will hear. They know, as well as you do, how children will do anything to protect their parents."

Desperate, I throw my darkest insight about her Amala's way, suspecting before I even speak that she'll dodge these arrows too. "But I know you're responsible for the deaths of Jacq. And Bea."

Amala's mouth drops momentarily.

"I gave you an alibi, remember? I'm sure I can prove you weren't at my place when you said you were. CCTV footage from the shop's camera near the entrance to my place, something else from the street that's time-stamped."

Amala views me with familiar collectedness. "There's no evidence to attach me to the sad and unfortunate events that led to the deaths of either your sister-in-law *or* my associate beyond your or Ginny's testimony. You're a fraud, not to mention someone who evidently failed to go to the police with information they felt pertinent to an ongoing investigation, and she's an alcoholic who I can put on the scene of the slaughter of a child."

She's right, of course. I have nothing to lose now from presenting her with the truth. "Bea. She wasn't much smaller than you, but so much more fragile. You're strong, I've felt that. Was it a struggle to get her over the railings, or did killing her come easy to you?"

"NOTHING!" Amala shouts. "*Nothing* has come easy for me!" She forces herself to take a long breath. "Bea barely had a life anymore to hold on to. If she'd talked herself into a state about things, made some poor choices, then I don't see how she has anyone to blame for what happened but herself." She examines me for my reaction, cool, unafraid, and without any trace of guilt.

"You told her you'd make her life a living hell, send her back to the brink again when she'd worked so hard to get out of where she was."

Amala shrugs. "You saw that state she was in. Her time had come. It was kinder to send her over the edge she was already teetering on."

"You pushed her?"

"It was her choice to put herself on the precipice." She hands me back the thick brown envelope that should have changed my life. "The same is true of you."

I look behind me. The door.

"It's locked."

Amala steps toward me.

I've never felt so small, so completely cornered in my life. Almost in slow motion, her hand reaches for me. A flash of gold and diamond in the corner of my vision. Amala presses her palm against the doorframe, so close now, her dark scent suffocates me.

"I'm going to do everything in my power to take your child from you."

"My son." The words leave my throat in little more than a gasp.

"Let's see how long you survive round here when I do."

A shot of metal on metal by my ear.

I'm tipped backward as the door falls open.

I've run out of cheats, loopholes, shortcuts, and cons to try to win the life I want to live now, to relieve Amala Kaur of her power. She has control over the only thing precious to me.

I stumble out of the front door and into the sickly lavender lining the path to the front gate. I stumble down Bryk Road, the ground that used to be mine, feeling like it's falling away from me.

Amala knew, she knew all along my dirtiest, most rotten secret, the thing I can never scrub myself clean of. I look around me and barely know where I am anymore, my whole neighborhood, my one home, a hall of mirrors, mocking me for thinking the vision I had for myself was ever real.

Then, it hits me.

The only thing left I can put on the line to stand any hope of claiming the final Hurrah.

There is one final roll of the dice. It would see me lose the last thing I just about have left, something she has already threatened to take from me.

The victory will be far from sweet, but it still has a chance of being mine.

Now that Amala has my son in her sights, I see no other way out.

43

LET MYSELF INTO THE MAIN GATE OF THE WOOLF AND CLIMB TO
the roof garden. A winter wind whips hard about me. The
city center's hotels and office blocks wink in the distance
among the darkness of the winter afternoon. Another blast of
freezing air seeks to take my breath with it into the blackness
immediately around me and it strikes me as perfectly apt. The
last time I felt like this, I was a child in peril, at my father's
command, about to work with him to end the life of Amala's
father. They were right to call me Rotten Rosie. And I deserve to be up here now.

Stepping up onto the concrete riser and tipping the top half
of my body over the latticed stone to peer at the black tarmac
below, I allow myself to explore the sickliness of the sensation.
I think now of poor Bea. She must have been in the exact position I am in, but when she reached the moment of truth, she
decided she had too much to live for; the lives of her children.
Without Charlie, what would anyone say was my purpose for
living?

"Amala, it's me. Where are you?"

I turn to see Ginny on her phone behind me.

"Oh God, you. Go away!" I call over the wind.

Ginny keeps her phone by her ear, but walks toward me. "I
don't know what you think you're doing—"

"I've been thinking." I look to the gloom of the tarmac that beckons five stories down, my head light, my soul heavy as lead. "It makes perfect sense the women who make others jealous with their seemingly blessed lives, their thriving children, their equally successful careers and lifestyles, their amazing husbands . . . it makes perfect sense they're all scam artists."

I turn away from the view below and to Ginny now. "I mean, it is one big con, isn't it? Being the average working mum. The lies you're fed about being able to succeed at work, win at home. It's all one massive, long con designed to get women to chase an impossible Hurrah, a world built to see you succeed in every bit of your life, and if you don't, it's not a problem out there." I gesture to the neighborhood around us. "It's because of a failure here." I thump my chest with my forearm and fist. "I thought being a mum, the overriding feeling above everything else would be joy. No one tells you the truth, that it's actually guilt."

"I have Amala on the line. She'd like to speak to you." Ginny holds the phone toward me.

"Why would I want to do that? Just tell her what I'm about to do. She should be happy. This is what she wants. Just like you wanted for Bea." I angle my head to the phone and shout, "You don't get your hands dirty this way! You should be THANKING me!"

Ginny turns her mouth to the phone. "She looks like she means it. She's going to jump. Hurry . . . I'll keep her talking. Stay on the line." Ginny takes a step toward me.

"If you get any nearer to me, I do it right now!" Even I am surprised at the persuasive volume of my voice as the wind carries my words into the night.

"Calm down, Amala, I *know* we can't have another fucking body in the playground. Think I don't know what this'll do to the school! For fuck's sake, get here and do something!" Ginny sounds desperate. She huffs a cold breath into the dusk, then says to me, "Rose, I know very well why you might hate me, but, honestly, I don't want to see you do this. There has to be another way."

I hold on to the latticed stone, imagining what it might feel like to fall through the sky, whether you're able to override the fear and experience any kind of joyful freedom from the flight to death.

"This is all I have now. I'm not living my life how she wants me to, in fear, in disgrace, without my Charlie. Even if I can't prove Amala murdered Bea and Jacq."

Ginny looks into the night and crosses her arm over her chest. Tears rumple her face before she swallows them down again to focus on me.

"Another suicide of someone close to her will do enough damage, played right. At least if I go down, I take her with me. She can't shake that off, not with the suicide note I'm ready to post just before I do what I need to do."

What must it be like when life is all over and done with? Do our spirits roam, stay attached to the people still living, as my father's did to me? Or do we disappear forever? When my last breath comes, will my soul know to find Charlie, to stick by him for eternity?

Moments pass before Amala bursts onto the roof garden. As usual, she's making herself appear wholly unafraid of whatever I might do next, calmly walking to my side.

"Do you honestly think anyone will believe the rantings of a suicidal no one who clearly got out of her depth when she tried to keep pace with the big girls? Look, if you just get down from there now, I'll make sure you—"

Amala startles as Ginny runs to her. She tries to step back. "Ginny, what are you doing? Get off—"

I jump down from the riser's ledge and do my part.

It is ugly. It is scrappy, but together we are careful somehow, determined to leave no sign of a struggle on her body, just as I instructed. If you want something done well, you could ask one busy woman, or you might get an even cleaner result by involving two.

Amala fights. I knew she would.

She squeals.

She goes to insert her fingers in the patterned stone, to cling to her life. As we restrain her limbs and get her legs above the concrete riser, she grunts, the buckles and zips on her boiler suit, her gold and diamond rings, clinking against Ginny's bangles. Just before we push her over the top of the stone, her deep brown irises somehow find the green of mine. For less than a breath, she sees me, and I her. A moment of silent, dreadful understanding: She would one day do the exact same to me if I do not do it to her. The knowledge is enough to power my final show of strength, to complete the unthinkable act of ending Amala's life. If I can see it in her eyes that it's a case of kill or be killed with Amala, then what I am doing now is little more than self-defense, the ultimate protection of my family against what more she would do to destroy us.

Amala plummets toward the ground. I turn away, but I hear her and I pray no one else does. Her final word: *No*.

But it's done now.

Ginny hands me the burner phone she's been using, which I'll dispose of on my way out of here, unseen, unheard, as is my way. Jo or one of the mums due to arrive to set up for tomorrow's fundraiser, a secondhand designer clothes sale, will find her first. Ginny's main job now is to expose all of Amala's financial scandals, not to mention her failed relationships, all of which she was escaping when she decided to end her life, once she realized that Ginny was about to break cover on how she'd been defrauding The Woolf from day one.

My dad always said that to carry out the perfect con, you need to know your mark perfectly. And that's what I did. I know perfectly well the secret shames of Amala, Tamsin, Ruby, and, of course, Ginny. The surviving women will never know mine. No one else will ever know, except Amala Kaur.

I may have beaten her, but I've lost too.

I realize this as I watch my hands dismantling the burner phone in my bathroom, disguising its pieces in an old Lego box, before I throw it out into the commercial recycling bin of the natural wine shop below.

Ever since I played my role in killing Amala's father, I've been finding ways to live my life simply and decently, keeping myself away from others in case they could see the wrong in me, the rot, until Jacq came along and only ever wanted to see the best in me; Pete, too, for all the good it may have done him. But now, any noble ideas I ever had of living my life purely are gone.

I have felt that version of myself leave me over these last months, cold air between me and my better nature when I threw my husband into my long con against Amala, my son at the front of this process; my damaged nature confirmed when I didn't bring Jacq's killers to justice. And now I've murdered a woman, not because my father forced me to, but because it was my own plan when I had no further choices available, ones that I could live with.

This will change me forever, but if I had not dealt with Amala, how could I have lived as she had wanted me to; how could I have lived with myself, guaranteeing that my son would never be able to thrive as he deserves? Unlike my father, I have done something evil not because I enjoyed it, or because I was motivated by what I might gain because of it, I've done it for the good of my family, my son. The falling man died because my father was a bad man. The falling woman joins him in those images that would replay themselves over and over in my mind if I did not shut them down for an altogether better reason: the desire to be a good mother.

But unlike causing the falling man to die, I made Amala fall wholly of my own volition. Perhaps somewhere I understand this means badness is likely my true nature, revealed to me in all its complex detail once I'd met Amala Kaur. Some days I believe I was indeed a mistake, something that shouldn't be in this world. I am, and always was, an aberration; my father's daughter.

But I am here, and here is where I belong and where I will stay.

THE JACOBS NETWORK RUNS A GROWING NUMBER OF FREE schools across the region. Its motto: *Inclusivity and Creativity.* These words are its values and a pledge to the communities in which it operates. The only expectation the Jacobs' schools make in exchange for their prized educational experiences is that pupils commit to working toward finding whatever potential they may have. The institutions run a no-uniform policy and provide their Beatrice Pascoe hardship funds and scholarships to the neediest pupils, all paid for by an endowment kicked off by a successful application for crisis funding made three years ago.

The Jacobs Network chief executive sits behind her desk in a grand office looking out over the hall at the very center of The Jacobs Primary School, once known as The Woolf Academy. Ahead of her next meeting, she slips her stockinged feet into a pristine pair of Christian Louboutin black suede boots, the heel not huge, but enough, together with the gravitas of her presence, to allow others to believe she is far taller than she is.

She hears a squeak-squeak of new leather outside her office and asks whomever it is to enter. Her son, more confident than his seven years may suggest, runs to embrace his mother. She allows him a brief hug before sending him on his way. She has business to attend to. Her husband emerges only to usher the boy out of the office, his expression not entirely approving of his wife's brusqueness, but she knows he won't call her to task for it. He, too, is busy, caring for their infant daughter, Jacqueline, named, like the school, after his late sister. He has brought Jacqueline into work today since their nanny is laid up unwell in her room at 43 Bryk Road.

Four women file in as he leaves with the children, each taking a seat at the other side of the CEO's desk. Ginny, Tamsin, and Ruby, plus a new woman, not nearly as smartly dressed as the others, who waits at the end of the semicircle nervously with a paper and pen on her lap.

Rose O'Connell looks at the members of her Circle in turn, each of them with their matching brooches, a circle of gold, no longer empty, but full in its center, savoring the moment as the four women wait primed, ready to do her exact bidding.

Acknowledgments

"It was like removing layers of crumpled brown paper from an awkwardly shaped parcel, and revealing the attractive present which it contained," wrote Diana Athill in *Stet: An Editor's Life*. The parcel I delivered to my editors in the first draft of this book was so oddly shaped, it would barely fit through the letterbox, and was so wildly out of whack with the recipients' expectations that while it contained the same characters and themes as the book you have just read, it was returned to sender. Twice. I've written more than a quarter of a million words in the name of this book. I share this not to have you wring my hankie, but to provide some context to the depth of my gratitude to my editors Clio Seraphim at Penguin Random House in the US, and Emily Kitchin and Abby Parsons at HQ HarperCollins in the UK. They pushed and pulled me until this book emerged from the sometimes ugly tussle with myself. I am so very grateful for their brilliant insights and unwavering belief that I would, in time, deliver a present of the right shape.

Thanks as always to my agent Hellie Ogden for sticking with me through this difficult gestation while also giving birth herself. My thanks also to Allison Hunter and everyone at the Janklow & Nesbit teams in the UK and US.

I'd also like to use this space to thank the brilliant PR, Media, and Marketing Teams at HQ and PRH and also to every book blogger and bookstagrammer who's supported me this far. Thanks also to all the authors who've been kind enough to say great things in public about my work and provide wise words behind the scenes. Naturally, massive thanks to every single reader who has read and enjoyed this or my first book.

My heartfelt gratitude to all the booksellers who've stocked and sold my work to date. Special thanks to my local Stoke Newington Bookshop for putting my debut in the window and for generally being brilliant and also to the wonderful Broadhursts in my hometown, Southport, for stocking my work and being gracious about the repeated shelfies by members of my family. Thanks also to Goldsboro Books, where I was thrilled to sign a stack of copies of my debut.

Many thanks to the brilliant and generous Stuart Gibbon of The GIB Consultancy. Liberties taken with police process are entirely on me.

Thanks so much to my good friend and Northernsoul .me.uk founder Helen Nugent for unending support through events and promoting my work on Northern Soul. I am so grateful for these opportunities and your friendship over the decades. And big thanks to my trusted readers who tolerated the early drafts of this book and my ups and downs to get to the version you have just read: my sisters Bernardette and Caroline, Rachel Stevenson, Frances Corrin, Emma Guise, and especially Victoria Lane, whom I'm so grateful to for reading the first draft, and the last. Thank you, Chloe Leland, for many things, not least your cheerleading and championing.

As always, thanks to my mum, Monica, for everything, but also for not objecting to my using her maiden name for Rose, and also to all my brothers and sisters and their families who have cheerleaded me at every step, in particular my twin sister, Ruth, to whom this book is dedicated. More than words, Ruth.

Thanks also to my husband's family, especially my mother-

and father-in-law, Gurpal and Gurmail, and also my brothers- and sisters-in-law for all their brilliant encouragement and enthusiasm for my work over the years, which means so much. Special thanks also to our cousin Amber Johal for her thoughts, including those on Amala's character.

Thank you to my daughters, Mohinder and Zora, for making every morning feel like Christmas, but particularly for embracing the fact I'd had to trash more than 150,000 words when creating this book. This began as an amusing parable about my rubbishness, but became significantly less entertaining after repeated airings during the lows and troughs of lockdown homeschooling (if I could bounce back after corrections of my magnitude on this book, then surely they could try again on a single sentence?).

Final and biggest thanks to my husband, Danny Takhar. So many things for which I'm grateful, including your genius characterization of this book as "Scarface for Mums." You are my most important critic, supporter, story editor, and about the best person with whom to split the family load down the middle, and to be locked down with.

Helen Monks Takhar, February 2021

SUCH
A GOOD
MOTHER

Helen Monks Takhar

Random House Book Club
Because Stories Are Better Shared ™

A BOOK CLUB GUIDE

Author's Note

Each Monday morning at my high school, children who qualified for free school meals queued up outside a horribly conspicuous room to collect their strip of utilitarian-looking lunch coupons. My siblings and I were all, frankly, ashamed of our "dinner tickets." Come lunchtime, we might whip them out of the cuff of our cardigans at the very last second or, I'm sorry to say, skip the meal.

My feelings of shame and inferiority from relative deprivations like this followed me all the way to university and into my journalism career and made themselves known in moments of doubt, even after I'd realized a lifelong ambition of publishing a novel with my debut thriller. For the next book, I decided I wanted to write about the power and persistence of such negative emotions, create a protagonist dominated by them, and place her in a setting precision-engineered to bring out the extremities of her character.

What if her childhood wasn't only characterized by having less money than her peers, but by trauma and rejection, and what if her neighborhood was moving on from the past, undergoing relentless gentrification, while she remained held back by her history? And what more fertile ground for her feeling less than the next woman than if I made her a working mum? This was how Rose emerged. By contrast, Jacq grew as not only the moral heart of the book, but the only person in its world living outside of any shame about who she is and what she had done, or not done, at the point in her life that we meet her.

Guilt, hopelessness, and that old friend shame were very much part of my life when I had my daughters in quick succession and returned to my job at the time. I'd often arrive at the office with a broken heart, having left my young children crying their eyes out at nursery for little in the way of financial gain. Why was such a routine life so hard, unhappy, and expensive? Why couldn't I do any better for my children and myself? I know firsthand why working mothers might be vulnerable to anything promising a quality of family life that on a bad day feels like the stuff of fantasy. The notion of "The Circle" came into focus, something that looks like a golden ticket, but in reality preys on a desperation that, all things being equal, should not be there. But all things are, of course, far from equal.

I started writing this book well before the Covid-19 pandemic, but the economic and gender inequalities at play in my draft were only heightened by the crisis. In particular, the Covid-19 calamity seemed to make it abundantly clear that the person who truly leads on keeping children fed, educated, and mentally well is too often an exhausted working woman who feels she should still somehow be doing more and better.

For too many working mums, every day can feel like a game rigged for them to lose, the notion of a joyful family life a con, where contentedness is robbed by their too-heavy emotional, mental, and physical workloads and the daily drip-drip of guilt. Research published in 2019 by the Universities of Manchester and Essex only confirmed what many women already know: Working mothers are under considerable psychological strain.

But as so often happens when women face macro inequality, we personalize it; we make it about our apparent individual failures to cope with the demands of work and home. We may be tempted to soothe ourselves by criticizing women who seem to be doing an even worse job than us, perhaps feel darkly entitled to "punch down" at those poorer than ourselves, or women with less inclination to commit themselves to the sometimes abject drudgery involved in ensuring a child wrings every drop of potential from their existence.

A word about my Punjabi antagonist. Amala was born of my desire to create a powerful adversary for Rose, someone with poise, charisma, self-made success, and an untouchable splendor guaranteed to both enthrall and intimidate Rose. I started to see her as a glamorous Punjabi woman with a taste for the finer things in life, and a tendency to weaponize the magnetic ways the Punjabi Sikhs I know make you feel you are part of their family.

Punjabis have a rich vocabulary to describe every relation. For example, your father's sister's husband is your Fufar ji and your father's older brother might be known to you colloquially as Budda Daddy (Bigger Daddy). The collapsing of these labels, when someone needs to know you are there for them simply as their sister or father, is also based on reality.

The same is true of the situational resistance to saying *Thank you*. It was my father-in-law-to-be who told me, with love, that I shouldn't say thank you so much when I was first introduced to my husband's family. Expressing gratitude for something, be it a meal or a lift to the station, suggests you didn't expect it would ever be given. In this way, *Thank you* becomes almost a slight on someone you should know is family and would do anything for you. I found this, and the many ways I've been made to feel at home in my husband's family from the off, comforting and sometimes fascinating. Being the kind of writer I am, however, I have ended up subverting this goodness to, I hope, create a uniquely textured and dangerous character in Amala Kaur.

This book does not set out to make devils of poorer or middle-class mums, or women from any social class, ethnic background, or sexuality, but to entertain while exploring how a wide diversity of women are contributing more than their fair share to families. I believe no woman should be swindled out of the happiness, rewards, and mental well-being that, given their endless and sometimes thankless efforts, should be rightfully theirs.

Questions and Topics for Discussion

1. What was your initial impression of Amala and the women of The Circle? Have you experienced a similar power dynamic, either in your personal life or in the world at large?

2. How are wealth and privilege portrayed in this novel? What attributes are the most prized social currency at The Woolf? How does this affect the characters?

3. What did you think of Amala and Rose's relationship? What were each of them getting out of it? How are they similar as characters, and how are they different?

4. The book takes place in a rapidly gentrifying neighborhood. How does this affect Rose and her family? Have you noticed any such changes where you live? If so, how have they affected your community?

5. What do you think Pete and Rose saw in each other? How has their relationship changed over the years, especially since having Charlie? Do you think their personalities complement each other well, or not?

6. How did you understand the book's title? Do you think it's ironic, or aspirational (or both)? How does author

Helen Monks Takhar engage with the expectations around what makes a "good" mother?

7. Do you think Rose had any choice not to be like her father, or was it really "hardwired into her," as she tells us? What influence did her upbringing have on her life as an adult, as a wife and mother?

8. What did you think of Rose's assertion that working motherhood is "one massive, long con designed to get women to chase an impossible Hurrah"? Did it ring true to you, either from your own experience or the way society treats motherhood in general?

9. How did Rose evolve throughout the novel, from her first meeting at The Woolf with all her insecurities on display, to her final showdown with Amala? What do you think caused this evolution? Or was she just revealing her true nature?

10. Monks Takhar says that she started writing this book before the Covid-19 pandemic, "but the gender and economic inequalities at play . . . were only heightened by the crisis." Did the way the book portrayed these inequalities resonate with you? How have things changed since 2020?